The Bourbon Street

Ripper

SINS OF THE FATHER: BOOK ONE

By Leo King

grey gecko press

Published by Grey Gecko Press, Katy, Texas.

www. greygeckopress. com

Printed in the United States of America

Design by Grey Gecko Press

Library of Congress Cataloging-in-Publication Data

King, Leo
Sins of the father: the bourbon street ripper / Leo King
Library of Congress Control Number: 2012950910

ISBN 978-1-9388210-6-6

10 9 8 7 6 5 4 3 2 1

First Edition

Boudreaux is innocent.

Truly innocent.

I promise.

— Leo King

Contents

Prologue

Date: **Wednesday, October 18, 1967**
Time: **12:00 a.m.**
Location: **A Basement in New Orleans**

It was the night of a full moon and a total lunar eclipse when a young girl with a weak heart was laid down on the floor amidst a circle of candles in a room of stone.

Barely five years old, she was a small girl with strawberry-blond hair and dark blue eyes, which were barely open due to the drug she had been given hours beforehand. Dressed in a simple white chemise, the girl was laid down by a gentleman with graying hair who wore a black long robe with a pulled-back hood.

All around the room, groups of people dressed in black-hooded robes, holding torches in their gloved hands, looked on. The girl, however, could not have seen the faces of those people even if she were not so heavily drugged, for each face was covered in a porcelain mask, the torchlight and candlelight reflecting eerily off of them.

As the older gentleman, the leader of the gathering, placed the girl down on the floor and started to stand, the girl made a feeble attempt to sit up and reach for him as a child would reach for its parent. The man, whose face looked emotionless in the flickering light, brought a finger to his lips and made a sound: "Shhh."

Reaching beneath his robe, he took out a small porcelain doll dressed in a Southern Belle's ball gown and placed it into the child's arms. She hugged the doll as if it were a life-line. The leader smoothed back her strawberry-blond locks before standing up and walking just a few paces to an altar draped in red velvet. The girl lay still, her limbs slack from the drugs she'd been given.

As the man reached the altar, he clapped his hands. Two hooded figures emerged from the shadows carrying a brazier that bellowed forth sweet-smelling pink smoke. The brazier was placed in front of the girl, who started to cough as the sweet vapors wafted about her. Upon the altar lay two wooden bowls, one filled with water and one with blood. Next to them was an ornate dagger with a golden hilt topped with a large red stone, and a book no bigger than a hymnal.

Picking up the book, the man leafed through it until he came to a certain page. Turning to face the child in the center of the candles, he began to lead the others in a chant in Creole.

"Papa Gede, nou mande w tanpri voye zye w sou timoun sa a nan tan fè nwa sa a. Tande vwa nou ak chante nou yo, pou gras ou kapab geri li."

On cue, the hooded figures around the room began to chant, *"Papa Gede, nou konjire ou!"* Each figure's foot rose and fell in time to the chant, keeping a measured beat to the words.

Putting the book aside and taking the dagger, the leader knelt down before the girl and cut off a lock of her hair. She rolled her head back to look at the man, a confused and anxious look on her small face, her mouth slightly open. She tried to sit up, but her movements were feeble and ineffective.

Standing, the leader returned to the altar, sprinkling the girl's hair into the bowl of water and the bowl of blood. As he did this, he continued to chant, his own voice ringing out over the chanting of the crowd. *"Larèn Brijit, nou mande w tanpri pwoteje saktite timoun sa a nan tan fè nwa sa a. Tande priyè nou k ap monte wo nan chason, pou kè li ka vin fòtifye."*

The chanting of the figures grew in volume, as did the strength of their stomping feet keeping time, the words changing to, *"Larèn Brijit, nou konjire ou!"* Some of the figures began gyrating their hips and torsos around lewdly, a few of them ceasing the chant to make guttural noises that bordered on obscene.

Taking the book in one hand and the bowl of water in another, the leader walked over to the girl, who was now looking around the room, clutching the doll, and starting to sob fearfully.

Pouring the water on top of the small child's head, causing her to cry out in a pitifully weak voice, he continued to chant. *"Bawon Samdi, Wa Lanmò, n ap mande pou pa fouye kavo timoun sa a aswè a. Tande vre entansyon nou, pou li kapab viv san laperèz."*

The figures continued to chant, some of them slithering around from where they stood, or crawling upon the ground like beasts, their voices saying, *"Bawon Samdi, nou konjire ou!"* The circle around the girl began to tighten, the figures drawing nearer to the trembling child.

Exchanging the bowl of water with the bowl of blood, the leader returned to stand above the girl, who was now crying in a terrified and choking voice. As he poured the blood around the child's head, making her huddle into a ball and cry out, *"Papa,"* he continued to chant. *"Sen Madonna, nou konjire Twa Gwo Lwa w yo. Nou mande ou pou yo bay pouvwa yo pou timoun sa a, pou maladi li an pa fini avèk li."*

The child continued to cry in terror, even as the hooded figures' voices rose to a fevered pitch, chanting, *"Sen Madonna, nou konjire ou!"* The figures crawling or slithering on the ground moved around the circle of candles that separated themselves from the trembling girl, some of them only pausing to make those guttural noises at her, making her flinch.

The leader raised his hands, looked toward the ceiling, and cried out, *"Kite yo tande vwa nou yo! Kite yo tande chanson nou an!"*

From the darkest corners of the room came the sounds of drums and tambourines. The figures who hadn't been crawling or slithering on the ground began a dance, moving lewdly and crying out, voices ranging from the high-pitched to the deep and grating. The torchlight, shining off the porcelain masks, gave them a haunting, if not outright demonic appearance.

Throughout all this, as the girl cried in absolute terror, crying out "Papa" over and over, the leader stood above her, arms raised to the heavens, his face contorted with euphoria. Over and over he screamed out, *"Tande chanson nou an!"*

As the dancing and music reached a crescendo, the small girl suddenly let out a horrific scream that tore through the room like a shot. Her tiny hands and feet began to punch and kick as if she were having a fit.

One small fist connected with the face of a figure slithering by her head, and with a resounding crack, the mask broke into the face of the dark-skinned man behind it, causing him to scream as he rolled back.

A small foot connected with the chin of a figure crawling by her legs, and with a snap, the person's head flew back with the impact, the mask flying off to reveal a Caucasian woman's face pale with shock. She slumped to the ground. The girl's strength suddenly seemed inhuman.

With another shriek, the girl knocked over the brazier, scattering sweet-smelling incense and red-hot embers all over the floor. The nearby figures jumped back to avoid catching their robes aflame.

The music stopped and a few surprised cries tore through the quickly sobering crowd of hooded figures, but no screams were as loud as those coming from the girl on the floor in the center of the circle of candles. Twisting around, she began to froth at the mouth, her eyes rolling into the back of her head.

As the tenor of the room changed from euphoric to concerned, the girl threw the doll with preternatural fury. It flipped through the air and hit a hooded figure in the chest harder than a five-year-old should have been able to throw anything. With a muffled cry, the figure sank to the ground.

"Princess!" The leader rushed to the girl's side and knelt beside her, trying to get his hands on her. Covered in blood, water, and sweat, greatly foaming at the mouth, she thrashed about violently.

"She's having a fit," the man called out. He motioned toward one of the hooded figures off to the side—it was a tall, slender person. "Get my bag, quickly!" He then pointed to three other strong-looking figures. "I need you to restrain her while I give her an injection!"

The three figures moved forward, albeit with obvious hesitation, and soon they were upon the small child. Two men grabbed her arms. The leader motioned to the third man, saying, "Hold down her legs!"

The figure seemed even more hesitant than the others, but he finally reached for her legs. The girl gave a sudden shriek and a jerk and drove both feet into the hooded figure's face. The mask shattered into hundreds of pieces, slicing the man's face open, and the force of the kick threw him back. As two figures tended to the fallen man, two more quickly came and held down the girl's legs.

Still managing to thrash about, the girl arched her back and thrust her pelvis into the air, crying out in gibberish as she began to choke. "Sir," said one of the men holding the girl down, "what's happening to her?"

"She's seizing," replied the leader, who had by now been given a black bag by the tall and slender figure. Taking out a vial and syringe, he quickly measured out a dose. "I believe it's from the stress of the ritual. I'm giving her a dose of Valium before she hurts herself."

Without another word, the leader plunged the needle into the child's arm. Slowly, the screaming and convulsing started to lessen. All the while, the men held the girl down, even though that appeared to be challenging.

Once her convulsions lessened to where she could be safely touched, the leader wiped the foam off her mouth and again smoothed back her hair. The girl looked up at him with an unreadable expression. This made the leader's brow furrow with both confusion and concern.

"What is it?" asked the same hooded man as before.

"I'm not sure," replied the leader. "I think she's fully aware. But she can't be. She should be asleep."

Reaching his hand out, the leader called for a candle. As soon as someone handed him one of the candles from the circle, he held it over the girl's face, close to her eyes.

The girl didn't flinch; she didn't even blink. She just stared at him. With concern in his voice, the man said, "Princess?"

The girl smiled and said, "*Li la a.*" With a small puff, the girl blew out the candle, leaving the leader with a puzzled look on his face. He leaned back and looked at the girl as her eyes slowly closed and she fell asleep.

"This was a mistake, Brother," said the slender figure next to him. She removed her mask, revealing an aged face with a pinched, tight-lipped, sour look. "Now you've gone and caused your precious heir permanent damage. She'll grow up broken now. Mark my words, Brother."

"Silence, Sister," muttered the leader, reaching down to take the child into his arms.

One of the men who had helped hold the girl's arms down said, "She's right. There's no way a person can recover from that. She's lucky if doesn't end up in a sanita—"

The man stopped as the leader turned and gave him a look that could only mean one thing—death. The figure retreated.

All around, the other hooded figures were removing their hoods and masks, revealing men and women of all ages and races. Many of them started to help the few who had been wounded.

Someone called out, "We're going to need an ambulance. Gerald Robichaux's face is cut to ribbons."

The leader walked through the parting crowd, not looking anyone in the eyes, to a large wooden doorway. Someone opened the door, and the leader walked up the staircase beyond it. The slender woman, still in her hooded robe, followed the man upstairs.

"Where do you think you are going, Brother?" asked the woman, her arms folded indignantly.

"To a hospital, Sister," replied the man in an annoyed tone, stopping in a well-appointed and brightly lit study. "The princess has had a seizure and needs to be looked over."

"You need to address what happened," said the woman as she pointed down the stairs, her tight lips twisting with growing anger. "You need to assure them that this will never happen again. Tonight was a total failure."

"Correction: tonight was an unexpected success," replied the man, his nose in the air. "I will have to take a day or two to analyze the data, and I may have to reference some things with Dr. Lazarus, but I believe we've witnessed a miracle tonight."

The woman looked as if she could spit, her lips snarling in obvious frustration. "A miracle, Brother? Really now? The child had a psychotic fit. Russell is right, the girl is fortunate if she doesn't end up chained to a bed for the rest of her li—"

"Do not say that again, Sister," the man snarled at the woman, making her gasp with shock and outrage. "Insult my princess again and I'll forget that you're family."

The woman seemed to lessen her anger at the man's outburst. Finally, she contented herself with just looking away in a huff.

The man turned to continue on his way out of the study, saying, "Anyway, next full moon, we'll be better prepared. We know what to expect this time."

"We are doing this again?" asked the woman, the surprise evident in her voice. "They will never go for it. The Priory isn't like that, Brother."

The leader chortled as he stopped at the door and turned toward the woman. "Ha! Those fools would jump off the Huey Long Bridge if I asked them. Face it, Sister, the Priory only lives because of our bloodline. Next full moon, we will try this again. This time, we should use one of the twins. Their mother is one of our priestesses. And they should take to the *tkeeus* nicely, don't you think? I'm anxious to see how they react to the ritual." The foreign word had an African-style *click* at the beginning.

As the man started to step out of the study, the woman called out, "Brother!"

The man stopped but didn't look back. "Yes? What is it?"

"There is no such thing as magic or miracles," she said with a scowl. "You and I both know these rituals are merely superstition to keep the others in line. So stop acting like they could really correct the girl's condition. It's madness."

The man turned to the woman and grinned widely. "The mind can do things so incredible it may very well be magic. Therefore, there is a fine line between magic and madness, Sister. You would do well to remember that."

And with that, the man left, the child in his arms, leaving the woman to stand there with a sour look on her face.

She only made one last comment before heading back downstairs: "No good can come from any of this."

Chapter 1
Twenty Years Later

Date: **Wednesday, August 5, 1992**
Time: **3:00 a.m.**
Location: **Corner of Dauphine & Ursuline**
                French Quarter

A steady rain was falling on the streets of the New Orleans French Quarter. It was a reprieve after an ill-tempered summer shower. The torrential downpour had ceased not too long ago, leaving a low-hanging mist over the cobbled streets. The droplets of water were all but invisible as they fell from the night sky, only becoming perceptible as they passed a streetlight or collected on the shingles of a nearby roof before cascading into one of many gutters.

The sound of the rainwater rushing down those gutters to the streets below, where they collected in fetid puddles, had a sloppy quality to it, an unclean sound. Mixing together the sights and sounds was the smell. Despite the recent summer showers, the stench of the French Quarter still lingered, the collective booze and bile of the New Orleans tourist hanging like a heavy blanket.

Detective Rodger Bergeron noted, as he stood deep in thought on the corner of Dauphine and Ursuline, that he loved that smell.

The smell was a way for Rodger to know that he was home. Born and raised with all the pride of a pure-blooded Cajun, Detective Bergeron loved his hometown. He loved every single flaw New Orleans had to offer. He loved the constant humidity that made everyone sweat even on winter days. He loved the run-down and dilapidated buildings that simultaneously preserved their French and Spanish heritage. He even loved the myriad forms of human decadence that flourished in the heights and back alleys of the French Quarter and the Lower Ninth Ward.

It was New Orleans. It was the Big Easy. It was hell. It was Rodger's home.

As Rodger stood on the street corner, coming out of his musings, he noticed that he was being watched. Looking across the street, he spotted three tourists looking in his direction from the second-story balcony of one of Dauphine Street's hotels. The men, two of them, were typical middle-aged tourists, wearing cargo pants and sandals, heads crowned with ten-dollar crew cuts, and a little too much chest hair.

The woman had two dozen or so lengths of plastic beads draped around her neck as if they were treasured pearls and gemstones. She wore a pair of blue jeans that looked like they took a machine to get into, and a revealing white shirt with the words 'I'll Tickle Your Pickle for a Nickel' written on it in bright pink letters. All three held large plastic cups.

Fortunately, the trio, who by now had noticed Rodger and were waving at him, were the only ones out tonight. Most of the French Quarter was either asleep or drunk, and the drunk people were mostly contained to Bourbon Street at this hour. As he gave the three tourists a nod of his head, Rodger felt relieved that no one else was around. Even the local news had yet to arrive, and with some luck, they could clean up and clear out before they did arrive.

Now facing down Ursuline Street, Rodger observed the flashing red-and-blue lights of the half-dozen or so police cars parked around the entrance to the crime scene—an inset door leading down into a basement. Next to the curb was a Mobile Crime Lab, its occupants absent. They were already in the basement.

Just another night in New Orleans.

"It's horrible," said a fresh voice beside Detective Bergeron. Rodger didn't look at his partner, Junior Detective Michael LeBlanc, but instead watched as a number of uniformed officers and CSI personnel scurried in and out of the crime scene's doorway. He absently raised a Styrofoam cup filled with piping hot coffee to his lips and sipped with expert dexterity, not even slightly burning himself.

The coffee was strong, and Rodger could taste the chicory, a strong, acrid taste that lingered. Lost in his thoughts, Rodger heard the voice of his partner again.

"It's horrible," Michael said again, as if trying to get Rodger's attention. "CSI is just finishing up, and the coroner is on his way. What do you think?"

Rodger turned and looked at his partner, who was his opposite in every way. Michael stood there wearing a gray Stanford suit, complete with a white shirt and navy blue tie, right hand thrust into his side pocket as if he was feeling himself, left hand holding his own Styrofoam cup.

From his freshly trimmed sideburns and bangs to his recently polished dress shoes, Michael looked as far removed from his partner, who was wearing a pair of old, worn shoes and tan duster thrown over whatever he'd worn yesterday, as a Persian cat from a common tabby. Despite their night and day differences, the duo had already closed over fifty murder investigations this year—and it was only August.

Rodger was silent for a moment as he examined his partner's face, which showed almost no emotion. Michael's brown eyes just barely moved, as if reading the pages off a typewriter.

Rodger had come to respect Michael's mental acumen. His partner had graduated top of his class with the highest honors. He rarely spoke needlessly or frivolously. His social skills sucked, and he had no concept of how the real world worked, but he was introspective and highly intelligent.

"What do I think?" Rodger paused and mulled over what he might say, only too certain he knew what to make of the scene. When Police Dispatch had placed the call for the two detectives, the words *gruesomely dismembered* had been used. Then, one glance inside the basement where the murder had taken place, and Rodger had had enough.

"Well, Michael," Rodger finally said, his voice gruff from years of smoking, his eyes heavy with years of seeing one horror after another. "What do you think?"

Michael exhaled and looked up at the rain, letting it hit his face for a moment, before looking back at his partner and beginning, "Victim is a Caucasian female, age twenty to thirty, with severe lacerations to the abdomen, chest, and throat by a sharp, but small, instrument. Most likely a scalpel. Arms and legs were bound with electrical wire, either to a metallic chair or table, and the victim was dismembered with some sort of hacksaw or buzz-saw. Eyes, teeth, and fingertips were removed after death."

Rodger nodded at Michael's analysis, impressed as always with his partner's ability to recall a scene simply by looking at it once. Michael paused for a moment before adding, "So yeah . . . I think it's horrible."

Rodger let out a snort. Then he was ashamed at himself for laughing even a little.

Finishing his coffee, Michael asked, "So why did you take one look and leave? It's not like you to just walk away from a crime scene, but"—Michael paused and a thoughtful look crossed his face—"it's like you've seen this before."

Rodger looked over at Michael and frowned sorrowfully as he gulped the final draught of his coffee. Placing the cup on the curb for the street cleaners to take away, Rodger looked back over the entrance to the crime scene and sighed heavily. It was twenty years ago this very night that he had stood outside this very same doorway.

"I have, Michael." Rodger didn't look at his partner as he walked to the doorway, past the groups of officers and members of Crime Lab scuttling outside with uniform pale and sickly looks.

Tracing his fingers over the doorway's frame, Rodger spoke as if addressing a distant memory. "The worst case I've ever worked. Solved some twenty years ago. The Bourbon Street Ripper murders."

At that moment, another police officer, a short woman who walked this area as her beat, came out of the doorway. Officer

Guidry exhaled and inhaled loudly, as if she had been holding her breath, before looking up at both detectives, shaking her head, and speaking in a thick Creole accent. "It's a downright nightmare in there, Detectives. Crime Lab is almost through, and the coroner should be here any minute. Sergeant's taken my statement and sent me back on my beat."

That said, Officer Guidry hurried off down the street, as if she couldn't get away from the crime scene fast enough.

Rodger watched her leave.

Michael shook his head and said, "It's a real shame that she's the one who found the body. She's about the same age as the victim. Damn. What a way to start your career on the force."

Despite his grizzled demeanor, Rodger had to agree with Michael's statement. Officer Guidry had been on the force for only six months. She was the one to discover the body. She was the one to call in the murder.

It was a hellish awakening to the horrors a police officer can face at any given time. Rodger shook his head as he walked away from the doorway. "It's a crying shame. But what's worse is that it looks like we have a copycat of the Bourbon Street Ripper murders."

Confusion showed plainly on Michael's face as he followed his partner. "Hold on, Rodger. You were the one who solved the Bourbon Street Ripper murders. So why do you think tonight's murder is a copycat?"

Rodger stopped several yards from the crime scene's doorway and leaned against the wall of the building. Protected from the stray raindrops, Rodger took out a cigarette, lit it, and moistened it between his lips. As he took a lingering drag and exhaled just as slowly, he looked to his partner, who was watching him with anxious anticipation, and began to speak.

"It was during the early seventies when those murders began. Back then I was a moderately successful detective with an unimpressive list of closed cases. By a stroke of fate or a case of rotten luck, however you want to look at it, my partner, Edward, and I were assigned the case. The first time I saw one of those murder scenes, what he did to one of those women, I was sickened to my soul."

The gravelly croak of Rodger's voice as he sank into his narrative was ripe with sordid memories.

"The pools of blood. The strips of flesh. The stench of bile. The gruesomeness alone had been enough to turn my stomach inside out. But what affected me to the core was the look on the victim's face.

It was as if someone had frozen a scream of incalculable agony on her once pretty face. Just one look, and in an instant I felt as if I had experienced every horror that woman was forced to endure before being allowed to die."

"I remember hearing about the Bourbon Street Ripper at a lecture on serial killers. The media named him that because the murders were similar to the old Jack the Ripper murders in the late eighteen hundreds," said Michael. "Awful. That a person can do that to another human being. It's disgusting."

Taking another lingering drag off his cigarette, Rodger continued without paying any heed to his partner's interruption.

"Correct. At that time, Moon Landrieu was in the mayor's office, and already his battle with City Council over desegregation had the police budget in shambles. My partner and I were the only ones sent after this sicko, and every time that it seemed we were closing in on him, he evaded us with ease. After a while, it was like he was mocking us."

Rodger looked up at a nearby streetlight, watching the raindrops fall silently past the yellow halogen corona. His normally furrowed brow was even heavier this evening, all that stress from twenty years ago crashing back with every second.

"But obviously you caught the Ripper, correct?" asked Michael, raising his eyebrows inquisitively.

Rodger nodded in response before taking a third drag of his cigarette. Unlike some people who took lingering drags from a cigarette before accenting a point, Rodger managed to make it look natural. Like Sam Spade or Lieutenant Columbo, being a grizzled and jaded detective looked good on Rodger.

"Yeah, we finally were able to piece together our killer," Rodger said as he scratched his shoulder blades against the brick wall behind him. "Dr. Vincent Castille, a surgeon at Southern Baptist Hospital in Uptown. Old aristocratic money. Real old. Not that he needed it. The guy was a real genius with the scalpel. It was said he could fix any injury and heal any illness. And he wasn't cheap. Rich folks would come from all over Louisiana just to place themselves under his care."

"A real saint," quipped Michael.

"And a first-rate psychopath. His personal life came out during the trial. Apparently, this monster had been collecting memorabilia from the Middle Ages or the Inquisition or some shit. Real torture equipment, like the kind you'd see down in the Wax Museum. I don't even know what some of that stuff was, or how it was used, but it looked downright evil. The doc, however, loved that stuff."

Michael grimaced and then asked, "So the Bourbon Street Ripper—I mean Dr. Castille—tortured his victims to death because he was reenacting scenes from his private collection?"

"That's what the newspapers wanted to believe," replied Rodger with disgust, taking a fourth drag of his cigarette, wearing the stick almost to the nub. He exhaled slowly and the smoke billowed out.

"The murders were methodical and well planned, much like a surgery. The wounds were cut cleanly. There was no passion in the crimes, no rage."

He made a scribbling motion in the air with his stunted cigarette and said, "And he took notes. Lots of notes."

A coarse voice coughed out a pointed "ahem" beside them. Both detectives turned to see an older gentleman with tired eyes and scraggly gray hair. His black suit and white shirt were crumpled, as if it needed a trip to the dry cleaners as much as its owner needed a trip to the day spa. The man himself looked grim and serious.

"Morton," said Rodger with a nod of the head to the New Orleans coroner.

"Dr. Melancon," said Michael. He held out his hand, which the coroner ignored.

"Rodger. Michael," replied Morton with the look of a man who would rather not be outside in the rain. "I'm sure you know what this looks like, right?"

"The Bourbon Street Ripper murders. It's obviously a copycat." Rodger looked over Morton's shoulder toward the doorway leading to the crime scene. A pair of EMTs were rolling out a covered gurney, a third one behind them holding a black garbage bag that looked mostly full.

"It's goddamn butchery! That's what it is," exclaimed the coroner quite suddenly, his charcoal eyes burning with indignation. "Whoever did this knew exactly how the Ripper did it, down to the amputations and living autopsy at the end. It's sheer barbarism!"

Rodger didn't let Morton's outrage affect him. He knew that Morton had a personal reason for feeling so passionate about these murders. And one glance over at Michael, who had flinched at the outburst, confirmed to Rodger that his partner had no idea.

"All the same," inquired Rodger calmly, "your assessment is that it's a copycat, correct?"

Morton thrust his wrinkled hands into his coat pockets and spat on the sidewalk. "If you're asking me if the victim died of exsanguination, then yes. If you're asking if there was severe physical trauma, then yes." Morton's voice had once again considerably raised, so much that the trio of tourists, who were still on the balcony, perked up their heads with interest.

"If you're asking me if she suffered, then hell, bloody yes." Morton was practically in a fit now, to the point where Rodger was holding out his hands to try and calm him. To the senior detective's dismay, the coroner just railed on, "But if you want the really gory details, Rodger, you're going to have to wait until I have the autopsy report ready. But don't worry, if this is anything like the Bourbon Street Ripper murders, we'll get plenty more where that came from! Until then, I suggest you go say some prayers at Saint Louis Cathedral, because Satan is back in the Big Easy!"

With that, Morton stormed off, drawing looks from the remaining officers and officials at the scene, some of whom shook their heads at the over-the-top outburst from the coroner.

Michael, who by this point wore an exasperated look, turned to his partner, and mouthed the words, "What the hell?"

"Don't worry about it," Rodger said as he took a final drag from his cigarette and tossed it into a nearby puddle. "He has his reasons for being so sensitive about this shit. More so than most of us."

With that bit of wisdom dispensed, Rodger grew silent, his mind working. He mulled over a way to start the investigation off. He was sure it was a copycat, even though he knew that they needed more than one victim before City Hall would consider it a real copycat murderer.

Goddamn bureaucracy.

Rodger frowned. There was one way to get a jump on this investigation if it was indeed a copycat. It would require bothering someone he didn't want to bother, but given the grotesque nature of the crime, he felt there was no other choice.

Rodger began moving to his squad car. "Come on, let's get going."

Rodger heard a quick "Hmm?" from his partner before hearing those polished shoes scuffling after him.

Like a duckling hurrying to catch up to its mother, Michael scuttled over the sidewalk to the passenger side of the car. "Where are we going?"

"To see someone who can help us get a leg up on this damn thing," responded Rodger as he slid into the driver's seat and strapped himself in tightly. The receptacle for the safety belt failed to catch a few times before finally clicking in place. Rodger paid it no mind. The department couldn't afford to give him a raise after five years, so why have them spring for new seat belt latches?

Damnable budget cuts!

"All right, I'll bite," replied Michael as he effortlessly latched his safety belt in place. "Who is this person? How can they help us?"

Rodger turned the key in the ignition, and with a roar the Ford Crown Victoria came to life, headlights spilling out over the back of Ursuline Street.

Putting the vehicle in gear, he replied, "Sam Castille, Vincent's only living descendant. Sam has some stuff of the doc's that police never got warrants for during the trial. Some bullshit red tape thrown up by the defense that ultimately did that scumbag no good. If we can get our hands on that stuff, it may help us understand how Vincent thought out his crimes."

With a nod, Michael leaned back in his seat, folding his arms thoughtfully. "I see. So we establish a pattern of behavior and use that to predict the copycat's next move."

"Exactly," replied Rodger with a small smile.

Michael's expression was still thoughtful as he asked, "And you think this Sam fellow will help us out?"

"I hope so," replied Rodger as he pulled off Ursuline and onto Dauphine Street, passing underneath the balcony where the tourists still watched the gruesome gallery below. "Sam and I . . . we go way back. Shouldn't be a problem."

In truth, however, the uncertainty was still there, along with a pang in his chest. Sam was a delicate matter to Rodger, but Sam was also the only one who could give Rodger what he needed. It was a real conundrum.

"Great," answered Michael as he relaxed and looked out the window. "So where does Sam live?"

"Uptown," replied Rodger as he stopped at a stop sign, checking both ways before proceeding forward through the intersection. "Near Tulane University."

The rain had started up again, coming down in sheets of water that made visibility nearly zero.

"Nice area." Michael looked out the window, before looking over at the clock, blinking a bit, and calling Rodger's attention to the time. "Will he even be awake at this hour? It's only three thirty."

Rodger chuckled to himself. If he remembered properly, Sam was an incurable night owl. As he turned out to the highway, leaving the French Quarter and its grisly murder behind, Rodger said, "Oh yeah. By the time we get there, Sam will definitely be awake."

By now, the summer storm was raging on in full force.

Chapter 2
Sam of Spades

Date: **Wednesday, August 5, 1992**
Time: **4:00 a.m.**
Location: **Sam Castille's Townhome**
Uptown New Orleans

With a shuddering series of clanks, the door to the medicine cabinet more or less slid open, revealing row after of bottles, each bottle filled with pills. Triazolam, Temazepam, Zolpidem, and other sleep aids shared the shelves with NoDoz, Vivarin, and other pills meant to do the exact opposite.

Only on the bottom shelf were pills dedicated to functions other than promoting or inhibiting sleep. One such bottle, a bottle of plain aspirin so old the label was half-worn, was the target of Sam Castille's search.

Sam spent a moment or two half-opening and closing the cabinet door, listening to the mirror as it shuddered in its track, before finally sliding it all the way open. To Sam, the sound was reminiscent of heavy rain on a tin roof, and that was very relaxing. Finally, with the cabinet completely open, Sam found and snatched up the bottle of aspirin. Then Sam closed the door to the cabinet, coming face-to-face with her own reflection.

Sam wasn't pretty by conventional standards. Her face was more gaunt than normal, her cheekbones were too high, and her nose was a little too big. Her blue-gray eyes didn't shine, and her sandy blond hair wasn't remarkable, especially pulled back in a tight ponytail as it was. Her frame was slender, with only her hips having any definition.

Many people had told Samantha Castille that she had that "hometown girl" look. She couldn't care less. People weren't something Sam was interested in.

After staring at her reflection for a few moments, Sam flipped open the bottle of aspirin with her thumb and popped a few pills right into her mouth. She stared again at her reflection before leaning forward to check under her eyes to see if the bags were as heavy as they had been the night before. They were. By the time the bitter taste of the pills dissolving in her mouth registered, Sam was already washing it down with a mouthful of cold coffee.

The vile combination of tastes made Sam's face crunch up into a comical pucker. The surge of bitterness passed within a few moments, and she swallowed the wretched mouthful and shuddered in disgust.

Leaving the opened pill bottle on the sink, she took her coffee mug, which was marked with the phrase, "If I gave a penny for your thoughts, I'd have change coming," and headed downstairs to her study.

Outside, the patter of raindrops softly rolled off the slated roof and down to the gutter below, sloshing out to the sidewalk of Uptown New Orleans.

It had been storming earlier, and Sam, after trying with all her might, had abandoned all pretense of trying to work and had contented herself with sitting outside on her back porch, holding a mug of cooling black coffee, listening to the torrents of rain, and thinking of as little as was humanly possible. Only when the rain had finally dwindled to a mere patter had Sam realized she had a splitting headache, and that she had daydreamed away two hours.

"Isn't that just lovely," Sam had said to herself before unfolding her legs, sliding her feet into her slippers, and walking back inside the house in search of some aspirin.

But now with the rain having lessened up, Sam returned to her study and the large solid oak desk that acted as a centerpiece to the room, taking a seat in a large red velvet chair. The desk, the chair, the house she lived in, and most of her belongings were keepsakes from her father.

Even the lonesome and frightfully old-looking typewriter resting on the desk was once used by her father. Sam's fingers lingered on the sides of the typewriter, lost in nostalgia for a moment's passing, before she ritualistically slid her fingers over the keys of the typewriter and began to type.

> Mortimer crept down the abandoned hallway, the creaking of the floorboards piercing the night's silence like a terrified caterwaul. The investigator's right hand stayed firmly wrapped around the butt of his trusty revolver, his left hand wrapped protectively around the flashlight that illuminated the path before him.
>
> Beads of sweat gathered on his brow as his eyes darted side to side, suspicious of every shadow. Soon Mortimer came upon the last door in the hallway. He took a deep breath. The answers to the Mystery of the Crimson Mask lay inside! Hands shaking, the investigator reluctantly forsook his gun and, with an audible gulp, opened the door, revealing . . .

Sam stopped typing in midsentence, her lips scrunching up into a pucker and shifting to the side. "Right," she said and moved from the typewriter to a pile of handwritten notes. There were scribbles, mind-maps, jots, and musings—all the notes of a mystery writer—and Sam shuffled through them several times before finally letting out a deep sigh. Her fingers slid from the loose-leaf papers and ceremoniously slid back to the typewriter. For a long moment, she just sat there, fingers on the keys, not typing anything.

After a few soft breaths, Sam's face crinkled in frustration and anger, and she quickly typed out:

> . . . nothing at all. Why? Because Sam is a dumb bitch who wrote herself into a corner six pages ago and has no feasible way for the Crimson Mask to be in this

room. It's in the bottom of the river with Mr. Dahl, the crooked attorney who stole it at the beginning, after being murdered by Rico-the-Freaking-Gay-Mobster.

Mortimer Branston fails at being a private investigator, leaves New Orleans, and moves in with Vinnie the Nose, Stinky Earl the Plumber, Jimmy with the Gimpy Leg, and every other character Sam has introduced but failed to tie in to the crime to provide cushioning in case she writes herself into a corner yet again!

Sam stopped the torrent of self-hate as she heard the clack of the typewriter's hammers hitting the carriage of the typewriter, the paper having run out. Leaning back and covering her face with her hands, Sam let out a long sigh before finally rubbing her brow.

"This sucks," Sam announced to herself. "What the hell is wrong with me? You think it would be easy to write a crappy mystery." Sighing with exasperation, Sam got up and, taking the litany of self-flagellation off the typewriter, walked away. A few moments later, the crumpled and balled-up paper landed in the wastebasket by the desk.

Sam was a mystery writer of mild repute, known locally amongst the natives of New Orleans by her pen name "Sam of Spades." Since she was old enough to work a typewriter, Sam had written mysteries, drawing upon her love of crime dramas and gritty detective novels to create worlds where smoke-filled interrogation rooms and back-alley information brokering were as commonplace as taxis and streetcars. While Sam of Spades had enjoyed a modest success within the metropolitan areas of New Orleans, she had never experienced true success.

One part of it was that Sam just had difficulty concentrating for long periods of time. Even when she didn't have coffee in her system, which was relatively rare, she would struggle to maintain focus for more than a few minutes. About the only thing that helped was alcohol. Consequently, Sam drank a lot of wine.

Another part of this had to do with Sam's sleep disorder. Ever since her father's death, when she was only ten years old, Sam had never been able to sleep soundly without medication.

Doctors and friends had offered Sam prescription sleep aids, over-the-counter drugs, and questionable home remedies to help her get a good night's sleep—with none of it working. After a while, any doctor who treated her for her sleep disorders would give up and refer her back to the psychologist who had been treating her since she was a child—Dr. Klein.

For Sam, going to therapy didn't help her problems sleeping, but it did offer her a weekly chance to express her frustrations to someone who'd listen, even if he was paid to do just that. As for tackling her sleep disorder, Sam continued to pop pills and drive herself to exhaustion, finally getting a solid six to eight hours of sleep about every three days.

Dr. Klein, whose goatee, monocle, and German accent made him look like the cliché of a Freudian psychologist, strongly disagreed with Sam's methods of getting sleep. He'd often state it would eventually deteriorate her "mental condition to the point of irrecoverable psychosis"—this statement usually said while the doctor puffed out his chest and pointed toward the ceiling knowledgeably.

Sam, of course, was basing a recurring villain in her stories off of him.

The final reason Sam of Spades enjoyed only a small regional popularity was that she was notoriously late on her deadlines. With the habit of being days to weeks late with submissions, no publishing company would dare touch her. Sam was fortunate that Jacob Hueber, one of the publishers for the *Times-Picayune*, the local paper for New Orleans, was a close friend of hers from college.

Sam didn't have many friends. People made her very uncomfortable, which was why Jacob getting her a job at the newspaper was such a big deal. She could work from home and only had to go out to mail her publications to the newspaper—whenever she could actually get them written.

Many times, Jacob would almost have to knock down Sam's door to get a submission on time, and the last-minute rush resulted in a noticeable lack of quality.

It wasn't that Sam was lazy or didn't like to write, nor was she without talent, but she was so often afflicted with writer's block that she'd go days, sometimes weeks, without knowing what to write next. That, combined with her terrible sleep schedule, held back what would otherwise be a very successful career. Her only solace was in drinking a local blend of coffee and chicory, or listening to the raindrops whenever a shower would spring up overhead.

Sam was just preparing to indulge in one of those pleasures, putting on a fresh pot of her favorite coffee, when the doorbell rang. For a moment, she just looked in the direction of the front door, startled by someone visiting this early in the morning. While it was no secret amongst those who knew Sam that she was a guiltless night owl, there weren't that many who knew her to begin with. She chose this life of seclusion and enjoyed it, and she wasn't so sure about an interruption at four fifteen in the morning.

Leaving the coffee to brew, Sam moved toward the front of the house, stopping for a moment in the hallway to look inside a ticking grandfather clock. There, on a wooden shelf just below where the pendulum hung, was a gun—a service revolver left to Sam by her father.

Whenever she answered the door, Sam always checked to make sure the weapon was present. She had never been the victim of a violent crime, and she did not want to take that chance. When she was sure the gun was in place, she headed to the front foyer.

"One moment," Sam called out to the person on the other side, fumbling with the old metal latch to the door. She'd see who it was and politely send them on their way. Even if she wasn't facing another bout of writer's block, she was in no mood to receive visitors. She never was.

The latch finally undone, Sam opened the door and started with, "Sorry, but do you realize it's four—"

Samantha stopped midsentence when she saw who was standing there. Glowering through the crack in the door, dripping with cold rainwater, was someone she hadn't seen in years.

"Detective Bergeron," Sam said with a start, staring at the older man. "What a pleasant surprise. Why are you here?"

Rodger nodded at Sam through the doorway. "Sam, yes, it's me. I need to speak with you. It will only take a moment."

Sam could make out another person with Rodger, someone dressed "to the nines." She figured that was most likely Rodger's newest partner. Had anyone else been there, Sam would have turned them away without a second thought. Her head aching again, she wondered why the detective who had put her grandfather away was here at four in the morning. Perhaps it was for a personal reason. He had once been an important part of her life, but he hadn't even so much as sent a birthday card in years. The thought made her tense with years of resentment.

No, thought Sam, *I need to give him a chance.*

Sam suddenly realized that she was just standing there, keeping the door cracked open while staring at Rodger and the other man. Sam would often do that—stare at someone absently while lost in her own thoughts.

"Sorry. One moment," she said.

Soon Sam was unlatching the door and letting the two detectives inside. By the time Rodger's partner entered, Sam was leaning against the wall of the entry hall, considering the men curiously.

"So nice of you to come calling on this rainy day, Detective," she said.

"Please, Sam, call me Rodger," the older man said. "This is my partner, Detective Michael LeBlanc."

Sam shook Michael's hand while sizing him up. His clean-cut look was offset only by the tense clench of his jaw. Sam immediately decided that this was one of those intellectual types, the kind that probably lived in their heads and had a rather noticeable lack of social graces.

"A pleasure, Ms. Castille," replied Michael, being very obvious about looking her over. "I'm sorry, I expected—"

"That I was a guy," interrupted Sam with a shrug, suspecting that Rodger had been ambiguous about her gender—a suspicion confirmed by a smirk from the senior detective. "It's all right. I go by Sam, so a lot of people get confused."

To Rodger, Sam then said, "So then, what brings you by so early?"

"Believe me, Sam," Rodger said, looking at his hostess's feet, "if this could have waited until the morning, I wouldn't be disturbing you."

For a moment, Sam's lips tightened as she looked Rodger directly in the face. It seemed he was avoiding eye contact with her. Sam had often wondered if Rodger had just stopped caring about her after he found out that her grandfather was a serial killer. His actions now made her believe that even more. With a soft sigh, Sam decided she was too tired to care and motioned toward the study. "Come on in. Hang your raincoats and hats up on the rack, wipe your feet, and have a seat." She started heading back toward the kitchen. "I'm about to make some coffee. Do you want any?"

Both men replied that coffee would be nice.

In the kitchen, as Sam got to work on preparing the coffee for her guests, she heard the two detectives talking in her study. Due to the open ventilation between rooms, Sam was able to make out bits and pieces of the conversation.

Sam's thoughts turned to Rodger, and for a moment she felt a surge of nostalgia. "Twenty years," she muttered to herself, frowning as she fought against the slowly rising feelings of panic. "Why is he coming back into my life after twenty damn years?"

Memories assailed Sam of halcyon days. First came memories of wearing a pretty blue-and-white dotted dress, playing on a swing set at New Orleans City Park, and laughing mirthfully. Another of her handsome father, whose gentle eyes and kind face watched her with love as she played, approaching her with his arms outstretched. Next, she was running into her father's arms and embracing him, burying her face in his chest, followed by the memory of offering her father a cypress blossom and placing it into the lapel of his jacket.

And then a different memory assaulted Sam, a flashback of sitting in a police station as Rodger approached her with a grim look upon his face. In this memory, Rodger held up a cypress flower, the petals ripped and torn from the stem.

With that, Samantha was shaken out of her thoughts by the sound of the coffeemaker beeping loudly, declaring its payload to be finished. She also heard Michael in the study expressing surprise that Samantha Castille was the author called "Sam of Spades."

The revelation that an actual police detective was a fan of hers made Sam smile inwardly. She thought to herself, as she lifted the tray and hurried into the study, that she might have to give him an autograph.

Michael had taken a novella from the bookcase and was flipping through it. As Sam entered the study, he quickly closed it and started to put it back.

"Don't worry about it. I don't try to hide who I am," Sam said as she placed the coffee tray on an uncluttered part of her desk and began pouring. "Actually, I'm surprised that Detective Ber— Rodger hasn't told you that he knew Sam of Spades, Detective LeBlanc."

"Call me Michael," said the younger detective, putting down the novella and reaching out to take a cup of coffee. "Truthfully, collecting obscure mysteries is a hobby of mine. You know, authors like Sam of Spades, Gino Elk, and Richie Fastellos—just to name a few."

Sam nodded in response to Michael's comments, pouring Rodger his cup of coffee. She wasn't at all surprised to be on the "obscure author" list, especially with an author like Gino Elk, who lived as a total recluse. However, one name did catch her off guard. "If I'm not mistaken, isn't Richie Fastellos on the *New York Times* best-seller list now?"

"He is, indeed," replied Michael, sipping his coffee and grinning wryly. "That's why I don't collect his books anymore. They're too mainstream. Too successful."

At that, Sam gave a short laugh, not sure what to make of Rodger's new partner. He seemed to be ignorant of the fact that his comments could be taken as insulting, and yet there was a sincerity to his candor that Sam appreciated.

"Well, Detective LeBlanc," she said as she poured her own cup of coffee, "I may be a far step away from Fastellos, but it's nice to meet a fan just the same."

Her own cup of coffee made, Sam walked around the desk and took her seat. "So, Detectives, what can I do for you?" Sam said after she took a long gulp of the hot, sweet brew.

Rodger took a long sip from his cup and then put it down on the saucer, looking as he if didn't want to have this conversation. That look reminded Sam of the same look he had given her at the police station twenty years ago. Sam did not like that look.

"It's been a long night, Sam, so forgive me if I'm brusque," Rodger started, looking her in the eyes for the first time since he knocked on her door. "There was a murder tonight in the French Quarter. The victim was killed in the same way as the Castille murders. I believe we have a copycat on the loose."

It was not what Sam expected to hear, and once again memories, both unpleasant and incoherent, assailed her senses. The memory that drew Sam in the most was of a long hallway with a single door at the end and a feeling of impeccable dread.

Sam felt as if she were once again a child in a blue-and-white dotted dress standing in that long hallway. At the same time, she saw frightening images of a bloody hospital room, with walls lined with streaks of bloody handprints, and clinging globs of meat covering a bone saw and a pair of forceps.

The memories assaulted Sam's senses—the memory of moving with legs like lead down that hallway, her heart pounding in her throat, her mouth dry with the exhale of terrified breath.

Then in the next instant, Sam felt as if she were once again standing in the doorway and staring at a table with a dismembered body on it. An old man stood over the corpse, a bloodied scalpel in his hand. He turned to her and said, "Isn't it wonderful, Sam? *Sam?*"

"Sam!"

Sam snapped back to reality, aware of the cool air of her study, aware of the clamminess of her skin—had she been sweating?—and aware that both Rodger and Michael were looking at her with concern, Michael halfway to his feet. The woman put down her coffee cup and shook her head as the two men passed a glance between each other.

"I'm sorry," Sam said, avoiding eye contact, "but that was probably the last thing that I ever expected or wanted to hear." Looking back up at the men, she offered a shaky smile. "So, how can I help you, Rodger?"

From his seat, Rodger leaned back, the look of concern on his face fading into silent understanding. Michael also leaned back, looking briefly once more toward his partner before turning his attention back to Sam.

Rodger immediately got down to business. "When your grandfather was put away, a box of his belongings remained out of police custody. Stuff from your father's townhome, here, that the police couldn't get a warrant for. I don't remember all that was in it, but it's the only evidence from the original case that we don't have."

Rodger finished off his coffee and leaned forward, partially to place the cup back on the tray, and partially to look Sam in the eyes. "It could really help us if we had that box, Sam."

At first, the request seemed unusual to Sam, who wondered why a stash of her grandfather's belongings could be helpful in finding a copycat killer. After a moment, however, she understood.

Sipping her coffee, Sam nodded and said, "I see. You're hoping that the contents of this box will help you think through how Grandfather committed his crimes. You're trying to profile the killer."

To Sam's surprise, it was Michael who replied. "Exactly. By developing a profile of the copycat killer, we hope to catch him before he claims another victim."

Rodger nodded to Michael before settling back in his chair again. "Can you do this for us, Sam? We may not be able to use it as evidence, but that's the district attorney's problem. Either way, if it helps us catch the killer, it will put this ugliness to an end."

For a long moment, Sam sat there and considered things. She had never doubted her grandfather's guilt. Even with all of her efforts to forget those events in her life, Sam knew that she was the granddaughter of the most prolific serial killer in the history of New Orleans, perhaps all of Louisiana. She also knew that, despite the ties of blood, she hated Vincent Castille more than she hated anyone else in the world.

After several long moments of consideration, Sam said, "The box is up in the attic. If I give it to you, do you promise—" Her voice caught for a moment as an inexplicable feeling of fear seized her heart. "Do you promise to never bring it back to me? Destroy it or seal it away in one of those police evidence rooms of yours if you like. I just never want anything of Grandfather's in my home again."

Rodger nodded, giving Sam the most sympathetic look she had received in a very long time, before replying, "Of course, Sam. I'll make sure it never gets released to you."

"Good. Then wait right here," was Sam's brief response before standing up and leaving the study. Heading up the stairs, which were conveniently located in the front hallway, Sam bypassed the second floor, where the guest bedrooms were located, went past the third floor, where her own bedroom was located, and went up to the attic on the fourth floor.

The attic was stuffed with boxes and chests, mannequins with dresses of all sorts, and more junk than fire safety codes should ever allow. Each box, each chest, each container was meticulously labeled—a product of Sam stuffing a mansion's worth of junk into a townhome's storage space.

She began to rummage, her brow furrowed and her headache back. By now, her thoughts were fully on the Bourbon Street Ripper murders. She was obsessively thinking about the vile things her grandfather had done to his victims.

"You bastard," Sam said between her teeth, "after all these years, you still haunt me. When the hell will you go away?"

Suddenly, Sam pulled back her hands as if her fingers had been bitten. When she came to her senses, she realized that she had recoiled the moment she had touched the very box she was looking for.

It wasn't a very large box, just two cubic feet, but it was old, was taped shut, and had written on it, very clearly, "Vincent Castille."

For another long moment, Sam kneeled back and looked at the box as if it were evil itself, her heart racing. The side of her head was pounding, her spine was tingling as if she was suddenly out in the cold, and she felt like she was going to pass out. It was like a memory was trying to force its way to the surface, one that carried nothing but pain.

Sam began to take deep breaths, pushing back the unpleasant memories, until she was calm. Only when she had calmed herself down did her cynical, tight-lipped smirk return. "There you are, Grandfather. The sooner you are out of my life, the better."

A few minutes later, Sam was returning to the study, carrying the old box. Without ceremony, she placed the box on her desk, right next to the coffee tray, and patted the top.

"Here you are, Rodger, and good riddance. Get this damn thing out of here." She was appreciative when he gave her a sympathetic nod. Then she headed over to the mantle and absentmindedly straightened a few pictures, letting thoughts of the box slip out of her mind.

Rodger said, "Thanks. If we have any questions for you as the investigation continues, we'll call you. No more reasons to show up unannounced." He motioned his partner toward the box. "Michael, can you take that out to the car?"

Michael nodded before standing up and, grabbing the sides of the box, picked it up. For a moment, he shivered as if he was cold, and then his hands jerked violently. That was when the bottom binding of the box, covered only in old tape, broke with a loud rip, and the contents of the box spilled onto the carpet below, much like the entrails would spill from a slaughtered pig.

Everyone just stared at the broken box in Michael's hands before looking down at the contents. Scraps of paper, half-chewed pencils, tattered remains of surgical masks, a golden pocket watch, a receipt book, a neatly folded map, and a miraculously unbroken jar of marbles all lay on the floor. A few objects rolled about the carpet, scattering in different directions.

"Oh, for God's sake, Michael," exclaimed Rodger as he got up to start gathering the miscellany together. "Don't you know you're supposed to hold old boxes by the bottom?"

Michael, who looked very flustered, apologized profusely before flipping the box over and helping his partner gather the contents to put back into the box. Sam soon joined them.

"It's not Michael's fault," Sam quietly remarked to Rodger. "Everything connected to Grandfather finds a way to bring misery to others. It's his curse." She then offered a small smile to Michael. "Just be thankful it didn't do this while you were outside in the rain."

Michael gave Sam a grateful look. In a matter of minutes, the contents were back in the box and the box was securely in Michael's arms. He was now holding the box from the bottom.

Sam looked around and said, "There, that should be everything. If I find anything else that rolled out, I'll let you all know."

"Thanks," said Rodger, looking at his pocket watch. "We should get going, Sam. We need to get started on sorting through this mess."

"And sorting through the box, too," joked Michael, his remark sparking a soft laugh from Sam.

"Indeed," said Sam, already feeling the relief of her grandfather's last set of possessions leaving her home. It was like a huge weight had been lifted from her shoulders.

Leading both men toward the front door, Sam said, "And I have a deadline to make."

At the foyer, Sam unlocked the latches and opened the front door. "So, if you have anything else that I can help you with, you'll call me?"

"Correct," Rodger answered, carefully stepping outside and down the front porch steps into the light drizzle, the raindrops pattering gently on his trench coat. Michael followed, looking like he was holding on to the box for dear life.

"Sounds good," Sam replied from the porch, arms folded as she leaned casually against one of the support posts. "Good luck catching the guy who's doing this. Lord knows the *Times-Picayune* is going to have a field day reporting it."

Roger shook his head. "You ain't kidding, Sam. It'll be a media circus all over again." Soon both detectives were getting into their car, Rodger fiddling with the safety belt for a few seconds before starting the car and driving off.

Sam watched them leave. For a moment, she was lost in thought, wondering why, after twenty years, this nightmare would return. Finally, she headed inside, latching the door tightly behind her.

"A Vincent Castille copycat," Sam said to herself as she headed back into her study. "Maybe—just maybe—this will have a silver lining, in that I'll finally be inspired." It was a horrible thought, to draw inspiration from something as gruesome and horrific as the Bourbon Street Ripper murders, much less a copycat.

"Still," Sam said, sitting at the desk and turning back to the typewriter, "if I don't get my ass, or my act, together, then Grandfather's inheritance will be the only thing I live off of . . . and God knows I don't want anything that bastard left behind."

With a firm resolution in mind, Sam laid her fingers on the keys of the typewriter once more.

"Okay, inspiration, come!"

Chapter 3
Four Names, Four Leads

Date: **Wednesday, August 5, 1992**
Time: **10:00 a.m.**
Location: **New Orleans Police Precinct, 8th District**
            French Quarter

Sounds.

A cacophony of sounds.

Merged together in anything but harmony, the sounds of the New Orleans Police Department's 8th District were as varied as they were discordant. The most obvious of the sounds were the voices—dozens of human voices, each having their own independent conversations, some of them outright raucous. Sinking beneath those voices was the hum and clatter of an old photocopier as it spit out papers at irregular intervals. Floating along with those voices were the sounds of fingers clacking on keyboards, doors opening and closing, and shoes clapping against the linoleum floor.

And finally, rising above the murmur of those voices were two shrill sounds that cut through the others like a knife. One was the incessant ringing of an unanswered telephone, while the other was the bleating cry of an ill-tempered infant. Not to be outdone by the sound was the smell, that humid and pungent odor of a building with too many sweaty bodies on a hot afternoon. The only thing keeping the atmosphere from being choking were the dozen or so ceiling fans running at full speed high above the floor.

The floor of the precinct was almost like a grid, rows upon rows of desks facing each other and forming walkways just big enough for two adults to walk side-by-side. Five by five the rows were laid out, giving a total of fifty detectives their floor space. The walls were littered with doors leading into the offices of sergeants and lieutenants, interrogation rooms, and storage closets. At one end of the large room was an office twice the size of the others, with two large glass windows framing either side of the door. It was the office of the 8th District commander.

Michael LeBlanc knew the layout of the precinct well, for on his first day he memorized where everything was located. Memorizing things was something of a hobby for Michael, who was almost like a computer, filing away facts, conversations, maps, and crime scenes into his mind, ready to call back later with perfect clarity. It was something of a gift, or so he had been told at an early age by his mother, who would go around announcing that her son would become the brightest neurosurgeon to come out of Shreveport. That was before Michael enlisted in the police academy, or applied for a transfer to New Orleans, rendering him more the family's black sheep than their pride and joy.

Michael didn't care. He had wanted to be a police detective as far back as he could remember.

Waiting at his desk for Rodger, Michael looked over the contents of the box they had procured from Samantha Castille, even though he had already committed the contents to memory. Most of it, Michael had to admit, was useful to prove more that Dr. Castille was a lunatic than a killer: stacks of notebooks with insane ramblings about how man's mortal soul can only achieve transcendence through ultimate suffering, printed clippings from occult magazines about consuming the soul of one's enemy, and diagrams of the human neural pathways.

Yeah, thought Michael, *this guy was whacked out of his gourd. It's as if he really believed that by murdering others, he could use their souls to extend his own natural lifespan. Not only that, but his philosophy that pain and suffering reinforced identity is as antiquated as it is barbaric.*

Michael's thoughts were interrupted by the sound of a loud, "Get your fucking hands off me!" Looking up quickly, he saw a rough-looking man wearing a jacket proudly displaying the Hell's Angels logo, his face as bearded as it was scarred, being forcibly escorted by two uniformed officers toward an interrogation room.

Trailing behind them was a senior detective barking orders to the two officers, saying, "Escort Mr. Jones to the interrogation room. And one of you, get his dumb ass a bandage."

Stopping an officer passing by, Michael inquired what was going on.

"Oh, that," replied the officer, a young man who was clearly trying not to get involved. "There was a break-in at the Riverwalk this morning, just before the shops opened. Keith Jones, one of the bikers who hangs out 'round there, didn't take kindly to Detective Aucoin questioning his girl about it. The two exchanged words, then Jones's fist exchanged personal space with Aucoin's face. Best to just stay out of it, if you ask me."

Michael looked toward Senior Detective Kyle Aucoin, who was trying to look as dignified as a man can look while blotting up a bloody nose. Aucoin soon disappeared into a side room, cussing with a level of vulgarity that made Michael's ears burn.

"Is Dixie still on vacation?" Michael asked the nearby officer. One of his closest friends, Dixie Olivier, Kyle Aucoin's partner, had been on vacation with her boyfriend for only a few days. As far as Michael knew, she'd be gone for at least another week.

"From what I know, yes, but the commander is thinking of calling her back after that murder in the French Quarter last night."

With that, the officer walked off, leaving Michael to wonder if both Rodger and the police commander were jumping the gun on declaring this a copycat, or if they were both on the right track.

The media was already calling it a Vincent Castille copycat murder.

In the background, the ill-tempered infant continued to bleat its cries. Michael looked over and saw that the infant belonged to a woman, most likely a battered wife, who was giving a report while trying to tend to her baby. He thought she should probably check that kid's diaper.

"I'm back," replied Rodger, making Michael abandon his thoughts once more. He saw that Rodger was offering him a Styrofoam cup of coffee. Michael didn't particularly care for coffee one way or another, but his partner, and everyone else in New Orleans, seemed to live on it. Not one to rock the status quo, Michael took the proffered cup with thanks, holding it for the moment. It was too hot to drink anyway. Michael recalled that Rodger had a habit of scorching his coffee, making what was normally a bitter drink particularly vile.

"Welcome back," said Michael as he pushed the crying infant, the bloodied Aucoin, and any other distractions out of his mind. Focusing on Rodger, Michael asked the question that had been on his mind since his partner was called down to the coroner's office two hours prior: "So, what did Morton say?"

"Well, give me a second to get out my notebook," Rodger said, sipping his coffee before leaning down behind his desk.

While Rodger was distracted, Michael quickly leaned over to a vacant desk across from his desk and opened a drawer. In it were several cups of long-since cooled and abandoned coffee. Placing the new cup into the drawer and closing it, Michael turned back to his partner before the latter noticed anything.

Rodger plopped down his notebook, then reached into his coat pocket and fished out a neatly folded coroner's report. Holding it out toward Michael, he said, "First off, we're lucky as shit that Morton bumped our body up to the top of the list. But I suspect that's more thanks to the chief's office than anything else."

"Probably," answered Michael, leaning forward and focusing on the paper in the older man's hands. "The media is already having a field day. One slip that last night's murder could be similar to the Bourbon Street Ripper murders and every talk show and radio program is running commentary, ready to theorize that this is everything from a copycat to the ghost of Dr. Vincent Castille."

Roger nodded grimly, with a disgusted look. Michael wasn't sure this was a copycat—not based on one murder—but Rodger had obviously already convinced himself that it was. Michael shrugged and said, "Well, the commander wants to know one way or another, and he's already leaning toward the copycat side of the argument. So, what did Morton find out?"

Rodger unfolded the report and handed it to his partner. "Well, the victim was in our system, so she's been identified. Her name was Virginia Babineaux, otherwise known by her street name, Virgin Baby."

Michael couldn't help but smirk at that name as he took the report and got himself oriented. "Lady of the night, eh?"

With a nod, Rodger leaned back in his chair and, scribbling in his notebook, continued, "This goes against the doc's MO, though. Dr. Castille never went for prostitutes or derelicts. His victims were always upstanding middle-class citizens. College honor students, well-mannered housewives, daughters of civil servants. Those sorts of people."

Putting down the report, Michael was caught by one of the phrases: *"daughters of civil servants."* In the depths of Michael's mind, a lightbulb suddenly illuminated. "Wait, you mean like the daughter of Morton Melancon?" One look at the frown that crossed his older partner's lips, and Michael knew that he was correct.

"Morton's daughter was the third victim," said Rodger, shaking his head in disgust. "It was actually Edward who told Morton what had happened. I didn't have the stomach for it. Sent Morton on a five-year sabbatical, nearly made the poor guy lose his mind. I suspect that even if the chief hadn't told Morton to bump our case to the top, he'd have done it anyway."

Well, that explains his reaction last night, thought Michael. He went back to looking over the autopsy report. His eyes moved like the scanner on a fax machine, taking it in line by line. When he set down the report at last, Michael closed his eyes and visualized the entire report. There it was in his mind, clear as day, down to Morton's accidental transposition of the letters *i* and *e* in *their.*

Opening his eyes, Michael rejoined his partner in the conversation. "So this killer is already doing something different from the doc. He chose someone who is less than an upstanding member of society."

"Correct," replied Rodger, sipping his coffee again. "Which means if another of these pop up and she's in the same social class as the first one, we've got us an MO."

Michael looked grim as he nodded in agreement. "Although, if we're lucky, this was a one-time situation, and there won't be another one of these 'popping up.'"

To Michael's dismay, Rodger immediately shook his head, saying, "I've been on the force over forty years, and my gut is almost never wrong. My gut tells me, Michael, that this is just the beginning."

For a long moment, Michael was silent. He heard the infant in the background still crying, although not with as much strain to its voice. *Someone must be trying to comfort it, at least,* thought Michael, who gave a sigh and began spreading out the various pieces of evidence obtained from Sam Castille. He didn't want to believe that Rodger was correct, but his own gut didn't offer any solace.

After a few moments, Michael began, "Well, Vincent took one victim every seven days, correct? That gives us six days to find and identify the killer before the next victim goes missing. Now, I've been sorting through this stuff we got from Sam and have come up with several things."

Michael produced a stack of receipts, bound together with a rubber band. "First, we have these receipts. All of these show the purchase of the hardware that the doc used to perform his murders. For each murder, he bought new power tools, new tubing, new everything."

"Except his scalpel," stated Rodger, taking the receipts and looking through them. "He used the same scalpel for every murder. He also used the scalpel, and not anything else, to finally kill his victims. Did the same kind of cut given for an autopsy. Everything else was either to torture during the killing, or to dismember afterward."

"Right," replied Michael. "And according to the autopsy report, the cuts on Ms. Babineaux were made from a hacksaw, a wire cutter, a circular saw, and a scalpel."

"Same as the doc," said Rodger, tossing the receipts back onto Michael's side of the desk.

"But not quite, Rodger," said Michael, tapping the upturned autopsy report. "Morton clearly states that the scalpel cuts were amateurish, that they didn't have the precision of a trained surgeon. That means that the killer doesn't have any training as a physician."

As Rodger nodded, Michael continued, grabbing a similar bundle of receipts. "Now these receipts are from various restaurants around town. Commander's Palace, Arnold's, and Café Giovanni, just to name a few. Each receipt is always from the same night that the body was discovered."

"That's no surprise," Rodger said, finishing up his coffee and tossing the cup into their already overflowing trash can. "At the trial, the doc was profiled as treating himself to a nice meal after every murder, sort of a reward for a job well done."

Michael couldn't hide his disgust at Vincent Castille as he continued. "The point I am getting at is that the doc's case was highly publicized twenty years ago. So all these facts would be available for someone who knew where to look, correct? So, if this is a real copycat, like we suspect, then he will do more than just murder like Vincent Castille."

Rodger looked up, the look on his face showing Michael that they were both arriving at the same conclusion. With a quick nod, the older man said, "Right, and since a copycat will want to emulate the full Vincent Castille experience, if we analyze lists such as recent hardware purchases and expensive restaurants . . ."

" . . . we can find our man," finished Michael with a smile. He and Rodger had solved many cases this way, arriving at the same conclusion over conversation. The younger man knew that he and his partner were as different as night and day, but when they worked together as a cohesive team, they could solve any case.

Michael sometimes wondered if Rodger, and not Edward, was the one who had solved the original case.

Rodger motioned toward the contents of the box Sam had given them. "So, then, what else do we have here?"

Michael gestured toward the stacks of notebooks, article clippings, and diagrams. "Well, all that stuff just shows the depths of Vincent's insanity. The guy seemed obsessed with studying how much people could be made to suffer, as well as dabbling in that occult nonsense."

Rodger picked up a few clippings and glanced over them, sighing softly before saying, "Yeah, the doc's defense tried to put a voodoo spin on things in order to go for an insanity plea. It didn't work, of course. The doc was too lucid, and never rambled about 'the occult this' or 'black magic that.' Still, they presented it really well. At times, voodoo almost made sense."

Michael wasn't surprised. Variations of "The devil made me do it" were centuries old. When facing the death penalty, especially for crimes this heinous, Michael supposed that anyone could be persuaded to try any defense, no matter how ludicrous.

Michael reached down to fish out a small pocket notebook from the pile of belongings. "Then there's this," he said, waving the small notebook. "It's just a list of names and old phone numbers."

Michael tossed the notebook to his partner. "Mean anything to you, Rodger?"

Rodger opened the notebook and looked at it. Within a moment, the older man's lips curled down into a frown. "These are aliases, Michael. No one, not even in one of Sam's detective stories, goes by the names Topper Jack, Mad Monty, Fat Willie, or Blind Moses."

With a chuckle, Michael shook his head. "I knew that. I also called the phone company and tried to get their records of who owned those phone numbers back then. Of course, I was told that this was too far in the past to . . . "

Michael stopped and grew silent as his partner suddenly slapped his desk.

"Oh, of course," exclaimed Rodger. "I think I know who these guys are!"

Michael, who rarely saw Rodger have a *eureka* moment, just stared.

Rodger continued, "The prosecution always contended that Vincent had to have one, if not more, accomplices. It makes sense, since a sixty-five-year-old man shouldn't have been able to carry out those murders alone. However, Vincent never gave anyone any information about who could have helped him. And since the stuff in this box"—Rodger waved the notebook—"was in his son's townhome, and thus was never under a search warrant, we never got an idea of who they could be."

Michael stood up and went to the side of his partner, looking at the small notebook again. "Accomplices, you say? This adds a new dimension to the investigation. So you think these aliases are those people?"

With a nod, Rodger looked up at his partner. "That's my hunch. And I happen to know who can help us. A retired cop by the name of Douglas Dugas. My mentor, actually. Back in the seventies, he had his hands on every Tom, Dick, and Harry that had any information in this town. If anyone, and I mean anyone, in New Orleans would know who these four were, and where we could find them, it would be him."

Their conversation was interrupted by an earsplitting crash. Rodger jumped up and pushed Michael back while putting his hand to his sidearm.

What the hell is happening? Michael thought as he hit the ground. Quickly, he got back to his feet, and immediately saw the cause of the commotion—the biker, Jones, had broken free of an interrogation room by knocking the door off its hinges. All around him was a swarm of uniformed officers, and the sheer violence of the biker's outbreak had caused everyone nearby to dive behind their desks.

In the background, the infant shrieked in terror.

"Holy shit!" exclaimed one of the officers as Jones grabbed a nearby chair and swung it at him, barely missing. "Someone bring this guy down, now!"

Three officers leapt on the biker, swinging their batons at his head. Jones seemed to ignore the repeated blows, and instead rammed his fists in two of the three's midsections. As the sound of cracking ribs resonated throughout the room, Michael heard the one uninjured officer saying, "Shit! It's like this guy's immune to pain!"

That comment got Michael's mind spinning, and he said, "Rodger! Sounds like this guy is high on something like PCP! Beating him with those batons isn't going to do anything."

Before his partner could react or protest, Michael was running toward the carnage.

The biker had just picked up the third police officer, who was screaming for someone to help him, when Michael reached the heart of the fray. All around were other detectives and officers, as well as citizens, most likely there just to file reports or follow up with investigations. Loosening his tie, Michael called out, *"Keith Jones!"*

Keith turned around and, seeing Michael, threw the officer he was holding to the side. Unfortunately, that happened to be just where Aucoin, who had emerged from the side room right after the mayhem started, was standing. The two crumpled into an ignominious heap.

As Jones turned to fully face Michael, the younger detective took a moment to calm his nerves. This man was huge—easily six feet tall and muscular—and high on something that made him immune to pain and fear.

Michael thought, *I have one chance to take this guy down. If I'm off by even a few inches, I'm screwed.*

With a frothing cry of "Up yours, copper," Jones ran at Michael, arms outstretched, mouth opened wide, tongue flapping out—generally making the man look like a maniac. His eyes, pupils heavily dilated, focused on Michael as a hunter does its prey. Michael stood his ground and watched, waiting, calculating.

A little more, Michael thought. *A few more feet. Come on, you sad sack, you're doing exactly what I anticipated, running straight at me.*

Just as Jones was within arm's length of Michael, Michael dropped down, his right shoulder dropping, and his arm getting in a relaxed position to strike. It looked, to anyone watching, like Michael planned on hitting the biker between the legs.

But just as Michael's body dipped down, he suddenly came up, bringing his right hand up as fast as a bullet. His hand opened and his palm connected with the underside of Jones's jaw, bringing his mouth shut so hard that part of the biker's tongue flew off and onto the floor nearby. Jones's eyes rolled up in the back of his head as Michael moved quickly behind him and, jumping up, brought his elbow down on the back of the biker's head.

The baby in the background stopped crying.

The hit was hard enough that blood spewed from Jones's mouth as he slumped forward into a heap. Landing from his elbow attack, Michael turned back and stared for a long moment at the now prone biker, his eyes still rolled back. Michael viewed him with remorseful pity.

In an instant, the other officers were all over Jones, cuffing him and dragging him away. Already the biker was conscious again and screaming about having bitten off part of his tongue, leaving a bloody trail on the floor as a reminder.

Joined by his partner, who whistled and patted him on the back, Michael did the only logical next step.

He straightened his tie.

"BERGERON!" came out a loud voice that reeked of authority. "LEBLANC! AUCOIN! GET YOUR ASSES IN HERE NOW!"

"Crap," said Rodger, giving a defeated sigh. "The commander wants to see all three of us."

Aucoin, who had since extricated himself from the inglorious pile, winced at Ouellette's voice, saying, "Shit, Rodger, we are going to get our asses torn apart!"

Michael said nothing, still coming down off of the high of the fight. All three men headed toward Ouellette's office.

Commander Louis Ouellette's office was what one would expect a police commander's to be—clean and orderly. In fact, the lack of ornamentation pointed to a spartan attitude, one that supported Ouellette's status as an armed forces veteran. On his bookcase, Commander Ouellette displayed a photo of himself posing with President Nixon, as well as a folded American flag in a shadow box. His desk had only two photos, one of his late wife posing in front of a Christmas tree, and one of his daughter and grandchildren playing in Audubon Park.

As for Ouellette himself, the only things that screamed military more than his spit-cleaned uniform and complete lack of hair were his ferocious gaze and his manner of screaming out half his sentences. And to Michael, as the three detectives entered their superior's office, it seemed that Ouellette was spoiling for a good ass-reaming.

"What the bloody hell, and I do mean *what the bloody hell* just happened out there?!" started off Commander Ouellette in his generally congenial way. Having spewed out his question, the police commander just stared at each man in turn, as if his gaze alone could result in a full confession.

Michael drew in a breath. Even though he had subdued Keith Jones without drawing his sidearm, he had beaten the hell out of a citizen. That kind of thing never went well. It was a sure-fire way to get Internal Affairs involved. Commander Ouellette had a policy of protecting his own, but only when his own kept him in the loop. Michael knew that, just as he knew that if he had taken the time to inform his superior of his plan, someone would have gotten severely injured. Or worse.

"It was—" Michael started to say.

"The blame is all on me, Commander," Aucoin interrupted. "I didn't have Jones frisked before being brought into the precinct. If I hadn't been negligent, he'd have never used whatever he's on and caused all this shit." Aucoin nodded his head toward Michael. "If the newbie hadn't jumped in with that karate shit, Jones woulda ripped someone's head off."

Michael was stunned into silence, even as Commander Ouellette's gaze moved from him to Aucoin and back. Everyone knew that Aucoin was a hard-ass who didn't respect rookies until they earned it. So for him to take the fall like this was shocking.

"Fine," said Commander Ouellette at last, nodding his head toward the door, "you're desked for the next two days. Get a report ready for Internal Affairs. You know they're going to be up our ass about this."

Aucoin left without so much as a glance toward Michael or Rodger.

Once he was gone, Commander Ouellette turned back toward the two detectives. Regarding Michael with the gaze of a drill sergeant, Ouellette asked, "So that was some fancy shit you did, LeBlanc. Where'd you learn it?"

Michael hated that his commander called him by his last name, but he knew that he referred to everyone that way. Even Rodger, who had apparently known Ouellette from childhood, was no exception. Michael answered, "Muay Thai kickboxing, Commander."

Commander Ouellette seemed impressed, sitting down as he gestured for the pair to sit as well. "You a black belt, then?"

As Michael took a seat, he explained, "Muay Thai doesn't have a ranking system. But yes, I'd be comparable to a black belt in something like karate."

"Very good, LeBlanc," stated the police commander. Michael knew that was the only praise he'd get and was unsurprised when his superior moved onward with the conversation. "So, where are you two on that French Quarter murder last night?"

Rodger picked up the conversation, something that didn't bother Michael at all. "Well, Commander, we've gone through a box of evidence donated by Samantha Castille, and we've found a potential lead on profiling the killer—that is, if the killer is a copycat."

With a *tsch* sound, Commander Ouellette shook his head. "Keep an eye out for that Samantha. The Castilles are nothing but trouble. But with the way that the chief's and district attorney's office is acting, it damn well better be a copycat. And don't get me started on the media. The newscast this morning is already calling this 'The New Bourbon Street Ripper.'"

"Pardon me, Commander," interjected Michael. "I understand that everyone is anxious to call this a full-fledged copycat, but we can't be sure just off of one murder. Serial killers have to establish a patt—"

"Yeah, LeBlanc, I know that," interrupted Commander Ouellette. "And not one single member of the brass, including the DA and the goddamn mayor, wants to wait for another body to show up. So what leads do you have to find this guy and put him away before the city gets plunged into hell again?"

Again Rodger led the discussion, causing Michael to sit back and wonder if respect was something that was earned in ways other than stopping a biker high on PCP without killing him.

"We've got a lead on some potential accomplices from the Castille murders," continued Rodger. "Potentially, the DA's office could have new people to charge with aiding and abetting those murders. Also, if this is indeed a copycat, perhaps one of these people knows something that can help us."

In the depths of Michael's mind, another lightbulb went off, but he kept his mouth shut for now, allowing his partner and their superior to finish.

"Good job, Bergeron," Commander Ouellette said. "You and LeBlanc get out there and see if you can make any sense of this madness. Report back to me when you have something—anything—new that I can push on upward."

Both men nodded in agreement and got up. A minute later, they were heading down the hall toward the garage. Along the way, Michael had to ward off a storm of applause and praise, fellow officers and detective patting his shoulder and calling him "Karate Kid." Michael got the reference, but he hated that movie with a passion, so his only reaction, even as he caught up with his partner, was an annoyed scowl.

"Hey, Rodger," said Michael as they made their escape.

"Hey, Kara—" Rodger started, stopping when Michael shot him a dangerous look. "I mean, hey, Michael, what's on your mind?"

Michael recounted the revelation he had in Ouellette's office. "I just had a theory. What if one of those four people in this notebook"—Michael patted his coat pocket—"is actually the killer? It would make sense if someone already associated with Vincent Castille would murder people like he did."

As Rodger opened up the door to the garage, he shook his head. "Michael, if we could only be that lucky."

Chapter 4
To Pen a Mystery

Date: **Wednesday, August 5, 1992**
Time: **1:00 p.m.**
Location: **Café du Monde on Decatur**
             French Quarter

"I really don't believe that you understand at all, Sam," said Jacob Hueber, editor for the *Times-Picayune.* "Caroline is ready to can you. You're underestimating your situation." He sipped his cup of café au lait.

As she sat across the patio table from Jacob, a plate of half-eaten, powdered-sugar-drenched beignets before her, Samantha Castille had to admit that she was indeed underestimating her situation.

All around them, the people of New Orleans, as well as its tourists, were finishing up lunch at one of the city's most popular places, Café du Monde. Exclusive to New Orleans, the café was known for its beignets—French-style donuts eaten with powdered sugar—its coffee, which was usually mixed with steaming milk, and its hot chocolate. It was a very popular place for rendezvousing couples, vacationing families, and businessmen on the go.

Under the covered patio, all manner of folk mingled, and Sam noticed them all. Nearby, a couple sat, the man's ringless hand caressing the woman's, avoiding her solitary ring of gold. Two children laughed as they chased each other around a table, only to be scolded by an exasperated mother who was trying, and failing, to hold a decent conversation with a woman her own age holding a baby.

In the back, near the entrance proper to the café, three men in business suits traded witticisms about their supervisor, as well as information on the latest football betting pools. To most people, it was the common noise associated with the outdoor patio of Café du Monde, but for Sam Castille, it was a launching point for many a tale.

In the back of her mind, Sam saw how each of those people's stories could possibly evolve into something unsettling, perhaps even ghastly. The trysting couple would go back to their hotel room, only to find the husband of the woman there, gun in hand. With one pull of the trigger, the man's brains would splatter upon the wall, leaving the helpless woman screaming in gut-wrenching terror.

The exasperated mother would be barely able to keep watch on both children as they walked home, and when one of them stopped near the trolley tracks to pet a stray puppy, she would turn her whole attention to him for a good scolding. The sound of screeching metal wheels would freeze her blood, and she'd turn to the other child just in time to see her cut in half by the oncoming trolley car.

The three businessmen would head back to their office to discover that they had been fired during their lunch break, and the pressure of losing their job in a slow economy would cause them to snap. The next day, they would go on the worst shooting spree the city had ever seen.

Sam Castille had some problems.

Sam's thoughts were interrupted by Jacob calling out her name, and the blond woman realized that she had been daydreaming again. The look Jacob was giving her was annoyed.

"I'm sorry, Jacob," Sam said, absently dabbing a beignet into a heap of powdered sugar. "My mind is just not on the conversation today. Too many people, you see."

It wasn't a lie. Sam hated being out in public, preferring the solitude and sanctuary of her townhome. People made her nervous. People made concentrating even more difficult. Suddenly noticing that two of Jacob's fingers were wrapped with gauze and bandages, Sam asked, "What happened to your hand?"

"Oh, this. I burned myself on the stove several nights ago. I really should stop trying to cook after working all day."

"You could let me cook for you," Sam offered. She fancied herself a pretty good cook. "I haven't cooked for anyone in a long time."

Jacob wasn't "people" to Sam. He was a friend, someone she had learned to trust ever since he befriended her in college, when she was even more reclusive.

Jacob didn't seem to be interested in talking about culinary arts, however. He shook his head, saying, "Look, we have to talk about your job, like it or not. It's come down to a simple, black-and-white situation, Sam. You're not making any deadlines, and Caroline is ready to cut you loose."

This time, the comment got Sam's attention. Caroline Saucier, the executive editor of the *Times-Picayune*, was a mirthless woman whom Sam did not like. Everything about Caroline, from her Jones New York business suits to her Prada knock-off shoes to her wide-brimmed glasses, screamed the word *bitch*. The woman seemed to be the most expressive when she was yelling at an employee, usually Jacob, about his "male incompetence."

And the few times they had met, Sam was pretty sure that Caroline was hitting on her.

With a sigh, Sam nodded her head, her ponytail bobbing about her neck. "I get the point, Jacob," she said. "I know I'm unreliable. Hell, I'd have canned me years ago. But I really hate to think that you're taking heat for me."

"That's the problem, Sam," said Jacob as he met her eyes. "We're both in hot water over this. I brought you in as Sam of Spades, and Caroline loved the idea of the *Picayune* having its own female mystery author. And your job isn't that hard. Five thousand words a week. That's all we ask for. Tell your stories about your detective, Mortimer Branston, and get paid for it. Not that difficult, right?"

Sam's lips grew tight. She knew where Jacob was going with this, and she knew it wasn't going to be pleasant. "So then why haven't you turned in anything in over four weeks? We've run out of filler, and our readers are sending in letters and calling us on the phone wondering when Sam of Spades's next chapter is coming out. It seems that half of New Orleans is waiting to see how *The Mystery of the Crimson Mask* ends."

At that, Sam let out a heartfelt sigh, averting her eyes and saying, "Look, Jacob, I just haven't felt inspired with a good ending lately. I want to give the readers something really amazing, and—"

"Don't give me that, Sam," Jacob said, a twinge of disgust in his voice. "You've never cared about quality before. Hell, your last Branston story, *The Mystery of the Gill-Slit Killer*, was so cheesy that the critics refused to pan it. You write campy mysteries, Sam. You don't have to go for a Pulitzer Prize here."

"Yeah, I know," Sam replied with a frown. "I know that I'm not taken seriously by most. But for this story, I really wanted to give the readers something amazing. I guess . . . " Sam struggled for a moment to find the right words. "I want to be like Richie Fastellos. I want to enter the big times."

At that, Jacob laughed—a short but hurtfully direct laugh— one that made Sam flinch. The expression on her face must have betrayed her feelings, because in the next moment, he was leaning forward and placing his injured hand gently on hers. To Sam, the scratchy and coarse bandages took a lot away from his warmth.

"Sam, I'm sorry." Jacob's voice had softened. "I'm not laughing at you because I think light of your situation. I just find it amazingly ironic that you, after all this time, want to be taken seriously as a writer."

As Jacob's hand left hers, the gauze scratching her skin, Sam gave her friend a wry smile.

She had met Jacob when she was only twenty years old, in a creative writing class. He seemed to take an interest in a short story she wrote about a young girl hitching rides across the country on trains and nearly falling out of one of those trains, only to be saved by the ghost of her dead companion. Up until then, no one had ever paid attention to her writing before.

They had continued to talk throughout the semester until Halloween, when Jacob had invited her, a recluse, to go to a Halloween Vampire Ball hosted by a famous New Orleans author.

Sam had originally declined, but Jacob was so earnest in his insistence that she'd enjoy herself, she eventually told him she'd go to this one party if he promised to never ask her out again. Jacob agreed, and so she went dressed as Elvira, and he went dressed as Gomez Addams. Three highballs and a sorry attempt at dancing the tango later, they were becoming close friends. Ever since then, Jacob had sort of looked out for Sam, even going so far as to vouching for her writing ability to Caroline.

Sam came back from the nostalgia and looked down at her hand. Jacob's bandage had scraped her skin, leaving white marks. She thought that he must have really hurt himself to be wearing such thick bandages.

"It's okay," she said. "I know I've been a real pain in the ass to the *Picayune* all these years. I miss deadlines all the time, my work has to be heavily edited, and I seem to go on a sabbatical every time I near a story's completion. I really am a bad investment."

To Sam's surprise, Jacob shook his head. "No, you're not a bad investment, at least not as a writer. Sam, I've read your stuff. You've got good ideas, you just lack organization. It's amazing that you've lasted this long. Don't you take notes on your stories?"

"Of course. I just don't organize them very well," answered Sam, looking guilty. "I think . . . " For a long moment, she sat there and thought, her brow furrowed with effort. "Honestly, I don't think I go into my stories with a good plan. I just sort of wing it."

With a nod, Jacob leaned back and sipped his café au lait, only to make a face indicating that the coffee was now cold. Putting the cup down, he shook his head and said, "Well, Sam, I can't make you get more organized. But I can tell you that Caroline wants something by tonight."

"Or I'm sacked?" asked Sam point-blank.

Jacob nodded. "Pretty much. But that may not be a bad thing. I mean, come on Sam, you're independently wealthy. Your father may not have been well off, but your grandfather left you wi—"

"Stop right there," Sam snapped at her friend, who withdrew hastily. "Never suggest I live off of that man's inheritance. I'd rather live on the streets than touch a dime that bastard left me!"

Sam soon realized that her outburst had gained the attention of almost a dozen people. Her ears burned as she turned back to her beignets, realizing that she had been mashing one against the powdered sugar this entire time, rendering it an inedible mess. Embarrassed, Sam wiped her fingers clean and washed them off in the small water glass near her plate.

"Sorry, Sam, I know how you feel about him. But if you don't start producing, you may not have a choice."

Finishing wiping off her fingers, Sam nodded in disgust, saying, "I know. Believe me. I know. It seems that no matter how hard I try, though, Grandfather's ghost won't let me be."

Now it was Jacob's turn to get silent. As he pondered, Sam stacked all the dirty plates to the side for a busboy to take away. She had an anxious desire to thank her friend for his time and head home.

"Sam, here is an idea," started Jacob, his tone very business-like. "Scrap the stories with Branston for now, and focus on a different series altogether. You may or may not know this, but last night a woman was brutally murdered."

Sam's heart started to pound in her chest, her blood pressure rising, her mouth going dry. *He isn't about to suggest what I think he's about to suggest. Is he?*

"The murder was very similar to the Bourbon Street Ripper murders. In fact, Caroline's already having us call it a copycat. It would be an incredible tie-in for the granddaughter of Vincent Castille to write about this copycat, give it her own—"

Something about Jacob's suggestion set off an explosion in Sam's skull. Her head started to ache, the veins in the side pounding like a blacksmith's hammer on the anvil. Closing her eyes tightly, Sam took in a short breath and clenched her jaw. The world around her seemed narrowed, as if she were looking through a tunnel. She felt like everyone was now looking at her and waiting for a response.

"I have to go," said Sam, moving quickly as if she were in a bad dream that she had to escape. Reaching into her jeans' back pocket, she threw out some money and gathered her things. In a heartbeat, she was walking out onto Decatur Street and heading toward the trolley stop.

"Sam! Wait," called out Jacob as he hurriedly paid for his own coffee, gathered his leather portfolio case, and followed. When he caught up to Sam, he added, "Look, I know that was in poor taste, but I'm just try—"

"You're damn straight that was in poor taste," snapped Sam again, turning to Jacob, her voice low and venomous. "You haven't the smallest clue how much it sucks being that man's grandchild. I live every day with the memory of what he did to those women. What he did to me . . . "

"Sam . . . I . . . " Jacob reached out to touch Sam's shoulders, only to have his hands swatted away.

"Just piss off, Jacob," Sam snapped for a third time, everything around her moving in slow motion as she focused on her shocked friend. "A real friend would never ask me to capitalize on that bastard's work. It's bad enough that your newspaper is already calling this a copycat. How long do you think it will be before reporters are knocking at Samantha Castille's door wanting an interview? You think I enjoy being known as a serial killer's granddaughter?"

By this point, Jacob was looking quite sick to his stomach. Sam, however, gave no indication she was going to let up, a rush of adrenaline pouring through her to the point that she felt like she was wading through a fog.

"So whose idea was it? Yours? Caroline's? Did you all have a group circle jerk and decide to ask Vincent Castille's granddaughter to create the next series about the Bourbon Street Ripper murders?"

"No," said a pale-looking Jacob. "Nothing like that at all. I just thought that—" He softened and lowered his voice. "I thought that it might help you deal with those demons. By, you know, writing about it."

"Deal with it?" asked Sam, turning and walking away, Jacob following in a meek manner. "Let me tell you something about dealing with it. I haven't slept well in over twenty years. I see and feel death all around me. Right now, every demon and dark loa in New Orleans is laughing at me. Tell me, how do I deal with that?"

By this point, Jacob had the look of a man who'd rather be swallowing razors than staying where he was. Somehow, he managed to say, "Sam, you're freaking out. Have you . . . have you taken your medicine today?"

"Have I taken my medicine?" Sam yelled at Jacob. By now, they were both at the trolley stop, and the trolley car had arrived, heading uptown. Sam got on board, paid the toll, and then turned to offer one final attack on Jacob. "Yes, let's just ask Sam the psycho if she's loaded up on her Lithium and Valium today. You're an asshole like every other person, Jacob. Good-bye!"

With that, Sam headed to her seat on the trolley as it began to speed away, leaving behind her distraught friend. As for Sam, as soon as she found a place to sit, her thoughts turned inward. She wondered how any friend could ever even dare to suggest she make a dime off of her grandfather's evil.

They are all the same. Jacob. Klein. Caroline. They hate me because I'm Vincent Castille's granddaughter. They all want to see me suck and die.

The fog around Sam thickened, the pounding in her skull like the screams of restless demons, as she got an image in her head. Again she was ten years old, standing at the end of a long hallway. The smell of blood and bile was faint but present. Walking down the hallway, her eyes were fixed on a single door, red luminance and smoke drifting from it. With every step, her heart beat faster. Her grandfather's words echoed in her head, *Why do I do these things? Because this is what you want, Sam.*

Sam's vision blurred as, in her mind, she saw the door open, then a close-up of her grandfather, in surgical scrubs and with a surgical mask on, holding a bloody scalpel. Behind him was a corpse with its chest opened in the manner of a full autopsy, the heart beating rapidly. The smell of blood and bile was much more intense. Vincent Castille's gaze was iron as he exclaimed, "Life everlasting through pain. Isn't it wonderful, Sam? Sam!"

The fog began to lift, to thin out, the pounding overshadowed by a voice calling out her name.

"Sam!"

Sam's attention came back to herself and her surroundings.

She was not on board the trolley as she had thought. She had not gotten up, had a nervous breakdown in public, and stormed off.

Instead, she was seated at the table at Café du Monde. Sam looked up and saw Jacob with a concerned expression on his face. He leaned back and frowned at her, saying, "So what do you think? I mean, I know it's crappy to ask you this, but what about writing about those murders? Give it your own spin. Any direction you want to go is fine. Do that, and I'm sure Caroline will give you a few more days to get yourself straightened out."

For a very long time, Sam sat there, her eyes focused on Jacob, her mind and heart racing.

God help me, I think I do need my meds.

After a long pause, one that got several uncomfortable "ahems" from Jacob, Sam gave a small nod and answered in a soft voice, "Let me think on it. I'll call you tonight."

It wasn't until later that afternoon, when Sam had gotten home, popped her medication for "hallucinations," and taken a seat on her back patio, that she thought about things.

At least the scene was familiar and therefore comforting. Her patio overlooked a small backyard garden adorned with popcorn bushes along its perimeter, a growing magnolia tree, and a water fountain, comprised of a naked cherub pissing into the basin.

For a while, she sat there and questioned her sanity, wondering if perhaps she had finally lost her grip on reality. After rationalizing that possibility away, she considered the possibility that she was suffering from severe sleep deprivation. Finally, Sam decided that analyzing herself was just a way of avoiding the real issue—Jacob's offer.

Every fiber of Sam's being hated the idea of giving her grandfather even the least bit of attention, and writing about a copycat killer would only serve to keep his memory alive. However, Sam reasoned, it was too late to stop the ghost of Vincent Castille from being empowered. Just from last night's murder, her grandfather's memory was already being given new life.

That thought sickened Sam, who had worked so hard over the past twenty years to bury her grandfather. But however sick those thoughts made her, she had to admit that the idea of Vincent Castille's granddaughter penning a mystery based around his grisly crimes was an amazing shtick. If done properly, it could be amazing.

Finally, Sam said to herself, "Okay, if I'm going to do this, I'm going to do this right. I need to organize myself and make sure I don't leave any loopholes."

After making another pot of coffee, Sam headed into her study for what she hoped would be a fruitful brainstorming session. It was as she was walking around her desk that she heard a small *crunch* and realized that she had stepped on something. Looking down and moving her slipper-covered foot, Sam saw something silver and shiny pressed into the rug below. Curious as Alice in Wonderland, she stooped down to pick it up.

What she had stepped on was a metallic pen, one of those expensive types given for a graduation or some other memorable event. It was older, probably from the seventies, and still in beautiful condition. The silver casting was hardly dulled. It had one word professionally etched across its body—"Castille."

She tried to remember where it was from. As far as she could tell, the only place it could have come from was the box that she had given the detectives earlier this morning, the one that spilled open.

But why is this pen so familiar?

Sam walked to her chair and opened her desk. After rummaging through a small pile of unused sticky notes, paper clips, and pencils, she found what she was looking for: a small pen case.

Taking the case out and opening it, Sam looked over the pens in the case. Just like the one she'd found, these were old fountain pens with a metallic finish and her family surname etched into the side. A gold one, a black one, and a red one were in the case—perfect matches to the silver one.

"Curious," said Sam to herself as she touched each of the pens. "These belonged to Father. I wonder where this one"—she again picked up the silver pen—"has been all these years?"

Uncapping the silver one, Sam took out a sheet of paper and ran the pen across the surface. Sure enough, dark blue ink flowed out smoothly, writing with ease. This got a small smile from Sam. "Well, if that isn't a stroke of luck," she commented. "Looks like the set is now complete."

Putting aside the case of three pens, Sam again rummaged in her desk, eventually pulling out several sets of five-subject notebooks. Inside each one were pages upon pages of notes, character relationship charts, and diagrams from over ten years of mystery writing. While the majority of the notebooks were filled with notes for Mortimer Branston's mysteries, some contained stories never finished. Tales of betrayal, torture, and murder scribbled hastily, ideas interlinked and then crossed out, and copious side notes denoting directions characters could take—all of that lined the pages of these notebooks.

Finally finding a notebook with considerable blank space, and putting the others away, Sam opened to a fresh page and, uncapping her newly discovered—or rediscovered—pen, began to write.

An hour later, she had five words on the page: "Bourbon Street Ripper Copycat Killer."

Feelings of self-deprecation began to rise again, forcing Sam to action. Getting up, she headed over to a bookcase and scanned for a certain binder. Finding it, she pulled it down.

It was an old binder filled with various notes from the original Bourbon Street Ripper case, a scrapbook of sorts her father had made. Sam remembered wanting to throw it away, but her therapist, Dr. Klein, had told her that by keeping it, she could one day confront the demons inside her and bury them.

By the time Sam was sitting down at her desk, her head was again pounding, and with some effort, she opened up the binder. Inside were newspaper clippings, scene photographs, and a myriad of notes, sketches, and diagrams—all of the details of the Vincent

Castille murders. Sam's eyes fell upon a picture taken from the crime scene—a woman's face, covered in blood and frozen in a look of incalculable anguish.

For a moment, Sam felt as if she was about to be sick, her headache pounding like the clash of a hammer against metal. Forcing herself, she turned to a far less offensive sight—a grouping of newspaper clippings with titles such as "Madman Strikes Metro Area" or "Satan Lives in the Big Easy."

As she looked at the headlines, Sam felt a tingle go down her spine, like she had gotten cold suddenly. The feeling was both odd and yet familiar, and Sam shivered from it. When it passed, she felt like it would be a good idea to stop stalling and start writing. Picking up the silver pen, Sam started to jot down notes, despite her headache.

She soon found herself immersed in scenario after scenario over who could be the copycat killer in her story, jotting down lists of people who were close to the actual murder, who could have acted as accomplices, or could have snapped due to the stress of the investigation. She even wrote down her name and Rodger's, intent on basing characters off of the two of them later.

It was after she had an entire page filled with notes on who the killer could be that Sam's eyes fell upon a particular article, the headlines emblazoned on the page: "Mother and Child Missing. Police Suspect Serial Killer."

Sam felt powerfully drawn to that article. Resist as she might, she found herself reading it with intense concentration. It was as if everything inside of her was telling her that this article would give her the inspiration she needed.

As she read through the article, Sam tapped the pen to her lips. Of all the murders attributed to Vincent Castille, this was the oddest and the most out of character for him.

And according to the notes scribbled in the margins of the newspaper clipping by her father, this was one of the last murders in the case.

A woman, Maple Christofer, and her ten-year-old son, Dallas, were kidnapped from their home on a summer evening.

Eventually, both bodies were found buried in a coffin in a field not far from the Castille Estate, underneath a cypress tree.

This last tidbit gave pause to Sam, who rubbed her eyes and thought out loud, "Cypress blossoms are used for funerals. Why so reverent? That doesn't seem like Grandfather at all."

Suddenly, Sam looked up, as if coming upon a moment of pure clarity. What if Grandfather was associated with Maple Christofer? What if she had been his lover, or was a kept woman, or something similar? Sam's mind raced as she jotted down the idea. Excitedly, she finished reading the article, reaching the biggest surprise at the end.

When the bodies were found, Dallas was still alive, but in a coma, having been badly beaten with a shovel. His mother, who had been executed in the same gruesome manner as all of Vincent Castille's other victims, was found in pieces in the same coffin, Dallas having been buried in his mother's own viscera.

Her headache gone, Sam felt elation as she scribbled furiously in her notebook, the silver pen a mere blur as she took down all of the information. When she finished dotting the last *i*, Sam triumphantly closed the binder. She had found her murderer.

Several hours later, Sam had finished filling up over a dozen pages of notes. She had written that Dallas Christofer was the copycat killer. She had given herself the alias Julia Castille, and Rodger was now Horatio Benoit. She had also assigned aliases for everyone else who was going to be involved in the story, with the exception of her killer. Something inside of her told her to keep that name as it really was.

Sam had also jotted down a timeline detailing Dallas's mental deterioration into psychosis, his subsequent escape from the mental asylum, and his murderous killing spree emulating the Bourbon Street Ripper.

The timeline came easily to Sam, every fact coming effortlessly, as if she were taking down dictation. When she finished coming up with Dallas's timeline, she stared at it, contemplating one of the most important questions in any mystery: Why did the killer do it?

Finally, Sam felt a lightbulb go off in her head, and with a victorious smirk, she put the tip of the pen to the paper. She would go with one of the oldest reasons for any sort of crime, other than money or love. *Revenge.* Sam thought to herself and wrote down: "Dallas Christofer is a copycat killer of the Bourbon Street Ripper because Dallas wants revenge on the Castille family's heir, the granddaughter of Vincent Castille."

As the silver pen dotted the final period of that sentence, Sam felt herself shiver again, that tingling sensation going down her spine. She was starting to like that feeling, equating it to the excitement of the story she was crafting. For once, coming up with ideas came easily, and while this surprised Sam, she figured it had everything to do with how personal this story was to her.

"If I was Dallas Christofer and I was the murderer, this is why I'd do it," Sam said out loud, high from the intense brainstorming session. "And I'd make sure that Sam—er, Julia—suffered until her very last breath."

Sam felt as if she had just starting penning her very best work.

The ringing of the phone on her desk pulled Sam from her reverie, the loud clanking of the bell indicative of the age of the phone. It was her father's, willed to her, and Sam liked the old-world style of it, with the receiver resting on the cradle and the large internal bell rung by the clanking of a metallic hammer. She felt all mystery authors should have a phone like this one.

Picking up the receiver, Sam said, "Hello?" and was delighted to hear Jacob on the other line. He reminded Sam that it was almost ten o'clock in the evening, and that Caroline needed an answer. With her grin widening from thoughts of how brutally delicious her story was going to be, Sam answered her friend, "Tell Caroline that she's got herself a deal."

Chapter 5
Stories and Shih Tzus

Date: **Wednesday, August 5, 1992**
Time: **3:00 p.m.**
Location: **Suburbs of Marrero**
Westbank, New Orleans

When Rodger pulled up to the small house in Marrero, a city on the Westbank of New Orleans, everything looked just as he remembered it: the flock of five or six pink flamingoes as tastefully arranged as is possible with such a decoration, the garden gnome with its red pointy hat discolored from years of rain and sun exposure, and the well-tended flower beds.

The sprinkler system was currently sputtering out water, due to a knot in the line. The house itself was in good repair and had a homey feeling to it Rodger liked.

"This is it?" asked Michael as Rodger parked the car. "Somehow, I expected more from the detective who taught you everything. Not something so . . . tacky."

Rodger looked at his partner and sighed, shaking his head at Michael's lack of social graces. "Well, when you've put in as many years on the force as Douglas, you go right ahead and have your house cleaner than a virgin's knees and your yard straighter than a nun's ruler. Until then, you can hush your mouth. Douglas is a good man."

Getting out of the car without another word, Rodger walked carefully along the walkway leading toward the house's front door. Michael was soon following, saying, "Man, Rodger, I'm sorry for being out of line there. It's just that I'm surprised, even shocked, that such a successful detective lives in such a downtrodden location."

"It's mostly due to cutbacks on pensions," replied Rodger as he got to the front door, having navigated the labyrinthine front yard. "Men like Douglas gave their all for this city. They struggled on a daily basis to clean up the filth that polluted the streets—from mobsters to murderers. They sacrificed their days, their health, their youth to make sure the bad guys didn't win. And all it took is one instance of them collaring the son or nephew of someone with a little too much power, a little too much money, and *bam!*" He clapped his hands together. "Their careers were over. No advancement. No opportunity. Just put in your time, get your gold watch, and hope no one's around to hold a grudge. That's why good cops like Douglas live in shit holes like this."

Michael nodded with an understanding look in his eyes.

Rodger nodded back, glad his partner "got it." It wasn't that the entire system was corrupt, but it was just corrupt enough that good people got punished.

Rodger rang the doorbell. Immediately, there was the sound of a small dog barking, followed by the sound of its paws scuffing at the other side of the front door. There was a long pause filled only with the yapping of the dog, before the sound of shuffling and moving could be heard.

"I'm coming," said a gruff old voice from the other side of the door. "Boudreaux! Get your damn ass back, dog, or I swear I'll put you in the stew, ya!"

A moment or so later, the door opened, revealing an old man with a strong build, a thin head of gray hair, and a clean-shaven face. He was hunched over some, as if his back had stopped working a long time ago, and he was wearing reading glasses, which slid precariously close to the edge of his nose as he stared at the detectives at the door.

"Well, holy shit," said Dugas, opening the door completely and embracing Rodger with a familiarity that was as warm as his voice was gruff. "Rodger Bergeron, you old goat! How the hell have you been?"

"Douglas," replied Rodger, embracing his old friend and former mentor before clapping him on the arm. "Damn, it's been how long?"

"Not since Christmas last year," replied Douglas with a pleasant smile. "What the hell have you been up to? Come on in, will you?"

Rodger started to move in, but there was a small shih tzu dog growling as it bit his pants leg, swinging its head from side to side rapidly with a mouthful of fabric. Looking down at the animal, Rodger said, "I'd love to, but I think Boudreaux has decided to eat my pants."

With an apology, Douglas dropped down and picked up the dog, who refused to let go of Rodger's pants leg at first. Growling with frustration, Boudreaux finally let go, and contented himself with applying his tongue liberally to Douglas's face, who replied with doting baby talk. Out the corner of his eye, Rodger saw Michael struggling to keep a straight face.

"Come on in," said Douglas finally as he carried the squirming dog into the house. "Mabel was just about to go making groceries for dinner, but I think she can whip up some coffee and cakes."

Rodger and his partner followed the older man into the house. Roger noted that the house hadn't changed much in five years. The walls and old wooden tables were covered in photographs of children and grandchildren, from infancy to graduations and weddings. An old grandfather clock stood in the living room. Old wooden consoles and coffee tables were littered with more photographs, including pictures of Boudreaux. The mantel had a shadowbox above it that contained an old badge labeled "Lieutenant Dugas," as well as a service revolver.

As he took it all in, Rodger felt a peaceful nostalgia flow through him. Some things didn't need to change with the times, and Douglas was one of those things.

"Mabel," called Douglas from the living room, putting down Boudreaux, who padded off to who knew where, "Rodger and his new partner are here. Come on out and say hello!"

Rodger, who had started to take off his coat, turned as a small, skinny woman came into the room. Mabel Dugas was, like her husband, on in years, but the sweet smile on her face never faded. She was the kind of woman who could be anyone's grandmother, and while she had a strong will—she had to, being married to a man like Douglas—she never lost that gentle nature.

Walking up to Rodger, Mabel put her hands on the sides of his head, pulled him down, and kissed him on the forehead. "Good to see you, Rodger," said Mabel with a kind smile. "It's been too long. What have you been up to?"

"Oh, the same old stuff, Mabel," replied Rodger, hugging the older woman back. "Breaking in a new partner, mostly. This is Michael LeBlanc. Michael, this is Douglas and Mabel Dugas, probably the two nicest people in New Orleans."

"Aw, now there's no reason to go insulting folks in their own home," said Douglas as he and Michael shook hands. He and Rodger had a good laugh at that, Mabel gave her husband a friendly swat on the arm, and Michael chuckled.

"Well, you have a really lovely place here, Mr. and Mrs. Dugas," said Michael, looking around the house. "I have to say, though, it's a real honor to meet the guy who trained my partner."

Douglas laughed sharply, giving Rodger a punch on the arm. "Is that what this old bastard had to say? Well, hell, did he tell you what a hellion he was as a rookie?"

"Oh, now, Douglas, there's no reason to tell Michael all that," replied Rodger as Mabel took their coats.

As Douglas motioned for the two men to sit, Rodger's tone got serious. "Actually, as much as I wish this could be a personal visit, we are here on business."

Douglas's demeanor changed at that. "It's what was in the papers this morning, Rodger, isn't it?"

Mabel excused herself from the room as Douglas continued, "So, is it true? Is there really someone emulating that devil?"

Among many other things, Rodger appreciated that Douglas never wasted any time in getting down to business.

Rodger nodded ruefully, saying, "We aren't one hundred percent sure on that yet, Douglas, but the brass want us to treat it like a copycat until we get proof otherwise."

Rodger noted the grim expression on Douglas's face before continuing, "We have a potential lead in profiling the killer." Rodger held out his hand to Michael, who gave him the pocket notebook. Rodger held it up for Douglas to see. "We think that some or all of the people mentioned in here were accomplices to Vincent Castille. If anyone could have a lead on who this new murderer is, it would be them."

Reflecting on Michael's most recent theory, Rodger mentally added that one of them might very well be the murderer. As he handed the notebook over to the older man, Rodger was not wholly surprised when Douglas said, "If one of them isn't actually the murderer, right? Because that would be my hunch."

For a few long moments, Douglas stared at the interior of the notebook, remaining still, his old brow furrowing in thought, even as Mabel returned. She was followed by Boudreaux, who now had a bow attached to the top of his head. Mabel appeared to pay no mind as the dog jumped up on her chair and sat with entitlement. The elderly woman focused on serving cups of coffee and a plate of sliced pound cake.

Finally, Douglas spoke. "I remember these four. Until now, I never would have connected them. I'm certain the first three are still alive, and I'm pretty sure that Blind Moses is, too."

Rodger couldn't have hoped for better news. As he moistened some pound cake between his lips, he asked, "So you know who these people really are? Their real names? Where they live?"

By this point, Mabel had sat down, after picking Boudreaux up, and placed him on her lap. The shih tzu busied himself with the important task of trying to filch pieces of pound cake off of Mabel's plate. Mabel didn't seem to mind as she kept the treats just out of his reach.

"Let me see . . . I know where they lived ten years ago, before I retired," replied Douglas, putting down the notebook and tapping the pages. "I haven't kept up with anything but my gardening since then." Picking up a coffee cup, the older man thought things over. "If I recall, Topper Jack has spent his life in the Lower Ninth Ward, in and out of rehab for cocaine. He's a career junkie, but he knows everything about everyone downtown, I shit you not. He even helped Narcotics bust up a few drug rings."

"An informant," Michael said as he sipped some coffee. "That could be useful." He made a strange puckered face, then put down the cup.

Boudreaux jumped off Mabel's lap and trotted over to Michael. The shih tzu sniffed Michael's leg before jumping into his lap. Michael looked down at the dog, who looked back up at him. It was apparent the two were evaluating each other.

"I think Boudreaux likes you," commented Mabel with a warm smile.

Michael replied, "Obviously."

Rodger shook his head, reconciling himself to the fact that Boudreaux liked everyone but him. Then he looked back at his former mentor. "What about the other three, Douglas? What can you tell me about them?"

Taking a large gulp from his cup, Douglas continued, "Well, Mad Monty is all over. He's run everything from drug rackets to car thefts. He's either in prison or out on parole. His real name is Tyrell Montgomery Jones. You probably remember him, Rodger."

Rodger clenched his jaw hard, a line of sweat forming on his brow. He remembered Tyrell Jones from years ago, during the 1980s. He also remembered investigating Tyrell for manslaughter, and putting him away for close to ten years. And he also remembered Tyrell saying that if he ever got the chance, he'd cut Rodger's balls off.

"Yeah, I remember him. Who else?" Rodger asked, his voice slightly hoarse.

"Fat Willie, or William K. Benedict, if I recall properly," said Douglas, "is serving a life sentence up in Angola."

Rodger was surprised that someone they were searching for was in the state penitentiary. "And what about Blind Moses? Where is he?"

Douglas gave a short laugh, as if something was very funny to him. "Whenever I've ever encountered the name Blind Moses, Jackson Square came up. So did a name: Dr. Lazarus. Might want to check those leads for your *man*."

"A fortune-teller or palm reader, eh," said Rodger, wondering what was so funny to Douglas. "All right, thanks for the tip." He wondered which of the four would be the most likely candidate as a serial killer.

"Let me ask you something," said Douglas. "Have you spoken to Samantha Castille yet?"

The room went silent, and a tension hung in the air like a low-lying fog. Rodger looked down at his plate and clenched his jaw a few times. While he had spoken to Sam, and even gotten a pivotal clue from her, he knew that wasn't what Douglas was talking about.

Looking up at Douglas, Rodger said, "Yes, we spoke to her recently, Michael and myself, about the case. No, I haven't talked to her about *that*." He couldn't help but sound disgusted on the final word.

While Michael seemed taken aback, Douglas just sat there and shook his head. "Rodger, you're going to need to talk to her about it sometime. You can't carry that to your grave."

"Yeah, well, you didn't have to look that sweet little girl in the eyes and tell her you failed," replied Rodger as he looked into Douglas's eyes. "Rhythm and blues don't have it right, Douglas, time doesn't heal all wounds."

While Michael sat there looking lost, and Douglas sat there scowling with disapproval as only an old man can, Boudreaux decided it was time to strike. The shih tzu made a quick pass for Michael's pound cake, only for Michael to lift it out of his reach. With a frustrated snuffle, the dog sat heavily on Michael's lap.

Quickly, Mabel acted, refilling her husband's coffee cup. "Now, Douglas, leave poor Rodger alone. He's a grown man. He can decide when to talk to that nice Samantha." As she finished with the coffee, she turned to Michael and said in the most conversational of tones, "They're just a bunch of boys sometimes, but they've got good hearts. It's like an old film noir, Michael. When they were younger, these two focused day and night on hunting down the bad guy. It was just like in a Humphrey Bogart film."

This seemed to alleviate the tension, as Rodger soon gave a low chuckle and sipped his coffee. "Well, I wouldn't say we were that cliché. Besides, I stayed out on the floor, while Mr. Big Shot over here got an office."

"Only because I broke up one of the Marcello boys' gambling rackets," said Douglas with a proud laugh, any trace of seriousness gone from his face. "Now that was a case worthy of a movie being made about it. Have you ever heard what happened, Michael?"

As Michael replied that he hadn't, and Douglas launched into a tale of how he single-handedly broke up one of the largest illegal gambling operations in New Orleans, Rodger leaned back, the tension gone from his aging face. While he was grateful to both Mabel and Michael for breaking up the tension, he knew that, sooner or later, he'd have to have a long, painful talk with Samantha Castille.

As Douglas continued to tell his tale, Rodger's memories hearkened back to the saddest day of his life. A large funeral held outdoors on a dreary and cloudy day, the world's colors so muted they were nearly just shades of gray. Rodger wore the same outfit as always, standing next to Sam, only ten years old, dressed in a simple black dress. Her blond hair was wrapped with a black ribbon, and she held a bouquet of cypress flowers. As "Taps" played in the background, Rodger reached down and rested his hand on young Sam's shoulder. The child looked up at him, and Rodger remembered seeing the blankest look he had ever seen on anyone's face.

A face devoid of life.

Coming out of those unhappy memories, Rodger became aware that Douglas was asking him a question. "Hey, Rodger! You listening? Remember the look on Ouellette's face when I brought in the train of bookies, all cuffed to one long bicycle chain?"

Rodger quickly drew himself back to reality and, with a forced chuckle, nodded and replied, "Yeah, he nearly crapped himself an entire building, Douglas."

As Douglas continued the story, the others laughing, Rodger forced away those unhappy memories. That's what he had done for the past twenty years, and it made it all bearable. What was one more day of avoiding the issue? With that thought, Rodger left the memories behind yet again and rejoined the conversation and lively storytelling.

A few hours later, Rodger and Michael were on the road, speeding along toward downtown New Orleans. The two detectives had come to the agreement to find and question Topper Jack first, and Rodger had suggested that they return to the precinct long enough to run a check on the informant's last known location. Michael had agreed.

After studying the notes in his own notebook for a while, Michael finally spoke. "You know, Rodger, I just realized something."

Rodger, who had the window rolled down and was smoking a cigarette, snapped out of his daze. "Hmm?" he replied. "Wait, what? What did you realize?"

"Let's say for a moment that we are dealing with a genuine copycat," Michael said, flipping through his notes to an earlier page. "In our first conversation, you mentioned that after a while, it seemed that Vincent Castille was toying with you and your partner, Edward, correct?"

"Correct," answered Rodger. "He would purposefully leave red herrings. For example, at one murder scene, he left a key that belonged to a locker at the Greyhound station. The locker contained a set of power tools, similar to the ones used for the murders. Of course, we immediately suspected the owner of the locker, and were even able to make an arrest, but it ended up being a false lead. The owner was out of town during the murder, with his mistress in Lafayette, and couldn't even remember losing the key."

This information seemed important to Michael, for he immediately jotted it down. "Well, was he a patient at the hospital Castille worked for?"

That question made Rodger give a short laugh, which trailed into a smoke-induced cough. Recovering, he said, "God, if it had been that easy! No, the chump had no relation at all to Vincent Castille, not even in casual passing. The guy worked on a dredger out on the Mississippi River. We could never connect how Castille got that key."

Michael seemed to slow down. He finally asked, "Is his name on file?"

Rodger found that to be an odd question, but he answered it anyway. "Of course, Michael, all suspects' names are always on the reports. I think it's on the report Edward filed. Why?"

"Just a hunch," answered Michael, closing the notebook. "When we get back to the precinct, I want to check his name and see if he's still around."

"I'll do that," replied Rodger, "seeing as how I have to run a check for Jack's latest whereabouts."

That seemed to satisfy Michael, who looked out of the car as Rodger turned off onto the interstate, heading over the Mississippi River. The mighty river, one of the largest in the country, was as brown as shit-water, and smelled twice as bad. But any New Orleans native would tell you that the mighty Mississippi was as much a part of the city as the French Quarter and the Superdome. It was another part of the hell that Rodger called home.

Finishing his cigarette and putting the butt out in the ashtray before rolling up the window, Rodger said, "So what was your initial hunch? The one you were mentioning before we got sidetracked?"

"Oh right," replied Michael as he seemed to snap out of his own thoughts. "My hunch is that if this is a real copycat killer, he's probably going to try to play us like Vincent Castille did. We need to be ready for anything, even the people in this notebook, to be a red herring."

"Question everything?" asked Rodger with a grin, knowing full well that his partner's answer would be yes.

"Of course," replied Michael with a nod. "If we're dealing with any kind of serial killer, even a copycat, then we need to expect anything. He may change the number of days between murders, the types of locations, even the age of the victims. All we can hope is that this person is trying to emulate the method of the original murders as closely as possible."

"Right," replied Rodger with an affirmative nod, "because if he does, then we still have the hunch about the receipts from the hardware stores and the restaurants to work with."

After a few minutes of silence, as Rodger drove the police car through the streets of New Orleans toward the precinct, Michael finally asked the question Rodger had been dreading.

"So, Rodger, what's the deal between you and Sam?" asked Michael as he looked out of the window, observing the afternoon traffic. "Why is it that whenever her name comes up, or you get in front of her, you get more withdrawn than a guilty suspect?"

Rodger grimaced at his partner's question, clenching his teeth and pretending to be too focused on the road to answer. This tactic did nothing to dissuade Michael, who spoke again after a few moments of silence. "I'm not trying to be nosy here, Rodger, but if this is something that could be significant in the future—"

"It's nothing, really," Rodger hastily interrupted, irritated even though he knew it was irrational. When he saw, out the corner of his eye, his partner looking at him, Rodger sighed and, stopping at a red light, turned to face his partner.

"I knew her father, and I made a bad judgment call that resulted in him getting killed," Rodger said, staring right back into Michael's unblinking eyes. "Sam's already forgiven me. She forgave me about ten years ago. On Christmas Eve, actually. Sent me a long letter and a card and everything. But—"

"But you never forgave yourself, correct?" asked Michael. His attitude was passionless, as if he were simply stating a fact, just as one would state that boiling water burned.

"Correct," said Rodger between his teeth, utterly irritated at his partner's know-it-all attitude. It was at times like this that Michael's brilliance was overshadowed by his lack of social skills. Resisting the urge to reply with an equally brusque comment, and partially because the traffic light chose that moment to turn green, Rodger instead focused on driving.

"So that's it, Michael. Really. It's one of those things that I wish I could forget, and yet know I'll always remember."

"Tough break, bud," replied Michael in an almost bored tone, already looking back at his notebook. "At least she's forgiven you by now. It would be really hard to work on this case if she was still pissed at you."

This elicited another clenched jaw from Rodger, who actively tried to avoid personal conversations with Michael for this very reason. Even though his countenance never betrayed how frustrated he was, Rodger took the rest of the drive to the station to calm down.

By the time they pulled up into the underground garage of the police precinct, Rodger had cooled off. He knew that Michael was right—if Sam hadn't forgiven him years ago, if she had held a grudge, they might not have gotten that box of evidence. Getting a court order when Sam was clearly not implicated in last night's murder would have been difficult at best. Sam's lawyer, Kent Bourgeois, was one of the best in the city, and he would block any attempt to force Sam to give up anything of hers that she didn't want to give up.

Rodger reflected on this as he got out of the car. His reason for avoiding Sam was guilt, and he knew that. He also knew that trying to hide that guilt was useless—Douglas knew about it, Ouellette know about it, other detectives like Aucoin knew about it, and Michael had figured it out without so much as batting an eyelash.

As Rodger walked alongside his partner into the building, he decided that once the time was right, he'd talk to Sam and bury the past once and for all.

Chapter 6
The Pale Lantern

Date: **Wednesday, August 5, 1992**
Time: **7:00 p.m.**
Location: **Ritz-Carlton Hotel on Canal Street**
             French Quarter

The lights flickered as they turned on, cutting back at the darkness with the efficiency of a razor. A man sat up in a king-sized bed. Looking around with bleary, half-sleeping eyes, he noted his surroundings. It was the same hotel room he had checked into three days ago, and not the darkest recesses of his dreams where he had been just a moment ago. Rubbing his eyes, the man gave an "ugh" sound, followed by a cough, one that cleared his lungs of sleep-induced gunk. With a final yawn, the sort given when one has no worries as to who might overhear, the man stood up and headed to the bathroom.

The room itself was posh, as was any room in the Ritz-Carlton—one of the more expensive hotels in New Orleans. It offered down pillows and blankets, Egyptian sheets, plush red carpets that hushed one's footsteps, a courtesy bar, and an executive desk and leather chair. The walls, papered in fleur-de-lis designs, were adorned with tasteful landscapes of fields, plantations, and the French Quarter.

The man had chosen the Ritz-Carlton on the suggestion of his publicist, who had stated that someone of his newly discovered fame should stay in nothing less than a five-star hotel. As the man stood in front of the toilet, relieving himself, he thought that he could have spent half as much for a nice bed-and-breakfast.

Business taken care of, the man flushed the toilet and looked in the mirror. "All right, Richie," said the man to his reflection, "you might as well get started. You got a long night ahead of you."

Richard Alfonso Fastellos, or Richie, as he was commonly known, was an author. Like many others, he had started out writing short stories and articles while he struggled to discover the real writer within him. One night, a horrific nightmare inspired him to write a sordid murder mystery. In less than six months, he had finished what would become his first best seller—*The Pale Lantern*.

Richie's chronic anxiety had finally worked in his favor. Seeing as how he'd been taking medication for it since childhood, he considered the book-inspiring nightmare to be a blessing.

Continuing to appraise his reflection, Richie scowled a bit, muttering about how awful he looked. His normally neatly combed brunette hair was as messy as a mop, those normally crystal blue eyes were bloodshot from sleeping too hard, and that normally smooth Caucasian skin was stubbly with a five o'clock shadow.

Standing up straight and giving a nod, he started to fix himself up. Richie Fastellos, as he was commonly known, felt he could look better than he currently did. On the upside, he thought he still looked like he was under thirty, rather than over.

A shower, shave, and grooming later, and Richie was back to his normally sharp-looking self, dressed in a short-sleeved mock neck and jeans—comfortable and functional. Smelling like Brut, his favorite scent, and having claimed a bottle of water from the nightstand, Richie moved over to the desk and took a seat. Turning his computer on and connecting to the Internet, the laptop's modem screeching to life, he took several swigs of water and started to check his e-mail.

The first were the usual e-mails from Gordon Rockway, his publicist, relaying pieces of wisdom on how to promote himself at the book signing tomorrow. Gordon's e-mails were tiresome to read, and Richie found himself skimming for high points at first, and eventually just not caring and skipping the e-mails entirely, "archiving" them in his e-mail client's trash bin.

"Gordon should be here tomorrow," Richie said to himself. "I'll talk to him then and see what advice he has for me. It's not like I'm going to blow a book signing."

Richie reached over and held protectively on to the bottle of pills near his computer. Having had anxiety attacks for years, the pills were a regular part of his life. Any high-stress situation could be made to disappear with one dose. In fact, just taking a pill made him feel better, even if they took a few minutes to actually start working.

Richie attributed that to the placebo effect. He was fine with it.

As he drew his hand back from the pill bottle, Richie's fingers touched the cover of a nearby book. It was his book, *The Pale Lantern,* his ticket to the big times. The story was centered on a New Orleans detective solving the murder of a wealthy couple.

In a twist that shocked his readers, the murderer ended up being the detective himself, and the mystery was solved by the detective's assistant. The novel became a hit almost overnight, making the *New York Times* best-seller list in only one week. Richie went from an unknown mystery writer from Pittsburgh to a millionaire.

One year and several talk shows later, Richie was in the city where the story took place, New Orleans, for a book signing at a local talk show. His publicist had arranged the book signing for the middle of the week, but Richie, who had always wanted to see New Orleans, came in a few days early.

So far, he had managed to get drunk two out of the three nights and get smashed a third time at a party held by a local author who specialized in books about vampires. Richie, who often enjoyed more than a few drinks, was already sick of daiquiris.

As Richie sorted through his e-mails, a particular one caught his eye. It had been sent by a man named Kent Bourgeois, an attorney in New Orleans. Richie wondered what a lawyer wanted with him. Anxiety beginning to churn in his stomach as he opened the e-mail, Richie saw that it was the result of an inquiry about a townhome in the Garden District—an inquiry he had apparently made several months ago.

"God, that was so long ago, I don't even remember doing it," said Richie to himself with a shrug as he read the e-mail. The contents of the e-mail, however, grabbed his complete attention.

Mr. Fastellos:

It is with regret that I must inform you that the property you have inquired about is not for sale. The townhome in question belongs to a legacy estate that is quite old in New Orleans, and cannot be broken up without express permission by the estate holder.

In this instance, the estate holder, Ms. Samantha Castille, uses the townhome in question as her primary residence. Ms. Castille has no interest in selling the property at this time.

We appreciate your courtesy in this matter.

Sincerely,

Kent Bourgeois, Esquire

For several minutes, Richie just looked at the e-mail, his mouth a straight line. He was a bit offended by its tone. He read the line talking about "Ms. Samantha Castille" over and over again. Finally, his expression melted and he rubbed his head. "Castille," he said tiredly. "God, I've heard that name before, but where?"

Being unable to place Samantha's name brought a nervous twitch to the corners of Richie's lips. Mind racing, he loaded up his web browser and typed in a search for "Castille New Orleans." A few minutes later, he was looking at the results—mainly newspaper articles from years ago on the Bourbon Street Ripper murders.

"Holy crap, that's right," Richie said to himself. "I remember this from when I was tinkering with the idea of doing a copycat killer story to the Bourbon Street Ripper murders from the seventies." Picking up a briefcase resting near the desk, Richie opened it up. Over a dozen notebooks lay inside, along with the usual assortment of important papers and credentials.

As he started to sift through the notebooks, Richie continued to talk out loud. "This psychopath butchered over twenty women in a ritualistic fashion. I was just starting to look into this before I decided to write *The Pale Lantern* first."

Finally finding the notebook he wanted, Richie opened it up and started flipping through it, revealing several pages of notes on the Bourbon Street Ripper murders.

Among the notes were four clearly marked columns: one was a list of the victims, another the names of the detectives investigating the murders, and a third was a list of suspects. A fourth column, titled "accomplices," had a large question mark underneath it.

"It's been awhile since I last looked at these," he said almost fondly, turning page after page. "I should probably speak with Gordon about this idea after the book signing tomorrow."

That course of action decided upon, Richie flipped to the final page of notes on the Castille murders. On that page was a single name—Samantha Castille—circled several times with an arrow pointing to it, and the label, "Only surviving descendant of Vincent Castille."

Again Richie stared at the name for a long moment, before finally closing the notebook and looking at Kent's e-mail once more. "Well, slap my face and call me Cousin Lenny," said Richie in a mixture of awe and disbelief.

"What are the chances that the same Samantha Castille who owns the townhome that I'm interested in is the last living descendant of Vincent Castille?" Deciding that those chances were good enough to risk responding to the attorney, Richie fired off a reply to Kent Bourgeois:

Mr. Bourgeois:

Thank you for the prompt response.

I appreciate your candor, as well as you looking out for the interests of your clients. However, I find it odd that Ms. Castille won't even reply to my offer, which is, as I have been told, a more than reasonable amount. Surely, Ms. Castille would be willing to hear my case?

Currently, I am in New Orleans on business. I will be by your office tomorrow after lunch, as I have a pressing morning engagement. I believe that a brief, private conversation will enable us to quickly put everything into perspective.

I look forward to seeing you tomorrow.

Sincerely,

Richie Fastellos

He hit the "send" button and leaned back in the chair. "Forget the property," he said to himself, "if I can somehow meet this Samantha face-to-face and talk to her about her grandfather . . ."

Richie's thoughts were interrupted by a loud ringing coming from the hotel phone, breaking his Internet connection. The ring was particularly loud, and with a start, he picked up the phone. "Good evening," he said into the receiver, "Richie here."

"Richie, good, you're awake," replied a tired man's voice on the other end, a voice Richie recognized as belonging to Gordon, his publicist.

"More or less," Richie replied with a chuckle, leaning back again into the leather chair and getting comfortable. "How's the weather over at Pittsburgh International?"

"It's fine, but I'm not doing so well," replied the publicist, his exhaustion apparent with every breath he took.

"Oh," replied Richie, biting on his bottom lip as his concern rose. "What's wrong?"

There was a modicum of irritation in Gordon's voice as he answered, "Somehow, I managed to lose all my reservations that we printed up last week. We're sorting things out here, but it looks like I won't be showing up until tomorrow evening."

Richie was no longer leaning back against his chair, but was instead sitting straight up. "Are you serious? Tomorrow evening? . . . What about the book signing? The talk show? The interview?"

"You'll have to do them on your own, Richie," replied Gordon, stifling a yawn and muffling the words "excuse me." "You got all my e-mails, right? They should more than prepare you for everything tomorrow."

Richie didn't immediately reply. As he clicked into his e-mail's offline trash bin and restored Gordon's e-mails, Richie responded in a calm tone, "Yeah. I read them. I'll read them again before going to bed, and again in the morning."

"Good. Then we'll be fine," was Gordon's firm reply. "You'll be fine, Richie. This isn't a roast. It's just an interview at a talk show, followed by a book signing. You'll be out and done by lunchtime."

Thinking to himself how well that worked out for his own plans, Richie couldn't help but grin. "Fantastic," he said, standing up and stretching his legs a bit. "So you'll be in town by when?"

"It's looking like I'll touch down at five, so expect to see me by six," was the short and tired reply on the other end of the phone. "For now, I'm going to go home and get some sleep. It's been a long day, Richie, and I have a long plane ride tomorrow."

Richie voiced his sympathy and exchanged a few more pleasantries before ending the call.

"Heck, yeah," he said to himself, grabbing his bottled water and finishing it off, then tossing the empty bottle into a nearby waste can. "I'll be able to swing by that Bourgeois's office and get back here in time to meet with Gordon. This is fantastic!"

Richie felt a shivering tingle go down his spine and attributed it to elation. He grabbed a pen from his briefcase and jotted his itinerary down. Feeling a secondary small shiver, he felt he must really care about seeing Kent tomorrow to bother taking notes on something so simple.

The elation was soon replaced by a sense of sincere hunger, his stomach growling loudly. "Right. I haven't eaten all day."

It was a small matter for Richie to get his watch, wallet, pill bottle, and shoes assembled before heading out the door. However, his thoughts of oyster po'boys and seafood gumbo were interrupted when he nearly tripped over the newspaper laid at the door of his room. Catching himself with a quick grab of the door frame, Richie looked down.

For the third time today, his eyes froze on some text laid out before him. Only this time it wasn't an e-mail, or a jotting in a notebook—it was a newspaper headline: "Woman Butchered Last Night—Police Suspect Bourbon Street Ripper Copycat."

For almost a full minute, Richie stood there and stared at the newspaper's headline. Again, the sides of his mouth twitched. In his mind, wheels were already turning, and his reasons for wanting to speak with Samantha Castille were just reinforced. When he finally came to his senses, Richie leaned down and scooped up the paper, taking it inside.

He read the articles on last night's murder, paying particular attention to the gruesome details of the crime scene. The more he read, the more fascinated he became. The story of a potential Bourbon Street Ripper copycat killer was thrilling to him. He was just about to get his pen and start underlining facts and details that he felt were important when his eyes fell upon a name he recognized from his notes on the Bourbon Street Ripper: "Senior Detective Rodger Bergeron."

Immediately, Richie recognized Detective Bergeron as one of the two original detectives on the Bourbon Street Ripper murders case, as well as the detective credited for catching Vincent Castille. His mind a whirl, Richie circled the detective's name several times before saying to himself, "I wonder if he'll actually talk to me about those murders years ago? Probably not, but it can't hurt to ask, right?"

Dropping the newspaper on the desk, Richie again headed out the door. His hunger had long since overcome his desire to continue researching the gruesome Bourbon Street Ripper murders, and besides figuring that he could think better on a full stomach, Richie needed to get out of the hotel room.

An hour later, Richie was sopping up hot sauce with the crunchy squishiness of a fried oyster that had fallen off his po'boy. Having walked about three blocks down Canal Street, one of the longest streets in downtown New Orleans, Richie had settled on a small family-owned restaurant that had come highly recommended. Run by an old, overweight woman named Mama Claire and her three sons, the Ragin' Cajun, as it was called, was quaint and intimate. Richie had received such good service there that he was already contemplating a 20 percent tip.

Having had a lot of time to think about the idea of writing about a Bourbon Street Ripper copycat, Richie had come to the conclusion that he really wanted to pursue this kind of novel next. The timing couldn't be better—with a real-life copycat killer on the loose, the media would love having a *New York Times* best-selling author release a book on the very same thing. *It's a bit gruesome*, Richie thought to himself as he swallowed the last bit of his po'boy, *but any free coverage is welcome. And if the controversy of cashing in on a serial killer's bloody trail gets me free press, then more's the better.*

Richie Fastellos didn't care what others thought of him, especially not the media. He wrote for himself, and if people thought he was a son of a bitch for capitalizing on a possible copycat, then let them think that—so long as they bought his books.

Slurping down the last of his iced tea, Richie paid for his meal and left the Ragin' Cajun, heading back toward the hotel. As he walked, he took in the sights of Canal Street and downtown New Orleans.

Ever since he was a teenager aspiring to be a famous author, Richie had wanted to visit New Orleans, the dark mystique of the city drawing him in like the summoning gesture of a Gypsy fortune-teller. He wasn't sure if it was the unique blend of Spanish and French architecture, the Creole and Cajun cuisine, or the year-round relaxed atmosphere that intrigued him, but something about the city fascinated him.

This was partially the reason why he was looking to purchase a townhome here, as Richie wanted a place specifically for him to stay in whenever he came to New Orleans.

Lost in his own thoughts, as well as the sights of the city, Richie didn't realize he was walking right into a group of strangers until a man's voice called out, "Hey, dick, watch out!" Quickly, Richie looked up and spun to the side, pressing against the side of a building, even as the group passed him. His heart immediately started racing, and for a brief moment, Richie was sure that the guy who had yelled at him would start kicking his ass.

Once he was sure that he wasn't about to have a full-blown anxiety attack, which he was prone to have whenever confronted by anything outside his comfort zone, he looked over at the group of people. It was just three people, two men and one woman, walking with the easily recognizable double stagger of those who have been imbibing all day. All three were holding forty-eight-ounce daiquiri cups.

As they passed, one of the men said, "Fuckwad," to Richie, but the woman stopped and slapped her companion's arm.

"Don't be a douche-mouth!" she said. Then she stumbled over to Richie.

As he was pressed against the wall, Richie noted three things about the woman. One, her chest was too big to be real. Second, the black T-shirt she wore had the words "Cock Teaser" on it. Third, she was pressing those silicon puppies against his own chest.

"Hey, good-looking," the drunk woman said, her breath rank with liquor, "don't let my stupid friends fuck with you. Here, have a drink . . . "

Richie opened his mouth to say "no, thanks." Instead, a spit-lacquered straw ended up in his mouth. Eyes wide, Richie sucked obediently for a few moments, tasting the distinct flavor called "Sex on the Beach" before tearing his mouth away and thanking the woman.

"My pleasure, sexy," replied Cock Teaser as she reached down and roughly manhandled Richie's manhood. Her two friends quickly tore her away, one of them apologizing for the woman's lewdness, the other wrapping his arm around her waist to keep her near.

The woman reared her head back and announced to the world, "I am drunker than shit and want to fuck some dick right now!"

The three stumbled off, heading toward the intersection of Canal and Dauphine. Richie shook uncontrollably as he gasped for breath. The encounter with the woman had been too much for him, and his heart was racing as panic seized him.

He struggled to keep his hands steady as he took out his bottle of anxiety medication and, popping the cover, slid two pills into his mouth. Dry-swallowing them, Richie slid down to the ground and sat there, protectively hugging the bottle against him as the medication took effect.

Once the pills had worked their magic,. Richie felt like he could function again. He took a few minutes to recover from what could only be described as a sexual assault by a drunk woman.

Inside, he felt nothing but disgust for himself and the woman. He couldn't stand trashy women, let alone *drunk* trashy women. And her roughly grabbing him started to bring back some memories he didn't want to have.

Straightening himself out, Richie, whose ears were burning red, wished he had reacted with more poise and dignity. By the time he got back to the Ritz-Carlton, he was thoroughly in need of a drink himself.

"I hate people like that," Richie muttered to himself as he wandered into the hotel's bar. "They're always out to mess up my mojo. I hope all three of them get run over by a goddamn truck."

Richie pushed those thoughts out of his head and focused on getting hammered. It helped dull the bad feelings.

It was ten to midnight, and Richie, seated alone at a table near a window, was on his third glass of scotch when he realized that a woman in a red dress had walked up to him. He had been lost in his own thoughts.

"Hey," she was saying, her voice on the tired side of sultry, her rose-colored lips still managing to pout out just enough to be alluring. Her fingers, manicured and painted deep red, ran over the chair opposite him. "You look lonely. Mind if I join you?"

Richie, who was already halfway intoxicated, looked the woman over. She had to be in her late twenties, had blond hair down to her shoulders, clear blue eyes, a single beauty mark just above her mouth on the left side, and dark lashes. She was dressed in a red cocktail dress right out of the fifties.

She smelled like exotic fruits, as if her perfume was made of mangos and papayas. Overall, she looked like she had stepped out of a film noir. For a moment, Richie expected a pug-nosed mobster to come up from behind, grab her roughly by the arm, and drag her away.

His lack of an immediate response drew an "ahem" from the woman, and Richie nodded and gestured toward the seat. "Please, please, by all means. They're not labeled." Once the woman had taken a seat, Richie asked if he could get her a drink.

Smiling sensually, the woman shook her head, saying, "No, hon, I'm good. I just needed some company, and you look like the only man here who won't try to take me up to his room."

Richie looked around the bar, admitting that at this hour, the majority of people here were either married, trying to hook up with a random stranger, or both. With a shake of his head, he turned back to the woman and said, "I'm too drunk and too preoccupied for that."

"Preoccupied?" asked the woman in red curiously, leaning forward and gazing into Richie's eyes. "With what, hon?"

"Oh," replied Richie as he sipped at his scotch, "I'm appearing on a talk show tomorrow morning."

At the woman's skeptical raise of an eyebrow, Richie quickly went on, "I'm serious. I'm a novelist, and I—"

Stopping, Richie reached into his pants pocket and whipped out his wallet. Fumbling embarrassedly with it, Richie pulled out his business card and slid it across the table toward the woman, who looked at it with mild disinterest, refusing to touch it. "See? Richard Fastellos. The author. That's me."

"How nice," replied the woman, looking back into Richie's eyes. "So you write mysteries then?"

"Yup," replied Richie, taking back the card and gulping down his drink.

Then she asked a question that Richie wasn't expecting. "Ever try to solve one?"

This elicited a pause from Richie, who peered at the woman through his tilted glass as he drank from it. He couldn't believe this was happening to him. It was so unreal, as if he were living out a gangster movie, complete with saxophone- and piano-laden background music.

Richie decided to go with it, figuring that if he was being pranked, or if this was some kind of alcohol-induced dream, he might as well have fun with it. Placing the glass down on the table, he shook his head, saying, "No. No, I have not."

"Well, you should," replied the woman, looking with boredom around the room, and then back at Richie. "They say that mystery writers would make great detectives. Why not try solving a mystery sometime?"

Richie laughed at that notion. Not a cruel, dismissive, or even sarcastic laugh, but a laugh of disbelief. "Really," he said, "and what mystery would I try to solve? The murder that happened last night? The one people are saying is like the Bourbon Street Ripper?"

With a shrug of her pale shoulders, the woman replied, "Why not, hon? It's as good a mystery as any. I'm sure you can offer your support to the police, you being a famous author and all. Get to know the facts about the case and see if you can"—she leaned in and accented her words slowly, her pouty lips sensually forming each word—"solve the mystery."

Entranced, Richie stared back at her for a while, even after she had leaned back and resumed looking over the bar. Finally, slamming back the last of his scotch, Richie gave a contented sigh and said, "Ya know, why the hell not, right? I'll solve this just like in one of my stories!"

His resolve drew a slightly pleased, if not slightly bored, smile from the woman in red. Standing up, she said, "I had better get back to my room, before the crowds thin out too much." She smiled again, a mixture of pleasantness and seductiveness in her look. "See ya around, maybe. Sleep well, hon. And thanks for the conversation."

"And thank you for the idea," Richie replied, "Miss—" But she was already gone before he could finish asking her name.

Richie sat there and mulled over the conversation for a few more minutes, until he became aware that someone was staring at him. He looked and saw the bartender, who was eyeing him curiously from across the bar. When their gazes met, the bartender shook his head in what seemed to be pity, and then went back to cleaning the bar.

Richie looked away, flustered. *Great, she probably is a mobster's woman, and the bartender is one of them, and now I'm suspected of putting the moves on her.*

Not wanting to wait around to find out if his fears were true, Richie quickly got up, tossed the requisite amount of money on the bar, and headed out to the lobby. Soon, he was back in his room, the alcohol fully in effect, hardly able to stand. It was all Richie could do to remove his shoes and get his pants off before falling into bed. As he did so, his eyes focused on his laptop on the nearby desk. An e-mail was waiting for him.

With a monumental effort, Richie got up, dragged himself to his computer, and clicked on the message to open it. It was a simple note from the office of Kent Bourgeois, one line saying only one thing: "I'll see you tomorrow at two o'clock. My office."

Richie grinned to himself and passed out on the keyboard.

Chapter 7
Topper Jack

Date: **Wednesday, August 5, 1992**
Time: **10:00 p.m.**
Location: **New Orleans Police Precinct, 8th District**
French Quarter

The police precinct at nighttime, while considerably less loud than it was during the day, was still neither peaceful nor relaxing. The humid smell was replaced by pine cleaner and Freon, the floors long since cleaned and the air conditioners finally turned on—the department kept them off during the day to save money.

The fluorescent ceiling lights still brightly illuminated the floor, although only a handful of detectives were still working—the ones with too many open cases, heavy workloads, or broken marriages. Among them was Michael LeBlanc, who sat at a computer terminal on a table pushed against one of the room's walls.

Michael had been there for several hours, running checks through the New Orleans police database for Topper Jack, while Rodger, using a computer elsewhere in the department, ran his searches on the poor guy whose Greyhound locker was implicated in one of the Bourbon Street Ripper murders.

Michael, who had already lost track of time, had scribbled several pages of notes in his notebook dedicated to Topper Jack. Amongst the notes were last-known whereabouts, other aliases, and a list of rehabilitation facilities he had been in and out of over the past twenty years. Satisfied with his work so far, Michael leaned back and closed his eyes, sorting out the information in his mind.

His inner thoughts were disrupted, however, by Aucoin loudly saying, "I don't give a shit that she's almost seventeen, Catherine! There is no way my daughter is going to The Point with some college student!"

Opening his eyes, Michael looked over to see Aucoin yelling into the phone. Sorting out his information on the senior detective, Michael remembered that Aucoin had a daughter, Cheryl, in her teens.

She had two bad habits: wearing inappropriate clothing and dating men in their midtwenties. Aucoin was getting into more and more fights with his wife over both his long hours and his daughter's behavior.

Michael had very little pity for Aucoin's situation. The way Michael saw it, men who wanted to be good detectives, especially in homicide, had no business being a husband or a father, let alone both.

"Wait, Catherine," Aucoin said, a sudden panic in his voice, "don't do that! I . . . we'll talk about it when I get home! Catheri—" The sudden silence from Aucoin was all Michael needed in order to know that the older man had been hung up on.

Quickly, Aucoin threw on his coat, put on his hat, and headed out the door. Michael didn't bother asking after the other detective—it wasn't any of his business.

When Aucoin's phone rang a few minutes later, Michael didn't pick it up, figuring it was Catherine calling back. However, a moment after Aucoin's phone stopped ringing, the phone at his desk rang. Looking up in surprise, Michael hurried over to his desk and picked up the phone.

"Hello, Junior Detective Michael LeBlanc," he answered.

"Michael? Finally, someone picks up," came a feminine voice on the other line, one he immediately recognized as belonging to Dixie Olivier, Detective Aucoin's junior partner. She was one of the few people he really got along with and was his only close friend. Right now, Dixie sounded ragged.

"Dixie," Michael replied, "yeah, it's pretty late. What's going on?"

"Is Kyle there?" replied Dixie, her voice momentarily muddled by the sound of what Michael figured was an airplane landing. "I've been trying to reach him all evening."

"No," replied Michael. "He and Catherine are having another fight about Cheryl. Hey, Dixie, are you at an airport? I'm getting a lot of background noise."

"What?" Dixie replied. "Oh yes, we're at an airport. I wanted to let Kyle know that I spoke with Ouellette about an hour ago. With the murder last night, I'm heading home early."

Michael frowned. If there was ever a couple who deserved time alone together, it was Dixie and her boyfriend. Since he'd known them both, they'd had very few successful dates. He couldn't imagine how that relationship was lasting.

"Dixie," said Michael, "I'd really rather you and Gi—"

Michael's rebuttal was cut short by a very loud sound, what must have been a large plane passing directly overhead. After the rattling in the receiver stopped, he heard Dixie say, "Hey, Michael, I need to run. We're going to try and get a plane home tonight, but we may be stuck over another day. I've got you a souvenir. Talk to you when I get back. Later!" And then Dixie hung up.

Hanging up his receiver slowly, Michael got up and shuffled back to the computer terminal. *A souvenir from Cancun. Dixie, you've gotten all tourist on me.*

Michael chuckled inwardly at that as he sat back down, remembering how the last time he and Dixie got stuck working late, they went out to a bar on Bourbon Street called Oz and shared about two pitchers of lager out on the balcony, complaining about their senior partners' bad habits and sharing funny stories until four in the morning.

That was a few weeks ago. She had promised him then that she'd bring him back a souvenir from her vacation in Cancun.

Michael smiled to himself and said, "Well, Dixie never breaks her promises."

Closing his eyes, Michael returned to sorting out the information about Topper Jack. He stayed that way for several long minutes.

His internal work was soon interrupted again, this time by Rodger's voice, saying, "Damn. Did you see Kyle before he left?"

Opening his eyes, Michael looked up at his partner, seeing the older detective leaning against the same wall as the table the computers were on, arms folded and looking at him. Michael nodded.

"His wife is packing up and moving in with her mother," said Rodger, even though Michael didn't ask. The older man circled around to where his partner was and, pulling out a chair, sat in front of him. "How many times is that this year?"

"Four," answered Michael with what he hoped was obvious disinterest. "Looks like they're on the way to getting a divorce."

"Probably," answered Rodger. "It hasn't been this bad in a long time. I may have to go out with him one night and, you know, offer a shoulder to cry on."

Michael recalled that Rodger and Aucoin were friends, having had a friendly rivalry over the years. Michael seemed to remember hearing that Aucoin was there for Rodger when Edward died.

The fraternity here is pretty strong amongst the old guys, Michael thought to himself, then said, "Dixie called. She's coming back home. Ouellette talked her into it."

Rodger leaned over Michael, facing the computer terminal. "Oh no, that sucks. I'd be pissed if my romantic two-week luxury vacation to the beach was cut short by something so trivial as a serial killer." His voice dripped with sarcasm.

Michael couldn't help but chortle. "Ass."

"So, what have you found out about Topper Jack?" asked Rodger, apparently done with the comedy portion of the evening. He looked over at the computer screen Michael was working on, the green hue of the out-of-date system casting light over the older man's face.

Michael slid over his notebook for his partner to see. "I came up with quite a lot, actually. Topper Jack, alias Tip Top, alias Jack Off, alias Toppers. His real name is Jackson Topman, he's forty-three years old, and his last known address was Odyssey House on North Tonti."

"The rehab clinic," Rodger replied with a nod. "So old Topper put his ass back in the House, eh? Feel like taking a trip there?"

"What, now?" asked Michael, looking at the time. "It's almost eleven. Don't you think Mr. Jackson will be asleep by now?"

The look from Rodger was one of sarcastic joy. "Then we'll do him a favor and wake his ass up. You know what they say, shock is good for the system." As Rodger gathered his coat and hat and prepared to depart, Michael was left wondering who exactly came up with statements like that.

Twenty minutes later, the two detectives walked into Odyssey House, one of the many rehabilitation facilities in the city. The lobby was clean and freshly vacuumed. The walls were adorned with portraits of happy families doing happy activities.

A large television showed a short video about Odyssey House and the "power of positive thinking," complete with campy music and even campier voice-overs.

Finally, the nurse on duty showed up. He was in his late forties, had a mostly bald head with a dark splotch of a birthmark on the side, was dressed in blue scrubs, and clearly thought, by the way he eagerly shook both detectives' hands, that a visit by the police was the most exciting thing in the world.

"Good to meet you, Detective Bergeron, Detective LeBlanc," he said, "and welcome to Odyssey House. I'm Gomer, Gomer Bernard, the head nurse and sort of a night manager around here."

He clapped his hands and rubbed them together, apparently savoring the moment. "So what can I do for you? One of our patients here implicated in criminal activity?"

Rodger said, "Not yet, anyhow, but we need to speak to one of your patients concerning recent criminal activity. Is the upstanding citizen known as Topper Jack awake and available?"

Gomer grinned a wide grin. "Mr. Topman is indeed awake and available. He's playing checkers, I believe, in the courtyard out back. Want me to bring him to you?" He looked eager to do so.

"That won't be necessary," replied Rodger, his voice flat. "Just take us to him. This won't take a moment."

As Gomer hastily agreed and bade the detectives to follow him, Michael matched his partner's stride. He hadn't ever met someone this excited about a patient possibly being a suspect.

"Is this gonna be one of those things where you gotta take him into one of those in-terro-gation rooms and sweat him out?" asked Gomer.

"Not likely," replied Michael hastily, wanting less to do with Gomer every minute. "If he doesn't act suspicious, there's no reason to treat him like a suspect."

The trio turned a corner and headed down another hallway, past an old African American orderly mopping up some puke and watching the detectives with disinterest.

"Was Mr. Topman implicated in something? Was he a witness? Will you have to escort him out of the building?" Gomer asked excitedly.

Michael felt himself getting annoyed at the head nurse.

Rodger said, "You don't have a lot of excitement in your life, do you, Gomer?"

After that, Gomer didn't ask any more questions.

Going through another doorway, Michael found himself outside, the hot and humid August night air hitting him full in the face. Within the inner courtyard, adorned with bushes and trees along the exterior walls, with only a break for the occasional doorway and a single fire escape, were about two dozen or so patients, and three orderlies—two Caucasian and one Hispanic. The patients, ranging from late teens to twilight years, both male and female, were reading, playing checkers, or quietly conversing.

Leading the two detectives into the thick of the courtyard, Gomer approached two older men in green gowns. The slightly younger man, who had skin the color of hot chocolate, had scraggly black stubble with specks of gray.

Michael knew from the photos that this was Topper Jack. The criminal was covered in sores, some of which had healed only to be broken open again, and he was still scratching. Michael noted that he had never seen anyone that skinny outside of an oncology ward before.

"Topman," said Gomer, tapping the skinny man's shoulder, "got some *police* here to speak with you." The needling way that the news was delivered made Michael's temperature rise. It was as if the head nurse was purposefully trying to get Topper Jack to clam up.

"It's not a good thing to talk to the poh-lice," muttered Topper, scratching a scab on his elbow. "Get a penny piece to keep an eye out. Just keep an eye out and you keep your penny piece. Gotta go and get me some Schlitz malt liquor. Penny piece to keep your eye out. Schlitz malt liquor. Keep your eye out."

"What the hell is he saying?" asked Rodger in a low, but surprised voice.

Gomer looked both apologetic and embarrassed. "Sorry. He's been having some bad shakes lately. He always gets like this during withdrawal."

Topper continued to pick at his elbow scab, starting to make it bleed, until Gomer removed his hands, making him stop. The junkie continued to ramble. "I said I'd keep an eye out, but for a two-penny piece. Get two Schlitz malt liquor, two-penny piece. Two. Keep an eye out."

"What is he talking about?" asked Michael, equal parts confused and irritated at the lost time he and his partner were suffering.

"I'm not sure," answered Gomer as he motioned for an orderly. "He hasn't ever babbled like that before. Usually, he just asks for his fix." Gomer completed that statement with a nervous chuckle, one that was not reciprocated by either detective.

When the orderly, a short Latino fellow, came over, Gomer whispered something, mentioning the word *morphine*. Michael unsuccessfully struggled to overhear the conversation between Gomer and the orderly while Rodger moved in and started to talk to Topper directly.

"Topper," said Rodger, "I'd like to ask you a few questions about Dr. Vincent Castille. Do you remember him?"

The junkie looked over at Rodger, his upper body twitching, and scratched at his neck with both hands.

"Castille," repeated Rodger. "Vincent Castille. The Bourbon Street Ripper. You worked for him, remember? You helped with those murders?" It wasn't a real accusation so much as a traditional police tactic. Get the suspect to admit to something, and then use that to get the real information out.

Michael was aware of this, but apparently Topper was not, since the junkie started to scratch really hard and mutter half-hysterically, "That's more than a two-penny piece, I said. But he said I should be grateful, since I get the good-night moon sugar and the Schlitz malt liquor. No penny pieces, just the good-night moon sugar. The sugar is sweetest, he said, when the Schlitz malt liquor is flowing. He told me to watch and I'd get the good-night moon sugar, but I wanted the ten-penny piece, so he told me to get the Schlitz malt liquor first."

The junkie's voice had elevated, and he was scratching his neck so hard the dark skin was starting to bleed. Both Rodger and Michael were momentarily stunned with horror as Topper gouged troughs into his flesh. "It wasn't good for a ten-penny piece! So I told him to give the good-night moon sugar! I'd get the Schlitz malt liquor! Just don't tell me to watch again! Don't tell me to watch again!"

"Holy shit," cried Rodger, grabbing the junkie's hands, even as Michael, now free from the shock, moved in to restrain Topper. It took a few minutes, but soon both men had stopped the skinny junkie from ripping his neck apart. By the time Gomer and the orderlies got involved, Topper Jack was as restrained as he legally could be restrained. Under Gomer's direction, two orderlies, one young Hispanic and one slightly older Caucasian, started to drag a kicking and screaming Topper inside the clinic.

"I don't get it," said an incredulous Gomer a few minutes later, as the detectives and he headed back up to the lobby. "Mr. Topman never acted this way before. What the—what the hell happened?" The head nurse sat down heavily, shaking his head in disbelief.

"He seemed to go nuts the moment that Rodger mentioned Dr. Castille," replied Michael in a levelheaded manner. While Michael wasn't sure if what Topper had spewed out was nonsensical rambling or not, he filed it away in his memory for later, just in case.

Rodger nodded in response as Gomer snapped his fingers. "Ya'll are here about that murder last night, right? That Bourbon Street Ripper copycat, right? Mr. Topman was involved with Dr. Castille, was he?" This revelation seemed to renew both Gomer's attitude and his annoying grin of anticipation.

Shaking his head, Michael answered, "We don't know that yet. How long until Mr. Jackson is lucid enough to talk?"

"Oh," mused Gomer, rubbing his pointed chin, "twenty, maybe thirty minutes, tops?"

Michael was just about to ask if they could wait in Topper's bedroom when an orderly—the Caucasian who had helped bring Topper inside—came in and said, "Mr. Topman has been strapped into bed. We've administered his medication."

Gomer gave the orderly a thankful nod. "Maybe not even until tomorrow, depending on how sedated we have to make him."

It was then that Rodger spoke up. "Well, this guy could be a material witness, so can you all keep an eye on him tonight?"

Gomer nodded and said, "Keeping watch on an important police suspect like Mr. Topman shouldn't be a problem."

He then turned to the reporting orderly and asked, "So, who is watching over him tonight?"

The orderly thought for a moment and said, "Oh, the new guy." This led to a look of concentration as the orderly thought on it. "I forgot his name. The black guy. Young dude with a tattoo. Just started a few days ago."

"Huh?" asked Gomer, scratching his head in confusion. "The only new guy is the Mexican guy I hired last week. Who is this new guy again?"

The moment Gomer voiced his doubt, something clicked in the back of Michael's head. He remembered seeing three orderlies out with the patients. Two were Caucasian and one was Hispanic.

His mind racing, he only remembered seeing one African American orderly, the elderly man who was giving a spiteful, bitter look as he cleaned up some vomit. And if Gomer didn't remember a new African American guy . . .

Michael moved forward, followed closely by Rodger, who said, "Take me to Mr. Jackson's room—NOW!"

They raced down the hallways. Once inside the room, Michael's suspicions were confirmed. Topper lay there on his bed, eyes open, mouth agape, while the heart monitor flat-lined. Not seeing anyone else in the room, Michael quickly looked around the hallway, even as Rodger moved to a nearby patient outside the room and hurriedly asked, "Have you seen anyone out of the ordinary?"

It was a dance the two detectives had practiced before, agreeing on certain roles should a subject ever be in danger. Rodger would look for the perpetrator while Michael secured the scene and, if applicable, got help for the victim.

Seeing Gomer move toward the bedside, specifically going for a syringe on the bedside table, Michael screamed, "Don't touch that, you idiot! Don't touch anything on that table!"

The head nurse jumped back as if struck by lightning. Michael immediately added, "Don't hesitate! Call for a Code Blue!"

Gomer nodded and sprang into action, his training overcoming his lack of common sense. As soon as he hit the emergency button on the wall, an alarm went off with a female voice saying, "Code Blue. We have a Code Blue."

Satisfied for the moment, Michael rushed out to the hallway where Rodger was, but his partner was nowhere to be seen. Michael looked around for any quick way to exit the building and could only see one—the doors leading to the courtyard.

Closing his eyes, Michael recalled the details of the courtyard. The tables, the chairs, the plants, the fire escape.

"Fire escape," Michael said out loud and rushed out to the courtyard. Once outside, he saw a young African American orderly running up the fire escape toward the roof. Rodger was trying to running toward the fire escape, but he was already clearly out of breath. Michael began to move. As he passed his partner, he yelled, "Call for backup, Rodger, I got this!"

"Michael, be careful," called Rodger. "You don't know if he's armed or not!"

"I'll be fine," Michael yelled as he reached the fire escape, his eyes locked upward at the fleeing orderly. "Just make sure they don't contaminate the crime scene!" With those words, Michael tore off after the perpetrator.

Michael raced upward along the fire escape, his heels *clanking* loudly on the corrugated metal stairs. It was five stories to the roof. Wary of the possibility that the perpetrator was armed, Michael stopped at the top of the stairs and peeked over the edge, reaching for his sidearm.

Greeted by the sight of the orderly running along the rooftop, Michael watched the way he ran. It was a full-on sprint, and Michael concluded that the perpetrator most likely was not armed.

Michael was glad of that as he let go of his weapon. He was certain he could move faster if he wasn't shooting. He jumped up the last few stairs, rushing after the orderly, his feet crunching on the gravel of the rooftop's surface.

Michael's blood pumped and his heart raced as he chased the orderly past skylights and air-conditioning units. The perpetrator just ran straight ahead as fast as he could go, heading directly toward the edge of the building.

What is that idiot doing? Michael thought with a growing since of dread. *Is he going to jump? That's insane! We're five stories high. That'll kill him!*

Michael suddenly felt cold, shivering as his spine briefly tingled with what he assumed was the release of pure adrenaline. Deep inside, Michael felt like he could make a difference if he put everything into an all-out sprint and tackled this guy. It was a gamble, and Michael knew it, but for that brief moment, he felt confident that he could pull off this feat.

"Stop," Michael cried out, putting everything he could into the sprint, his muscles burning as he rushed forward to catch up to the orderly. With his quarry just a few yards from going over the side of the building, Michael pushed himself with everything he had—and jumped!

The sky was very black, and the wind hot and muggy, as Michael and the orderly tumbled down to the surface of the rooftop.

Christ! Michael thought as he rolled, holding on to the perpetrator with a death grip fueled by determination and fear. His face rubbed against the gravelly surface of the rooftop as he and the orderly rolled several times. The world spun, and then Michael saw an elbow coming right for his face.

The rush of adrenaline was still there, and Michael felt like he had an incredible amount of energy. Instinctively, his hands came up to block the blow, the sheer force enough to make his own hands hit his face. Michael grunted as he rolled away from the perpetrator, who was scrambling to get to his feet.

"The hell you do," he screamed and, spinning his body around on his back, kicked the orderly's feet out from under him. As he did this, Michael felt and heard his jacket rip down the back. This only served to make Michael angry, and with another spin on his back, this time using the momentum to flip over on his stomach and then up to his feet, Michael jumped up and slammed his knee into the orderly's back, hitting him in the kidney.

The perpetrator cried out, his eyes bulging and his face going deep purple, before going limp. Keeping the pressure on the man's back, Michael reached into the pocket of his now ruined jacket and pulled out a pair of handcuffs. As he clicked them into place, Michael told the unconscious man, "You have the right to remain silent, asshole."

Ten minutes later, Michael was back on the ground, looking over his ruined jacket in disgust.

"Hey," said Rodger, coming up from behind. "You okay? Your jacket is ripped to shreds."

"No worries," Michael replied, tossing the jacket into a nearby garbage bin. "I've got five more like it at my apartment." He turned to his partner and folded his arms before asking, "So, did Mr. Jackson make it?" With the way things were going, he honestly expected the answer to be no.

To Michael's pleasant surprise, Rodger nodded. "Topper will live. EMTs got here when backup did, and aside from having a splitting headache, and a heroin addiction, he'll be all right. That sick bastard who tried to kill him pumped him full of morphine, the drug that helps heroin addicts deal with the withdrawal symptoms. Luckily, morphine isn't lethal in the dosage he was given, but I doubt the perp knew that."

Michael nodded to his partner, then looked back at the interior of the clinic. "Probably a contract killing, then. It's not like the gangs here hire professionals to do this sort of thing."

Rodger nodded. "Agreed. Any idiot with a gun can be a hired killer nowadays."

"I doubt this had anything to do with the Bourbon Street Ripper murders."

"Yeah. This was most likely a hit by the drug ring Topper helped Narcotics bust up a few weeks ago. However, just to be safe, let's interrogate the perp back at the precinct later."

The door to the clinic opened and Head Nurse Gomer came out. "Detectives," he said. His naïve enthusiasm was long gone, his bloodshot eyes and red face showing that he was taking things seriously. "Mr. Topman is awake and wants to talk to you both."

Michael and Rodger looked at each other before heading inside, Michael thinking to himself that this was a night when they were blessed (or cursed) with the devil's luck.

Both detectives followed the nurse to the infirmary where Topper lay, hooked up to about half a dozen machines, some of them monitoring his vitals and others administering time-released dosages of medication.

"Detectives," said Topper Jack in a raspy voice as they approached him, "looks like I owe you all for saving my life."

"Don't mention it, Topper," said Rodger, standing at the edge of the bed and resting his hands on the side railing. "The doctors say you'll live. How are you feeling?"

At that, Topper gave a short cough that had a laugh buried somewhere deep inside. "I suppose I've been better, but thanks all the same." The junkie cleared his throat and coughed a bit more before continuing. "Mr. Bernard tells me you all have some questions for me?"

"That's right, Mr. Jackson," said Michael, standing to the side of Rodger, his arms folded. "We'd like to talk to you about Vincent Castille."

"Vincent Castille," said Topper, looking up at the ceiling. "Now there is a name I haven't heard in many a year."

"So," said Rodger, "you knew the doc back then?"

"Knew him?" asked Topper as he coughed out another laugh. "He was my doctor."

This revelation came as a shock to Michael, and apparently to Rodger as well, for his eyes widened as he exclaimed, "Wait, what? Dr. Castille was an expensive doctor. How did you afford him? And why didn't we find your name on the patient list?"

"Because his kind of help was the kind a respectable doctor don't give an undesirable like me," said Topper with another cough, his raspy voice strangling a bit from exhaustion and effort.

"So, he supplied you," said Michael. "With what, heroin? Cocaine?"

"Morphine," answered Topper without hesitation. "Same shit I'm on now. He said if I was going to kill myself, to at least do it with a gentleman's drug."

This seemed to satisfy Rodger for the time being. "And what did the doc want from you in exchange for these . . . special prescriptions?"

At this, beads of sweat began to appear on Topper's brow. "Look," said the junkie, "I don't wanna go to jail. I spent twenty years trying to forget that shit. I didn't know, and I don't wanna know. All I know is he paid me in cold cash and Miss Emma."

"Miss Emma?" asked Michael, who felt green for having to ask.

Rodger said, "A street name for morphine or heroin," before returning to Topper. "Look, you aren't a suspect in anything, Topper. We just want to know what the doc wanted from you in return for his medical services."

Although tense as a board, Topper relaxed some, perhaps more from the medical drip than from Rodger's assurance. After looking up at the ceiling for a long few moments, the junkie finally said, with the voice of a man with a twenty-year weight on his chest, "He had me watch certain women." Topper's voice cracked some. "And tell him where they'd go."

Already, tears were forming in Topper's eyes, and in that instant, Michael was assured of the junkie's innocence in the murders twenty years ago. *Vincent Castille obviously didn't tell this guy what he was doing. Why risk it? This guy is a junkie and a huge liability. Really, Mr. Jackson is lucky he wasn't murdered himself.*

"And now you've been in here for the past two to three weeks?" asked Rodger, focusing on the junkie's eyes. "Has anyone come to you and asked you to do anything like that again?"

Much to Michael's surprise, Topper suddenly got indignant. "Sir, I may be a waste of human life, but I am not going to make the same mistake twice when it can wreck other people's lives." Looking back up at the ceiling, Topper added, "But to answer your question, yes, I received the same offer about a week ago."

You could have heard a pin drop in the infirmary.

"Wait, what?" asked Michael, leaning forward on the side rail of the bed. His mind raced, preparing to sort the incoming data. *If Topper was contacted by, or even saw the murderer, this entire case could be solved in a matter of days.*

"Topper," asked Rodger, sounding calm, "how did this guy contact you? What did he look like? What did he say?"

"He didn't say nothing," said Topper rather briskly, "and he didn't look like nothing . . . He sent me a letter." Topper pointed with his thumb to an ambiguous area behind him. "It's in my room, in the tank. But don't tell Mr. Bernard about it, okay? It'll get me in huge trouble if you do."

"Our lips are sealed," replied Rodger with a grateful grin, before turning to his partner. "I'll finish up with Mr. Jack here, Michael, if you go and get that letter."

Michael, who recognized that Rodger had better rapport with this witness, nodded and headed down the hallway to Topper's room. It was a simple matter of going back to where the junkie was nearly murdered, as the scene was still marked off with yellow police tape. Entering the bathroom area, Michael lifted up the tank lid to the toilet. Sure enough, a plastic bag was floating around inside the water, and despite the unsavory odor, Michael fished it out and opened it up.

Inside the plastic bag were a number of things one would expect a junkie to have: a bottle of pills, a wad of cash, and a small notebook filled with phone numbers and Bible verses. He decided none of that was any of his business. Also in the plastic bag was a folded-up envelope. After carefully putting the rest of the contraband back in the bag and sinking it back into the toilet's tank, Michael unfolded and looked over the envelope.

It was a plain white envelope, the kind one can get at any office supply store. It had been taped shut with Scotch tape, and had a stamp glued in place. Looking it over, Michael immediately saw two things that stood out. For one, the envelope was a security business envelope, the kind that obfuscates the contents, rather than a small stationery envelope. Another was that the address on the envelope was typed up using a typewriter.

A typewriter, thought Michael, looking the envelope over, *not a computer, but a typewriter.*

Michael hummed to himself, tapping his lips with the corner of the envelope. *That's significant. Typewriters are not like computers. What does this mean?*

Before Michael's wheels started turning too much, he remembered that the envelope had contents. Hastily, Michael opened the envelope up and scooped out what was inside.

Inside the envelope was the Polaroid picture of a woman on a street corner, a lady of the night, looking off to the side with disinterest. The photograph was obviously taken from a distance, so that the woman wouldn't know she was being stalked.

"Miss Virginia Babineaux," Michael said to the photo. It was the murder victim from the night before. The last time he had seen this woman, she was tied to a table, her body vivisected with cruel precision, a look of agony and fear on her face that still curdled Michael's blood. And here she was, in this photo, looking bored, jaded, and very much alive.

Turning the photo over, Michael saw nothing of interest on the back of the Polaroid, so he instead looked over the letter. The language was simple, but the message was chilling.

Mr. Topman,

You don't know me, but I know plenty about you. Twenty years ago, you offered your services to Dr. Vincent Castille, aiding in a great experiment. I now ask you to do the same for me.

Enclosed in this envelope, you will find the photograph of a woman. I want you to follow her and determine when she is alone. You can leave the information I need at your usual drop-off point.

For your services, I will give you what you have been craving. Don't let the orderlies catch you with them.

Signed,
The Nite Priory

Michael reread the letter two more times before tucking it back into the envelope and tucking the envelope into an evidence bag. He noted that the envelope didn't contain anything else, but assumed it had held morphine pills. *The guys in the lab can test for residue*, Michael thought as he pocketed the evidence bag and headed out to join his partner.

Rodger was waiting for him in the lobby, lighting up a cigarette, a tired look on his face. Before Rodger could ask, or say, anything, Michael asked, "Is Topper still awake?"

Rodger shook his head, and Michael knew they'd be waiting another day before finding out about Topper's "usual drop-off point." With a sigh, Michael said, "I'll tell you what I found on the ride back to the station."

It took the detectives ten more minutes of signing incident reports for the clinic before Gomer Bernard allowed them to leave, and by that time the squad car with Topper's would-be assassin was already gone. On the way back to the precinct, Michael read the letter out loud.

"The Nite Priory, what is that?" asked Rodger.

Michael pondered for a moment and said, "An alias. A clue, I guess, like Zodiac or BTK."

Rodger harrumphed. Michael looked over and noticed that his partner's eyes were getting bloodshot. Both of them had been awake for over twenty-four hours. They'd need to rest soon.

"So when Topper wakes up, we'll ask him where the usual drop-off point is."

"Right. And when we get back to the station, we can interrogate that sonabitch that you caught up on the roof."

Rodger half-turned to his partner, which was a splendid feat considering he was driving the squad car, and said, "That reminds me . . . what on earth did you do up on the roof that ripped your jacket and nearly broke the perpetrator's ribs?"

Michael, despite being tired, gave a small chuckle. "It was the weirdest thing, Rodger. I had to tackle him just before he jumped off the roof, and I suddenly felt all my inhibitions and concerns melt away. I felt invincible."

That got another sideways glance from Rodger, who replied with, "Invincible? That's crazy talk, Michael."

"I know," said Michael, nodding in agreement. "It must have been a serious adrenaline rush, Rodger. I have never felt so confident."

"Confident, huh?" Rodger gave a bit of a laugh as he turned to the street where the precinct was located. "Just promise me one thing, Michael."

"Oh?" replied Michael, curious. "What's that?"

"That you won't take chances like that again," Rodger said, adding with a smirk, "I don't believe the department will send me any more partners."

Michael was surprised to find that he laughed out loud at that one.

Chapter 8
No More Fake Smiles

Date: **Thursday, August 6, 1992**
Time: **3:00 a.m.**
Location: **Sam Castille's Townhome**
Uptown New Orleans

Clank. Clank. Clank. Ching!

With a final ring, Sam's typewriter clanked out the last line of her first chapter, and the writer, eyes transfixed on the last word of the page, spoke two relief-filled words: "I'm done."

It seemed almost surreal for Sam, that she would have completed five thousand words in one evening, but even as she sat there and stared at the last page of her manuscript, the reality hit her. She had done it! She had finally made a deadline. Her first installment would go out on time.

She had always wondered what she would do if she completed a project on time, and the theoretical responses ranged from a shout of joy to a New Orleans "Who Dat" to a fist pump conjoined with a rowdy chorus of "whoops."

However, in the face of actually completing the task, Sam found herself just leaning back and giving a heartfelt sigh of relief.

"I'm done," she said, leaning her head back and looking up at the ceiling. "Thank. You. God."

After a few minutes of silent reverie, Sam leaned forward and began to collect her pages, arranging them in order. Once that was done, the blond woman got up and headed across the hallway from her study, into Sam of Spades's "office."

It wasn't really an office so much as a place where she handled her business, as Sam disliked technology newer than the seventies. Only at the behest of Jacob, as well as the urging of her lawyer, Kent Bourgeois, did Sam get devices such as a personal computer, a television, a fax machine, and a copier. She had adamantly refused, however, to write her manuscripts on anything but a typewriter.

So Sam's office contained over five thousand dollars of equipment only used to send and receive faxes, copies, and e-mails. She wasn't even sure where the equipment had come from—Kent had handled the details of their purchase, delivery, and installation, and also made sure she got a sizeable tax write-off for them. This did nothing to enhance the communication between her and the outside world, however, as Sam rarely used e-mail, preferring the phone, and had never quite figured out how to work the fax machine.

But she did use the copier to make copies of her manuscripts, and often called Kent when the toner (or ink, as she called it) ran low. Even though her attorney consistently reminded her that he wasn't her secretary, he would end up getting the order placed, delivered, and installed anyway. All this made for a very grateful Sam, and a very satisfied Kent got to bill his client two hours each month for "miscellaneous services."

Turning on the lights and the copier, Sam leaned against a wall and waited for the machine to warm up. As she waited, Sam read over her draft. She had to admit she had never written so well before. Even though this was just the first chapter, she managed to capture the spirit of the mystery, as well as the gruesomeness of the murders, in stark detail. Without being too graphic, she placed the reader in the role of the victim, creating the tension of being stalked, of being hunted like prey, and the terror of finally being caught. Then there was the murder itself.

Sam had wrestled for a while with how to handle the murder, knowing that she could, all too easily, go too far into the graphic detail of a torture murder at the hands of a serial killer. She had tapped her newfound pen to her lips several times, considering the shock value it would present to readers to read the vivid details locked away in her memory of her grandfather.

However, she had finally decided against it for now, cutting away from the victim's point of view right before the first cut. With a loud rolling sound, and then a short *beep*, the copier signaled that it was ready. Sam busied herself with making two copies of her manuscript. One would go into a file here in her house, to keep in case she needed to refer to it later.

Another would go to Jacob, and ultimately Caroline, at the *Times-Picayune*. The original would go into Sam's safe deposit box at her bank, locked away with all her other manuscripts. It was Sam's way of securing herself against plagiarism, or so she told herself. The truth was, she didn't fully trust anyone but her attorney or Rodger Bergeron, and hadn't for years. And with Rodger still avoiding her, Kent was the only person who seemed to actively look out for her.

Kent had been her family lawyer since her grandfather's time. He had been a man of thirty when Vincent Castille was arrested for serial homicide. Sam remembered that Kent was just the estate law attorney, and while he had nothing to do with her grandfather's trial, he had been there for her when she was literally left alone—her father dead and her grandfather accused of heinous crimes.

As Sam watched the copier's light sway back and forth, copying her manuscript, her thoughts drifted like eddies in a river. Soon, the swaying light of the copier was the swishing of wiper blades, and the repetitious hum and stutter of the machine was the monotonous patter of rain on a windshield.

Samantha was ten years old, dressed in a simple black dress, her long hair in a black ribbon, and was seated in the back of a black Mercedes-Benz, leaving her father's funeral. In the front of the car, a chauffeur named Reginald Washington, a well-groomed and well-dressed man of color, drove. In the back of the car with Sam was Kent Bourgeois.

"Don't worry, Samantha," Kent said softly. He was dressed in a black Armani suit, streaks of gray already visible in his hair.

"All we need to do is find a guardian who will agree to act as executor for your estate, and who will grant you access to your trust fund. You won't be without, I promise."

Samantha said nothing, her hands resting motionless on her lap. The funeral had seemed so distant, like she was watching herself on the television, and even as she had laid the bouquet of cypress flowers on her father's coffin, it hadn't felt real.

It had been only when the coffin had started to lower into the ground, the sound of a lone trumpet playing a lonesome song, that Sam had finally reacted to her father's death.

She had fallen to her knees and screamed.

"Samantha," Kent said, his hand resting on her shoulder, "don't feel like you shouldn't cry. It's perfectly okay. In fact, I'd say it's healthy to cry."

"I don't want a relative to watch over Grandfather's money," Samantha suddenly interrupted.

This appeared to surprise Kent. He pulled his hand away. "What do you mean, Samantha?"

"I don't want any relatives to watch over Grandfather's money," Samantha repeated, looking out the window as they passed through the rain-swept streets of New Orleans. "I don't want anyone spending that man's money. I want it put away."

"Put away?" asked Kent, who then rubbed his chin in thought. "You mean, like in a bank?"

"In whatever you have to put it in to lock it away," Samantha said, her voice devoid of any emotion, save for a trace of hostility. "I don't ever want anyone to benefit from Grandfather's life. Ever."

Kent adjusted his glasses and looked at the ten-year-old girl. "Well, technically your grandfather's money doesn't pass to you until he's dead—"

"Oh, you know he's going to get the death penalty, Mr. Bourgeois," piped up Reginald, looking at the pair through the rearview mirror. "They are going to find him guilty and light him up like a Christmas tree. I am just so glad he never did nothing to my Constance. Let me tell you!"

Kent snapped, "Reginald! Will you please refrain from such commentary in front of Miss Castille here!"

"No, it's okay," Samantha said, turning to face Kent, feeling devoid of almost any emotion. "Reggie speaks the truth, and I hope my grandfather *burns in hell*." Her voice was so harsh, so hateful, that Kent, his glasses sliding down his nose, recoiled from the girl.

She immediately turned back to looking outside the window, her fists tightening as she continued, "I don't care how, but I want my grandfather's money locked away. Forever."

Kent straightened his glasses and replied, "I understand that, Samantha, but assuming that your grandfather does indeed pass everything on to you—because you know I cannot divulge that information—and you do 'lock it away,' you will still need to live. Remember, we read your father's will last night, and he only left you that townhome in the Garden District, as well as a few choice belongings.

"Your grandfather could potentially leave you his entire mansion on Lake Pontchartrain, all of his automobiles, as well as access to his various accounts and holdings. That could amount to"—the attorney cleared his throat before finishing discreetly—"a great deal of money."

It was as if someone were playing a broken record, as Samantha just replied, "I don't care. I don't want anything of his. Ever. Lock it away. Seal it away from everyone."

"But, Samantha," said Kent, the exasperation much more clearly prevalent in his voice, "you need to eat. Houses require upkeep. And don't forget"—the attorney motioned toward the chauffeur—"you have five servants. Reginald. Your housekeeper, Miss Patterson. Your butler, Mr. Mason. And Tania and Violet, your two maids. What are you going to do, fire them?"

"Oh, don't mind us, Miss Castille," chimed in Reginald as he braked for a traffic light. "We'll all manage somehow. You do what's best for you, you hear?"

"I swear, Reginald," retorted a clearly disgusted Kent, his voice thick with fatigue, "it's almost like you *want* to get fired."

"Oh, I don't want that," replied Reginald hastily. "I just want Miss Castille to be happy, that's all. She's always been so good to us who run Mr. Cast—I mean, the doctor's—house. We all just want her to be happy, that's all. We don't want to stop working for her, but if that's what she wants, that's all fine by us. We'll get by."

Samantha, who had been silently listening to her lawyer and her chauffeur, finally spoke.

"Reggie," she said softly, her blue eyes looking up at the black man through the rearview mirror, "I don't want to punish you and the others. It's not right. You all have been like family to me and my . . . "

Samantha's voice trailed off, and Reginald looked to be choking up, when Kent jumped into the conversation. "Well, Samantha, there is a way to help 'Reggie' and the others, you know."

"Oh? What do you mean, Mr. Bourgeois?" asked the girl, feeling neither a glimmer nor a sparkle within her.

Kent folded his arms, looking thoughtful. "Well, Samantha, there is your trust fund, the one your grandfather established when you were born. It's worth several million now, and will grow as time goes on."

Looking at the child to make sure she was following him, the lawyer continued, "You can 'lock away,' as you said, your grandfather's estate, when and if he wills it to you. I'll take care of that. I'll put it in so many different places that no one will ever get it again. And you can use your trust fund to live off of, pay for Reginald and the others, and keep your house running."

With a nod of her head, Samantha said, "Okay, let's do that."

"Not so fast," said Kent, again adjusting his glasses. "This is where things get tricky. You see, Samantha, since you are a minor, even though it is your money, the law requires you to have an adult manage your money. That is what the courts call a 'trustee.'

"Your grandfather's trust specifically states that you will have full control of your money on your eighteenth birthday. But until then, you need a trustee. And you'll need a guardian. Someone to take care of you."

"So you'll be my trustee and my guardian," Samantha answered, "and you can manage my money, like you did for Grandfather, until I'm eighteen."

Kent chuckled, patting the girl on the poufy shoulder of her black dress. "I wish it were that simple, Samantha, but your grandfather names your trustee, not you. And he named your great-aunt Gladys. And only a family member can be a guardian."

For the first time since before the funeral, Samantha's voice had emotion in it, a pouty sort of huffiness, as she said, "I hate Auntie Gladys. She locks my dolls away. She's mean."

"Well, then, Samantha," replied Kent, thinking for a moment, "if you had a choice with a family member, who would it be?"

For a long while, Samantha sat there, her young brow furrowing with effort. Finally, she said, "Auntie Marguerite. She's much nicer."

Nodding, Kent sat back and exhaled, lost in thought for a moment. As he sat there, Samantha looked outside the window again, and noticing how heavy the rain was falling, found herself wondering if her father's grave was going to flood.

Finally, Kent spoke up. "All right, I'll see what I can do, Samantha. I'm going to have to talk to your grandfather anyway, especially if the verdict comes back as we all anticipate."

"You mean," said Samantha, a rising bitterness evident in her young voice, "that he's going to be executed."

Kent didn't answer that, instead saying, "He'll need to get his affairs in order. I'll bring up transferring trusteeship from Gladys to Marguerite. Guardianship, too, okay?"

"Okay," replied Samantha, quickly adding a polite, "thank you."

Kent opened his mouth, and out came the sound of a bell ringing once.

Sam was jarred from the deep recesses of her memory by that sound, the singular bell ringing coming from the copier as the copying of her manuscript completed. For a long moment, Sam stood there, blinking, breathing, and coming back to reality. Back to the nineties. Back to the present.

"Nice," Sam said to herself as she removed her finished copies. "My imagination is on fire tonight."

Three copies in her hand, Sam moved over to a cabinet next to her computer table and opened it up. Inside were dozens of types of office supplies: envelopes, paper tablets, stamps, binders, paper clips, and much more.

Taking out three sizable manila envelopes, Sam headed back into the study. Once there, she placed a copy of the manuscript into each one and sealed it up. Taking out a permanent black marker, Sam wrote on the upper left-hand corner of each one: "The Bourbon Street Ripper—Chapter 1."

That task complete, Sam stood back to admire her handiwork, smiling the first genuine smile she had in quite a while. "You did it, Sam, old girl," she said to herself. "You totally did it."

After filing away one of the copies of the manuscript, Sam looked over the notebook with all her notes on the story so far. Picking up her silver pen, she tapped the notebook pages several times, glossing over them to make sure that she had a good plan for the rest of the story.

Her notes included it all—a quick-paced investigation racing against the clock to stop the murderer, interrogations gone wrong in the police precinct, rooftop chases high above the city, hair-raising escapes from mechanical death traps, clandestine organizations, and a climactic final confrontation between the murderer and the surviving detective for the life of the heroine.

The entire story had come so easily to Sam, both while she penned the notes and typed it out. Even though that fact alone was odd to her, since she had always struggled with outlining and following through with stories, she just chalked it up to her sudden burst of inspiration.

"I'm brilliant," Sam said to herself, capping the pen, tossing it on the notebook, and leaving the room.

Deciding it was time to celebrate, Sam headed to the back of the house, to the kitchen, and over to a cabinet over the stove. Inside was a bottle of Valdespino Sherry, 1975, with a note taped to it reading, "For when you finish a work on time. Go for it, girl!" On the neck of the bottle dangled a small keychain, with a plastic red shoe attached to it.

Taking the bottle of sherry out, as well as a wineglass, Sam proceeded to uncork the bottle and pour herself a glass. Holding the glass, Sam swished the drink around a bit, then sniffed it, then sipped it delicately. With a joyful smile, she nodded her head and took the glass, and the bottle, to the back patio.

The night air was hot, and unlike the previous evening, the sky was clear. She placed the bottle of sherry on the patio table and sat back on the glider. She closed her eyes, sipping the sherry occasionally, and feeling good for the first time in a long time. If she had to put the feeling into words, it was like that first morning of being healthy after you've been sick for a very long time.

As she sat there, rocking back and forth, sipping her sherry, and relaxing, Sam's mind turned back to her very realistic flashback. At first, she wondered if she should tell Dr. Klein about her recent flashbacks. Quickly, however, Sam decided that she shouldn't.

Dr. Klein was quick to prescribe medications for anything Sam reported having that was new or different. When she said she couldn't sleep, he prescribed Trazodone. When she said she was having terrible nightmares, he prescribed Prazosin. When she said she was dizzy all the time, he prescribed Dramamine. And he loved prescribing Lithium to her, like it was some sort of wonder drug. Thanks to Dr. Klein, Sam had a small pharmacy in her bedroom medicine cabinet.

Sam frowned, finding that she was tensing up again, and quickly gulped down her entire glass of sherry. For a moment, she coughed and hacked hard, having swallowed too fast. Once the coughing fit was past, she exhaled, shook it off, and poured herself another glass. Then she leaned back and looked at the label on the bottle.

The label was old and worn with time, but it clearly marked the brand and the year, 1975. The shoe charm dangling from the keychain had the word "Comus" etched on it in finely detailed gold-leaf lettering, all of which was in surprisingly good shape considering how old it was. Looking intently at the bottle, Sam suddenly remembered where she had gotten it from.

Again, her mind drifted, aided by the mental fuzz brought about by the alcohol, and without realizing it, she gave in to the feeling. Her mind traveled back to the time she had looked up at this very same bottle. The swaying of the glider was her ten-year-old body in motion, swaying back and forth, rocking on her heels, as she looked up at the bottle of sherry on the mantle, underneath a landscape portrait.

She was standing in one of the lounges of her grandfather's mansion on Lake Pontchartrain. She was wearing a nice dress, dark blue velvet with black-and-white accents, her long blond hair tied back with a dark blue ribbon. While she no longer felt devoid of life, she had completely shut down her heart, refusing to allow herself any more pain.

"And what are you looking at, Samantha, dear?" asked a pleasant voice from behind her. Turning around, Samantha saw the pudgy face of her great-aunt Marguerite, one of her grandfather's sisters. The older, heavy-set woman was in her Sunday best, complete with an old-fashioned white bonnet she was currently removing with white-gloved hands.

"Auntie Marguerite," said Samantha with a faux smile, turning and curtsying as a proper Southern lady should, "I'm so glad you could make it today."

Marguerite seemed a little surprised, but kept that pleasant smile as she asked, "What, no hug for dear Auntie Marguerite?"

Samantha shook her head. "I don't feel much like hugging people lately, Auntie Marguerite. Sorry."

Marguerite gave her a sad smile and an understanding nod of the head. "Well, if you should ever want a hug, Auntie Marguerite is giving them away for free. Now what were you looking at, my dear?"

Turning, Samantha pointed up at the bottle of sherry. "That bottle. I've seen it somewhere before. Where have I seen it, Auntie Marguerite?"

Squinting a bit, Marguerite looked at the bottle and hummed to herself, before saying quietly, "I believe that was the brand of sherry your mother used to drink."

"Mama?" asked Samantha, her blue eyes widening. She had hardly ever heard her mother spoken of, other than to hear her father call her "a beautiful woman who could turn the heads of kings and paupers alike."

"You knew my mama, Auntie Marguerite?" asked Samantha, pressing her hands in front of her in an almost prayer-like fashion. "You knew her when she was alive?"

"Well, not especially," Marguerite said, a twinge of ruefulness in her voice. "I mean, she died soon after you were born, and she wasn't exactly from, well, that is . . . "

"She wasn't from good stock," answered a similar, but much harsher-sounding voice from the doorway of the room. Samantha's face drew into a tight pucker, as if she were being forced to taste something particularly sour. Turning, she faced a wrinkled woman with a gaunt face, lips that had probably never smiled a day in their life, and a dress that would make a Catholic nun look like a stripper.

"Auntie Gladys," replied Samantha in a particularly nasal voice. She spoke that way whenever she wanted to show courtesy that wasn't genuine, and her curtsy was more of a nod than anything else.

"Still not able to show our elders their proper respect, are we, Samantha?" replied Gladys as she approached the child, her eyes like two pieces of coal. "I can see that even with the ridiculous amount of money spent on your etiquette lessons, you cannot manage a single curtsy to your great-aunt Gladys?"

"Oh, come, sister," interrupted Marguerite. "Samantha is only a ten-year-old girl. And she's been through so much recently. First her father is murdered, then Vincent is—"

Marguerite's words were cut short by Gladys. "Do not speak that name before me again, Marguerite. Our brother is dead to us, in name and spirit, despicable man that he was. May the devil feast nightly on his soul."

"Sister, please." Marguerite tried to wave the taller and sterner great-aunt off, "not in front of Samantha."

Feeling a sudden urge to speak, Samantha asked, "Auntie Gladys, what did you mean by saying that my mother wasn't from good stock?"

While Marguerite looked anxiously between the child and the living mummy that was her older sister, Gladys replied, "I will not fill your head with stories of that irrelevant woman. But suffice it to say that when your father brought her into this house, he committed the second of two grievous sins against the noble Castille family name."

"Grievous sins?" asked Samantha, honestly curious. "What do you mean? What was the other one?"

"His profession," replied Gladys, who suddenly looked as if she smelled something very unsavory. "Imagine a Castille, stooping so low as to become a—"

"Sister," Marguerite said with more vim, "stop it!"

This outburst surprised both Gladys and Samantha, as the latter had always known her younger great-aunt to be meek and easily cowed by her older sister.

Marguerite continued, "Who cares what her mother was? Or what her father did? Samantha is a Castille and"—the pudgy woman winked at the girl—"is growing up to be a fine Southern lady."

Samantha gave another placid smile, nothing behind it but manners, and curtsied to her great-aunt. This appeared to disarm Gladys enough that the strict-looking woman huffed, said something about being late, and turned, leaving the room with her head tilted up fifteen degrees.

"Don't mind her," Marguerite said after her sister was gone. "She's been angry since . . . Well, since she was born." Marguerite winked again at Samantha.

Normally, that kind of joke would make Samantha giggle, but instead she just nodded.

Marguerite offered her hand, saying, "Come on, I think they are about to begin."

Samantha took her great-aunt's hand and allowed herself to be led to the drawing room.

There, in that room, were over three dozen people: men and women all dressed up in their Sunday best, children dressed as if going to Easter service, and the five servants who cared for the Castille estate. At the front of the room, near a mantle with a portrait of Vincent Castille in his doctor's garb, was Kent Bourgeois, dressed in a tailored suit and rifling through a large and impressive-looking document.

As Marguerite led Samantha through the crowd of people, conversations stalled and heads turned. Voices were hushed, but Samantha could make out a few of them. "I bet she's going to get it all," said one voice.

"She always was his favorite," said another voice.

"Lucky little bitch is about to become the richest person in Southern Louisiana," said a third voice.

"Don't you mind them," whispered Marguerite with obvious annoyance in her voice. "They are all jealous of you. Samantha, never forget that you are the star of this story."

Samantha didn't respond, only looking out at the sea of faces and wondering who these people were. She knew the Castille family was large, but she had never seen any of them before.

Finally getting to the front, Marguerite joined her sister, Gladys, on a sofa, next to some older gentlemen in expensive-looking suits. Samantha recognized them as her grandfather's associates from Southern Baptist Hospital. She curtsied to them and got a stern look and a stiff nod in response. With that placid smile, Samantha headed up to where Kent was standing.

"Mr. Bourgeois?" Samantha asked as she approached the lawyer, who stopped what he was doing and looked down at her. Samantha looked around the room to confirm that the face she was looking for wasn't there. "Where is Mr. Bergeron? Where is Rodger?"

Kent looked troubled as he leaned in some, saying, "He's not coming, Samantha."

"What? But why not?" asked the young girl, feeling hurt.

With a small sigh, Kent kneeled down, drawing a few murmurs of disapproval from the crowd. The lawyer put a comforting hand on Samantha's shoulder before saying, in a low voice, "Well,

Samantha, do you remember how you said you couldn't go to your grandfather's funeral?"

"Yes," answered the girl, who remembered adamantly refusing to go.

Kent nodded and said, "It's similar to that with Rodger. You see, just as you didn't want to see your grandfather because you . . . hate him . . . Rodger doesn't want to be at the reading of his will because he wants to forget him."

That made sense to Samantha. She gave the lawyer a small nod and whispered, "Thank you." That done, she walked over to where her great-aunts were sitting and took a seat next to Marguerite.

"All right," said Kent, clearing his throat and rapping his knuckles on the mantle. This had the desired effect of getting everyone in the room to stop talking and focus on him. "Let us begin with the reading of the Last Will and Testament of Dr. Vincent Gilles Castille."

Later that night, young Samantha was on the back porch of her grandfather's mansion. The guests were long gone, and with them, their sighs of relief or indignant declarations of fighting the will in court.

Samantha sat on the white bench that hung from the ceiling of the back porch, swinging in a halfhearted attempt to lighten her spirits. Nearby, a small plate of angel food cake, her favorite dessert, lay mostly uneaten. A small trail of ants marched triumphantly to and from the confection, carrying off bits and pieces in an almost cartoonish fashion.

"Samantha," said a soft voice.

Looking up, Samantha saw her great-aunt Marguerite, looking more serious than usual. Sitting down next to the small girl, Marguerite added, "Or should I now call you, 'Madame Castille'?"

"Call me Samantha, please," replied the girl quietly. Her gaze cast out over the lake before her, the brackish waters managing to look beautiful in the setting sunlight.

"Okay, then, Samantha," said Marguerite, inhaling softly. "I wanted to thank you. For having me named your trustee and your guardian. That shows you have a great deal of trust in me."

"You're welcome," replied Samantha, still staring out over the water. "I'm sure you'll do a great job."

The pudgy woman smiled as pleasantly as one could under the circumstances. "Do you want to . . . talk about it? Anything, I mean. Your father, your gra—"

"No," Samantha replied, looking over at Marguerite, feeling utterly lifeless on the inside. "I want to forget it. I want"—again Samantha gave a smile just for show—"to be happy. That's what a lady is supposed to do, right?"

To Samantha's surprise, Marguerite shrugged. "To be honest, Samantha, I don't know what a lady is supposed to do. I've never been good at it like Gladys has, I've just"— the woman paused and sighed, shaking her head—"I've just kind of had others lead me through all that. But now, I can't do that. Now, I have to lead you. Which means I have to learn how to be a lady, a mistress, and a mother."

Samantha slowly turned and looked up at her great-aunt. She felt tears welling up in her eyes, her heart aching. Marguerite looked back, her own eyes tearing up.

"So," continued Marguerite, "I'll make you a deal. I'll do my best to be all those things for you, dear. In return, you don't smile if you don't want. You don't be happy unless you want. You don't do anything you don't want to do. Ever. Can you promise me that?"

Samantha looked back out over the lake and thought. A lot of it didn't make sense, but neither did anything in her life these past few months. Her father had died at her grandfather's hands. Her grandfather had sabotaged his own trial, waived all his appeals, and gone to the electric chair with a smile.

And here she was, all alone, her own family hating her, and all of New Orleans fearing her. The only people she could trust were her overworked lawyer, her great-aunt, and the detective who had destroyed her family by fingering her grandfather.

And one of them hadn't spoken to her since he had caught her grandfather and lost his own partner in the process.

"Okay," Samantha finally said. "I promise. No more fake smiles."

"Good," replied Marguerite, who then presented something to her ward.

Looking at it, Samantha was surprised to see that it was the bottle of sherry she had been looking at earlier. Looking up at her guardian quizzically, Samantha said, "But I'm not old enough to—"

"I know that, dear," said Marguerite with a smile. Handing the bottle to the girl, Marguerite pointed to a piece of blank paper taped to back of the bottle. "This is for when you are happy again. Even if it's a small, fleeting happiness, when you finally smile, for real, this bottle is yours to drink."

"All right," said Samantha, trying to take it all in, and looking quite confused about the whole thing. While she was glad to be given her first bottle of alcohol at such a young age—most young ladies in New Orleans's elite society didn't get more than a small glass of wine occasionally until they debuted at sixteen—she didn't see what this had to do with her becoming happy again.

"Happiness is all your mother ever wanted for you," Marguerite said as she opened her purse and took out a small keychain. On the metallic chain was a lovely, sparkling red plastic shoe, the word "Comus" etched onto it in gold leaf. She showed it to the girl.

Samantha looked over at the charm, then up at her aunt, then back at the charm. "What's this?"

Aunt Marguerite smiled as she said, "A keepsake from your mother. Your father, a few years before you were born, took her to the Comus Ball on Mardi Gras. These"—the pudgy woman slipped the free loop of the keychain over the neck of the sherry bottle—"were used to decorate the wine bottles. She thought they were beautiful and begged your father to get one for her. He slipped one off and gave it to her right before the captain's toast."

Samantha looked down at the sherry bottle and touched the charm. "What kind of person was my mother? Was she beautiful?"

At that, Aunt Marguerite frowned a little and looked away from Samantha. "She wanted to live in a world she didn't belong in, dear. Her life was smoke-filled lounges and nightclubs, not caviar and cocktails. But she was a kind woman, at least to your father and grandfather, and yes, she was very beautiful."

She smiled at Samantha. Those words made little Samantha feel better, and the girl, looking away again, felt a little less dead inside as she hugged the bottle of sherry close to her small body.

"Here, write a reminder on it," said Marguerite as she took out a fountain pen from her purse. "I write notes to myself all the time. It always helps." She winked at the girl.

Nodding, Samantha took the pen and, resting the bottle on her knees, started to write, slowly and methodically. The calming waves of the lake crashed on the shore, the lulling sound genuinely comforting, like the pattering of rain on the roof. Samantha loved how the lake was so large that it could actually have cresting waves like the sea. It was very soothing.

But it wasn't the waves of Lake Pontchartrain that Sam heard. Instead it was the splattering of raindrops on the roof. Coming out of her memory, Sam realized she was still outside on the back porch of her townhome, and a small summer shower had broken out. For a long moment, Sam sat there, looking down at the label on the sherry bottle. Her thoughts were, for the moment, not jubilant at all, but instead were those calm and almost docile thoughts that young Samantha was having, the void of feeling nothing at all.

Then Sam moved, placing the wineglass down on the patio table, and removed the charm, hooking the keychain with one finger to almost wear it like a ring. Then Sam flipped the bottle over to look at the back, where her note to herself was taped, the one that said, "For when you finish a work on time. Go for it, girl!"

For the first time in days, Sam's head didn't hurt at all. And for a long moment, she just looked at the label, her mouth tightening and her lips starting to shake. She squeezed the plastic charm a few times. Then she started to peel back the note.

Memories assailed her as she did so. Memories of playing at the park with her father, memories of her grandfather sitting her on his knee and telling her stories, memories of Great-Aunt Marguerite reading bedtime stories to her, and so much more.

When the note from ten years ago was peeled off, Sam saw it. A single, smaller piece of paper, secured with old tape that had long since fused to the glass of the bottle. Written on it, in a child's well-styled handwriting, were the words: "For when you're happy again."

Sam reached up with her free hand to cover her face, fingers and plastic charm soon getting soaking wet. It was in many ways the beginning of true healing, as Samantha Castille, for the first time in twenty years, began to cry.

Chapter 9
Why a Snake Is Dangerous

Date: **Thursday, August 6, 1992**
Time: **10:00 a.m.**
Location: **New Orleans Police Precinct, 8th District**
            French Quarter

Steam rose from the ceramic cup in Michael's hands as he brought it toward his mouth. The moment the sting of heat reached his lips, however, he pulled back. He blew on the drink to cool it off, then raised the cup to his lips and sipped. It was a chocolate almond herbal tea, with a perfect mix of flavors, and as the drink greeted his taste buds, he knew a peaceful feeling of Zen.

"Ah," said Michael to himself. "There's nothing like a cup of herbal tea in the morning."

Glancing around as he waited for his partner to show up, Michael noted how cluttered Rodger's desk was. Old receipts for Chinese food, validated parking stubs, sticky notes dating back to the Reagan administration, and a curious stain that was probably made from that noxious coffee all littered the surface. It was a disaster area, in contrast to Michael's own desk, which was as pristine and organized as an altar.

It's amazing someone as disorganized as Rodger managed to crack the Bourbon Street Ripper murders, thought Michael as he sipped his tea. *I wonder if his partner, Edward, was as organized and methodical as I am.*

Michael decided he'd have to ask Rodger about that later.

He found himself wondering how late Rodger would be coming in to work. *He's probably still sleeping, and after last night, I won't be surprised if he just calls me and asks me to meet him someplace.*

Reflecting back on the previous night, Michael closed his eyes and sifted through the events, one after another, in the same manner that one would watch a slide show. When he and Rodger had gotten back from the rehab clinic, it was late, and the officers were finished booking T-Dawg, the gang member who had nearly succeeding in silencing Topper Jack once and for all.

Of course, T-Dawg had pretty much clammed up on the officers after screaming that Michael's subduing of him was "police brutality," so Rodger volunteered to go in and interrogate the suspect himself.

With Rodger as tired, frustrated, and stressed out as he was, the interrogation went about as well as it would on an episode of any crime drama show ever created.

T-Dawg's snide comments and disrespect seemed to wear on Rodger's last nerve, and when the suspect spat in his face, it seemed to put him over the edge. After putting T-Dawg in a full nelson, Rodger was extricated from the interrogation room by Commander Ouellette, who bellowed his disapproval and told him to go home and get some sleep before he was suspended.

Michael, who had been watching the interrogation from the other side of the one-way mirror, had made a move to enter when Rodger's temper got the better of him, only to be trumped by Ouellette. After Rodger was sent home, Michael had the wrath of his commanding officer turned on him.

Michael had handled himself calmly, simply stating that neither had slept in twenty-four hours and both were under stress. After calming down enough to impress upon Michael the importance of reining in his older partner, Ouellette had sent Michael home as well.

Having had a solid night's sleep, Michael was in a good enough mood, and he was enjoying his tea when he heard a *clunk* from Rodger's desk. Looking up, Michael saw his partner, looking haggard, but better than before. A lit cigarette dangled from his mouth. Rodger had dropped a paper bag on his already cluttered desk.

"Bagel?" asked Rodger.

"Sure. Thanks," replied Michael.

As Rodger took out the bagels, plastic dinnerware, and cream cheese, Michael looked over at his partner for signs of whether he had slept. While the bags were still present under Rodger's eyes, they weren't as heavy as they were before, and the bloodshot was gone from the whites. Satisfied that his partner had actually slept, at least a few hours, Michael finished off his cup of tea and took a bagel.

"You know, Rodger," Michael said as he cut his bagel in half and smeared a measured portion of cream cheese on it, "I was thinking that, before we go for Mad Monty, we should check out that guy whose locker key was left at one of Vincent Castille's murder scenes. The offshore worker?"

Rodger nodded as he glopped a much more generous portion of cream cheese on his bagel. "How do you figure?"

"Well," said Michael, "I think it's somehow important that a serial killer who did such a professional job of covering his tracks would do such a poor job of throwing suspicion onto another person." He took a bite from his bagel.

"The original Jack the Ripper covered his tracks and was a murderous ghost that was never seen. Only the aftermath of his victims proved that he even existed. Vincent Castille was methodical enough to do just the same thing, and yet he deliberately implicated someone else—and only one other person, and not someone who would actually be found guilty. Why?"

"That's really good, Michael. Ya know, Edward said the same thing after we crossed off that offshore worker as a suspect. He believed we should investigate more into the person, his background, and factors that could lead to why he was chosen to be Castille's patsy."

Michael nodded, a small smile crossing his lips as he was compared to Edward. It wasn't the first time Rodger had done so, but it was a very rare compliment, and Michael had learned to appreciate it when it was given.

It was obvious, from both Rodger's stories and the way people like Aucoin and Ouellette spoke of him, that Edward was admired and respected as one of the best detectives to ever work for the New Orleans Police Department.

"Well, then, what is this man's name?" Michael finally asked. "You were finding that out last night, while I was looking up Mr. Jackson's information."

"Ah, yes," Rodger replied, and he opened his desk drawer, taking out a piece of paper. Michael frowned. How his partner was ever able to find anything in that mess was well beyond him. Rodger handed him the paper, saying, "His name is Robert Fontenot, and he still lives down in Bayou Lafitte. Here." He ate his cream-cheese-slopped bagel in four bites.

Ignoring his partner's messy eating habits, Michael looked over the paper. On it was just a name and an address. "Bayou Lafitte, eh?" said Michael, mulling over the sparse information. His gut told him it was important, but he just couldn't put the pieces together.

We don't have enough information, Michael thought to himself, *but I am sure something about this man will be key to breaking this case.*

Michael was suddenly aware that he was starting to clench his jaw, the frustration of having his gut tell him one thing and logic tell him another starting to raise his stress level. Unlike his partner, who operated primarily on his intuition, Michael always relied on logic. Cold, hard facts broke a case, not gut instinct. So when his own gut nagged at him this badly, Michael got anxious, needing to know why he felt this way and how logic could back it up.

Michael's thoughts were interrupted by the sound of Commander Ouellette calling out, "Bergeron! LeBlanc! Office, now!" With a small sigh, and another nibble on his bagel, Michael headed with Rodger to their commander's office.

Inside, Ouellette, who was standing up, had them close the door, but didn't motion for them to sit down. "All right," said Ouellette as he looked over both men. "I've convinced T-Dawg not to sue the department or you, Rodger."

Rodger nodded and opened his mouth to speak, when Ouellette cut him off. "But you two are not to go near him or his gang. Narcotics has him now, and he's out of our hands. Understand?"

"With all due respect, sir," Rodger said, drawing a surprised look from Michael, "we need to make sure that T-Dawg doesn't have any link or information to the murder we're invest—"

"He doesn't," interrupted Commander Ouellette. "After I sent you two home, I interrogated him myself last night. The attack on Jackson Topman was purely narcotics-related. It had nothing to do with the murder you're on now, or the murders from twenty years ago.

"It was a good thing you two were there, or else that witness for Narcotics would be dead right now. Because of that, I'm not going to squash your sorry ass over this, Bergeron."

Rodger seemed to tighten up. But he nodded and dropped the argument. "Yes, sir."

"Good," replied Ouellette, sitting down at his desk. "So the investigation is coming along well? Any more leads?"

"Plenty," said Michael, before his partner had a chance to speak. "In fact, sir, we need to get moving. We have to travel south to Bayou Lafitte today."

"Bayou Lafitte, eh," said Commander Ouellette, rubbing his chin, then nodding. "That's Jefferson Parish. I'll give them a call and let them know you're coming."

"Thank you, sir," said Michael. His partner said the same, and with a dismissal from their commander, the two were off to their desks.

"Thanks for getting us out of there," said Rodger as the two collected their belongings. "I really didn't want to talk to the son of a bitch anymore."

Michael, who was only trying to be efficient, shrugged.

The two soon headed out of the room and toward the garage.

On the way out, they passed Aucoin, who, despite looking like he had slept last night, still managed to look haggard. Although it was obvious to Michael that Aucoin did not want to discuss last night, Rodger spoke to him anyway, and was able to determine that his wife, Catherine, and his daughter, Cheryl, were staying at Catherine's mother's house for a few weeks. Rodger gave the other senior detective his condolences, which were received with a grunt, before he and Michael headed out to the garage and their car.

A few hours later, they were driving along a dirt path in the middle of Bayou Lafitte.

The August sun beat down through the foliage, the cypress and tupelo trees hanging like thick canopies overhead. The filtered sunlight through the branches created a beautiful cathedral effect, which helped to detract from the oversized mosquitoes and the large wolf spiders that seemed to be everywhere.

"There's the cop Ouellette was talking about," said Rodger, jarring Michael out of his thoughts.

Michael had been scribbling in his notebook, furiously trying to come up with ideas and theories as to Robert Fontenot's role in this mystery. Now Michael looked up and saw they were approaching a Jefferson Parish deputy sheriff's car, and leaning against it was a deputy sheriff.

The man was, from what Michael could tell, in his midthirties. He had swarthy tanned skin, an expressionless face, and a thick black mustache. He also wore those aviation sunglasses that hid most of his upper face, and a short-sleeved brown uniform. He got up from leaning on his car as Rodger slowed down and stopped.

"All right, it's showtime," said Rodger as he put the car in PARK, leaving the engine idling.

Michael nodded and got out of the car. As he and his partner approached, the deputy sheriff unfolded his arms and reached out his hand to shake Rodger's and Michael's.

"Morning, hello there, and welcome to the lovely Lafitte Bayou, gentlemen," said the deputy sheriff in a voice so Cajun it had its own unique spice. "I'm Deputy Jean-Luc Thibodeaux, but you can call me J. L. Now who do we have here?"

Michael had met plenty of Cajuns before, but this was the most cliché one. After Rodger introduced himself, Michael did the same. To his surprise, J. L. looked at him funny and said, "LeBlanc, huh? You don't sound like any LeBlanc I know. Where you from?"

Disinterested, Michael said, "LeBlanc is a very common last name, sir. And if you must know, I'm from Shreveport." He stared at the Jefferson Parish deputy, wondering what any of this had to do with the case at hand.

"All right, all right," J. L. said, holding up his hands in a lack-adaisical way. "I'm just asking. Just being friendly." The deputy turned to Rodger. "So ya'll here to see Old Man Fontenot, right?"

"Right," said Rodger. "Were you able to call and verify that he's home?"

"Ain't got no phone," said J. L. "Ain't got no computer or television neither. Man just lives on his houseboat and eats moccasins."

Michael found himself blurting out, "He eats what?" Moccasins could mean anything from shoes to water snakes.

J. L. turned to Michael and said, in a voice as disinterested as Michael's must have been earlier, "He eats snakes, Shreveport."

Michael began to feel snubbed.

"All right, then," continued Rodger, as he motioned to their respective cars. "Let's go pay Old Man Fontenot a visit then. Lead the way, J. L."

As soon as they got into the car, Rodger turned and said, "Hey, Michael, there is something you need to know about these guys."

Michael, who had started to retreat into his thoughts on Robert Fontenot, just said, "What's that?"

Rodger continued to look at Michael, who found his partner's gaze more and more unsettling.

"These guys are all about clan, family, and conversation. You can't just go rushing into a meeting with them, and you can't take offense if your last name is the same last name as a family they've known since childhood, even if it's in no way related to your own family. It's just their way."

"I see," said Michael, filing the information away for later consideration. His mind was focused solely on the task at hand now, and he found the pep talk about Cajun etiquette to be superfluous. Looking back at his partner and matching his gaze, Michael said, "I get it. Let's get going."

Rodger sighed and shook his head as he took the car out of Park. Michael returned to his notes, creating potential links between Vincent Castille, the victims, and the accomplices. *Nothing links this guy to anything. Could this truly be a red herring? No. There is no way that this is not somehow important.*

The two detectives followed J. L.'s car down the dirt road another few miles, until they were deep in the bayou. The thick canopy of trees made the noonday sun almost like twilight. Like an optical illusion, the road seemed to go on forever. Michael, who had stopped working in his notebook, watched the Jefferson Parish deputy's car with complete boredom.

Suddenly, the car in front of them veered off to the left, the action jarring Michael out of his parked mental state. Before his mind could catch up to the rest of him, Rodger was veering to the left as well. But instead of going off the road, the two cars merely went onto a smaller, even more rural dirt path, and were suddenly driving alongside the glossy waters of the Lafitte Bayou.

The beauty of the natural waterway was breathtaking, with the branches of the cypress trees, heavy with moss, dipping down into the clear surface of the bayou. The water was still, the current so slight it could be nonexistent. Only the occasional ripple of animal life disturbed the otherwise mirror-like surface.

Michael observed a single water moccasin slithering across the surface toward the far bank. In the middle of the waterway, two small bumps, set with two small eyes, betrayed the presence of what was most likely a sizeable alligator.

Michael was taken aback by the sight before him. "It's beautiful."

Rodger smiled as he replied, "Yeah, Michael, it is beautiful. One of the few unspoiled natural beauties left in this country. There ain't nothing here but gators and natives, and with the only export being mudbugs and catfish, no one is interested in tearing this place apart."

Leaning back into his seat, Michael nodded, adding, "Well, mudbugs—I mean crawfish—and catfish comprise what, two-thirds of Creole cooking?" The question got the chuckle from Rodger that Michael expected. "But yeah, it's pretty nice out here. Very peaceful. Very secluded."

The perfect place to dump a body, he thought.

Soon the deputy sheriff's car stopped in front of them right outside a small wooden path with railings. Off the road some, pulled up right near the embankment and on a wooden deck of sorts, was an old beat-up pickup truck, filled with all sorts of junk, and half-covered in a rotted blue tarp. Deputy J. L. got out of the car and, adjusting his britches, walked over to Rodger's side of the vehicle.

Rodger rolled down the window, and J. L. bent down, sunglasses still on.

"Okay, Rodger, Shreveport. Here's the thing. Old Man Fontenot—well, he's half-crazy. And he hates visitors. But he knows me, knew my mamma, too. So I'm gonna go and let him know the two of you are here, okay? If you don't wanna get shot at, just sit back until I come to get you."

"Wait a second," said Michael, ignoring the second jab at his hometown, "if we go and introduce ourselves as police, he might take a shot at us?" Michael could hardly believe that such a thing would happen, even out here.

J. L. just sniffed derisively and said, "Well, Shreveport, Old Man Fontenot's hearing ain't too good, so he might not hear ya. Wouldn't want you to mess up that fancy suit of yours. Just you sit tight. Ol' J. L. will make sure it's safe for you."

With a smirk and a pat on Rodger's shoulder, J. L. stood up and headed down the wooden path.

"Man, what an ass," said Michael.

Rodger just shook his head and shrugged, saying, "Don't drag me into this, Michael."

The minutes passed, and soon J. L. came back up the path. Motioning for the detectives to come, the deputy sheriff hollered, "All right, Detectives, we're good. Come on!"

Michael got out of the car and followed Rodger down the wooden path, which ended up turning out to be a wooden pier leading out to a small houseboat on the water. The houseboat was old, but in good repair, and looked like it had been anchored for many years. The front door was shut only by a screen, but the darkened inside seemed to lead into a kitchenette area. Dirty pots and pans of all sizes rested on a countertop just beyond the doorway, which was as far inside as the detectives could see. The outside front porch, that being the starboard side of the boat, was adorned with drying snakeskins hanging from the ceiling, and a wall that looked to have hundreds of small ornaments attached to them.

As Michael approached, he saw that the ornaments were actually hundreds of snake skulls, mouths open and fangs bare, nailed to the wall. Michael decided that was the creepiest thing he had seen in quite some time.

Sitting on the front porch, near the front door, was a man who looked like he was in his sixties. His body was skinny, but it was obvious from the definition to his arms that he was not weak. Next to him, propped up, was a double-barreled shotgun. Sitting on his lap was a large nutria, and the old man stroked its fur while peering up at the detectives with suspicious eyes.

"Robert," said J. L., "these are the two detectives from the city I was talking about. The young one here is Michael LeBlanc, and the older one is—"

"Rodger Bergeron," Robert said with a spit to his voice. "I remember you, ya. You and that partner of yours, what was his name, sent my ass to jail some twenty years ago."

Rodger seemed to be expecting this, as he didn't flinch, but instead rubbed the back of his neck. "Yeah, we both, and the city of New Orleans, have apologized for that many times, Robert. You were a suspect in a murder investigation, and we had to hold you in custody while we ruled you out."

J. L. quickly chimed in, "Old Man Fontenot was a murder suspect, you said?"

Michael, who was at his limit with the Jefferson Parish deputy, said, "The Castille murders, you dunce. Didn't your superior tell you why we were here?"

To Michael's surprise, J. L. seemed almost apologetic, saying, "Sorry 'bout that, Shreveport, but I guess I wasn't listening too good when he mentioned it."

With a sigh of frustration, Michael started to step forward to take control of the questioning, and to his surprise, Rodger held his arm out to stop him.

Rodger quickly said, "We have a few questions about that incident, Robert. It will really help us out if you would cooperate."

"Shit, Bergeron," Robert said, spitting on the ground, "my wife left me soon after that shit. Took my baby girl with her, too, ya. I ended up coming out here because half my family thought I was responsible for those murders. It was bullshit, Bergeron. Bullshit."

"And yet," said Rodger, "you never sued the city. Why is that?"

That question seemed to stop Robert in his tracks. He huffed and looked away from the two detectives. "Man, Bergeron, go fuck yourself, ya."

After an exhale, Rodger spoke again. "Look, Robert, Mr. Fontenot, I am sorry for what happened. A lot of people were under a lot of pressure back then. You caught a bad break, and it messed your life up. For that, I am sorry. But I'm not sorry that I did my job. If there had been even the smallest chance that you were the Bourbon Street Ripper, I had to get you off the street. And for the record, you were off in Lafayette cheating on your wife. *That* is why she left you, not because we arrested you for Castille's crimes."

This seemed to calm Robert down some. He just snapped, "So what do you want, ya?"

Rodger stopped and turned to Michael, who had been just waiting for his chance to speak.

"Mr. Fontenot," began Michael, "what we want is information on anything relevant to why you were chosen by Vincent Castille to be his patsy. Anythi—"

"I already done said years ago," spat out Robert, "to Rodger's partner himself, ya. I said that I had never known Vincent Castille, that I had never heard of him before they arrested him. It was years ago, and I was spending most of my time offshore on the dredger, digging up shit. So what do I know of why Vincent chose me? Maybe it was funny to him, ya?"

Michael implored, "Are you sure? No matter how trivial, any reason can be—"

"For God's sake, Shreveport," said J. L. with a disgusted singsong to his voice, "the old man said he don't know, okay? Quit busting his ass over it."

"Deputy Sheriff Jean-Luc," Rodger suddenly said in a manner so curt and cross that it even took Michael by surprise, "will you please shut the hell up and let my partner do his job?"

There was a moment of awkward silence before J. L. quietly apologized and backed off.

Michael thought for a moment, then asked, "Mr. Fontenot, do you remember where you lost your key?"

"I already said I don't remember where," Robert replied.

Michael, however, refused to let up. "What were your days like when you were not offshore?"

"With my family, like any good Catholic would be," said Robert, perhaps more indignant than he needed to be.

Michael smiled inwardly. *He's being too defensive. First off, that means he's hiding something. Second, he knows we suspect that he's hiding something. Third, it has to be something embarrassing. There is no other reason for a man to act this way.*

Michael asked, "Okay, then tell me this, Mr. Fontenot. Where did you meet your mistress?"

"You leave her out of this, ya."

Robert nearly spat venom at Michael, his eyes showing a growing, testosterone-driven anger.

I knew it, Michael thought to himself. *It has something to do with his extramarital affair. Somehow, some way, Vincent Castille is linked to that.*

Michael then said, "Okay, okay, then tell me this. You obviously were not faithful to your wife—did you have any other affairs?"

"I don't see how it's your business, boy," said Robert, now full-blown indignant. The nutria in his lap bristled at his master's tension and hissed at Michael.

He did have other affairs, thought Michael. *If I can just get him to name where he'd go for his affairs, I'd have it.*

"Hey, Old Man Fontenot," chimed in J. L., "you need to answer their questions, or people here gonna think you ain't made right. Now you've done a good job of showing folks around here that you made good, but you start dodging police questions, and people gonna think you hiding something." It was, in Michael's eyes, J. L.'s first bit of real help all day.

This elicited a scowl from Robert, who leaned back and said, "Fine. But I answer this and you fuck off for good, ya?"

"Sure," replied Michael, staring down at the older man, waiting for his answer.

Robert closed his eyes and said, "It was a place called the Jean-Lafitte Theater. That's where I met her. I'm pretty sure that's where I lost my key, ya."

"Jean-Lafitte Theater?" asked Michael, now feeling a bit confused. "You mean the bar on Bourbon Street?"

Rodger answered this, shaking his head. "No, although I wouldn't expect you to know what he's talking about, Michael. Jean-Lafitte Theater was a nightclub on Toulouse Street that operated back in the seventies. It was burlesque. You know, a cabaret."

"Oh," said Michael, having indeed never heard of such a place before. "Well, what happened to it?" A sudden feeling of panic started to work its way into Michael. What if this place had been burnt down? Or flooded? Or was sold and turned into a bed-and-breakfast? Would their best chance at cracking this case be gone?

Rodger alleviated all those worries by saying, "It was closed down after a disgruntled ex-employee took a submachine gun to the performers and clientele one night. It was a real mess. Owners closed it down and, as far as I know, never sold it. Should still be there, just closed up."

Michael felt hope again that this was not a red herring, but something deliberately planned out. Turning back to Robert Fontenot, Michael said, "Thank you so much, Mr. Fontenot. We won't bother you again."

"Agreed," said Rodger, nodding his head to the older man, "and sorry about your loss, again. We won't come back."

As the two detectives turned to leave, Robert suddenly said, "Rodger."

Stopping, Michael and his partner turned around. Robert had reopened his eyes and was looking at them. "Do you know why a snake is so dangerous?"

This question got a blank stare from both detectives.

Robert answered, "People think that it's because of the snake's bite, but that's not it at all. The snake is the most dangerous creature because the snake knows. It knows what you are going to do. It knows when you are going to do it. The snake knows everything."

Michael took it for what it was seemed, a threat from a bitter old man, but Rodger seemed to be more tense about it. Once they were inside their car and pulling around to leave, Rodger lit up a cigarette and said, "You get what that meant, right?"

Michael shook his head. "It's not just Robert trying to get the last word in, then?"

"No," replied Rodger, setting his eyes on the road. "It hearkens back to the religion back here. A Haitian religion called voodoo."

"Seriously?" asked Michael, cocking an eyebrow at his partner. "Voodoo? You're bringing voodoo into this investigation?"

"No," growled Rodger as he swerved left back onto the main road. "But the people of the bayous take it seriously, and if we're going to deal with them, you gotta know how they think. Anyway, in voodoo, there are these powerful spirits called *loa*, and the snake is one of the most powerful, often associated with—"

"Wow." Michael cut his partner off, shaking his head. "Look, Rodger, I appreciate you trying to educate me in bayou culture, but this has nothing to do with the investigation. Unless you're actually superstitious about this stuff?"

Rodger, who momentarily looked upset at his partner, seemed to fight it off and managed a smile before saying, "Well, I've had my fair share of jackrabbit feet, but fine, if this is something you don't want to hear about, then I won't go there. But I'm telling you, Michael, a lot of people put a lot of stock into that stuff. But anyway, Mr. Ace Detective, what should our next move be?"

"Honestly," Michael said, getting his mind back on track, "I think we need to check out that abandoned nightclub. Then we need to go and hunt down that Mad Monty."

That seemed to get a concerned expression from Rodger, who said, "Yeah, about Mad Monty. Michael, there are some things you need to know."

There was a serious tone to Rodger's voice, one Michael had heard before. It was several months ago, but Rodger had spoken a warning in that tone just before they went to arrest a suspect in the Marcello family, who had murdered an ex-girlfriend in a very violent way, leaving her body to rot in the Mississippi River. The serious tone had stuck with Michael afterward, because when they went to arrest the suspect, they ended up in a firefight that resulted in three cops wounded and four gang members dead.

Suffice it to say, when Rodger spoke in that tone, Michael listened.

Chapter 10
Darkness Rising

Date: **Thursday, August 6, 1992**
Time: **12:00 p.m.**
Location: **Ritz-Carlton Hotel on Canal Street**
             French Quarter

"I loved your book so much, Mr. Fastellos," said a portly woman as Richie handed back her signed copy of *The Pale Lantern*. She smiled at him with that sort of admiration that borderlines on maniac, and for a short moment, he was afraid that she'd lean forward and try to kiss him. Instead, she just giggled, covering her mouth with pudgy little fingers, and tripped off into whatever world she'd come from.

As he sat there at the book signing, Richie was amused to think that he had just met his biggest fan—in more ways than one.

Reaching over to a tall glass filled with ice water, Richie took a long drink before motioning for the next person in line to come forward. A skinny, awkward-looking guy approached, offered his book, and immediately started to stammer about how *The Pale Lantern* had inspired him to become a writer, and asked if Richie had any advice, as well as a host of other questions that were quickly drowned out in the novelist's mind.

Autographing the inner cover, Richie mentioned a few token things such as "keep on writing" and "believe in yourself"—stock answers that were given to him by his publicist, Gordon. As the gangly youth departed with what Richie could only imagine were new aspirations, he suddenly realized that he was bored out of his mind.

The morning talk show had gone extremely well, the local celebrity talk show host asking only the most general and friendly of questions. Never once did the interview get hostile, and never once was a question asked that Richie wasn't coached for. He'd answered all questions briefly and succinctly, and in the end, several rounds of applause were given to the man being heralded as "The Next Dean Koontz."

Richie, who wasn't a Koontz fan, just smiled and thanked his host, reminding himself that one man's junk is another man's yacht—or something like that.

After the show, he was treated to a short brunch before being set up in the lobby of the Ritz-Carlton for a two-hour autograph signing. With luck, he'd be finished by one o'clock, giving him enough time to head over to the office of Kent Bourgeois and, hopefully, get in touch with Samantha Castille.

Richie's mind kept flipping back to the previous night's events, especially his conversation with that woman in the red dress. He had even tried to find out who she was, heading down to the bar the next morning and inquiring from the bartender the name of his mysterious companion. Unhelpfully, the bartender had looked at him like he was a lunatic and refused to give him any more information, even when money was placed on the table. This did nothing to alleviate Richie's suspicion that the woman was connected to organized crime. He had left with the bartender shaking his head.

But Richie thought that, so long as he didn't end up with a pair of cement boots on, he'd be all right.

Richie was interrupted by an "ahem" from one of the security guards present. He was suddenly aware that a woman was standing in front of him, holding out a copy, not of *The Pale Lantern*, but of *Darkness Rising—Ten Short Stories* by Richard Fastellos.

"Oh my goodness," Richie said as he took the book, genuinely surprised. It was a bit older than his first novel, having been published through a subsidiary publishing company about a year or so before his big break with *The Pale Lantern*. Richie remembered that since the publisher was of the subsidiary kind, it had cost him a great deal to publish that book, and less than ten thousand copies were made. To see someone with a copy of it really made his day.

"Well, I never thought I'd see this thing again," he said.

It wasn't that Richie wasn't proud of his collection of short stories. He was very fond of them. He wasn't, however, known for them, and with the book in very limited circulation, he had been certain he'd never see a fan with one in their hands.

"I'm afraid I haven't read *The Pale Lantern* yet," said the woman who handed him the book. Richie deigned to look up at her. She wasn't remarkably attractive; however, she had a hometown prettiness about her. And something about her really stuck out in Richie's mind.

Maybe it was the circles under her eyes, the kind indicative of a person who sleeps very little. Maybe it was the way she made a blond ponytail work. Or maybe it was the way she pulled off wearing a pair of black jeans and boots along with a red blazer over a black shirt. Whatever it was, Richie liked what he saw in this woman.

"Well, you'll have a good time with it, I'm sure," Richie said, opening to the inner cover and uncapping his pen. "Who should I make this out to?"

"Sam," said the woman, who paused for a second, squeezing what looked like a red plastic something in her free hand. "Just Sam." She looked around as if someone was distracting her.

Looking up at her, Richie noted that the woman was carrying a manila envelope with some words on it, but he could only make out the word *Bourbon*. He found himself wondering what had her so distracted. Shrugging, he quickly adopted a pleasant smile and said, "All right, Just Sam, one Richie Fastellos autograph coming up."

Scribbling quickly, Richie wrote out, "Just Sam, pleasure to finally meet a <u>real</u> fan," in the inside cover of her book.

As soon as he handed Sam her book back, she smiled at him. It was a small smile, but it had a sincerity to it that every other smile around him seemed to lack. For a moment, her hand touched his as they handed off the book, and Richie felt his entire body tingle. As Sam pulled back, he could see a small look of confusion on her face as well. He wondered if she had felt the same thing.

The look of confusion was quickly masked by that pleasant smile, however, and with a nod of the head, "Just Sam" wished him the best and headed off. Richie's eyes followed Sam's back for a few moments, noting that she had an attractive posterior. Realizing that he was staring, Richie arched his eyebrow and chuckled to himself.

I need to get laid.

Richie shook his head at his own sudden rush of maleness before looking back to the next person in line, an extremely heavy man who smelled of Cheetos and Diet Pepsi.

Richie groaned inwardly. It was going to be a long ninety minutes.

It was one thirty when Richie was finally able to tear himself away from the autograph table, the line having been much longer than he, or the more-than-patient staff at the Ritz-Carlton, had anticipated. As soon as the line closed, Richie waved good-bye to the remaining fans, quickly threw them enough canned responses, love, and praise to fill a book on being fake, and rushed up to his room.

Once inside, Richie immediately called the concierge desk and requested a cab to come pick him up, giving the destination address as Kent Bourgeois's office. Finding out that the office was only ten minutes away, Richie scaled down his panic from frantic to furious and changed his clothes. Soon, the fancy dress clothes were replaced with a more casual set: a button-up white shirt with a dark navy-blue tie and a pair of casual dress pants of the same color. The bottle of his anxiety pills went straight into his pants pocket.

In record time, Richie made his way downstairs and, sneaking out the side door so as to avoid the mob of his fans, got to the concierge desk. He was greeted by a gentleman in a full tuxedo who looked like he was perpetually smelling something foul.

"Ah," said the man at the concierge desk, "Mr. Fastel—"

"Shhh," Richie said, "let's keep that on the down-low, okay? I want to get outside while avoiding"—he pointed to a gaggle of his fans, congregating at the bottom of some stairs and theorizing about his next book—"things like that."

The concierge, while initially looking offended, gave Richie an understanding nod and said, in a lower voice, "We have a few side entrances that celebrities like to use. Shall I have the cab come around to one of them, sir?"

"Yes," replied Richie, sliding the man a ten-dollar bill. "Take me to one of those private exits."

The concierge looked at the ten-dollar bill with an inscrutable expression, but he picked it up. Richie just smiled. He knew that tipping well was a way to gain favor with hotel staff, and ten dollars was a pretty good tip as far as he was concerned.

Tucking away the money, the concierge motioned for Richie to follow him. "This way, sir." As he led Richie through an unmarked door, the concierge snapped at one of the bellhops, "Tell the cab to meet Mr. Fastellos at the Number Six Exit."

The bellhop snickered and ran off. Richie wondered what was funny. As the two men wandered through what Richie was certain was a maze of halls, the novelist, who was struggling to keep up with the concierge, said, "Number Six Exit? What's that?"

Without looking back, the concierge replied, "It's a place for guests such as yourself who wish to exit the hotel in privacy. Trust me, no one will ever think to look for you at the Number Six Exit. Your privacy is assured."

"Ah, good," Richie said as he and the concierge passed by more hotel staff.

"Here we are, sir," said the concierge as he came to a door marked EXIT. Opening the door, the man smiled once more and motioned for Richie to step through. "Your cab will arrive momentarily. When you return, let us know if there is any other way we can serve you."

Richie gave the man a nod and muttered his thanks before going through the doorway and stepping out into the back alley behind the Ritz-Carlton.

Richie splashed down into a pool of pink and orange liquid that smelled like spicy meatballs, and as he turned, the door closed behind him. Looking around, he saw a heap of trash bags overflowing from the two green Dumpsters, several rats crawling around the refuse with twitching noses. His ears perked up as he heard the caterwaul of two alley cats fighting for supremacy. And as the cab turned into the alley, a pack of dogs started barking in the distance.

"Wow," said Richie to himself as he waved toward the cab, gingerly shaking off his shoes. "I wonder what I get for a twenty?"

Ten minutes later, Richie was stepping out of the cab and heading up to the office of Kent Bourgeois. The building was impressively large and housed a number of businesses, including a mortgage corporation, a technology company, and over two dozen different legal and medical practices.

Taking an elevator to the fortieth of sixty floors, Richie had to admit that he had a twinge of vertigo as he exited the elevator. Remembering that Gordon Rockway's office was only on the tenth floor of his building, Richie figured he had never been this high in a building before.

Following the directory on the wall, Richie soon reached impressive oak doors that had the words "Kent Bourgeois, Estate Law Attorney" written on them.

At the door, Richie inhaled deeply, closed his eyes, and focused on his thoughts. He reminded himself that the point wasn't to buy the townhome, it was to meet Samantha Castille. With that determined, Richie entered.

He didn't have to wait at all, as Kent Bourgeois was more punctual than even Gordon Rockway. Just as Richie entered the office, it turned two o'clock, and the receptionist on duty, a pretty young lady with the whitest teeth he had ever seen, said, "Mr. Fastellos?"

Richie nodded, and the woman kept that bleach-white smile up. "Mr. Bourgeois is waiting for you. Please head through that door. At the end of the hallway." She motioned toward a large door to the side of her desk, and Richie, smiling politely at her, traveled through the doorway and into a hallway with rather expensive-looking artwork. He soon reached an open doorway leading into a huge office.

"Mr. Fastellos," said an older gentleman's voice from within the room, "please come inside, sir."

Taking everything in, Richie entered the office. His initial impression was correct—it was huge. The room was easily the size of a studio loft apartment, and sported a soft carpeted floor with area rugs of a Persian design. The walls were, once again, adorned with expensive artwork, and a few marble busts appeared to serve no other purpose than to break up the monotony of wall art.

Seated behind a solid mahogany desk, in a leather chair, was Kent Bourgeois. The man was dressed in what Richie assumed to be a tailored Armani suit. He wore spectacles. His hair was a medium gray, and he looked, above anything else, like a man who meant business.

"Yeah," said Richie, not sure what he was saying "yeah" to. "I'm Richard Fastellos, the writer. I'm glad you responded to my e-mail, Mr. Bourgeois."

Kent offered Richie a small smile before motioning to the seat in front of him. "Please, take a seat. I wish to talk with you for a while."

"Right." Richie, a bit overwhelmed at the sheer size of the office, took a seat. For some reason, Kent looked like a mob lawyer, and Richie suddenly felt that he had come here unprepared. "Look, I don't want to cause any trouble for your client, Mr. Bourgeois. I'm just here on business."

To Richie's surprise, Kent chuckled and shook his head. "Ah, Mr. Fastellos, if you were perceived as any trouble, you wouldn't be here." The attorney slid his fingers together and rested them over his lips, which made him look positively villainous. "I just want to feel you out some before introducing you to Samantha."

The response confused Richie, who leaned back and, wearing a perplexed look on his face, said, "Yeah? Is that so?"

"Mr. Fastellos," Kent said, leaning back in his chair, "you are familiar with Vincent Castille, are you not? Known in his time as the Bourbon Street Ripper? The most famous serial killer in the history of New Orleans? Surely you know he was Samantha's grandfather."

"Well, yes," admitted Richie. "I mean, I've heard about him, but I was just a kid when that happened, so it's not like I followed the events or anything."

"Yes, yes," Kent replied, lowering his folded hands down to the surface of the desk. "Well, I handled the Castille estate during Vincent's lifetime. In a way, I still do. I also handle Samantha's personal estate, and that makes me, in many ways, her advocate."

"Advocate, huh," said Richie. "What, is she a recluse?"

"Of the highest variety," Kent answered. There was a certain sadness to his voice as he gave that response, or so Richie thought, but it was quickly covered up.

"She keeps to herself, communicating only with myself and a few choice people. She also leaves the handling of all her property and investments to me, and since she has given me no indication that she wants to sell any of her properties, I have had no reason to negotiate with you."

"Ah," replied Richie, leaning back in his chair and folding his arms. Kent went on to talk about his responsibility to watch over Samantha's interests, and that he'd bring up the idea in a few weeks, or something or other. Richie wasn't listening, but instead was in the deepest of thought.

This guy is way too protective of Samantha's interests for a mere estate lawyer. There is something else here, something that's just off about the entire thing. But what is it? What reason would an estate law attorney have to stop anyone from having any contact with a client?

A sudden thought entered Richie's mind, and even as Kent was beginning to wrap up the conversation, Richie blurted out, "Mr. Bourgeois, are you the executor for the Castille estate?"

That question seemed to shock Kent, who froze for a second before saying, "Well, I don't see how that is any of your business, Mr. Fastel—"

"Yes, but it is a matter of public record," interrupted Richie. "I mean, I could go down to City Hall and find out, so you might as well just tell me."

Straightening up, Richie started to feel anxious. He slipped his left hand into his pants pocket where his bottle of anxiety pills were and ran his fingers over the bottle, the smooth plastic surface reassuring to him.

"Very well," stated Kent. "Yes, I am."

"So, you are the executor of the Castille estate," Richie said, pointing animatedly at the attorney, feeling that Kent had just opened himself up wide for a good verbal rebuttal. "And are you the executor of Samantha Castille's estate? Again, matter of public record. Don't think you can lie to me."

Kent looked confused as he said, "Yes, as a matter of fact I am."

"So, you are the estate law attorney for two separate estates under the Castille name. And I assume then that Samantha is the beneficiary of Vincent's estate?" said Richie, feeling anxiety start to well inside him. He knew that if he took the conversation the wrong way, Kent would toss him out on his ear.

"What are you getting at, Mr. Fastellos?" replied Kent, with more than a hint of irritation in his voice and his eyes narrowing.

Richie felt a rush of elation that matched his gnawing anxiety. He knew nothing about law itself, just that if he let Kent retake control of the conversation, he'd never get what he wanted—a chance to meet Samantha Castille.

"Well, if you are still overseeing the distribution of the estate of Vincent Castille to his granddaughter after twenty years, then she must, for whatever reason, not be using that estate." Richie's mouth flew faster than his brain, much like words flew from his fingers when he was on a writing binge. He squeezed the bottle of pills in his pocket more strongly.

"That means her own estate, for which she has turned the daily operations over to you, is what she lives on. I can only assume that estate is finite. I can also only assume that the sale of the townhome in question would expand the financial value of that estate. Samantha hasn't said that she wants to sell anything, but she also, according to you, hasn't said that she *doesn't* want to sell anything."

"The point?" Kent said, boring holes into Richie's skull with his eyes. There was something almost dangerous in Kent's gaze.

Richie gripped the arm of the chair and leaned back, pushing his anxiety down to his gurgling stomach. "This just smells a lot like a conflict of interest, that's all. I don't suppose we should audit the Castille estate and find out, should we?"

Richie, who was pulling most of what he was saying out of his ass, did not expect his bluff to have any effect, but it had come out before he had even realized what was going on. He got this way sometimes, and was aware that this anxious method of talking a person to death rarely worked. Fortunately, it only happened when he got stressed out.

Unfortunately, just being in the same room as Kent stressed him out.

To Richie's surprise, however, Kent just stared at him with narrowed eyes, looking more frustrated by the moment. The effect was significantly more unsettling than he had anticipated.

Finally, Kent spoke. "Your knowledge of the law is a bit flawed, but your basic accusation is disturbingly accurate. All right, Mr. Fastellos, the truth." Leaning in, the lawyer looked right at Richie, his face once again masking any emotion. "The truth is, I've known Samantha since she was a child, and I've seen that girl suffer in ways most people will never understand. That, paired with the fact that her own family loathes her has made me, well, very protective of her. I'll admit I'm going far beyond the duties of a family attorney, but dash it all, someone has to look out for Samantha."

This confession took Richie completely off guard, and with an "Oh," he slumped back, unsure of what to make of the situation. He couldn't tell if Kent was bullshitting him back or not. Every knot in his stomach told him it was time to leave the office.

Finally, he sighed, leaning forward and looking at the lawyer in a frank manner. "Okay, I see why you're doing what you're doing, and I promise not to do anything to harm her. I just want to talk to her. If you can make that happen . . . I promise not to bother her if she says 'no.'"

Richie felt irritated at having to hand-hold a seemingly all-powerful lawyer through what he felt was tantamount to pinkie swears. But the alternative wasn't even possible. After a confession like that, telling Kent he wanted to talk to Samantha about a book involving her grandfather would seem like pure exploitation.

"Deal?" Richie prompted.

After a long moment of silence, Kent nodded. "Deal. I'll contact Samantha this afternoon and arrange a meeting between the two of you for tomorrow. Is that satisfactory?"

"Of course," replied Richie, who struggled to keep the smugness off his face. The anxiety was gone, and in its place was the feeling of how awesome he was.

Kent nodded, showing no more emotion. "I can reach you by e-mail, then, Mr. Fastellos?"

"Of course," responded Richie, "or just call the Ritz-Carlton and ask for my room."

"Leave your room number with my receptionist," Kent instructed, then reached down to pick up a pen. The stern-eyed lawyer started going through a stack of papers on his desk, then stopped when he noticed that Richie was still there. "Thank you for stopping by, Mr. Fastellos. Have a good day."

Richie finally took the hint and left, making sure to drop off his room number with the receptionist, who almost laughed when he made sure to explain that it was for Kent to call him and not some attempt to pick her up.

Once in the lobby of the building, Richie popped a pill, washing it down with some water from a nearby fountain. While he didn't feel a panic attack coming on exactly, he felt anxious enough that his stomach and head were starting to hurt. It was a dull, throbbing ache, like someone was walking around inside his skull.

Despite all that, Richie was in a fantastic mood when he got back to the hotel. He even tipped the concierge twenty dollars, which the man looked at with what appeared to be mild interest. Heading up to his room, he busied himself with answering e-mails, having an hour-long conversation with Gordon about the morning's interview and signing, and looking over the dinner menu of a local pizzeria.

It was five o'clock, and Richie was just settling down to order a pizza and then watch some television, when the hotel phone rang. Picking it up, he said, "Hello?"

"Mr. Fastellos," said the unmistakable Bond-villainous voice of Kent Bourgeois, "I just spoke with Samantha Castille."

"Great," replied Richie, his heart starting to race. "What did she say?"

"She wants to meet with you tonight"—Kent's voice sounded like someone had taken away his plate of cookies—"at the restaurant at the Ritz-Carlton."

"She what?" Richie said in a voice that was completely incredulous, before quickly recovering. "Oh, that's fantastic! Tell her I'll meet her. What time? What will she be wearing?"

Kent's voice continued to sound disgruntled as he said, "Seven o'clock. Yes, I know that is a bit later than usual for dinner, but Samantha is somewhat of a night owl. As for what she'll be wearing, don't worry about that. She's already reserved a table for you and her. When you get there, just give your name, and you'll be seated. Samantha will join you shortly."

"All right," said Richie, getting a sense of cloak-and-dagger intrigue that was quite enjoyable.

"Be there no later than seven o'clock, Mr. Fastellos." Kent's voice suddenly took on a tone of warning, one that made Richie's breath quicken. "Do not make my client wait for you."

"Oh, I won't," replied Richie, jotting down notes of where, when, and what concerning his dinner with Samantha Castille. "Thank you again, Mist—"

"And Mr. Fastellos," Kent added dryly, his voice becoming menacing, "you upset her, and I'll make sure you never have another cent to your name again. Good night, sir."

The lawyer hung up, leaving Richie sitting there, holding the phone, and wondering what kind of bug had crawled up Kent Bourgeois's ass and turned him into a raging dick.

Richie shook it off and set about the task of getting ready for his dinner. Richie took a shower, shaved his stubble, brushed his teeth, and put on a clean suit. A spray of cologne later, and Richie was headed downstairs to meet up with Samantha Castille.

Chapter 11
Mad Monty

Date: **Thursday, August 6, 1992**
Time: **5:00 p.m.**
Location: **Jean-Lafitte Theater on Toulouse**
              French Quarter

Smoking a cigarette and leaning against a brick wall, Rodger stood outside the closed-down building that once was the Jean-Lafitte Theater. Michael sat in their nearby car.

Rodger mulled over the events of the last hour in his head. He wasn't sure what Michael had expected to see in the run-down building, but as far as Rodger was concerned, the entire side trip was a colossal waste of time.

They had both been hopeful when they had discovered the building to be closed and still standing. The small pathway leading from Toulouse to the courtyard where the entrance lay was badly overgrown, and it was obvious from the flea-ridden blankets and used drug paraphernalia scattered throughout the courtyard that the outside of the Theater was being used as a crash space for addicts and derelicts. However, against all odds, the building hadn't fallen into a permanent state of disrepair.

With just wooden planks nailed over the entrance of the building, getting in was an easy matter of tearing them down. Fortunately, Rodger always kept a toolbox in the trunk of his car, a habit he had gotten into during his days with Edward. The hammer in the toolbox was old, and the head was a bit rusty, but it did the job. It had taken only a few minutes for them to gain access to the old cabaret.

Inside the theater, it was very dark, even at four o'clock in the afternoon in August, the interior of the club having always had minor exposure to the outside world. Flashlights in hands, both detectives shone their beams around the front entry room, light reflecting off of tarnished brass and absorbed by moth-eaten velvet. Michael had made a comment about what a dump this place had become, but to Rodger, it was a cornucopia of memories.

Rodger remembered the splendor of what was once New Orleans's most famous cabaret. The courtyard had been lit with gas lanterns that reflected off the surface of two large glass windows, which were draped on the inside, as well as reflected off the water from two enormous lion-head fountains, one on either side of the courtyard. The double doors from the courtyard had opened into the splendid front entry room, the smell of expensive cigars and even more expensive cognac wafting as soon as one entered.

Rodger remembered the weasel-like host standing behind a podium made of solid oak. He would look down his nose at you while checking "the list" for your name. The detective also remembered the pug-nosed bouncer with the sloped forehead and arms the size of small frigates who would ensure that only those on "the list" would get inside.

Rodger also remembered that back in the seventies, fifty dollars got you on "the list."

Now, two decades later, Rodger had to agree with Michael's assessment. Compared to its former glory, the Jean-Lafitte Theater had become "quite a dump."

The brass was now tarnished, the black velvet divider was long gone, the red velvet drapes were moth-eaten, the carpet had more bald patches than a cat with mange, and the posters on the walls were faded and only partially legible. The smell of mold and dust was as thick as the specks in the air.

Only a few things were left to remind Rodger of the once proud and exclusive nightclub. The oaken podium still stood, an effigy to the weasel-nosed host and his list, and there were still two posters, one on either side of the room. One showed two lovely blond lasses in red dresses blowing kisses and winking for the camera, and the other showed a man who looked suspiciously familiar, with slicked-back hair and startling blue eyes, grinning like the devil himself.

Michael had shone his flashlight over at the two posters, first on the one of the two women, then on the one of the suspicious-looking man, and had asked who they were. It took Rodger a few moments to remember, as the posters were in bad condition.

"Ah yes, the M and M Sisters," Rodger had said. "They were a staple here. A pair of twin sisters with the kind of beauty about them that could melt men's hearts. Their golden hair and sapphire blue eyes were contrasted by their deep red velvet dresses. It's said that any man they looked at would lose their hearts, and their souls, to those sultry vixens."

When he noticed Michael staring at him, Rodger had chuckled and said, "What can I say? I'm a sucker for blondes."

Michael had smirked, shaken his head, and shone his light on the blue-eyed gentleman, asking who he was and why he looked suspiciously like Frank Sinatra.

"Oh yeah," Rodger had said, shining his light on the other poster, especially on those unsettlingly beautiful blue eyes. He had a sudden venom in his voice. "Giorgio Marcello, grandson of Carlos Marcello, of the New Orleans Marcello family. They called him Blue-Eyed Marcello. The guy made himself out to be the South's version of Old Blue-Eyes, but . . . "

After Rodger's voice trailed off, Michael had pressed him for further details. Taking the light off Giorgio, Rodger had walked around the room, absently focusing his beam of light on other places. "Giorgio was, to put it lightly, a serial rapist. The story was always the same: The women would be lured into his limousine with promises of expensive gifts and 'a night they would never forget,' were taken to an expensive hotel in the French Quarter, and not seen again for several days."

When Michael had asked what had become of the victims, Rodger responded, grim-faced, "Well, the bastard would leave them in the hotel room he raped them in, tied to the bed, blindfolded and gagged. He'd pay for the room for three days, so the woman would only be found, usually lying in her own shit, by the hotel staff after the room's occupancy had expired."

The story had seemed to make Michael upset, as he scowled at Rodger and shook his head, a look of disgust on his face. He had asked, "When was Giorgio arrested?"

Rodger had shaken his head. "Apart from using a different associate with a different name to reserve the hotel room, using the back entrance, and threatening each woman's life should they speak to the police, Giorgio was part of a very powerful and influential crime family who could throw money and violence around to get anything they wanted."

That had ended the conversation for the moment, and both detectives had headed deeper inside, past the red velvet curtain that stank of twenty years of mildew, and into the main floor of the cabaret.

What they found, however, really sank their spirits into the ground.

Given the incident that had resulted in the Jean-Lafitte Theatre being closed down—the shooting up of the cabaret by a disgruntled ex-employee—even Rodger was surprised that the main floor of the building had been completely cleared out. As the flashlights swam around the two-story interior of the nightclub, shining from the wooden stage across the tiered floor to the balconies above, they could see that every piece of furniture was gone. Only the brass chandelier, thick with cobwebs and dust, remained of the once-great cabaret that was haunted by New Orleans's upper echelon.

"This is insane," Michael had remarked, disappointment and anxiety thick in his voice. Rodger, having agreed with his partner's sentiment, had agreed that they needed to search the rest of the club anyway. The two spent approximately the next hour checking the side rooms, hallways, and offices.

From the private booths and rooms, where exclusive clientele did God knows what, to the dressing rooms, where talent would prepare to go on stage, to the offices, where money was counted and employees and police alike were paid—everything had been long since methodically removed. Only the front entryway remained decorated.

By the time both detectives had reached the manager's office, their flashlight beams shining on the indentation where a safe must have been, it was painfully apparent what had happened.

Even as his partner seemed to tense up over what was rapidly becoming a red herring, Rodger had said, "After the place got closed down, Carlos Marcello must have had his men come in and clean the place out. They only left the front room, the chandelier, and the bullet holes behind."

It was after that statement that Michael had left in disgust, although he barely showed it. As he followed his partner back outside and toward their car, Rodger thought to himself that Michael was taking the apparent dead end badly. Knowing that his partner almost never followed hunches unless they had facts to back them up, Rodger figured that Michael probably felt like he had detracted from the investigation.

As Rodger stood outside, finishing his cigarette, he decided that Michael just needed some encouragement. The senior detective headed back to the squad car, reminding himself that he had had his own fair share of bad hunches during his career.

As he got inside the car, Rodger said, "Hey, Michael, don't let it get to you, all right? We all have false leads from time to time. Don't beat yourself up over—"

"I'm fine," said Michael as he finished scribbling in his notebook. "I think I just figured out why we needed to be here."

For a moment, Rodger just stared at his partner, who had been making a real habit lately of interrupting him. Being a gentleman, if nothing else, Rodger refrained from punching his partner in the face, but the interruption did raise the senior detective's blood pressure. Rodger sometimes had to remind himself that Michael was, after all, still just a kid compared to him.

He'll learn to get along with others in time.

Brushing the rude behavior off, Rodger asked, "What do you mean?"

"Well, it's obvious this was an exclusive nightclub," Michael said, tapping the tip of his pen to his notes. "I'm assuming it was run by the Marcello family, given what you told me about Carlos Marcello being the one to clear this place out. Correct?"

"Correct, but that's not a big surprise," replied Rodger, not sure where his partner was going with this line of thought. "In the seventies, half this town was owned by the Marcello family. Even after his stroke in ninety-one, he was still the most powerful man in the city."

"Right, but that's just it, Rodger," replied Michael, again tapping his pen to his notes. "This was an exclusive nightclub for the socially elite to congregate. Why on earth would a common offshore worker like Robert Fontenot be allowed in a place like the Jean-Lafitte Theater?"

Thinking about that for a moment, Rodger replied, "Could have been the chauffeur for a client here, for all we know. Mr. Fontenot wasn't exactly forthcoming with the details of his life, you know."

"True," replied Michael, who paused for a moment. "But if that were the case, why would he have met his mistress here? Under what pretense does a guy who has nigh a penny to his name not only get into an exclusive club, but also attract the attention of a woman here? Especially when you figure that any woman frequenting this place would only be attracted to a man with money, power, or both."

Rodger looked at his partner and, for a moment, saw Edward sitting there, pointing to a similar notebook with similar notes. Shaking it off, Rodger admitted to himself that Michael, despite being a total ass, was brilliant. "It seems that Mr. Fontenot has played us, Michael. Either he's lying about this place, or . . . "

" . . . there's more to him than he's admitting," said Michael.

For a moment, Rodger sat there with Michael, the synergy between the two buzzing like the arc of a Tesla coil.

"Well," said Rodger at last, "we have to be extra-careful with this guy." Starting up the car, and fighting again with the latch of his safety belt, he elaborated, "We got one free interview with him. Any follow-ups, especially after he made it clear just how much he 'loves' us, will just bring out his suspicion. And we don't need to give this guy reason to vanish into the bayou for good."

"Agreed," replied Michael as Rodger finally pulled the car away. "We need to check up on Robert Fontenot. Find out everything we can about him. Who this man really was, what he did, and where he went when he wasn't working on the river."

Rodger nodded and pulled off Toulouse, heading to the interstate. "We should also check the civil records for Mr. Fontenot's divorce, and see if we can't find out the name of his mistress. If she's still living, and still in Louisiana, she may know some things as well."

"Good idea," Michael said, giving a small smile to his partner. "Good to see you're still in the game."

"Shit," Rodger replied with a smirk. "I wasn't the one who was about to cry when he saw the club was empty."

"Oh, piss off," Michael said with an answering smirk. The tension previously felt was long gone.

Once on the interstate, Rodger headed toward New Orleans East, the part of the city between Orleans and St. Bernard Parish. New Orleans East was not known as the safest part of the city, although, like the Lower Ninth Ward, it was more due to a history of gang violence than anything else. Pulling off on Chef Menteur Highway, Rodger started to get his mind in the zone for his next objective.

"So, according to the system's records," Rodger said, "Mad Monty owns a warehouse not far from here, correct?"

Michael, who had already taken out a computer printout made at the precinct, nodded. "Yes, turn right at Old Gentilly Road, then again at Paris Road." Those directions given, Michael turned to his partner. "Given what you've told me about Mad Monty, Rodger, will the two of us and Monty's parole officer be enough?"

Rodger gritted his teeth, recalling his conversation with his partner on the way back from Bayou Lafitte. After talking over not only Mad Monty's violent past, but his personal beef with Rodger, both detectives had agreed that going in alone would be foolish. They had contacted Commander Ouellette, who had gotten them in touch with Horace Blanchard, Mad Monty's parole officer. A brief call with Horace, and the oddly nerdy-sounding officer had agreed to meet the two detectives outside of the warehouse that Mad Monty owned.

Rodger was torn, as part of him wanted to go in there with an entire posse, rounding up Mad Monty and any of his friends, like the lawmen of the Old West. The other part of him knew Monty and knew that if anything more than a single police car and his parole officer showed up, he'd be gone before they could stop their engines. And since Mad Monty was more of a witness in this situation than a suspect, anything more would look like the New Orleans police were deliberately antagonizing him.

Rodger thought, with a disgusted shake of his head, how much the *Times-Picayune* would love a story of the police abusing a suspect, especially an African American one, and especially after the Los Angeles riots earlier that year.

"Let Ouellette know we're almost there, and that we'll check in within thirty minutes," Rodger said. "And if we don't, to send in the cavalry."

As Michael put in the call, Rodger thought to himself that while he didn't plan on dying today, he didn't plan on letting Monty walk away without answering his questions.

If that means I have to bring half the SWAT team out, so be it.

By the time Rodger pulled off Paris Road and into the old warehouse district, Michael had placed the call to Ouellette, who had once again expressed the need for extreme caution to both detectives. While Mad Monty had no official record of assaulting police officers, he was known to be a violent type. Having been arrested and tried on three counts of manslaughter, the only reason Mad Monty wasn't still behind bars was because only enough evidence was gathered to convict him for one count.

Rodger was the person who had collected the evidence needed to convict Monty on that single count of manslaughter, sending him to Angola State Prison for ten years. The rage in Mad Monty's voice on the date of his conviction—the venom with which he'd sworn he'd emasculate Rodger—had haunted the senior detective to that very day.

Those thoughts were still in Rodger's mind as he pulled past the gateway into Mad Monty's warehouse. A single hand-painted sign outside the gate, labeled "Monty's Auto Detail," looked rather fresh.

Otherwise, the entire property looked about as run-down as one would expect. The chain-link fence was overgrown with weeds, the siding on the warehouse was rusted and corroded with age and neglect, and the large sign above the entrance into the warehouse was so old it could barely be read.

"Metal works," said Michael, reading the sign aloud with obvious effort.

"Yeah," replied Rodger as he spotted a dark brown sedan with civil tags parked halfway between the gate and the warehouse. Pulling up behind the sedan, Rodger added, "Monty loves him some cars. I remember that. This warehouse used to be a factory where they made car bumpers. Back when they used to make bumpers out of real metal, not that crumple-shit they use now." Rodger put the car in PARK.

"Lovely," said Michael as he peered through the windshield at the warehouse. "All sorts of lovely things inside a metal-works factory that can kill you."

Rodger looked at his partner and contemplated a snarky comment, but settled on saying, "Thanks for settling my nerves about meeting this guy, Michael. I really appreciate the camaraderie here."

Michael smirked. "You're welcome." He stepped out of the car.

"Ass." Shaking his head, Rodger stepped out of the car as well.

As the detectives exited their car, the brown sedan's door opened up, and out stepped a short, bald man wearing a tweed suit. He wore a pair of wire-frame spectacles on his pointed nose and carried a brown leather suitcase in his arms. The man's nose was tilted up just enough to show that he had a rather sizable sense of self-importance.

Rodger was already annoyed with Horace. Not only did the man come across as a first-class nerd, but he seemed to have an unwarranted sense of self-importance. Those thoughts did nothing to make Rodger feel any less anxious, and with a look to his partner, he said, "Keep your piece ready, Michael," as they approached the parole officer.

"Horace Lancaster Blanchard," said the man with a stereotypical nasally voice, offering a hand to Rodger and then Michael. "I'm Mr. Jones's probation officer. So you two detectives are here to question Mr. Jones on that nasty murder that happened the other night, correct?"

"That's correct," said Rodger, shaking Horace's hand and noticing how clammy it felt. "My partner and I have just a few questions for Monty regarding the Castille murders. Then we'll be out of his hair."

"Mr. Jones has been well-behaved since his release from prison," said Horace, as he started walking toward the warehouse, the detectives following him, "but he gets rather . . . what's the word . . . indignant at times."

Rodger couldn't help but smirk. "That hardly comes as a surprise. Does he know we're coming?"

Horace nodded, not bothering to turn and look at the detectives. "He's aware of the situation. I told him to meet us alone outside."

"Does Mr. Jones know that it's Rodger who's coming?" asked Michael, walking alongside Rodger, stride for stride.

Another nod from the probation officer, and Rodger felt his stomach drop.

"Mr. Jones expressed surprise that, after all these years, Detective Bergeron would come and visit." At that, Horace stopped and turned toward Rodger, looking up at him, his tone as condescending as it could sound. "I know you and him have an unfortunate history together. It would be best if you didn't mention it, okay?"

Rodger stared for a moment at Horace for stating something so obvious in such an arrogant way, and finally just shrugged, palms out, and said, "I'll try to keep that in mind. Thanks, Horace."

The trio headed toward the door of the warehouse, which, with a loud creaking sound, suddenly opened up.

Out stepped a tall man with skin the color of dark chocolate, head and face clean-shaven. His hardened, chiseled face was accented by a large, angry-looking scar that started over his left eye and ended just beneath his thick jaw.

The rest of Monty was equally imposing: a broad chest rippling with muscles, two thick tree trunks for arms, and forearms that looked like they could lift a truck—all of it covered in tribal tattoos.

His chest was covered with a T-shirt that sported a lewd picture of a woman on a stripper pole with text reading "I Support Single Mothers." His lower half, covered in dirty jeans and army boots, was just as well-built as the rest.

Rodger felt his johnson shrink.

Jesus Christ. He's gotten bigger.

Alongside Mad Monty, two other men, similar in look but not nearly as big, stepped outside the warehouse. One, also clean-shaven, had his shirt off and sported two bullet scars on his chest. The other, wearing a black do-rag over his head, wore a wife-beater with some questionable stains on it, and had a goatee.

Rodger thought the situation was not a good one, and looked over at Michael, who seemed to be cautious but otherwise betrayed no other emotion. Then Rodger looked over at Horace, as if he expected the short parole officer to somehow manage this situation.

"Now, Mr. Jones, we agreed on the phone that you'd meet with the detectives alone," said Horace, seemingly unflinching in the presence of a man three times his size and many times more dangerous, even without friends.

Mad Monty gave Horace a toothy grin, his pearly whites shining, before saying, in a voice that rumbled like thunder, "Aw, hell, Mr. Blanchard, I'm sorry. Me and my boys here were just having a beer, and I plain forgot what time it was." Monty then motioned inside the warehouse. "Ya'll wanna come in?"

Horace must have shared Rodger's thought that such an action would be stupid, because the probation officer retorted, "Now you know that's not a good idea, Mr. Jones. Your friends can come back later, once we're finished speaking with you."

"A'ight," replied Monty, who then turned to the two other men and, after clasping hands in a series of grabs, slaps, and shakes, said, "When I'm done here, I'll give ya'll a ring at Leroy's house. We'll head to the lake and get fucked up tonight."

As the two men left, Rodger couldn't help but wonder if that was code for "wait until the stupid cops aren't looking and then help me beat them to death." His senses on high alert, he followed a satisfied Horace Blanchard after Monty and into the warehouse.

The interior of the warehouse did nothing to dissuade Rodger's feelings that they were walking into a trap, as the assumption Michael had about lots of stuff in there being able to kill them seemed spot-on. From the ceiling hung a series of hooks on chains, all of them arranged on a track that led around the warehouse. In the corner of the warehouse was a large vat, set into the ground, with steam and the stink of sulfur fuming from it. A set of stairs led up to a catwalk and over to an elevated area with rows upon rows of metal presses. And finally, in the center of the room was a conveyor belt leading into a large box-like machine that looked to be made of mangling, crushing murder.

However, off to one side several folding lawn chairs sat circled around an ice chest. Nearby was a folding table with a boom box playing Beethoven's 6th symphony, a tune that seemed totally out of place for either the location or the man. As soon as Monty reached the largest lawn chair, he took a seat and offered one to each of the detectives.

"Ah, I see you took my advice and started listening to classical music," said Horace as he took the proffered seat. "Is it helping that rage problem of yours, Mr. Jones?"

"Huh?" asked Monty as he opened the ice chest and took out a beer. "Oh yeah, that. Yeah, that shit's cool. That Beethoven, man, he was a hardcore motherfucker." Glugging down the beer and then crushing the can with minimal effort, Monty took out two more cans and offered one to Horace.

Horace shook his head, saying, "No, thanks, I don't drink. And how many have you had, Mr. Jones? You know the judge said you aren't supposed to imbibe too many spirits."

"Relax, it's nonalcoholic," thundered Monty as he tilted the cans of beer to show the brand. "Seriously, Horace, I need to get your ass laid sometime." He made the same offer of beer to Michael, who refused, then to Rodger, saying, "For old time's sake, Detective."

"Sorry, I'm on duty," said Rodger, looking Monty in the eyes as much as he dared.

"Suit yourself," Monty said with a shrug as he put back one beer and popped the top off the other. Taking a seat on one of the lawn chairs, legs spread as if inviting the detectives to take in the view of his crotch, Monty spoke directly to Rodger. "It's fucking amazing, ain't it? Last time I saw you, Detective, I said I was gonna rip your balls off . . . "

Instantly, Rodger tensed up, his jaw tightening.

" . . . but ya know," Monty said, shrugging with a sort of bored indifference, "nowadays I just don't feel like it." He sniffed at the air derisively. "I dunno, it's old shit, and I got other stuff going on."

Rodger relaxed some, and sensing that Michael was relaxing as well, nodded to the man who had once threatened his life. "Yeah. Old shit. We're too old to be playing those games, ain't we, Monty?"

"Now I never said I was too old," Monty said with a sudden life, his white teeth like the jaws of a shark. "I fuck three hos a night, Detective, and between that and my detailing business, I ain't got time to go ripping the nuts off of police."

"Well, that's a fucking relief," said Rodger with a hint of sarcasm. While he didn't want to antagonize Monty, he didn't want to look like a coward. He knew that men like Monty pounced at the first sign of weakness.

"If you two are done fanning out your plumage like two pea-cocks," said Horace, in a voice that sounded both cowardly and whiny, "I believe there were some questions for Mr. Jones?"

"Right, right," said Monty as he settled down. He looked Rodger over. "Horace here tells me you have some questions about the Bourbon Street Ripper. That so?"

"Yes," replied Rodger, sitting up and focusing on the task at hand—the interrogation of a potential witness to the Castille murders. "We're investigating the murder that took place two nights ago. We think this is a copycat killer."

"Yeah, I figured the same thing," Monty said, sniffing again at the air and looking over at the large machine in the center of the warehouse. "Read about that shit in the *Picayune*. Yeah, it's fucked up. The devil is back in the French Quarter, eh?"

Rodger nodded again, deciding that Monty was beating around the bush. Not wanting to waste time, the detective got straight down to business.

"So, Monty," Rodger said, leaning forward and looking him in the eyes in a challenging way, "your name was found in one of Vincent Castille's notebooks, along with a list of other accom-plices. What kind of dealings did you have with the good doctor back then?" He stared unflinchingly at Monty.

"I can't believe after all these years that shit's come back to haunt me," Monty said. He leaned his head back and stared at the ceiling. "Well, if this is some shit to get me back behind bars, I'd better give my lawyer a call."

Rodger shook his head. "Nothing like that at all, Monty. We're not out to bust you over something that happened twenty years ago. We are, however, looking for information on the doctor from the point of view of any . . . associates he may have had at the time. So, we'd like to know what you did for him. Strictly for the purpose of profiling this new killer."

"Ah," said Monty with a nod, his squashed nose sniffing the air a third time. "Well, that makes sense." He rubbed his thick lower jaw. "Well, I've always known of good places to hide shit. The doctor wanted out-of-the-way locations. Hell if I knew what he wanted it for. Hell if I cared. The doc supplied me with enough cold cash to make me think of retiring from my regular job."

"You mean the car theft rings, Monty?" asked Michael suddenly, giving Monty an icy stare.

Monty turned to face Michael and scrunched his face up. "Yeah," he said, "something like that, kid."

Rodger smirked, finding Michael's lack of social graces appropriate for once. "So, what else did the doc have you do?"

Looking back at Rodger, Monty grimaced and said, "Nothing else, Detective. I was the one who gave the Ripper his murdering locations. After the first one, I knew what was up. After all, some bitch gets cut open in one of my stash-houses, what the fuck am I gonna think? But the doc's money was too good, so"—he gave another toothy white grin—"I had me a bad case of amnesia about what my shit was used for."

Rodger leaned back and nodded in response to Monty's last confession. "So this is what you did in the past, Monty," he said. "But what about the present? Anyone contact you looking for new hiding places to torture victims?"

Mad Monty again scrunched up his face, puckered his lips, and furrowed his brow, then scratched the side of his head while making a *Hmmm* noise. The overall effect made the large black man look as stupid as possible, and Rodger suspected that at this point, Monty was messing with him.

"Ya see," Monty finally said. "I don't 'member. It's been a rough couple of days, Detective, and I've been getting fucked up every night on Jack Daniels."

"You really expect us to buy that?" Michael suddenly asked, straightening up. "Seriously, Rodger, let's run this guy in for helping the Ripper out. I'm sure we can get the DA to send his ass up the river for the rest of his life."

"That will be enough of that, Detective," Horace said, jumping in. "Mr. Jones is speaking to you in confidence, and I don't think threats are the way to resolve this matter."

Rodger felt utterly undermined. He and Michael were playing the good cop and bad cop routine perfectly, and here was Horace

"Poindexter" Blanchard messing the whole thing up. Their one chance just went up in a puff of nerd-smoke. One look over to Michael, who looked like he wanted to karate-chop Horace in the head, and Rodger knew his partner felt the same way.

"Yeah, ya'll coppers infringing on my civil rights," said Monty in a voice that would sound innocent if the tone weren't utterly mocking. "And here I was trying to be helpful."

By the time Monty pouted out his bottom lip like a child would, Rodger knew that the interview was over.

Standing up and dusting off his coat, Rodger said, "Sorry about that, Monty. You've been a great help to us. We thank you for your time."

Monty stood up and offered his hand for Rodger to shake. "My pleasure," he said in his boomingly large voice.

Rodger, still not wanting to show any fear, shook Monty's hand. Not surprisingly, Monty's grip was as strong as steel.

Monty grinned his white, toothy grin down at Rodger, released the grip, and then started to show everyone out of his warehouse.

"I want you to know, Mr. Jones, that you performed admirably today," said Horace as he waddled in front of the group toward the warehouse's exit. "I'll be sure to note this in my report to the Board."

"Aw, that's mighty white of you, Horace," Monty said with a low chuckle. "Let them know about the nonalcoholic beer, too, a'right? I want them to know I only drink that shit at night, like we agreed."

As Horace confirmed that he would add such information to his report, Rodger and Michael traded looks. At that moment, Rodger decided he would give Horace the dressing-down of his life once they were out of Monty's earshot. As Monty opened the large open door of the warehouse for all three officers, Rodger swore that for every two steps forward he and Michael took with this investigation, something stupid pushed them three steps back.

The fresh open air outside was a welcome change from the stuffy interior of the warehouse. Horace was the first one out, then Michael. As Rodger started to step out, Monty said, in a lower tone, "Hey, Detective. About all that shit I said I'd do to you at my trial. You know that was shit-talk, right?"

That made Rodger stop, turn around, and look at Mad Monty, who had his hands stuffed in his jeans.

Monty nodded and said, "I was really pissed about shit, lots of shit. Just want you to know that I don't want to rip your balls off."

Rodger found himself actually relieved, nodding his head and saying, "Well, that's good to know, Monty. I'm kind of attached to them. But thanks all the same."

"Yeah," said Monty as he looked up for a moment, then looked back down at Rodger. "I'm gonna kill you a whole lot worse."

For a surreal moment, Rodger just stood there, his eyes widening as his brain registered what was just said. Then suddenly there was a loud *whoosh* sound as a steel car bumper, attached by two chains, swung down from the interior of the warehouse and struck Rodger directly in the chest. Like a sack of potatoes, he hit the ground, his jaw slack and his eyes unfocused, all the breath gone from his body and his ears ringing loudly.

Through the haze, he saw Michael, already turning and reaching into his coat to grab his pistol, as one of Monty's friends, the bald one with the bullet wounds on his chest, rushed behind him with a metal baseball bat. With a single swing, Michael was disarmed.

Even as his vision began to blur and darken, Rodger mentally screamed for Michael to run away and get help.

Michael had already turned and was engaging the baseball-bat-wielding thug with his bare hands, even as the other one, the one with the wife-beater, came up behind Michael and hit him with a lead pipe in the back. Rodger watched as his partner cried out and fell to one knee.

Rodger again screamed in his head for Michael to run away.

While Rodger doubted that Michael could hear his thoughts, he was relieved to see that his partner was doing something.

Rolling to the side, Michael rushed toward the back of the ware-house, the thugs giving chase.

Good. He got away.

Meanwhile, Horace was shouting shrilly at Mad Monty, "This is going on my report, Mr. Jones. You, sir, are heading back to jail!"

Rodger's vision started to grow dark, the blow to the chest finally overwhelming him, even as he saw Mad Monty step over him and, with one punch, knock Horace to the ground.

As darkness stole over him, he saw Mad Monty turn and look him in the eyes, his white teeth glaring like the fangs of a wolf.

The last thing Rodger thought before unconsciousness over-took him was the word *shit.*

Chapter 12
Dinner at the Ritz

Date: **Thursday, August 6, 1992**
Time: **7:00 p.m.**
Location: **Ritz-Carlton Hotel on Canal Street**
               French Quarter

It was seven in the evening, and Richie was sitting at the table near the window, overlooking Canal Street, wondering why he had come down so early. He was at the restaurant an hour early and had since downed two dry martinis. Richie was already feeling a strong buzz. Glancing at his watch and seeing that it was now just turning seven o'clock, he made a promise to himself to never be that early again.

"Excuse me," said a voice that was frighteningly familiar. For a moment, Richie feared that he would turn his head and see that woman in the red dress again, this time with an older, stern-looking gentleman—probably Kent Bourgeois—glaring at them both and whispering to a pair of slick-haired "associates" who would nod and vanish into the darkness.

Instead, Richie was pleasantly surprised to see the woman he knew as "Just Sam" from earlier that day. She was dressed in an elegant black cocktail dress, which looked brand new, her blond hair out of her ponytail and cascading about her shoulders, and she was wearing low-heeled black shoes.

Her left hand was still wrapped around something that looked red and plastic. Her cheeks were flushed, as if she had been drinking. She was smiling that small, pleasant, and sincere smile at him, and suddenly Richie felt like the world's biggest boob.

"Sam," Richie said, gripping his forehead with both sets of fingers. "Samantha. God, I am such an idiot."

Samantha, or Sam—whichever—gave a genuinely pleasant laugh, a short and melodious one that held no hint of malice.

"Don't let that bother you, Richard," she said as she took her seat, motioning for a nearby waiter to bring a menu. "I get that, literally, all the time. I'm used to it."

"Fine," Richie said with an exasperated sigh. "Just . . . what do I call you, Sam or Samantha?"

"Sam, please," she said before pointing to a drink on the menu and nodding confirmation to the waiter, who quickly departed. "And what should I call you?"

"Call me confused, bewildered," Richie said, surprisingly getting another small laugh out of Sam. "Richie, please. I hate it when people call me Richard. It makes me nervous."

"Nervous?" Sam said, cocking an eyebrow at him. "Why so?"

"It's just a thing, ya know? It's who I am," Richie said, shrugging and leaning back, playing it cool. "And anyway, this morning, I thought I had no chance in hell of meeting you, and now we're having dinner. Who wouldn't be nervous?"

Sam again laughed, this one lingering a bit longer, and looked away. "Wow. And here I thought I was going to be the nervous wreck meeting you."

There was a hint of anxiousness behind her voice that Richie only made out because he himself often had experienced the same thing. He saw her squeeze whatever she was holding in her hand.

Arching an eyebrow, Richie leaned forward and asked, "So what, were you stalking me earlier at the autograph table? Because here I thought I'd have to hunt you down, Sam."

That comment got a bit of a shy grin from Sam. "Actually, I saw a notice in the newspaper this morning about your appearance. I had to head downtown to the *Picayune*, and the Ritz was on my way, so I figured, why not get an autograph from one of my favorite authors?" She shrugged.

Richie felt his cheeks get warmer at that compliment. He remembered that brief moment of electricity when Sam's hand had touched his. Sitting back, he said, "That's very flattering, Sam, but there is no way you weren't scouting me, not after all those e-mails I exchanged earlier this week with Mr. Bourgeois."

"I'm not sure I follow," Sam replied with a nervous-sounding chuckle, rapidly squeezing the plastic object in her hand. "I had no idea you were in contact with my lawyer before this afternoon. I called him after running errands, he told me about your visit, and I agreed to have dinner with you."

"Oh," replied Richie, and then sat back. For a moment, he wondered just how much information Kent was keeping from Sam, all under the pretense of "keeping her safe." Richie was surprised that the notion of someone abusing Sam in any way made his temperature rise.

He also wondered if Kent had even told Sam that he, Richie, wanted to discuss purchasing a townhome from her. Richie decided that Kent likely did not, given that Sam hadn't even brought it up. While this was fine with him, as it was really just a pretext, Richie felt it further cast Kent into a negative light.

Pushing those thoughts away, Richie looked back at Sam and saw that she appeared anxious, like a timid animal about to run, and that she was squeezing the plastic object in her hand much like he would squeeze his bottle of pills. A sudden feeling surged up inside him, a desire to shield this anxious-looking woman from whatever ailed her.

Richie wasn't sure where this desire came from, as it wasn't one he had ever had before, but it was extremely strong. With that desire came an uncanny feeling of attraction toward her—that frightened face, framed by that sandy blond hair, looked very sexy to Richie.

Richie didn't have a problem with women—well, not with getting in their pants—but it was usually just a matter of playing the game until they "opened up." He rarely felt emotionally invested. While he felt similar desire toward Sam, it was overtaken by an even stronger desire to keep her safe and secure, and near him.

"It's all right," Richie said. "I'm probably overanalyzing things, Sam. I am a mystery writer, you know, and I have to look at things from a suspicious and unorthodox angle. It's what I get paid to do."

That seemed to satisfy Sam, who relaxed in her chair, her shoulders lowering. "That makes sense."

After a few long moments of silence, Sam added, "I've been a recluse most of my life. This, that is, meeting you for dinner, is a big thing for me." Sam idly ran her free fingers over her black dress. "I even went out and bought this thing because, well, I don't even own a dress, or heels. So, I'm still a bit like a rabbit in a trap, you know?" Looking down at her hand squeezing the object, Sam covered it as if protecting it from the world.

Sam's analogy excited Richie even more, and his desire to put his arms around Sam and ward off all the ugliness in the world increased. It was like she was begging for someone to help her. Having never figured himself as a "savior" type, Richie was surprised that he felt this strongly. Maybe it was just a chemistry she gave off.

"I think I get it," replied Richie, offering his most charming and gentle smile to Sam. "So, I'll tell you what then, Sam, let me give you a dinner you'll always remember. If I'm your favorite author, then we'll talk about my books. If you want advice, I'll give it away. Want an autograph, I'll give you a hundred. Let's have this dinner on your terms, to celebrate you coming out into the world."

At that moment, the waiter returned with Sam's drink, a glass of wine so dark it was almost black, like her dress. Richie raised his nearly empty martini glass and said, "A deal, then?"

A soft hue of pink rose to Sam's cheeks, lighting up the otherwise hollow face with a splash of real color. She said, "Yeah . . . I think I'd rather just have dinner than all that, if it's all the same. Are you this way with all women, Richie, or just the ones who like your older books?"

This honestly caught Richie off guard, and for a moment, he was at a loss for what to say. When he had finally gathered himself back up, he said, "All right, then, that will work, too, Sam. And to be honest, I prefer that, because . . . Okay, well, I'm actually a lot like you. I keep to myself a lot, and I, how do I say this . . . "

A sigh escaped his lips, and he took a few moments to gather his thoughts before continuing. "A lot of people have pushed me into the spotlight really fast, and before this happened, I was nobody special. Now, suddenly, I'm at center stage and I have to act a certain way, talk a certain way, and respond to things a certain way."

Leaning forward, Richie continued, "So I've been pretty much coached on how to be a 'celebrity,' such as it is, and, in fact, most of the personality that people see is a façade created by my publicist. And Sam, you are"—Richie stopped, wanting to say one thing, but instead saying another—"someone I feel I can be the real me with."

The blush that had initially appeared on Sam's cheeks crept back even stronger than before. She nodded her head in understanding and said, "I guess we're kindred spirits, then, Richie."

There was a hesitant moment before Sam exhaled and asked, "So, then, would you be surprised to find out that I'm a writer as well?"

As Sam sipped her drink, Richie thought about what she had just asked. It made sense. Who else could understand a writer as well as another writer? Finally, he said, "Okay, I'm not surprised. But I'll bite. Sam, what have you written? I've never read anything by Samantha Castille, or even Just Sam."

"I write under a pen name," Sam replied, bringing her glass to her lips. "Sam of Spades."

"Never heard of her," replied Richie in a candid manner, as he ordered another martini.

Sam removed the glass from her lips and licked them silently before saying, "Ah well, that's okay. I should have seen that coming. I'm local at best."

"Oh, that's fine," Richie said, giving Sam a wink. "I mean, I was local, at best regional, before *The Pale Lantern* came out." He let that last statement linger, before pushing to segue the conversation toward his book topic. "So then, are you planning anything bigger? Looking for a way to get published outside of New Orleans?"

What Richie heard next, however, was not what he expected to hear.

"I'm writing a series about the killings that started up two nights ago," Sam said, a bit of an annoyed look on her face, "from the standpoint of it being a Bourbon Street Ripper copycat."

If Richie had been drinking at that moment, he would have spewed it all over the table. Immediately, his eyes cast downward and his fists, now in his lap, tightened. *What the flying hippopotamus fuck! This was an idea I've had for months,* months, *and this bitch is going to come along and swipe it out from underneath me?*

As he felt himself getting more and more upset, he remembered his conversation with the woman in the red dress the previous night. She had plainly asked why Richie didn't try solving the murders himself. That made him think—why write about a fictional copycat, when the real one would be just as, if not more, lucrative?

Immediately, Richie's brain went into overdrive, forming a plan to work this situation to his advantage. There was a genre similar to mystery, called True Crime, where the author examines a real crime, including the evidence and the people involved, and lays out the entire investigation for the reader to follow. While it was essentially nonfiction, it was a very profitable niche.

Richie figured that he could write the True Crime story based on the current real-life investigation, while Sam could write her fictionalized version.

And we could use each other as resources. That will work.

"Sam . . . " Richie finally said, looking up and seeing that she was watching him cautiously. He realized that he was getting anxious again, and he had left his pills up in his room. The sudden desire to swipe all his goals to the side and protect Sam flooded back into his mind. He pushed down his rising anxiety and focused on the woman before him.

"The truth, Sam," Richie began, "is that I've been toying with the idea of a Vincent Castille story myself, but I for one think it's an excellent idea for the granddaughter of the original

Bourbon Street Ripper to write a copycat story, or whatever it is you are doing."

That seemed to disarm Sam, who nodded and placed down her drink. "Okay," she said, "go on."

"Well, Sam," continued Richie, his mind and mouth going into autopilot, "I'd like to help you with your endeavor. Not as a co-author or anything, just as a coach. You know, impart some tips on what I did to make *The Pale Lantern* so successful."

Richie moistened his lips. Here was the big part of the whole deal. "In return, I want to write about this real investigation that the New Orleans police are doing, especially if the killer ends up being a real copycat."

"Ah," said Sam, nodding to show she understood. "So you will help guide me in writing the fictional story, and in return, you want me to help you with a True Crime version of this story?"

"Exactly," Richie replied, the talk of business pushing the last of those anxious bubbles out of his mind. "You can help by allowing me to access anything of your grandfather's that you may have, allowing me to interview you about him, and helping me get in touch with the detectives who were originally on the Bourbon Street Ripper case."

Sam leaned back and gave a long *hmmmm*, finishing with an inhale through the nose, before saying, "Well, this is definitely forcing me to face these issues head-on. So, as long as we help each other, and not just ourselves"—she offered her hand to Richie—"you have yourself a deal, Mr. Fastellos."

Taking the offered hand and shaking it, and noting how smooth it was, Richie said, "All right then, Miss Castille, we have an accord. Shall we drink on it?" Richie raised his glass.

Sam *clinked* her glass against Richie's, but then added, "Well, drinking is good, too, but I'd prefer if we ordered some food as well. I haven't eaten since noon today."

Richie laughed and said he thought ordering dinner was an excellent idea.

At eleven fifty at night, with the restaurant nearly closed, Richie and Sam were still going, laughing over stories of their managers and publicists.

Beneath their glasses, which *clinked* together with whatever they were drinking at the time, was a double plate of mostly eaten bananas Foster. All around, the restaurant was being cleaned, the staff giving the two writers a wide berth.

Richie had consumed several martinis, and was tipsy enough that his speech slurred. He could tell from looking at Sam that she was quite drunk.

He had adopted the same mannerisms as her, to appear just as drunk to her. It was a charade he was used to when with a woman—if he acted as drunk as her, she'd be more comfortable around him.

"Wow," Richie said, his speech just garbled enough to make him sound like he had his own Cajun accent. "So this Caroline chick is always busting not only your hump, but your buddy Jacob's as well?"

"Yeah," replied Sam, her own speech muddled as she sipped her fifth Crown and cola. "She is . . . Richie, she's a real bitch. I mean, I try to get along with her, but the more I give, the more she takes." Sam rested her free hand over her heart in a melodramatic fashion. "I'm only one person. I can only do so much."

Richie positively howled with laughter at that. "That is why—right there—that is why I never wrote for newspapers." He paused. "Unless I had to." Another pause. "For money."

Nodding, Sam finished off her drink and sat back. "Richie, I'm going to be totally honest here."

This got Richie's attention. He sat up as straight as he could and looked Sam in the eyes.

Sam continued, "I really thought you'd be a dick, but you turned out to be pretty cool. Thank you."

That got a sharp laugh out of Richie, who slammed back his fourth martini. "I don't know what you're talking about, Sam. I'm a totally likeable fellow!"

As Sam snickered at him, Richie continued, "But that's okay, because from the way Kent described you, I thought you would be a psycho-chick who would be ready with a lawsuit in one hand and a gun in another!"

That made Sam laugh out loud and gulp down the last of her wine before saying, "I'm not that bad. Okay, maybe I *was*, but dammit, I went out and had dinner with someone tonight. This is the first time I've come outta my shell since I was twenty. I'm proud of myself."

As Richie smiled to himself at Sam's comment, she added, "We should do this again, Richie." She reached out and touched his hand for a moment. "I mean, if you want to, that is . . . "

Richie again felt a charge rush through his body at Sam's touch, stronger than the first time. For a long moment, he stared at his hand where she had touched him. Her touch felt so strange and yet so familiar. He had never felt anything like that sensation before.

Richie looked up at Sam, who was smiling back at him. His anxiety was replaced by the confidence only brought about by alcohol, and he felt very masculine.

Clearing his throat, Richie reached over and touched his fingers to Sam's hand, saying, "Tell you what, Sam. How about we have coffee tomorrow morning? We can go over the book ideas together. And let's choose someplace you are comfortable with, like your place."

"Coffee, huh?" Sam asked, tapping her bottom lips with her finger. "Sure, why the hell not! Come over to my house tomorrow morning."

Sam reached into her back pocket and pulled out a card with an address. Sliding it over to Richie, Sam said. "How does eight o'clock sound? We can have breakfast, fresh coffee, and work on our book ideas."

Richie, who was certain that a sober Samantha Castille would never have invited him over for breakfast, thought that was a fantastic idea. Just as he was about to suggest that he pick something up for their breakfast, the head waiter approached the table with their bill.

"Pardon me," the waiter said in a cordial voice, "but we are closing in five minutes. Can you, please . . . ?" Holding out the bill, he offered a pleasant but tired smile.

Before Richie could do anything, Sam reached out and tossed a plastic card onto the plate. "Here. On me," she said, winking at Richie.

Richie was stunned. He hadn't seen the bill, but he was sure the total had to be over two hundred. Two filet mignon dinners, not to mention that many drinks, couldn't be cheap.

Remembering his conversation with Kent earlier that day, he realized that Sam must be extremely wealthy.

"Sam," Richie said with a twinge of guilt for all those martinis he had drunk, "I'll pay you back tomor—"

"You'll do nothing of the sort," Sam replied, tilting her nose up. The waiter brought the receipt and Sam started to factor in a tip.

"At least let me handle the tip, Sam," Richie said, reaching into his jacket pocket and taking out his money clip. Sam seemed to agree with that, as she zeroed out the tip column and signed the slip. Richie quickly tossed a fifty on the table, then another ten, just in case the concierge might somehow get involved.

Soon, the two writers, tired and with varying degrees of intoxication, stumbled out into the hot air of Canal Street, Richie reaching out an arm to hail Sam a cab. Finally succeeding, he opened the door for Sam and helped her inside. Once inside the cab, Sam regained her composure before thanking Richie for a wonderful dinner.

"My pleasure, Sam," Richie said with a smile. "I'll see you tomorrow in time for coffee. I like mine with sugar and cream, all right?"

"All right," Sam said, then leaned back against the seat, clearly still very drunk.

Closing the door, Richie watched as the cab drove off. He gave a happy sigh as he headed back into the hotel lobby. With a skip to his step, he headed into the elevator and clicked his floor number. Leaning against the back wall of the elevator, Richie took several long, deep breaths to push the tipsiness back, no longer having to pretend to be drunk in order to keep Samantha comfortable around him.

It was on his third deep breath that Richie realized he wasn't alone.

"You look happy," said a sultry voice beside him. Richie turned his head to see that the woman in the red dress was his elevator companion.

"I am," he said, and then he looked at the elevator doors again. "So where are you heading?"

"Top floor," she said, with a sigh that was mournful, like a lonely saxophone's final exhale. "People aren't doing their jobs properly."

"Oh," Richie said before looking over at the woman again. The way she phrased her problem only reinforced his belief that she was somehow involved in organized crime. "Sounds kind of suspicious. You're not in any trouble, are you? Do you need any help?"

"Not really," she said, her naturally sultry tone suddenly bitter. "The help I was looking for didn't come when I needed it. And I've already suffered for it." Then she smirked almost devilishly. "But now I get to pick up the pieces."

Richie said nothing to that. He just looked forward again. "Sorry. I have a habit of trying to rescue women. It's an annoying trend I think I've just developed today."

"Then go solve that murder, writer-boy," the woman said, her pouty lips curving into a sweet, sexy smile. "You are going to do it, aren't you?"

"Yeah," Richie said, nodding to himself as much as to his strange companion. "I'm going to do it. And I'll have help, too."

Richie then thought of Sam. *And I'll help her, while I'm at it.*

The woman looked upward as she sucked on her bottom lip for a long moment, almost as if she were nearing climax. "Mmmmm, so what's your plan?"

"I've got some work to catch up on," Richie said with a chuckle, even as the elevator stopped and the doors opened. "Quite a bit before I head to bed. But that's just how I roll, lady. I burn the midnight oil to do what has to be done."

"We all do," she said as Richie left the elevator. "We all do what needs to be done."

"Right," said Richie, giving the woman a nod of thanks. "Good night."

She just stared up at the ceiling of the elevator and smiled as the doors closed.

The Lady in Red. Who the hell is she?

Once inside his room, Richie stripped off his clothes and got into his robe, laying out a pair of jeans, boots, and a T-shirt for the next morning. He was already thinking about his breakfast with Sam.

"I may not be able to write about the Bourbon Street Ripper copycat murders," Richie said to himself, "but I can sure as hell help solve them."

The alarm was set for six o'clock in the morning, and once that was done, Richie sat down in front of his computer. Cracking his knuckles, he started to load up his web browser.

"All right," Richie said to himself once more, "time to get to work."

Chapter 13
Rodger's Bad Day

Date: **Thursday, August 6, 1992**
Time: **7:00 p.m.**
Location: **Mad Monty's Warehouse**
                Ninth Ward

When Rodger's consciousness and vision returned to him, he was back inside the warehouse with the door tightly shut. He wasn't sure how long he had been out, but judging by the daylight seeping through the windows of the warehouse, it couldn't have been that long. Rodger quickly realized two things: he was tied up with a chain, hands bound in front of him, legs bound at the feet, and he was suspended in the air by virtue of one of those hanging hook-chains attached to the chain binding.

"Good," said the booming voice of Mad Monty from the center of the warehouse. "You're awake."

Rodger swiveled a bit by swinging his lower body, turning to face Mad Monty. The large man was over by the conveyor belt, leaning on an equally tied-up Horace, pushing one hand on his face and another on his knees. The parole officer was tied up pretty tightly, and the conveyor belt now had raised sides, so rolling off would be impossible. Between Rodger and the machine was a small table. On that table lay Horace's briefcase and Rodger's coat and sidearm. Rodger could see that the weapon still had its clip in it.

Monty grinned that toothy, fanglike grin again, saying, "Man, you have no fucking clue how happy I was to hear that you were coming over today. I've been thinking for years about how

I'd do you. You can't even imagine how hard it's been to wait for the right moment."

Rodger screamed, "Monty!" Just the act of screaming made Rodger start to rotate away from the scene, and like a flailing fish, he struggled to return to facing Monty again. "You think you'll get away after this? You know I got backup coming!"

Monty laughed a great booming laugh and said, "Shit, you mean that skinny bitch kung fu partner of yours? My boys are chasing his ass down by the river. He's gonna get a real lesson in being a bitch." He sniffed once more. "But you and nerd-boy be dead long before that."

Rodger knew how bad the situation was. Without any way to call for help, he had to wait for the thirty-minute time limit they'd set with Ouellette to run out. By the time the police commander acted, he and Horace could already be dead.

Deciding the best chance he had to keep them both alive was to keep Monty talking and killing time, Rodger started up again. "You don't have to kill Horace, Monty. Your beef is with me, not him."

Spitting to the side, Monty said with a growl to his voice, "You think I care about this limp-dicked pussy? You can't imagine how annoying it's been listening to his wimpy voice tell me what I should and shouldn't do. Fuck, man, you know how hard it is to be a bad motherfucker when you have to drink nonalcoholic beer and listen to Beethoven? Hos don't respect that!"

"Like your woman didn't respect you when she fucked your best friend?" asked Rodger. He had played this card before, and it worked perfectly. Monty was pretty much emasculated when his old girlfriend had had a child with Monty's best friend. Only through crushing the guy's windpipe did Monty regain his manhood, as well as earn himself ten years in prison. It was a topic Monty was always sore over.

Much to Rodger's surprise, however, Monty just smirked and shook his head. "Man, I am well over that shit. I've had so many bitches since then it don't matter no more. Besides, I fuck guys now, too." Mad Monty leaned forward on Horace, resting his elbows on him. "White, lily-assed guys like your pussy-boy partner."

Rodger knew his face betrayed both his horror and his disgust, Monty's threat of making Michael "his bitch" suddenly making sense. Rodger started to speak again when Monty suddenly cried out in pain. Looking over in surprise, Rodger saw Monty withdrawing his hand from Horace's face, a large bite mark on it. Monty screamed, "YOU FUCKING TWITCH!!!"

Rodger stared at Horace in horror. *Horace, you stupid idiot!*

He felt desperation grow in his chest as he struggled for a way to turn attention back to him. Like a car's transmission might do at the worst possible time, Rodger's brain locked up, and he could only utter idle threats. "Monty! You hurt Horace, and I swear I'll hunt you down like a dog!"

That only made Monty cackle, and with a roar of laughter, he pushed a button on the side of the conveyor belt. With a sudden *clank* and *whir*, the machine came to life, a constant clanking and crashing coming from the interior of the large metal container that the conveyor belt fed into.

The belt itself started to slowly move Horace toward the machine as Monty called out, "Watch closely, Detective, this shit's gonna happen to you next!"

"What the heck is that thing?" cried out a panicked and terrified Horace as he struggled to get free from his chains.

"That is something of my own design," said Monty. "I use it to shred metal into bits so I can melt it down easier. To be honest," he mused as he walked alongside his struggling parole officer, "I have no idea what it'll do to a human body."

"Have you lost your mind, Mr. Jones?" cried Horace. "You know you'll get the death penalty if you do this!"

The fact that someone like Horace was trying to psych out Monty restarted the fuse in Rodger's brain. The detective screamed, "Yeah! You know we've got backup coming, Monty! We're not stupid enough to come in here without a Plan B. Assault and attempted murder is bad enough, but if you actually kill us, you're killing yourself."

Booming out more laughter, Monty said, "Shit, you think I don't know you got your little butt-buddies coming? This is why I'm using this thing on you and not giving you an acid bath. I know I ain't got time. But once you and nerd-boy here are dead, I'm outta here. I've had an escape plan in place since I built this fucking warehouse, just for this occasion. I'm heading to Mexico. Fuck this fucked-up city! Fuck this serial killer shit! And fuck the fucking Nite Priory!"

Rodger's eyes widened at the mention of the Nite Priory. He recognized that as the name that sent Topper Jack his letter.

Rodger's thoughts were interrupted by Horace screaming to be let go, pleading for his life, blubbering in gut-wrenching terror. Horace was halfway to the machine, and while from this angle Rodger could not see what the interior must look like to the parole officer, his imagination filled in some horrific blanks.

"It's okay to scream," Monty taunted Horace, his sweat dripping down on his parole officer's face. "It's okay to cry. It's gonna hurt real bad. So go ahead and scream for me. Scream like a bitch."

"Monty." Rodger's voice thickened with panic. "Don't do this! For heaven's sake, don't do this!"

This just spurred Monty on to laugh more maniacally and slap Horace repeatedly in the face, knocking his glasses off. "Gonna die, pussy," Monty started pseudo-singing. "Gonna die real bad, pussy! Scream like a girl for me, pussy!"

Monty stopped slapping Horace as the parole officer cried, snot and tears running down his face, begging for his life. The front of his pants had gotten very dark, and he struggled in vain to get free, unable to roll off the conveyor belt due to its side guards. He even tried to push himself back.

"Stop it!" Rodger's voice was just as frantic as he struggled to break free himself. It was like struggling against a one-ton weight. He couldn't think of what to say, what to do, to make this situation stop. He had never felt so helpless.

With his feet inches from the machine, Horace looked down and started screaming, "NO! NO! NOOOOO!" while trying to curl his feet back. Monty stood back and laughed cruelly while rubbing the front of his jeans and panting like a dog. As Horace's feet entered the machine, blood sprayed everywhere. The parole officer's scream was shrill and girlish.

Rodger forced himself to look away, closing his eyes and gritting his teeth. The sounds of Horace's screams, accompanied by the *clanking* of the machine and the sound of bones crunching, meat tearing, and blood squirting, lasted an obscenely long time.

One of the more shrill screams turned into outright crying for his mother, which squelched into a choking and gurgling sound, and then only the gruesome sounds of a body being mangled.

When Rodger finally looked back at the machine, Horace was nothing more than a mess of red meat and blood slopping from the back of the machine, out of a small metallic chute, and into a trough.

Rodger felt sick to his stomach, trying hard to hold back the bile. He really wanted to vomit. Instead, tears of rage came down his face. As the machine shut off, Monty let out a loud whistle, having come around to the rear of the machine and seen the bloody mess.

"Fucking hell," Monty said as he headed over toward Rodger, snorting with laughter like he had just heard the best joke of his life. "There is no way in shit I can clean that up before your buddies get here."

Standing in front of Rodger, Monty cracked his knuckles and said, "Too bad I don't got enough time to really enjoy doing you in, old man. But you'll scream for me like a bitch, too, won't ya?"

"How could you do that to another human being?" Rodger said through his teeth, with shock, rage, and many more emotions coursing through him. Turning to Monty, Rodger spat in his face and cried out, "You disgusting animal!"

Wiping the mess off of his face, Mad Monty smirked and said, "Yeah, you my bitch now, Rodger." With a single swing of his massive hand, Monty slugged Rodger in the gut hard enough to knock all the air out of his lungs.

Rodger's eyes rolled into the back of his head, and while he was barely conscious, he was aware of being lifted up and carried over to the conveyor belt. When his senses returned to him, he was face-up and pointing, feet-first, toward the machine.

The interior was too messy with Horace's guts to see clearly, but it looked like someone had merged a car crusher, a wood chipper, and a mass-killing machine into one terrifying contraption.

Looking up, Rodger saw Monty's face grinning down at him.

"Bye-bye, Detective. Fuck you."

With the push of a button, Monty started the machine up, and Rodger soon saw himself heading, feet-first, toward the jaws of the machine. As the mists of being knocked about left, the severity of the situation hit.

This is it. I am going to die.

In Rodger's mind, images flashed by. Clinking glasses with Edward in a bar after work. He and Michael catching a man who had murdered his own wife for insurance money. Ouellette giving him a commendation. And, finally, Sam greeting him for the first time in years and offering him a cup of coffee.

Rodger's mind then focused on Sam, specifically young Samantha, and that look of a child devoid of life, who needed someone, anyone, to make the bad stuff go away. That snapped Rodger back to reality.

Fuck this! I can't die until I solve this case! For Sam. For Edward. For Michael. And for me.

Rodger looked around, seeing that he was halfway to the jaws of the machine. Walking alongside him, Monty was talking trash. Ignoring the taunts, Rodger looked around for something—anything—that would help to save his life.

The conveyor belt's side guards were too high for him to roll off. The chains around his chest and wrists severely restricted his upper torso. His lower torso, apart from being bound at the ankles, was much more mobile.

Rodger thought as quickly as he could. Even if he managed to sit up, Monty could easily just punch him out and lay him back down. Since Monty was by his head, Rodger couldn't kick him.

His only hope was to stop himself from entering the machine.

Looking down at the entrance of the machine, Rodger saw something that could potentially be helpful: a grate, suspended over the mouth of the machine, held in place by a latch. As he drew closer to being turned into compost, Rodger figured it was probably an emergency latch and a safety grating.

Rodger moved his feet some from side to side, and realized that the chains were just loose enough for him to kick his feet up. He reasoned that if he could get the grating down, it might buy him enough time to sit up and jump off the conveyor belt.

Remembering that his weapon, which was on the small table, still had the clip in it, the detective quickly formed a plan.

I've got one chance at this working. It's a slim one, but it's all the chance I've got.

Rodger's thoughts were interrupted by Monty slapping him in the face, like he'd done to Horace.

"Hey, bitch," taunted Monty, "no looking away." With a rough grab, Monty forced Rodger's head to look down at the mouth of the machine, holding his neck and head in place.

"See that?" Monty hissed into Rodger's ear, his breath like beer and onions mixed into an unsavory stench. "That shit's gonna tear you into little pieces."

Monty rocked Rodger's head back and forth. "I musta done something right when I made it, 'cause Horace didn't die until that shit ate his most of his guts and lungs. So you get to watch it rip your balls off."

Rodger watched the approaching opening of the machine, his eyes on the latch that held the safety grate open. Just a few more feet and he'd get his one chance.

Monty leaned in more and said, "Hey, Rodger, I just realized something." He tilted Rodger's head up to face him. "I'm gonna rip your balls off anyway! Ain't that the shit?"

Rodger started to laugh—possibly somewhat hysterically—at that comment, then said, "Yeah, I guess the joke's on me, ain't it? Hey, Monty, before I die, there's something I gotta tell you!"

"Oh?" said Monty, leaning down to look into Rodger's eyes. "What's that, bitch?"

Rodger felt himself get cold, a tingle going down his spine, and his thoughts focus. He could feel the power coiling in his legs, ready to spring, and his concentration centered on the latch that would drop the grating.

Most importantly, he felt an overwhelming feeling of confidence in pulling off the escape plan. As he flashed a grin at his enemy, Rodger said with a laugh, "You're gonna get your ass kicked by an old man."

With that, Rodger quickly threw his head upward, his forehead crashing hard into Monty's mouth. Rodger felt the flesh of his forehead split open as those white teeth cut into him. Every part of him felt invincible and empowered. This desperate attack did the trick, as Monty flew back, and his hands, which were keeping Rodger from looking at the machine, let go of his head.

Quickly, Rodger looked down and saw that his feet were inches away from the jaws of the machine. The exposed grinders and blades whipped and whirled, caked with the bits of blood, flesh, and meat that used to be Horace. Still feeling that incredible focus, along with that chilly sensation, Rodger lifted up his legs and, with every bit of strength in his body, slammed his bound feet up at the latch holding the safety grate open.

There was a loud *crash* and suddenly Rodger's ass was smooshed against the safety grating.

Rodger rolled back onto his knees as the conveyor belt, still moving, pushed him into the grating. He soon found himself face-first against the front of the machine, the metal grating cutting at his cheek, as his body, unable to go inside, kept being being pushed into the metal framework.

This was not part of the plan.

He heard Monty roaring, and he leapt into action. With another grunt, Rodger threw himself off the conveyor belt and onto the floor.

Hitting the concrete hard, Rodger felt pain explode in his arm and stars explode in his head. And even though the chilly calming sensation was gone, the rush of adrenaline in his body was so strong that the pain left very quickly.

Thinking that Michael made stunts like that look easy, Rodger got up and, kicking his legs a bit, started trying to loosen the chains around his ankles.

To his pleasant surprise, Rodger felt the chains loosen, and as he slipped one foot out, then another, he saw Mad Monty come around the far side of the machine's conveyor belt, murder in his eyes. He roared at Rodger, "You're dead, bitch!"

That was all the motivation Rodger needed.

Rodger quickly ran to the table where his gun lay. In one motion, he grabbed the gun and kept moving. He could hear Monty's heavy footsteps behind him and could hear him taunting, "You think you can aim that shit with your hands tied up, bitch? I'm gonna tear you apart with my bare hands!"

Stumbling forward, Rodger hated to admit that Monty was right. With his hands and chest bound this way, he could only shoot down at an angle.

As he moved from behind the machine, leaping over the trench that held most of Horace's remains, Rodger decided to take the battle to higher ground. Taking a right, he headed toward the stairs leading up.

As he rushed forward, his legs aching, holding on to the gun for dear life, Rodger heard Monty give another roar. This was followed by the sound of a large man's body hitting the ground. Rodger smirked to himself that the dumbass had slipped on his own victim's gore.

Reaching the stairs, Rodger started to head up. The movement of climbing stairs after such a beating made the detective's lungs, legs, and hips burn. He felt as if he would pass out again at any moment. Twice he nearly slipped and fell face-first into the corrugated metallic steps.

All Rodger could think about, as he stopped for a moment when he reached the top step, was that he was too old for this shit.

As he took his third deep breath, he heard heavy footfalls on the stairs coming up, followed by, "I'm gonna rip off your nuts with my teeth! I'm gonna twist off your arms and eat them! I'm gonna—"

Monty's threats were cut short when Rodger shot at him, the bullet ricocheting off the steps above him. Monty stopped and nearly jumped back, but then laughed. "You can't shoot for shit, old man! Who's gonna kick whose ass now?"

Rodger aimed and shot again, this time the bullet hitting the side railing nearby. Thinking that Monty was right, Rodger quickly decided that if he was going to shoot the bigger man, he had to get right up next to him—without getting grabbed.

For a few moments, Rodger waited to see if Monty would come up the stairs and close the distance, but the large man had already figured out the same thing as the detective and was waiting. He even held his arms out and laughed up at Rodger, begging him to shoot.

Rodger realized he needed to lure Monty in. Looking around, all Rodger saw were rows upon rows of large metal presses. They were tall machines, with the presses activated by a button on the side of them. Looking them over, Rodger figured they were his best chance at surviving.

Hearing the heavy steps of Monty, Rodger quickly turned. Monty stopped, less than half the distance away now, and mockingly held out his arms again, laughing, his white teeth flashing like the fangs of a wolf playing with its prey.

Rodger fired the gun again, sparks flying as the bullet ricocheted near Monty, the sparks making the large man flinch. With his enemy distracted, Rodger headed in between the metal presses and, hearing Monty run up the stairs, waited for the sound of Monty drawing near.But no sound was heard, not even breathing, and after a few seconds, Rodger looked around a corner and saw that Monty had vanished from view. Then the detective heard it, the sound of heavy breaths—echoing all around him.

He was being stalked.

Looking around, Rodger ducked between another set of presses, even as he heard Monty's voice ring out. "I'm coming for yooooou, bitch!"

Concentrating on his surroundings, Rodger looked around, trying to sense what direction his attacker was coming from. Try as he might, however, he couldn't sense where Monty was. Only the sounds of breathing and laughter gave him any clue that he was still being stalked. When Monty got silent, all Rodger could hear was his own shallow, anxious breathing.

Coming across an end row of presses, Rodger suddenly saw something, a flash of white moving in between two of the presses. Quickly, he went on the offensive, ducking around to the interior of the rows of presses, gun ready.

Nothing.

Rodger crept forward, looking around, when he smelt it. The stench of beer and onions, right to the side of him. Looking to the side, Rodger saw Monty's grinning face looking at him through one of the end row presses. Even as Rodger turned to try to face Monty, the large man reached through the metal press and grabbed Rodger's jacket, calling out, "Got you, bitch!"

With a hard pull, Monty yanked Rodger forward, slamming the older man's face into the top of the metal press. Another pull, and Rodger's head was suddenly in the press itself.

"Guess I gotta make it quick, bitch," said Monty, reaching for the button to turn on the press. "Too bad. I really wanted to rip your balls off."

"What is your fascination with my balls, you freak!" said Rodger as he pulled back, his jacket ripping.

With a final tug, the left lapel of Rodger's old jacket ripped right off, and Rodger flew back. Seeing Monty's arm thrusting forward and grabbing at him again, Rodger quickly jumped to the side. Immediately, Monty's left knee came into view.

Roger shot at the knee, and with a popping sound, it exploded, blood and liquid coating Monty's jeans. The large man cried out, a loud guttural cry, then he leaned forward, his right arm braced inside the metal press. Monty roared out, "GONNA KILL YOU!"

Rodger kicked the side of the press, hitting the activation panel, and the machine lit up.

With a loud *whirring* sound, the metal press kicked into gear. Rodger saw the press come down quickly and, along with the sound of bones crunching and meat squishing, he heard the sound of Monty screaming.

As the press came to a halt, blood leaking out of it, Rodger leaned back against another press and caught his breath. His body hurt all over, his lungs were on fire, and he had never needed a cigarette so badly. Only when he heard the continued screams of Monty did Rodger come back to reality.

Taking his gun and pressing it against the chains around his wrists, Rodger fired. The chain fell limp. Another shot and the chains around his chest were gone. He had two burn marks from the bullets that freed him, but for once, Rodger didn't care about the pain.

All he wanted were answers.

Stepping around the side of the press, and pointing his gun at Monty, Rodger felt every fiber in his being wanting to pull the trigger and end the man's miserable life. But when he saw Monty, his forearm crushed in the press, his left knee shattered beyond repair, Rodger realized that living would be far more painful for Monty.

"Help me, man," said Monty, gasping for breath, obviously in terrible pain. "My fucking arm. Help me!"

"Help you?" said Rodger, glaring down the sight of his gun at Mad Monty. "You think after what you did to Horace, what you tried to do to me, I'm gonna *help* you?"

"Fucking help me, man," Monty whimpered. "I'm fucking . . . My fucking arm, man!"

"Oh, that," said Rodger, his voice dripping with sarcasm and venom. "Let's see what we can do about that." Heading over to the side of the press, he hit the button to release the press. With a *whirring* sound, the press lifted up, revealing the mangled mess that was once Monty's right forearm.

With another scream, Monty fell to his back and grabbed his ruined arm. Fresh blood leaked out in alarming amounts. Holding his destroyed arm, the man who was, just a few minutes ago, taunting a dying man to tears, started crying himself.

Rodger felt a mixture of disgust and satisfaction at this sight and at the same time was revolted by his own pleasure in Monty's misfortune. He had known exactly what releasing the press would do, and knew he now had only minutes to get what he wanted out of Monty and stop the bleeding before he died.

"Fucking help me," Monty whimpered, crying like a little kid. "Gonna bleed to death."

"Yeah, I know," said Rodger, still holding his gun on the other man. "I *could* go to my squad car and call for an ambulance to come save your miserable life."

Rodger kept his gun trained on Monty, but his eyes were focused on the blood coming out of that wound. He wouldn't let Monty bleed to death, but if he was going to get the information he wanted, before hospitals and lawyers and God knows what else got involved, he had to make Monty believe otherwise.

"Oh God," cried Monty. "Help me. Please. Help me, man. I'm gonna die. Gonna die!"

"First things first," said Rodger, glaring at Monty. "What is the Nite Priory?"

"Fucking gonna bleed to death," Monty continued to whimper. "Help me, man. Gonna die, man."

"Yeah, I get that, asshole, you're dying," Rodger said, his voice louder and angrier than before. His anger stemmed from knowing that if Monty didn't spill the beans soon, he'd be saving his worthless ass—and getting nothing out of it. "And you *will* bleed to death if you don't tell me what the Nite Priory is!"

"Fucking dying, man," whimpered Monty, sobbing pitifully.

"Hell on you," said Rodger, making a half turn away, as if planning to leave Monty to die. It was a feint, and his last one.

Monty cried, "Wait, Rodger! Nite Priory! That's them who did that ho in a few nights ago!"

Stopping, Rodger turned and nodded at Monty. "Go on, Monty, and no tricks."

Monty sputtered as he spoke, obviously weakened from blood loss. "It was someone. Wrote me a letter. About a week ago. It's in the black car out back. Under the hood. Wanted me to give him the exact location of the first murder of the"—Monty's lips trembled—"Bourbon Street Ripper."

"And you did, right?" asked Rodger.

Monty nodded.

"I saw that ho go in there," Monty said with shallow breaths.

Rodger wasn't sure he had heard Monty correctly. Starting to apply pressure to the wound, to stop Monty from bleeding out, Rodger said, "She went in to the place where she was murdered?"

Monty gave a weak grin. "Yeah. Musta . . . musta lured her there . . . An hour earlier . . . someone used a pay phone . . . right on the corner of—"

Then a shot rang out, and Monty's head exploded like a watermelon.

Rodger was stunned only for a moment before he twirled around and looked up, his police instincts kicking in, gun at the ready, hammer pulled back. Up on one of the ceiling skylights, looking down into the warehouse, was a figure dressed in a dark indigo hooded robe, hands covered in black gloves, face covered completely with a white mask painted to look like a skull.

The masked figure held a large rifle in its hand, the barrel still smoking. A moment later, the figure leapt with seemingly superhuman speed and agility out of the skylight and along the roof of the building. Rodger fired three shots at the retreating figure, succeeding more in hitting the ceiling and making the shots ricochet than anything else.

Rodger wondered what the hell that was. *Maybe it's the light playing tricks on my eyes, but that figure seemed to jump around like they do in the movies.*

Leaning back against the same metal press that had taken Monty's right arm, Rodger closed his eyes and concentrated on nothing at all, the adrenaline wearing off and the pain starting to rise. As his heart rate finally lowered, Rodger thought to himself once more, *I'm getting too old to do shit like this.*

Rodger stayed this way for a while, just breathing in and out and letting his mind empty. It was the only way he could deal with everything that had just happened.

Only when Rodger heard the door open to the warehouse did he open his eyes. Having his gun ready, in case it was Monty's henchmen, Rodger limped forward and carefully peered over the balcony down at the warehouse floor.

Light flooded into the warehouse from outside, and Michael came inside, walking with a distinct limp. Behind him were Captain Ouellette, Detective Aucoin, and several other uniformed officers of the New Orleans Police Department.

Chapter 14
The Investigation Continues

Date: **Thursday, August 6, 1992**
Time: **7:30 p.m.**
Location: **Mad Monty's Warehouse**
              Ninth Ward

Despite backup coming later than he would have liked, Rodger was grateful to see them. He was also grateful to see his partner alive, injuries aside. As he watched his fellow officers discover the gruesome scene below, Rodger drew himself to his feet. Now was not the time for rest—that could come later.

"Rodger," Michael called out, limping around, gun in hand, looking for his partner. "Rodger, answer me!"

"My God in heaven," Ouellette said as he looked upon what Rodger assumed was the gory remains of Horace Blanchard. "What the hell happened here?"

Even as an officer shut off the machine that had nearly killed him, Rodger waved his hand and called out to his frantic partner and disgusted commander. As soon as he saw Rodger, Aucoin rushed up the stairs and helped Rodger downstairs. He was grateful for the help—his body ached all over.

"Jesus, Bergeron," said Commander Ouellette as Rodger reached the lower level. "What happened? What is that mess over there? Where the hell is Mad Monty?"

Still supported by Aucoin, Rodger replied, "Sir, the mess you see there is what's left of Monty's parole officer, Horace. As for Monty, well, he's upstairs, missing a hand and a head."

As Ouellette looked the scene over, Rodger knew they were all keeping their cool only because they had already seen far too many gruesome murders over the years. Ouellette just shook his head.

"For God's sake, Bergeron, can't you ever have a normal interrogation?"

Wryly, Rodger said, "Commander, next time, I'll leave the questioning to someone else."

Ouellette said, "And leave me with more bodies to clean up? At least I know *you'll* survive this kind of crap, Bergeron. Good job."

Rodger wasn't surprised at the compliment. It was an unspoken understanding between him and his commander that if he could arrest the Bourbon Street Ripper, he could survive almost anything.

Rodger mentioned to Ouellette that there was an important piece of evidence, an envelope, underneath the hood of a black car out back. Ouellette said he'd get a uniformed officer to retrieve it, then headed off to manage the cleanup of the warehouse. Aucoin helped Rodger limp to Michael, who was standing over the mess that was once Horace.

Rodger could tell Michael was upset, but hiding it.

"We should have seen this coming, Rodger," Michael said as his partner approached. "We're trained police detectives. We should have anticipated this trap. We should have done something about it."

"Michael, please," said Rodger, not in the mood to give emotional pep talks. He wanted nothing more than a shot of whiskey, a hot bath, and his bed. "There is no way we could have known about—."

"We should have!"

Michael's uncharacteristic outburst seemed ill-timed, if understandable. After all, if Rodger or his partner had been just a little more vigilant, Horace Blanchard would be alive right now, they would be uninjured, and a material witness wouldn't be dead.

As the two limped out of the warehouse, heading toward the dozens of police cars outside, Rodger asked his partner what had happened to him after he ran off.

"Oh, that," said Michael, limping in time to Rodger's limp. "First off, sorry if it looked like I abandoned you, Rodger. The moment the trap sprang, I knew I had to shift things back into our favor."

Rodger gave a soft laugh, that motion alone making his ribs ache. "I figured as much, partner. I also figured that once you took care of those guys you'd come back and rescue me."

Michael nodded. "Exactly. It took me longer than I expected, though. Those two were really fast and nearly caught me several times. In the end, I ran down to the riverside and engaged them in a game of hide-and-seek." He chuckled. "They didn't win. One is cuffed and presumably being carted away right now. The other is . . ."

"Swimming with the fishes?"

"More like crawlin' with them mudbugs," Michael replied in his best fake Cajun accent.

This made Rodger laugh out loud, and despite the pain, the laughter felt good. He had learned twenty years ago that a morbid sense of humor was all that kept a person going sometimes.

The two detectives were soon swarmed by EMTs, who took them over to an ambulance and began treating them for their wounds. They were lucky to have nothing more than some major bruises, and in Rodger's case, a mild concussion.

As the EMTs tended to both detectives' wounds, Rodger told his partner everything that had transpired in the warehouse.

"Amazing," Michael said while the EMT wrapped up his left shin. "So the victim was contacted by the killer the night of her murder. That means somewhere is a pay phone that the killer used. Furthermore, there is this 'Nite Priory' that keeps coming up."

"Right," replied Rodger as his head was getting bandaged up. "I'm not sure exactly what a 'priory' is, but it seems to denote an organization of some kind. Perhaps, given that an assassin was sent to kill Monty, this Nite Priory is more than one person."

Nodding his head, Michael leaned back. "It's possible, Rodger. All we know is the following." He started to count off on his fingers. "One, the killer contacted Miss Babineaux personally, meaning he was either a past customer or knew how to contact her. Two, the killer is contacting the previous accomplices of Vincent Castille, calling himself, herself, or themselves the Nite Priory.

"So whoever they are, they knew that the Bourbon Street Ripper had accomplices, as well as what they did. Three, we know that this killer is either a trained assassin or can retain the services of a trained assassin to stop people from talking. Therefore, he must have either some kind of military or police background, or he must have strong finances."

Rodger nodded, again impressed with his younger partner. "The only problem is that we are, as of yet, unsure as to which of those variables you mentioned are true. Is the killer one or more people? Is the killer wealthy or highly trained? Is the killer aware of the accomplices or is he himself an accomplice?"

"Right," agreed Michael, who was finally being released by the EMTs and getting up and ready to depart. "We'll need to start checking those variables out tomorrow. I'll look up what this Nite Priory could be."

After being helped off the ambulance, Rodger joined his partner as he headed to their car. "And as for the accomplices," he said, "if Topper Jack and Mad Monty were involved, you can guarantee that Fat Willie and Blind Moses are as well. Who knows, with Fat Willie behind bars, Blind Moses could be the killer."

"Could be that Blind Moses was the masked assassin," said Michael as they got into their sedan and he buckled himself in. "Could also be that Dr. Castille's accomplices are being played as much as we are, you know?"

Having momentary difficulties with his safety belt, and finally clicking it in place, Rodger nodded before starting up the car, which roared to life. He pulled out of the warehouse courtyard and turned toward Old Gentilly Road. "We should also check up on the pay phones around the murder site, see if anyone has seen anything."

As Michael agreed with him, Rodger turned his attention to driving. He didn't know what his partner wanted, but Rodger wanted to get home, have a stiff drink, and go to sleep. Today's ordeal felt like it should have given Rodger half a head of gray hairs, and he wanted to put it behind him, hopefully in an alcoholic daze.

It was 10:00 p.m. when Rodger finally trudged into his apartment, a two-room place tucked away on Barracks Street in the southeast part of the French Quarter. After parking his car and squeezing through the alleyway's tight entrance into a residential courtyard, Rodger turned right and headed to the second door down—the door to his home. As the detective fumbled tiredly in his coat pocket for the keys, he heard a voice behind him that sounded as crotchety as it was old.

"Rodger Bergeron, there you is!"

With an internal groan, Rodger turned around and managed a weak smile for the diminutive African-American woman standing before him. She was standing at the doorway to the first apartment down, leaning on a black metallic cane and gumming her dentures. One bony hand pointed up at Rodger as the old woman looked at him through a single squinty eye.

"You owes me rent, Rodger Bergeron, and don't go thinking that just because you with the poh-lice, you gets a free ride."

"Of course, Ms. Parkerson," replied Rodger, keeping that smile. "You know I'm good for it. I've just been too busy to—"

"You been too busy to take all of thirty seconds to write me a check, Rodger?" interrupted Ms. Parkerson, wagging her finger in a very dismissive fashion.

While he kept smiling on the outside, inwardly Rodger sighed.

To be fair, Ms. Parkerson was probably one of the kindest and most considerate people he knew. One Christmas, when the heat went out in his apartment, she invited him over to her apartment to have dinner with her and her son and his family while putting a rush order on the repairs. When his water pipe broke, the old woman went and woke up Earl Mastadon, the portly plumber who lived two doors down, and paid him fifty dollars to fix Rodger's pipes that evening, even though it was Earl's day off. When Edward died, Ms. Parkerson sent an impressive arrangement of cypress flowers to Rodger at work, expressing her condolences.

She treated all of her tenants that way, saying that if she couldn't be a friend as well as a landlord, then there was no point. However, there was one thing Ms. Parkerson was an absolute tyrant about—the monthly rent.

"All right, Ms. Parkerson," Rodger said in a tired voice, "give me one minute and I'll write you the rent check."

Getting out his keys and opening the door to his apartment, Rodger stepped inside. In the front hallway, which only went in a few feet, there was a small writing desk that belonged back in the thirties—a keepsake from his father, Edgar Bergeron, a successful detective in his own right. Inside the desk was Rodger's mostly unused checkbook, the last several dozen entries centered solely around his monthly rent.

Quickly writing out the check, Rodger headed back outside, not the least bit surprised to see Ms. Parkerson standing right outside his door, tapping an impatient foot. "Your rent, Ms. Parkerson," Rodger said with a less forced smile.

Snatching the check in a brusque manner, Ms. Parkerson looked it over. Satisfied, she gave Rodger a denture-filled grin and thanked him. Rodger started to close the door when the old woman suddenly asked, "I noticed you were limpy, Rodger. Are you okay?"

This made Rodger smile a more genuine smile, opening the door and leaning on the frame. Despite being the Rent Gestapo, she honestly cared for her tenants. He shrugged off his pain and replied that it was simply a job-related injury.

"Hmm," Ms. Parkerson mused, looking the detective over, "you need some of my famous chicken and dumplings. I'll cook you up a batch tomorrow morning."

Rodger opened his mouth to protest, and almost got an old wrinkled finger in it for his troubles. "And I won't hear a word against it," Ms. Parkerson said before turning around to head back inside. "Thank you for keeping us all safe, Rodger. You have yourself a good night."

"Good night, Ms. Parkerson," Rodger said as he closed the door. He was certain that she would indeed cook up a batch of chicken and dumplings, and he was equally certain that it would be the best chicken and dumplings he'd had in months—since her last batch. As he headed into his apartment, he couldn't help but be glad Ms. Parkerson was his landlady.

Like Rodger, his place was disorganized, with old books and newspapers all over his front room, boxes of half-eaten cereal closed up but not put away in his kitchen, and last week's laundry on his bedroom floor. Rodger engaged a maid service to come in once a month to clean up the apartment, throw away the old food, and sort his laundry.

Rodger threw his coat over a coffee table, took off his shoes and slid them underneath the television stand, and poured himself a glass of whiskey. Then he sat back in an oversized comfy chair, resting his tired, battered body with a deep sigh.

The ice cubes rattled in his whiskey glass as Rodger leaned back, put his feet up on a small Victorian ottoman, given to him one year by Ms. Parkerson as a Christmas present, and tried to unwind. With every sip of the bitter liquor, Rodger felt more and more relaxed, his body sinking farther and farther into the comfy chair.

Only when he looked over to the side, at the side table to his right, did the detective sit up again.

On the table was a framed photograph, in black and white, of him and a man about his age, dressed in a neatly pressed suit and tie, clanking whiskey glasses together and smiling like a bunch of fools. The photograph was signed, "Edward and Rodger, good job catching the bad guys—Commander Ouellette."

Nostalgia filled Rodger's head as he reached over and picked up the photograph, looking it over.

"Edward, I'm sorry. You came to me during a time of crisis, and I turned my back on you. If only I had listened instead of being an obstinate old fool, you'd still be here. I'd be going over to your house for dinner and would probably be sitting for your grandchildren by now. I'm really sorry. When you needed me the most, I wasn't there for you. I won't make the same mistake twice. Not with anyone. Rest in peace, my friend."

The detective toasted his long deceased partner and slammed back his drink. With a shake of the head from the burning, bitter liquor, Rodger plopped down the glass, slid back in his chair, and fell immediately to sleep.

His dreams were vague and troubled and rapidly turned into a disturbing nightmare. In this tortured dream, Vincent Castille had him tied down to a conveyor belt that went toward a series of rotating scalpels and then into Monty's gaping, laughing mouth. Monty laughed as he chomped on the conveyor belt, and Vincent Castille, who looked like the old British actor Christopher Lee, had a dead, ghostlike pallor to him.

"That is right, Rodger," said Vincent as he walked alongside the tied-up Rodger, "this is what you want to do to every criminal you've ever failed to catch, isn't it? You want to tie them up and feed them into 'The Machine,' do you not?"

Looking forward, Rodger saw that the machine was no longer Mad Monty's face, but a giant typewriter, the keys slamming in a crushing manner along the length of the conveyor belt. Looking back at Vincent, Rodger was shocked to see Sam Castille there, her eyes looking distant and possessed. She continued to speak in Vincent Castille's voice, saying, "Maybe you should have let me die that day, too, Rodger. You can't trust a Castille. Didn't you say that to my father before you killed him? Didn't you?"

Rodger closed his eyes and shook his head, muttering something that could be an apology. When he opened his eyes again, the typewriter was now the machine from Mad Monty's warehouse, and the rotating scalpels were now steak knives on machine-like human arms, stabbing into the conveyor belt.

Looking back at where Vincent was, Rodger instead saw Mad Monty holding Michael's decapitated head. The head's eyes rolled forward to look at Rodger, and the head spoke in his partner's voice, saying, "You aren't very good at this, are you? Are you sure you solved the Bourbon Street Ripper case? I think you lied about it."

Mad Monty then threw Michael's head over his shoulder and leaned forward, saying in Mad Monty's voice, "Damn, Rodger! You lied about solving that murder case? You a meaner bitch than me!"

The knives began stabbing into Rodger's legs, chest, and arms as Mad Monty started to shake him by the shoulders, roaring, "What's wrong with you, Rodger? What's wrong with you, Rodger? Rodger! What's wrong with you, Rodger? Rodger!"

Rodger just flailed and screamed, the knives turning him into a bloody mess.

"What's wrong with you, Rodger? Rodger! RODGER!"

Suddenly, Rodger was awake, and instead of lying on a conveyor belt, he was lying back in his comfy chair. Instead of being shaken by Mad Monty, he was being shaken by Michael, who looked concerned. It was still dark outside his window, and Rodger was safe in his home.

Holding up his arms to ward off Michael, Rodger said, "Michael, Jesus Christ, what time is it? How'd you get here? What are you doing in my apartment?"

Michael leaned back, still looking concerned. Straightening his tie, he said, "I took a taxi. And you gave me a key, Rodger, and told me that if you ever failed to answer your phone three times when you should be home, to come over and check."

"Right, right," said Rodger, sitting up and stretching. "So you called me three times and I didn't wake up?"

Michael shook his head. "Not me, Commander Ouellette. He told me to come wake you up and, to quote, 'Get his sad ass out of bed.' So here I am. Are you okay?"

There was an unusual tone of concern still in Michael's voice, and Rodger suspected that in his stupor, he was so deeply asleep that he could have appeared to be comatose—not too far a stretch given that he had received a mild concussion earlier that day.

Now stretched, Rodger just cracked his back and neck, then looked over at his partner again. Michael was fully dressed in a new suit, and judging from the slight moisture about his hair, it seemed that he had showered off, too.

"Well, aren't you ready for work," replied Rodger, getting up and immediately wishing he hadn't. His body was sore all over, and he felt like the raw piece of meat that Mad Monty had made him last night. Again he asked his partner what time it was.

"Quarter to five," Michael said, getting up and following Rodger out into the hallway. "Go and get showered off and changed. I've got breakfast waiting."

"Whoa, whoa," said Rodger, turning to his partner and holding out his hands. "We don't have to go in until ten, and I aim to get some quality sleep in my bed." He then turned to head to his bathroom, intent on taking the longest piss he'd had in days.

"Yeah, you're starting work right now," said Michael as he continued to follow his partner like a baby duckling. "So go on and get cleaned up."

Rodger, who was in front of the toilet, stopped short of unzipping in front of his partner. His hands on his zipper, he looked over at Michael and said, "Oh yeah? Give me one good reason why I shouldn't just take my piss and pass out for three more hours?"

"Because we were right," said Michael as he folded his arms. "It's a copycat killer."

As Rodger stared blankly at Michael, the younger man added, "Another woman was found this morning in the French Quarter, eviscerated alive. Whoever it is, they have killed again, just like the Bourbon Street Ripper."

Chapter 15
The Magic in Your Mind

Date: **Friday, August 7, 1992**
Time: **7:30 a.m.**
Location: **Sam Castille's Townhome**
Uptown New Orleans

With a series of sharp ringing sounds, the egg timer in Sam's kitchen went off, calling her attention away from doodling in her day planner. The smell of bacon and eggs wafted throughout the room as the blond woman, dressed in a loose white blouse and relaxed-fit blue jeans, hopped up and headed toward the skillet.

"Hmmm, was almost in there too long," Sam mused, looking over the singed edges of the bacon.

She turned off the heat from underneath the skillet and, using a pair of tongs, removed the now quite crispy bacon, placing it on a plate simply covered with paper towels. The dozen strips still sizzled, smelling of cooked pork fat, a simply sumptuous smell. That done, she moved over to the eggs, cooking scrambled in an adjacent pan.

After seeing the texture was perfect, not too runny and not too solid, Sam stirred the eggs up some more and placed them on a plate next to the bacon. The aroma was intoxicating, and despite herself, she stole a bite of both.

As she munched the tidbits, Sam reflected on how different she felt on this sunny morning. Forty-eight hours ago, she was in a hellish place, memories of her grandfather assailing every waking moment. And now here she was, about to have a man over for breakfast for, honestly, the first time in her life.

It was not a situation Sam had expected to find herself in, not by a long shot. After the catharsis she'd had the night before, through the powerful memories brought about thanks to the sherry bottle and red plastic charm, Sam had vowed to finally come out of her shell.

Originally, she had just planned on dropping off her manuscript and then heading to a local park to read. However, when she learned that Richard Fastellos was in town, she decided to get him to autograph a copy of *Darkness Rising*, one of her favorite books by one of her favorite authors. After doing both tasks, Sam spent the rest of her afternoon reading that signed copy, enjoying the feeling of being a part of the world again.

Sam had never expected to find out from her lawyer that the very same Richie Fastellos wanted to meet with her. Kent hadn't even given a reason, which was all right with Sam, as she just wanted to meet the man. Although she decided to go and have dinner with him, Sam wasn't sure what to expect. She even drank a few glasses of wine before going to make sure she could concentrate on her dinner companion. And although she was nervous, the dinner went remarkably well; Richie was far more interesting than Sam ever could have expected.

Sam also wasn't expecting him to be so handsome, and even though she had gone through most of her life without giving men much thought, she couldn't get that smile of his out of her head. Her cheeks starting to pink, Sam came out of her thoughts and looked at the time. Seeing it was already eight o'clock, she realized Richie would be there any minute. She hurried to finish cooking breakfast.

She raced across the kitchen to prepare the toast. Six pieces of bread were torn from the womb of their bread box and crammed into the toaster oven. She busied herself with putting out a spread of preserves and butter. Then her nose caught the whiff of burning toast.

"Crap," Sam exclaimed and hurriedly opened the toaster oven door. In her haste to rescue the last part of breakfast, she touched part of the hot metal grating, and she snatched back her hand and cursed.

She removed the slightly burnt but still edible toast, and placed it on the same plate as the preserves. She then quickly moved to the kitchen sink to run cold water over her burn.

The pain wasn't excruciating, but already Sam could feel the throbbing associated with a minor burn from hot metal. She chided herself for being so clumsy.

Well, at least I didn't touch a hot coil this time.

After a minute or so of running cold water over her finger, Sam took a look at the wound. A red mark was visible and the skin was already tightening—a first-degree burn. Sucking in her breath through her teeth, Sam looked at her hand with disgust, trying to remember the last time she had actually burned herself. As she concentrated, she felt the world around her grow dim.

Soon Sam was no longer in her kitchen but her grandfather's, standing on a wooden stool. The sounds of sizzling bacon and the smells of sausage gravy assailed her senses. She was no longer an adult, but eight-year-old Samantha, in a little rosy day dress, her blond hair tied back neatly by a red ribbon. And all around her, the house staff, including the cook and housemaids, were screaming up a fuss, young Samantha having burnt her finger on the hot coil of an old toaster.

"Miss Samantha," cried out Tania Patterson, a pretty black girl dressed in a traditional maid's outfit. "Miss Samantha, are you okay?" In a blur, Tania was at Samantha's side, grabbing at the young girl's hand to look at the wound.

Samantha held out her finger, looking at the deep red mark with a mixture of fascination and horror. Tears were already forming in the girl's eyes, but she hadn't start crying—yet.

Miss Cooper, the cook, a heavyset white woman with a sizable hairy mole on her chin, bounded over and swatted Tania away from Samantha, saying, "Back off, girl! You don't grab at Miss Samantha's hand when she done burned herself. You go get some aloe right now, before I box your ears!"

The young servant girl nodded and slinked away, whimpering.

Nearby, stirring a pot full of grits, Violet Patterson shook her head. Her gray eyes, focused forward, looked expressionlessly over the stove as she cut a pat of butter off the stick and plopped it into the hot mixture.

"Tania's so stupid," Violet said as she reached to stir the sausage gravy. "It's just a burnt finger."

"Hush, you," Miss Cooper snapped at Violet. She then tousled Samantha's hair, as the young girl started to sob. "Now, it'll be all right, Samantha. Tania's gonna get you some aloe to put on that."

Samantha, who by now was registering what had just happened to her, shook her head, trying hard not to grow hysterical. The pain was increasing with every second, and already she felt a hot throbbing in her finger. As the stinging started to overwhelm her, she suddenly felt a calm and gentle presence behind her, a strong but firm hand on her shoulder.

"Sam," said Vincent. He was dressed for comfort in a dark red velvet robe with the initial *V* embroidered on it in gold. He smiled warmly down at the tear-streaked face of the girl in front of him before kneeling down and taking her hand from Miss Cooper.

"That'll be all, Miss Cooper," Vincent said in a sterner voice. Miss Cooper nodded and retreated to the stove, flipping over the bacon and cracking a few more eggs on the skillet. He then looked Samantha's finger over as if appraising a gem of the finest quality.

After a few moments, Vincent looked into Samantha's eyes. He reached up and, using the sleeve of his robe, wiped her tears away. As he did this, he asked, in a gentle tone, "How did this happen, Sam?"

By now, Samantha's finger throbbed in pain, and the girl wanted to scream. But having her grandfather there filled Samantha with a sense of calm and safety. She mustered up the best smile she could and responded with, "I wanted to make you toast, but I burned my finger on the toaster."

"Toast, you say?" Vincent asked, leaning up to see the plate of half-cooked toast lying on the counter where Samantha had dropped it after burning herself.

He smiled softly and said, "I'm sure this will be the best toast I've ever had."

"Violet"—Vincent turned to the Patterson girl, who cocked an ear in his direction—"put some honey on that toast and make sure it's served to me."

"Of course, sir," replied Violet, who returned to her work at the stove, eyes focused forward.

Vincent, turning back to Samantha, was about to say something when Tania hurried up and, holding out a bottle, announced that she had retrieved the aloe.

Samantha saw her grandfather's brow furrow, and as he stood, he said, "She doesn't need aloe. I have just the thing. Back to work, Tania."

As Vincent led Samantha out of the kitchen, holding her uninjured hand, Tania looked to shrink half a foot and scuttled over to the stove to help her sister finish cooking. Samantha was sure that she heard Violet call her sister stupid again, and that made her giggle.

Everyone in the Castille household knew that Tania was all heart, but she had very little in the brains department, while Violet was almost robotic, but was very keen in intellect. Being six years older than Samantha, the Patterson sisters had worked for the Castille family since childhood, and they were as much a fixture in the household as any of the other servants.

As Vincent led her into his study, Samantha's thoughts of Violet and Tania were replaced with the throbbing hot pain of her burn. She looked at the red mark and frowned, even as her grandfather led her to one end of the room, near a fireplace and large bookcase. Vincent led Samantha to his wingback chair in front of the empty fireplace, sat her down in it, and got up to search his bookcase.

"Here we go," Vincent said as he came back with his doctor's bag, kneeling again before Samantha. "I have just the thing for burns. Aloe will help the dryness, but it will do nothing for the pain."

Rummaging through his bag, Vincent pulled out a small bottle with a bunch of medical writing on it. Samantha looked over the bottle curiously as her grandfather opened it up, took a cotton ball, dabbed some liquid on the cotton, and moved to swab it on Samantha's burn.

When she pulled her hand back reflexively, Vincent paused and looked his granddaughter in the eyes. "I'd never hurt you, Sam. Trust me."

That was enough for Samantha, who nodded her head and offered her wounded finger to her grandfather. A few dabs of the cotton, and the pain vanished. Samantha was amazed.

"That's like magic, Grandpa," Samantha said, awe in her voice.

Her exclamation made Vincent chuckle as he capped the bottle. "Magic? Perhaps. Maybe there is magic in things such as Lidocaine, or maybe the magic is in your mind."

Samantha scrunched her nose at that comment. "Magic in my mind?"

Applying a bandage, Vincent nodded. "You'd be surprised what kind of powers are locked away within that mind of yours, Sam."

As Vincent stood to put away his bag, Samantha looked over her now-bandaged finger. Her grandfather continued, "We humans do not utilize our complete mental potential. If we could unlock the full power of our minds, imagine what we could do."

This concept seemed as alien to Samantha as some of the words her grandfather was using. Standing up, the young girl followed her grandfather, asking, "What do you mean, Grandpa? What can we do?"

Vincent offered his granddaughter a smile as he swept across the room to an oak desk while continuing his lecture. "All manner of things, Sam. You could remove the limitations of your body, transcend your conscious self into pure thought, or even . . . "

Sitting down behind his desk, Vincent patted his knee. " . . . or even live forever."

Samantha walked over to her grandfather, taking in what he said. Most of it didn't make any sense; however, the last part got her attention. "Live forever? You mean never die?"

With a deep chuckle, Vincent pulled Samantha onto his knee. "Yes, that's exactly it. Keep that old baron from digging your grave." He tilted her face toward his. "What would you do, Sam, if you never had to live with the fear of death?"

Samantha thought really hard about it, sucking on her bottom lip as she furrowed her brow. Finally, the girl answered, "I'd become a doctor like you, Grandpa, and cure all the diseases of the world!"

Proud of herself, Samantha folded her arms and nodded her head emphatically. This made Vincent laugh out loud. It was a warm laugh; however, given his age, it had a growling element to it. To Samantha, it always sounded like how that cartoon dog she liked on television laughed.

"I see, you'd be a doctor like your gramps, eh," Vincent said as he nuzzled the girl's hair affectionately. "Not wanting to follow in your daddy's footsteps?"

Again, Samantha scrunched her nose and shook her head. "Daddy's job keeps him up all hours. Besides, Missus Patterson says it's real dangerous, and he could get hurt someday."

"Missus Patterson is right, I'm afraid," said Vincent, a rueful tone to his voice. "Your daddy takes a great risk doing what he believes is right. But . . . " His voice trailed off, and for a moment he looked genuinely sad. " . . . we all have to do what we believe is right, Samantha, regardless of the cost."

Unable to understand what could make her grandfather so sad, Samantha just hugged him. To her delight, he hugged her back, and for a long moment the two just held each other. Samantha loved the way her grandfather smelled: he had a scent of fine tobacco and clean velvet. She liked those smells.

Soon, Vincent detached himself from Samantha and took her injured hand into his, looking over the bandage, softly asking the girl if it still hurt.

Shaking her head, Samantha said, "No, not at all. Thanks, Grandpa. I don't like it when it hurts."

To Samantha's surprise, Vincent chuckled. "Nobody likes pain, Sam. But that doesn't mean pain isn't important."

This elicited a confused look from the girl, who tilted her head to the side and asked, "Pain important? No way, Grandpa!"

"Yes, way," Vincent mused, his tone momentarily matching his granddaughter's, a feat that made the girl giggle. "Pain is your body giving important information to your brain. When you are in pain, your nerves are fully active, your brain is fully aware, and your entire being is fully focused."

As Samantha looked up at her grandfather, confusion still on her face, Vincent said, "In fact, Sam, when you are in pain, you are at your most alive."

Vincent ended that statement with a tight-lipped look, slowly staring down at his granddaughter. Leaning forward, he started to widen his eyes, and Samantha, who was nervous from the look for a moment, started to lean toward him and widen her eyes as well.

At the same time, both grandfather and granddaughter yelled, "Boo!" A few moments later, both were leaning back and laughing. It was a game that had been played many times, and Vincent was never successful in scaring his granddaughter.

"That's my fearless Sam," Vincent said triumphantly as he lifted the young girl off his lap and got up. "Nothing frightens you, does it, hon?"

"Nope," replied Samantha, holding out her uninjured hand for her grandfather to hold. "Like you and Daddy say, I have nothing to fear but fear itself."

"That's right, Sam," said Vincent, taking his granddaughter's hand and leading her out of the study. "If you remember that, you'll never be afraid. Besides, I'd never let anything happen to you. I want you to live a life without fear."

Samantha felt her heart brim with happiness as she walked with her grandfather down the hallway. "I love you, Grandpa!"

"I love you, too, Sam," Vincent replied tenderly, giving the child's hand a squeeze. "Now, let's go see if breakfast is ready. I can't wait to try your magnificent toast."

As the pair walked down the hallway, a bell rang.

The bell jarred Sam out of her memories, the sound coming not from the Castille mansion, but from the front door of her townhome. Looking around, Sam took a few moments to realize that she was an adult, in her own home, in the nineties. Reaching up to rub between her eyes, Sam sucked in her breath and muttered, "I didn't used to have such vivid flashbacks. Ever since the murders started up again." She sighed. "I swear, it's like Grandfather's spirit is haunting me in my dreams and when I'm awake."

The front doorbell rang again, and Sam moved into action. She placed all the breakfast components on a large serving tray, covered them with plate toppers, and carried the tray to her study. Placing the tray on a stand, Sam looked over everything and, with panic, realized she had forgotten the coffee in the kitchen.

She was just about to head into the kitchen to retrieve it when the doorbell rang again. Sam was a bit annoyed at herself for acting like this was some kind of a date, and she took a moment to grab the red plastic shoe charm. Then she headed to the front of the house, stopping only to make sure that her father's gun was still in its hiding place in the grandfather clock.

At the foyer, Sam took a moment to check herself in the mirror. While she wasn't dressed up as a Southern lady should be, she doubted that Richie, a Yankee from Pennsylvania, would care too much. Before the bell could ring another time, she unlatched the door and opened it.

Standing there was Richie, dressed in jeans and a button-up short-sleeved shirt, holding two bags up for Sam to see, and smiling cheerfully. "Good morning," he said in a morning person's voice. "It's early, so I brought breakfast. How are bagels and lox?"

Sam's face fell.

Chapter 16
Breakfast at Samantha's

Date: **Friday, August 7, 1992**
Time: **8:00 a.m.**
Location: **Sam Castille's Townhome**
             Uptown New Orleans

For a long moment, Sam looked at Richie with a defeated expression. Here she was, having scrambled to be the perfect hostess for her first guest in years, and Richie had gone and gotten breakfast! For a brief moment, Sam considered retreating. She didn't want to make any more mistakes.

No, Sam, she thought to herself. *You've moved past that. Don't beat yourself up!*

Sam noticed that Richie was starting to look uneasy, and realized that she needed to let her own anxiety go before she ruined both of their mornings. Taking a deep breath and recovering, Sam smiled, opened the door fully, and motioned for Richie to come inside. "Good morning to you, too, Richie. You won't believe this, but I cooked breakfast for us."

Richie's anxiety relaxed from his face and was replaced with genuine surprise. "Oh, really?" His lips tightened as he looked down. "Sorry. I guess I'm not good at this Southern hospitality thing. I figured it would be polite to bring something."

Instantly, Sam felt at ease, knowing that Richie was bumbling as badly as herself. Suddenly, her own worries didn't seem so bad. Giving her new friend a smile, even leaning down to capture his gaze, Sam softly replied, "It's okay, really. This just gives us more of a variety."

Sam's reply seemed to perk Richie up, and he nodded before following Sam into her study.

"Oh, by the way," Richie said, producing a bundle of paper wrapped in plastic from underneath his arm. "I found your morning paper on the front walkway. Where should I put it?"

Sam motioned for Richie to put the newspaper on one of the chairs in the study, then placed the bags of bagels on the tray with the covered breakfast.

"I need to get the coffee from the kitchen. Wait right here a moment?"

Richie nodded and started to look around the study as Sam headed into the kitchen. Once there, she placed the coffee, cream, and sugar, along with two cups and saucers, onto a coffee tray.

As she readied the last necessary bits for breakfast, she heard Richie walking out in the front hallway. Sam smiled to herself, figuring he was like her and couldn't help but look around.

When Sam emerged from the kitchen, however, she was surprised to see Richie staring into the glass case of her grandfather clock. Her eyes widened as Richie hummed to himself curiously and leaned down, looking near the bottom of the clock.

Sam cleared her throat, and Richie looked up, smiled, and gestured toward the clock. "Hey, I hope you don't mind me asking, but do most Southerners keep revolvers in their grandfather clocks?"

Walking past Richie, Sam smirked and replied, "Only those with nosy Yankees snooping around."

This got a chuckle from Richie as he followed Sam back into the study. "Well, I do apologize if I offended you. It's just as a mystery writer, I kinda think to look in odd places, and—"

"Don't worry about it," Sam interrupted, her smirk turning into a soft smile. She poured Richie some coffee. "I am a single woman living alone in New Orleans. I'd be a fool not to have a gun with me. Do you want sugar and cream with your coffee?"

"Yes, please, two spoonfuls," replied Richie, taking a seat.

Once the coffee was poured, he asked, "So was the revolver your father's? That model is—"

"Richie Fastellos," Sam said, turning to him with a mixture of amusement and annoyance on her face, "do you have a habit of asking such intrusive questions of those whose houses you visit?" She handed him the coffee.

As Richie took it, he cleared his throat and said, "Sorry. Like I said. Writer. Notice stuff."

"Well, yes, it was my father's," replied Sam, sitting in a chair across from Richie. "And the rest is my business. I don't like thinking about the past."

As she uncovered the plates and started serving them both breakfast, Richie said, "And yet you are writing about your grandfather."

That made Sam stop for a moment, before shaking her head and handing Richie a plate of eggs, bacon, and somewhat burnt toast. "Sorry about the toast," she said automatically, before starting to serve herself. "That's different. Like I said last night—"

"I know," interrupted Richie. "I get that it's therapeutic. Sorry. I won't pry anymore."

Sam nodded to Richie and rested her plate in her lap. She couldn't even be upset at his interrupting her, seeing as how she had done it to him twice. As she picked up her fork, Sam thought that Richie was a nice guy, just a little obtuse and a little too nervous.

Still, he's not bad-looking.

For a minute or so, both writers sat and ate breakfast in silence, not a word spoken between them. The feeling in the room, to Sam at least, was relaxed—like they were old chums, or family.

Finally, Richie cleared his throat and said, "Ya know, the toast ain't so bad, Sam. I like the jelly you got here."

"Preserves," Sam replied with a chuckle. "Surely you Yankees have preserves up north?"

"We do," Richie confessed. "And I'm not really a Yankee, so you can stop saying that."

This drew a surprised reaction from Sam, who regarded Richie with an appraising look. "Really? You're not from up north?"

"Well, my parents are actually from Northern California," Richie said, looking around the room as if forming his words carefully. "I was born there and moved to Pittsburgh when I was, what, nine, maybe ten years old? I don't remember. I was a kid at the time."

Richie seemed to grow quiet and contemplative. His face looked a bit tense for a moment, and then relaxed.

Sam nodded and munched on some toast. His sudden quietness made Sam wonder what caused him and his mother to leave their home out west. But she wasn't keen on prying.

Sam made a face as she took another bite. The toast was awful, even with the preserves. Looking over at Richie happily eating his own, Sam thought he either honestly didn't care how burnt the toast was, or he had the world's best poker face. Either way, her new friend had scored some points with her.

As he continued to eat, Richie got a thoughtful expression on his face. It was the real-life equivalent, Sam thought, of a cartoon character's lightbulb going off over his head. Sam watched him eat, appreciating how expressive his face was.

After a moment, Richie said, "Sam, mind if I ask you a few questions? About, you know, the current case?"

Sam, who was opening one of the bags and sliding a pre-made bagel with lox out of a wrapper, arched an eyebrow at Richie. "What makes you think that I know anything about the case?"

"Well, if I recall, one of the detectives who worked on the Castille case twenty years ago is working on this case. Correct?" replied Richie. He slid some scrambled eggs onto his toast and gulped it down.

"Yes, Rodger Bergeron," replied Sam, avoiding eye contact with Richie, looking instead down at her half-eaten bagel. It was not a topic she wanted to get too in depth about.

"Right," said Richie as he reached over, opened one of the bags he'd brought, and fished out his own bagel. Unwrapping it, he gestured with the breakfast item, saying, "And if I remember from the newspaper clippings I recovered on the Castille case, he was a close friend of—"

"You have newspaper clippings from back then?" Sam interrupted, giving her guest a most curious look. "Whatever for?" To Sam, for an outsider to have that level of interest in the Bourbon Street Ripper case, to go so far as to find old newspaper clippings from the seventies, was a bit odd.

Richie must have picked up on Sam's questioning gaze, as he visibly blushed. He fumbled the bagel out of his hand, and it dropped to his plate and opened up, lox falling over his eggs. He let out something that sounded a lot like *"Gwah!"*

This display of awkward, almost teenage silliness made Sam laugh, a soft but genuine chuckle. Shaking her head, she couldn't help but feel that Richie, despite everything, was as harmless as a kitten.

As Sam looked over and watched as Richie stumbled to slide the smoked salmon back onto the cream cheese–laden bagel, she wondered what on earth he was doing getting involved in this situation. To Sam, Richie seemed so completely out of place it was both amusing and intriguing.

Having recovered his breakfast and given a *heh* of triumph, Richie addressed Sam. "To answer your question, I have a bit of a confession to make."

"A confession?" Again, Sam looked at Richie curiously, a bit apprehensive. It was like the previous night. For every ten comforting things Richie said, one thing came off as almost sinister. Sam quickly looked over at her desk where the red plastic charm was, wanting to grab it in her hand, but she fought back the urge. She was in her home. She was safe.

Sam's gaze turned again to Richie. In the back of her mind, Sam wondered if Richie was truly being honest with her; however, in that same instant, Sam wondered if this was just her being paranoid and pushing others away like she had done for years.

Inhaling and then exhaling, Richie explained, "Last night, when I said I had been toying with the idea of writing a book about a Bourbon Street Ripper copycat, I wasn't being totally honest. The truth, Sam"—Richie got a resolute look—"the truth is I've been dabbling in the idea of doing exactly what you're doing—that is, writing a story about a copycat Bourbon Street Ripper—for a while now. I hadn't given it a lot of thought, what with *The Pale Lantern* and all, but I was still toying with the idea. Last night, when you mentioned that you wanted to do this, it really took me by surprise. So . . . "

Richie inhaled softly, then exhaled and said, "I came up with the whole"you write one thing and I write another thing' bit to cover up my surprise. But the more I think about it, I really like the idea of you, Vincent's granddaughter, writing this mystery. As for me, I'm just happy to help you out."

Sam's lips tightened as she looked at Richie, her face stern, otherwise expressionless. She hadn't suspected that it could be something like this; however, Jacob had often warned Sam that people might try to steal her work. She couldn't help but wonder why Richie was offering to help, when all he had to do was finish the story first, and the entire world would believe he alone had come up with the idea.

Why help a nobody like me?

Richie must have sensed Sam tense up, and he hastily set down his plate and, gesturing with both hands, continued his explanation. "However, the moment you told me your plans last night, I realized that I couldn't go through with it. This story has too much raw emotion behind it, too much anger. I don't want to get involved in that. To be honest, if I hadn't come up with the idea of writing a True Crime novel based on the current investigation, I'd probably be on my way home today."

Still tight-lipped, Sam nodded. His explanation made enough sense to relax her, but she couldn't help but think that Richie was unaware of how horrible the situation actually was. Finally, she asked, "So, do you realize what you're getting yourself into?"

Again, Richie got a pensive look, and Sam could almost imagine a thought bubble floating above her new friend's head. Finally, Richie said, "Ya know, I'm not sure anymore. I know this guy, Vincent Castille, committed some of the most atrocious torture murders in American history. A real modern-day Jack the Ripper. And I know there is a good chance we're dealing with another sicko who is doing the same thing. I don't know how far this goes, Sam, but it's ugly."

He rubbed the back of his neck and continued, "And, if my writing about the investigation helps put it to rest, or even solve it, then I've done my part."

"Solve it?" Sam asked, arching an eyebrow. "That's a bit out of left field. Do you really think you can help solve this?"

His face again resolute, Richie nodded. "Yes. Well, I mean, I'm no detective myself, but I have to think like one to write about crimes. As a mystery writer, you have to understand what I'm saying. The idea of seeing the evidence and coming up with a solution is rather exciting to me."

Shaking her head, Sam replied, "Look, Richie, this isn't some prime-time mystery hour. You aren't the brave consulting detective who helps the police solve crimes. This is a real murder investigation, possibly a serial one, and if you get too involved, you could get yourself killed."

Locking eyes with Richie, Sam continued, "Look, I understand you are a writer. I get that. I'm a writer, too. We both have to think like what we're writing about—killers and detectives. But this is some ugly shit, Richie, and if you're thinking of becoming like a character in one of our stories, all you're going to do is get hurt."

To Sam's surprise, Richie chuckled, giving her a wink. "Sam, I'm a dreamer and an optimist, but not an idiot. I don't plan on stalking the back alleys of Toulouse at night, or skulking underneath the Riverwalk for clues. But I do think that by looking over the evidence, and collaborating with you, we can come up with something plausible."

Sam nodded at that, giving Richie a wry smile. "Well, I'm a pessimist. I've been that way since my grandfather was arrested. I just want this to be over with, Richie, that's all."

To Sam's surprise, Richie smiled, leaned forward, looked her in the eyes, and said, "So let's do our part to help find out who this sicko is and put him away. You can't be so jaded that you don't want to help before someone else ends up dead. You're a brilliant person, Sam, and you can make a difference. *We* can make a difference."

Sam stared at Richie for a moment, her new friend's words having struck a central nerve.

He's right. I am jaded. I'm jaded as hell.

Looking down at her plate of food, Sam wondered how many more opportunities she'd let pass her up while being so disenchanted with people, and with life in general. Up until a day ago, she'd hadn't cried in twenty years. And now, in the span of a few hours, she was realizing that she had all but slept through the past twenty years of her life.

Sam also realized this was the longest and most coherent conversation she remembered having in a long time. She hadn't gotten distracted once. With only two conversations, Richie had drawn Sam out more than even Jacob had. Sam looked back up at Richie, who was smiling gently at her. Her cheeks flushed deeply as she looked away, muttering, "You're a damn fool."

She wasn't sure whether or not she was talking about herself.

Finally, Sam said, "Well, one step at a time. And don't you go running off on me, Richie Fastellos. I'll never forgive you if you abandon me or screw me over, not after drawing me out like this."

Richie kept that soft smile. "Nah, I won't, Sam." Leaning back, he continued eating. "I get the feeling we've both been through our own private hell. We'll both see this through to the end."

Sam gave a small smile. "Thanks." She took a few more bites. "So, we finish breakfast and then get to work, right?"

"Right," agreed Richie, who was happily eating his eggs, which had to be cold, seemingly without a care in the world.

After a few moments, the young man made an *"Mmmm"* sound and gestured to get Sam's attention. When she looked at him, he said, "So, my original question. Rodger Bergeron. Do you think he'll share any inside information with us?"

Sam, who was finished trying to eat the cold eggs and was just focusing on the lukewarm bacon, considered Richie's question for a few moments before replying. "I doubt Rodger would reveal anything confidential, even to me. He's a good cop, and a good man."

"But you know him, right?" asked Richie, obviously fishing for information.

Sam thought about that for a bit. After a moment, she shook her head and said, "I do, but we haven't really spoken since I was ten years old. It's personal."

"Of course," said Richie, nodding his head and crunching on some bacon. "No problem. Well, I guess it is newspapers and bothering constables for us. God, sometimes I feel like I should have been a journalist. Ya know, my mother wanted me to be one, but the closest I ever got was being a paperboy."

Sam chuckled inwardly at that, envisioning a young Richie trying to ride a bike and toss papers at the same time. The image in her head was one of him falling off his bike and skinning his knees, all with a bulldog latched on to his butt. As Richie continued to talk about his very uninteresting past, Sam looked over at him. He had an almost schoolboy charm to him, one that Sam found genuinely appealing.

Dreamers like him are a rare breed. I can't let anything bad happen to him.

Breakfast was soon over, and both writers were on their second cup of coffee. That's when Sam cleared her throat and said, "So, ready to start hashing out the details?"

Richie nodded, smacking his lips softly as he finished his coffee. After the second *smack*, he slowed down, looked thoughtful, and then said, "I mentioned newspapers earlier. Why don't we check the one I brought in and see if there's anything new?"

"That's a good idea. If there's nothing there, we can turn on the television in my office and see if there's anything on the morning news."

Setting down her coffee cup, Sam motioned for her guest to open up the newspaper. As Richie did so, she said, "Also, we can see if they've published my first chapter this morning. It could be posted today. After all, I just turned the manuscript in yesterday, and sometimes it takes . . . a whole . . . day . . . "

Sam's voice had trailed off when she spotted the headline to the morning paper. Richie, who had unfurled the paper, was staring at the headline as well. There it was in bold black print on the front page, right above a photograph of the side of a building in the French Quarter.

"SECOND VICTIM. POLICE CALLING NEW MURDERER A COPYCAT."

"Oh my God," said Richie, setting the newspaper down. "So it is a serial killer, isn't it?" Standing up, he walked to the open doorway, shaking his head, looking pale for a moment. "I mean, a part of me was holding out that this wasn't a real serial killer, but . . . " Richie's voice trailed off and he looked away.

Sam was calm. Richie's reaction hardly surprised her, though, and it only cemented in her mind that he was someone special, someone who needed to be kept safe.

Quietly, Sam picked up the paper and began to read the article.

All the while Richie stood to the side, regaining his composure. He asked who the victim was.

Sam didn't reply until she was a few paragraphs deep. Finally, she said, "This victim wasn't a native. She was a tourist. See?"

Sam pointed to the picture of the woman, and Richie came over to look at it. As far as Sam could see, the woman, named Rebecca Clemens, from Austin, Texas, was like any other tourist, right down to the gaudy beads and the skimpy T-shirt with the words "Cock Teaser" across the chest.

To Sam's surprise, Richie paled considerably. "I know that woman."

Sam looked up at Richie and blinked. "You knew the victim?"

Gritting his teeth, Richie replied, "Well, I mean, I ran across her the night before last. Her and her friends. On Canal Street."

Sam turned back to the paper and read over the information about the victim. Sure enough, she had two male friends she was traveling with. After confirming that, she offered the paper to Richie. "Wanna read about it?"

Richie backed away and held out his hands. "Give me a second to catch my breath. It's kind of freaky, ya know? You meet someone one night, and a day later they're a murder victim. First time this has happened to me. I don't really know what to make of it, you know?"

As Richie rambled on, he took out a small medicine bottle, popped the top, and gulped down a pill. Sam watched the action with interest. She didn't need to be a doctor to figure out those were panic pills, the kind people with anxiety disorders usually took.

She had taken enough medication in her life to be familiar with the mannerisms of one taking those kind of pills to ward off an impending panic attack.

While some people might have been turned off by Richie's behavior, Sam found it drawing her even closer to him. *It's like we're kindred spirits. We've both got problems.*

Sam found herself wondering what had happened to Richie to make him that way.

After taking a moment to breathe, Richie put away the pill bottle and held out his hand. "Yeah, let me see what it says about her."

Sam smiled gently and tossed the paper into his hands. "Here you go. See for yourself. The last person to see her was the hotel clerk. The report looks like it gets pretty detailed."

As Richie unfurled the paper and took a seat again, Sam shrugged and went over to her desk, took out her silver pen, and started to take some notes. The pen felt comfortable in her hand, and as Sam started to sketch out some random ideas, she felt them flow forth from her mind. She was learning to like this feeling, of being able to pour the ideas outward so easily.

"I guess I'm desensitized to this whole 'someone you met on the street was murdered' bit," said Sam. "I'm more concerned that there is a copycat of my grandfather going around than in coincidences."

"Right," replied Richie, who had started reading the article. "They have a lot more information about the victim's movements a few hours before the crime. Want to hear them? The guy who wrote the article, Jacob Hueber, was really thorough."

Sam had been jotting down ideas for her next chapter, cross-referencing her notes, and remembering that she had to tie everything back to her copycat murderer. At Richie's question, Sam looked up and smiled. "Jacob's covering this story? He's a good friend of mine. What does he say?"

Richie began to read. "Right, she had been partying with her friends all evening in the French Quarter. At eleven o'clock, she started to feel sick and had her two companions—her brother and her boyfriend—take her back to her hotel room on Dauphine Street. The boyfriend stayed and the brother went out for more drinks. At half past midnight, they got a call from the brother, who was piss-ass drunk and wandering the back streets of Chartres. The boyfriend left to go get the brother. At one fifteen in the morning, the clerk of the hotel where they were staying said that the victim came to the front desk, asking where the nearest twenty-four-hour pharmacy was. The clerk told her, the victim left, and she wasn't seen again until her body was discovered in an abandoned apartment next to the Faulkner House in Pirate Alley."

As he finished reading, Richie shook his head. "Pirate Alley is a tourist attraction. Seriously, don't you think someone would have heard her screaming?"

But Sam didn't reply, and in fact, she hadn't focused on anything since Richie started divulging the timeline of the crime. Instead, Sam was sitting there, her entire body shaking. Her head pounded in unbelievable pain, and her mouth and throat were mothball dry. Her right hand clutched tightly on to her pen and her left hand clutched tightly on to the red plastic charm as if her life depended on it.

Richie looked up, saw Sam, and blinked. "Sam. You okay?"

"How the fuck is that possible?" Sam muttered, the pounding in her head like hammer strikes on an anvil.

Richie shifted in his chair, looking noticeably concerned. Finally, he said, "Okay, you're freaking me out. What's wrong, Sam?"

Sam felt herself withdraw from both Richie and the world around her. Once again, she couldn't focus on anything but the horrible sensations she was feeling. "The murder. The victim. Her last hours alive. Where her body was found."

Richie, still with a confused look, nodded. "Yeah, what about it? It wasn't all that gruesome or anything."

"You don't get it," Sam replied, fighting the urge to start screaming, her entire body shaking. "That's exactly what I wrote in my story yesterday!"

Chapter 17
Introducing Dr. Klein

Date: **Friday, August 7, 1992**
Time: **10:00 a.m.**
Location: **Office of Dr. Klein, St. Charles Avenue**
              Uptown New Orleans

"I don't buy in to this shit at all," said Rodger, a huffy air of indignation about him, arms folded and brow furrowed, as he sat waiting with Michael in Dr. Klein's office. Rodger's usual gruff tone was several degrees more severe, and it was apparent to Michael that his partner was in a bad mood, good reason for it or not.

Michael didn't answer Rodger, and instead focused on his notebook, where he was busily sorting through notes he had scribbled down about the latest murder scene. Having recently come from the scene itself, Michael was anxious to get this interview, which he regarded as a waste of time for many reasons, over with, and continue with the actual investigation.

"I'm telling you, Ouellette is way out of line this time," a still gruff and disgruntled Rodger said. "I mean, really, don't you think the entire thing is ridiculous? Michael?"

Michael, who was now aware that his partner was looking at him, gave a small sigh and partially closed his notebook. Without looking toward Rodger, Michael replied, "It doesn't matter what we think, Rodger. It's our job to follow every single angle. And you have to admit, at this point, it's the strongest one we've got."

Rodger huffed, arms folding even tighter—if that were possible—and sank down into his chair. Michael had to admit that as shitty as the situation was, and as much as he agreed with his partner on what a waste of time this side trip was, the facts were too stark to ignore.

Sam Castille was now being treated as a suspect.

The morning had started off routinely enough, with Michael and Rodger reaching the crime scene and checking in with Ouellette. Michael had been a bit surprised to see Detectives Aucoin and Dixie already there, speaking to Officer Guidry, who had found the victim's body.

However, Ouellette had soon explained that, feeling increased pressure from the top brass to solve this case, he had decided to put both pairs of detectives on the case. Michael had been fine with that, feeling that having those two, especially Dixie, on the case would increase their chances of a swift conclusion.

However, it was at eight in the morning, just as the five policemen prepared to leave, that the real trouble began. Dixie, who had just picked up a copy of that morning's newspaper, gave a gasp. The source of her shock was revealed to be a completely accurate recounting of Rebecca Clemens's last hours alive, including some details withheld by the police, in the form of a serial story chapter written by none other than Sam of Spades.

Michael could hear the investigation derailing, and saw Rodger's psyche punch itself out.

The next twenty minutes had been exceedingly uncomfortable for Michael, who wasn't sure how Sam Castille was able to detail a murder so well before it happened, but he was certain there had to be a rational explanation for this occurrence.

His partner, however, had abandoned rationality almost immediately, becoming so defensive of Sam that Ouellette almost sent Rodger home. Fortunately, Michael had been able to calm his partner down enough to avoid a formal reprimand.

Still, Michael hadn't been able to argue that this didn't make Sam Castille into a suspect, and he had been not at all surprised when Ouellette ordered them to investigate her. Almost immediately, it had come out that Sam saw a psychiatrist. And given the rising profile of the crime, it hadn't taken long to get a court order compelling Dr. Klein to divulge information about Sam to the two detectives. Aucoin and Dixie were left to continue working the current crime scene. Michael drew back from the mental review of the past several hours, finally having sorted the facts out in his head, as Rodger asked, "So you know that Sam is innocent, Michael, and that this whole thing is bullshit, right?"

Nodding, Michael replied, "Well, while I don't think Sam is the murderer, Rodger, this is pretty damning evidence. After all, she had details in her story that we never released to the public. How can you explain that?"

"It has to be a trick," Rodger said, arms tightly folded in a doubting manner. "Someone is trying to frame Sam."

"Rodger, we should withhold any more judgments until we speak with Dr. Klein, and, I dare say, Sam herself," Michael said, his eyes finally sliding over to look at his partner. It was no secret that Rodger cared for Samantha Castille, but in this case, Michael thought that not enough information was present to make any kind of a decision.

"Damn straight we're meeting with Sam," Rodger said gruffly.

Michael sighed inwardly. *This is going to be a long day.*

About this time, the phone on the receptionist's desk buzzed, and she picked it up. A moment later, she said, "Dr. Klein is ready to see you, Detectives. You may head inside."

Gathering up his belongings, Michael followed Rodger into the office of Sam's psychiatrist.

Michael knew, from his dealings with psychiatrists and psychoanalysts alike, that mental health doctors' offices always had a modicum of what he referred to as OCD. Michael had surmised many years ago that this nearly obsessive level of neatness and organization was mostly there to calm the patients.

However, Michael had also surmised that there were some doctors who just had neurotic issues with things being orderly. Either way, he had come to expect it.

However, Dr. Klein took this to a frightening new level. Every book on his shelf was arranged, not by author or title, but by height, from shortest to highest, with each row alternating. The various knickknacks on his shelves were arranged in exact intervals and tilted at identical angles facing the desk. Every portrait on the wall was of the same height, and every item on the desk was arranged in perfect rows.

But the *coup de grâce* was that the two chairs facing the desk were arranged with their outer legs aligned with the desk's outer legs—and the chairs were bolted in place.

And people think I'm anal-retentive, Michael mentally commented to himself as he laid eyes on the doctor behind the desk.

Dr. Klein was a small man and was proportionately skinny. His face had an angular cut to it, the sharp nose accented by the well-groomed, if not equally pointed, mustache and beard, and his eyes, sunken in just a bit behind two uncomfortably squinty eyelids, were best described as beady. His hair, the same dark red as his beard, was slicked back to just above his shoulders. He was dressed in a stylish, if not dated, dark charcoal-gray suit with tails, red shirt, and black tie. And he had a monocle covering his right eye.

Michael, who was a fan of Sam of Spades, instantly recognized Dr. Klein's visage as the one used to describe Detective Mortimer Branston's arch-nemesis, Dr. Notoriety.

Michael shook off the thought as Dr. Klein approached from around the desk in a series of steps that looked rehearsed. His thumbs were symmetrically hooked behind the lapels of his jacket, and as he approached Rodger, who still had his arms folded, he presented his right hand at a right angle for the other man to shake.

"Detective Bergeron, I presume?" asked Dr. Klein in an accent that was more stereotypically German than Michael even could have imagined. "Commander Ouellette told me that you und your partner, Detective LeBlanc, vould be coming. Thank you for waiting for me to finish with an important phone call."

As Rodger finally unfolded his arms and shook the doctor's hand, Michael said, "Dr. Klein, we thank you for your time today. We won't be long. We wanted to talk to you about Samantha Castille."

In the same methodical fashion, Dr. Klein reached out to shake Michael's hand, but instead was handed the court order. Michael continued as the doctor unfurled the paper and read it.

"The court order to divulge patient information is there, along with the court order to turn over Samantha's medical records. I must advise you that if you refuse, you will be charged with obstruction of a police investigation."

Folding the papers up, Dr. Klein looked at Michael with a passionless expression. Turning around and heading back to his desk, while tapping the papers against his midsection, the psychiatrist motioned for both detectives to sit before saying, "Going straight for ze threat of arrest, are we, Detective? You have much to learn about ze slow und methodical pace in which people do things here in New Orleans."

Turning at a sharp angle and sitting at his desk, Dr. Klein continued, "I have very powerful friends at City Hall, Detective LeBlanc. I am sure I can refuse your court order und get away with it if I am so disposed." The psychiatrist's tone was confident to the point of being caustic.

Michael felt his pulse race, and also felt Rodger tense up. For a moment, Michael remembered some conversation he and Rodger had yesterday, something about how he should talk to others, but as it hadn't been relevant to the investigation, Michael couldn't remember the details.

However, feeling that he was on the verge of royally messing up the investigation due to his lack of grace, Michael surprised himself with two words: "My apologies."

Seeing his partner turn to him and look in surprise, Michael struggled to find the words to complement his apology. "This case has everyone . . . on edge. And we . . . we're just doing the job we've been . . . told to do. Nothing personal . . . was meant by it."

Michael's brow furrowed. Those words didn't come naturally. They felt contrived, and he didn't like that feeling at all. But what Michael liked even less was the feeling he'd been having lately that his lack of understanding social cues had contributed to the entire situation with Mad Monty.

He really felt that if he had been more emotively on par with Rodger, he could have seen the trap coming and stopped it. Seeing that Rodger was nodding with approval, Michael gave a small smile back. *That took a lot out of me, Rodger. Make sure you get over your own mood soon, so you can carry the emotive half of this team. I don't think I can do that again too soon. This is something I'll really need to work on in the coming days.*

The apology seemed to be enough for Dr. Klein, who nodded and again motioned for the two detectives to have a seat. Michael obliged and sat, finding he had to rotate his body to directly face the psychiatrist. Another look over at Rodger, who was struggling with the same revelation, and Michael concluded that both he and his partner were of the same mind—this was a ludicrous setup designed to make Dr. Klein, and only Dr. Klein, comfortable.

Another strike against Dr. Klein, thought Michael as he took out his notebook. *How can Sam, or anyone, get therapy in this situation? This office doesn't even have a couch to lie down on. Is Dr. Klein trying to cure psychological disorders or create them?*

Michael's thoughts were interrupted by Dr. Klein. "So, Detectives, vhat do you vant to know about Miss Samantha Castille?"

Michael thumbed through his notebook and found the page where he had scribbled down copious notes about Sam. Since he and Rodger had come to the agreement that he should handle the questions, with Rodger only chiming in when necessary, Michael asked the first question.

"All right, Dr. Klein, so Sam—"

"Samantha," interrupted Dr. Klein. Before Michael, whose mind had hit the brakes, could recover and answer, the psychiatrist said, "It is very important that you call her Samantha."

Okay . . . Michael thought to himself, growing less impressed and more annoyed with the doctor's nuances every passing second. *This guy has held on to his medical license for this long how?*

Shaking it off, Michael continued, determined not to get waylaid again. "Very well. So Samantha has been your patient for how long?"

"Since she vas ten years old," Dr. Klein replied, tilting his head up as if about to crow. "Right after Dr. Castille vas found guilty of being ze Bourbon Street Ripper, ze courts appointed me her psychiatrist as a condition of being ze heiress to her grandfather's fortune."

Michael nodded and, despite thinking that was a bit extreme, scribbled down the notes. "Really? Why did the courts make that decision? Do you know?"

"Of course I know," replied Dr. Klein, puffing his lips on a nonexistent pipe. "I know everything about Miss Castille. After ze murder of her father, ze young Samantha vas suffering from severe post-traumatic stress disorder. She vould not eat. She could not sleep. Und she vould be prone to ze horrible fits, much like schizophrenics having ze convulsions."

Shit, are you serious? thought Michael. One look at Rodger's steely expression, and Michael knew it to be true.

"So, wait," he said, looking back over his notes. "I know that Sam . . . antha's father was murdered by her grandfather, and I know that Samantha was the sole heiress to her grandfather's estate, but what caused all these disorders?"

Dr. Klein, again methodically puffing on a pipe that was not present, replied, "Ah, you see ze reality that vas hidden from public record is that Samantha saw her father murdered."

"Yes, I know that," retorted an increasingly annoyed Michael. "The reports state that Sam came across her grandfather right after he had murdered her father."

"I said, call her Samantha," Dr. Klein loudly snapped at Michael, before leaning in and resting both arms on his desk in two precise spaces obviously reserved for his elbows. He linked his fingers together and stared down his nose at Michael. "Und your reports are not accurate. Ask your partner, Detective LeBlanc. Samantha Castille vas in ze room to watch her grandfather torture und murder her father."

Michael sat there, stunned, staring back into the beady eyes of the psychiatrist. Slowly, Michael turned to his partner, wanting to hear that Dr. Klein was a quack, mistaken, or otherwise wrong.

However, upon seeing Rodger's grim face, Michael realized that this information was accurate.

"Sorry, Michael," Rodger said quietly, his voice tense, most likely from a dry throat. "Dr. Klein is correct. He . . . that evil bastard made her watch him kill her father."

The hell, Rodger? Michael thought, his blood pressure starting to rise. *What the hell else aren't you telling me?*

Michael sighed softly, keeping his cool, and asked, "So, Dr. Klein, how does someone make a ten-year-old girl watch as they butcher their father?"

Dr. Klein leaned back, hooking his thumbs again under his lapel, and said, "With a low-level general anesthetic. You see, at ze right levels, an anesthetic will produce ze paralysis within ze victim. They will be completely aware of vhat is happening around them, fully conscious und fully capable with all five senses, but completely unable to move or communicate to ze outside world."

Michael quickly jotted down the information. He had heard of such a thing, but only in passing. As he wrote, Dr. Klein continued to speak.

"Samantha, immediately upon her grandfather's arrest, was placed under State care at Acadia Vermilion Hospital."

Michael flipped back through his notes, and, finding the note on Sam during the Castille trials, saw something that didn't make any sense.

Immediately, Michael spoke up. "But wait, this doesn't add up. Samantha was present at her father's funeral a week later."

"Ah, yes," replied Dr. Klein, puffing on his imaginary pipe. "This is where things get odd with Miss Castille. Three days after she vas admitted, ze fits stopped und ze girl vas completely normal."

"Completely normal?" asked Michael, finding the idea to be utterly ridiculous.

"Well, not *completely* normal," answered Dr. Klein, with a tone that was more admitting than smug. "She vas emotionally devoid, but had no memories of seeing her father murdered. Und ze hysteria had stopped."

"What?" asked Michael, looking squarely at Dr. Klein and finding the entire situation to be completely contrived. "She developed some form of amnesia?"

Dr. Klein unhooked his fingers and waved his hands at Michael in a most dismissive gesture, saying, "No no. Nothing stupid like that. Samantha repressed everything, burying it so deeply in her psyche as to convince herself she never saw anything. Once she had done this, she vas soon released und ze rest is history."

"No, the rest is not history for me," replied Michael, his tone starting to take an aggravated quality about it. As Dr. Klein continued to stare down his nose at him, Michael collected himself. He felt he was being deliberately kept in the dark on key pieces of information that, as he had now convinced himself, were essential to solving the crime.

Getting himself together, Michael continued, "What I mean, Dr. Klein, is that I don't have all the facts about Samantha Castille. Can you tell me everything? Don't leave out any details."

Dr. Klein nodded and leaned back, looking even more full of himself, if such a thing were possible. "Well, Samantha repressed her memories to ze point where it killed her emotional side, turning her into a sedate child, devoid of life. Acadia Vermilion Hospital vas no place to treat her. I wanted her to be transferred to ze Tulane Mental Hospital. But her family lawyer, Mr. Bourgeois, had other intentions. He used me to get Samantha out of Acadia, but when it came time to transfer her, he betrayed our agreement. Mr. Bourgeois vas most persuasive und, winning ze argument in court, had her discharged from ze hospital completely."

As Michael scribbled down those notes, Dr. Klein continued. "But after her father's funeral, after ze grandfather vas executed und willed her his heiress, I vas able to intercede for ze child's mental well-being. Despite repeated blockage by Mr. Bourgeois, I vas able to get ze courts to force Samantha Castille into my outpatient care. I have been seeing her ever since then."

Michael put the information down in his notebook. "Right. So what is your diagnosis of Samantha? Has she still repressed those memories?"

"Well, this is ze difficult part," Dr. Klein said, reaching up to stroke his goatee. "You see, Samantha Castille still has many of ze repressed memories. While normally she is functional, even thought she has ze short attention span, ze repressed memories come out in times of great stress. Zherefore, I have been slowly, over ze past twenty years, using a combination of therapy, pharmaceuticals, und hypnosis to bring these memories to ze surface."

Rodger half-stood and cried out, "You what?!?"

Immediately, Michael, who was in no mood to deal with Rodger's emotions, put a hand on his partner's shoulder and, using his martial knowledge, tightened his fingers dangerously close to a pressure point. This made Rodger sit, although Michael could feel his partner tense up even more.

Seeing that they were about to lose the interview with Dr. Klein, Michael turned to his partner and said, "Rodger, let me handle this. You wait outside at the car."

As soon as Michael loosened his grip, Rodger smacked his hand away, got up, and, with a glare at Dr. Klein, left the office. Michael watched Rodger leave, then turned back to the psychiatrist to apologize for his partner. However, Dr. Klein was already shaking his head and talking. "It is a shame that Detective Bergeron is so attached to that girl," he said with an almost rueful tone.

Looking into Michael's eyes, Dr. Klein lowered his voice to almost a whisper. "There is much to your partner I suspect you don't know. He has not been forthright about ze events twenty years ago, has he?"

Michael exhaled, focusing his mind on the task at hand, and restoring himself to the stoic detective he tried so hard to be. "I am here to find out about Samantha Castille. In your opinion, is she capable of murder?"

Dr. Klein leaned back and smirked, saying, "Ah! Do I think Samantha is capable of murder? More importantly, Detective, I think you want to know if she can murder like her grandfather, yes?"

Michael, who was beginning to tire of this man, nodded his head. "Yes."

"Samantha Castille is not capable of murdering anyone," began Dr. Klein. "Deep inside that troubled soul, that frightened ten-year-old girl is still there. Why do you think she never leaves her father's townhome? Why do you think she is so socially shy und hides behind that villainous Mr. Bourgeois? Because deep down inside, Samantha is stuck on that same day her father died."

Michael could see that being true.

"That is vhat I hope to accomplish with my methods. One day, she will fully relive that horrible event of watching her father tortured und murdered. She will be ready to cope with it. Und on that day, Samantha Castille will be able to truly move on."

With a nod, Michael finished his notes and said, "Thank you, Dr. Klein, for your—"

"I am not done," interrupted the psychiatrist, motioning for Michael to sit back down. "I said that Samantha Castille is not capable of murder. But I said nothing about Sam of Spades."

Michael blinked, tried to process what he just heard, and shook his head. "Wait, what do you mean? Her pen name?"

Dr. Klein leaned forward again, this time his elbows pushing several pencils aside, and said, "Detective LeBlanc, who do you think told her to become a writer?"

Thirty minutes later, Michael left Dr. Klein's office and headed toward the parking lot nearby. He found Rodger leaning against the squad car and smoking a cigarette.

"Are you feeling better?" asked Michael as he approached his partner.

"Not really," replied Rodger, tossing the cigarette to the ground and stomping it out. "I really wanted to punch that guy's face in for doing that shit to Sam."

Rodger unlocked the car doors. "But thanks for stopping me. Punching out well-connected doctors would probably get me suspended."

As they got into the car, Michael shrugged it off. "You need to get those emotions under control, partner. I know that you care for Sam, family friend and all, but we have to approach this logically."

As he fumbled with the seat belt, finally getting it to *click* in place, Rodger said, "Oh, piss off."

Michael smirked and shook his head, thinking that sooner or later, he and his partner would have a very uncomfortable conversation. Right after that thought, he decided to test those waters.

"Rodger, I don't like getting blindsided by information you know and I don't," Michael stated they pulled out of the parking lot. "Finding out that Sam witnessed her father's murder was an unpleasant surprise. So, before we go any further, is there anything else you aren't telling me?"

"No, nothing else like that," replied Rodger a little too quickly. "There is some minor shit about Sam's father that isn't relevant. I was close friends with him, and he often confided in me."

Michael frowned, wondering if any of those things told in "confidence" was vital information. However, he decided to trust his partner, and nodded his head in understanding. "All right, that's good enough for me. If anything comes to mind, tell me, okay?"

Rodger didn't say anything, but his nod was enough for Michael. He took out his notebook and said, "Okay, now I am going to tell you what Dr. Klein told me after you left, and I don't want any outbursts from you, all right?"

"Fine," replied Rodger as he started to head uptown.

"Good," started Michael, who began to recount the information to his partner. "Dr. Klein is using those techniques to force Sam to, eventually, relive the murder of her father. His belief is that Sam cannot move on with her life until she remembers her father's murder, comes to terms with it, etcetera. He is adamant that this is necessary to bring Sam to full mental health.

"He does not believe Sam is capable of murder. However, in his twenty years of treating Sam, he has noticed a mental anomaly."

"A mental what?" asked Rodger.

"Yeah, I asked the same thing," Michael said. "Apparently, during times of great stress, Sam will appear to have a second personality, a sort of dissociative identity disorder. This other personality, which Dr. Klein has named 'Sam of Spades,' revels in the tortures that Vincent Castille caused, calling them things like 'beautiful' and 'works of art.' Dr. Klein believes this second personality is very capable of murdering just like Vincent did."

This news seemed to make Rodger more tense, and Michael, who hoped his partner could keep it together, waited a bit for him to calm down.

Finally, Rodger asked, "So Sam has multiple personalities or something?"

"Well, that is where Dr. Klein and I disagree," continued Michael, closing the notebook. "If this were true dissociative identity disorder, Sam would switch between these two personalities. It seems more like the violent 'Sam of Spades' personality piggybacks on and torments the 'Samantha Castille' personality with disturbing visions, flashbacks, and hallucinations. To me, it seems more like her psyche is beating itself up."

"Or she's possessed by demons," Rodger said.

Michael shot his partner a look and cocked an eyebrow. "You believe in that kind of stuff?"

"It was a joke, Michael," Rodger said, shaking his head. "Poor Sam. I know the girl has problems. How do you figure it's not true multiple personalities?"

"Partner, I came a hair's breadth from becoming a profiler for the FBI. Still might, after you retire."

"You'd make an excellent profiler," replied Rodger. "You've got the mind for it."

Michael, who was genuinely touched by the compliment, smiled and said, "Thanks. I appreciate that."

Michael reopened his notebook and continued. "So, Dr. Klein felt that being a writer would help Sam with this 'dark side,' and so Sam of Spades was channeled into the cult author New Orleans knows and loves. Luckily for Sam, a friend from school, Jacob Heuber, has a job at the *Times-Picayune*. So a few negotiations, and probably some bribes later, and Sam had an outlet for those darker tendencies of hers."

Michael furrowed his brow and thought to himself.

Jacob Hueber. Wait, wasn't he the editor who published the report on the murder? Where have I heard that name before? Jacob Hueber. Sounds familiar.

Michael's explanation of Sam's disorder seemed to satisfy Rodger, who nodded and asked, "Does Dr. Klein feel that Sam could be the copycat killer?"

"Dr. Klein is being unsurprisingly noncommittal there," replied Michael. "I believe he is more concerned about his ego and professional image than Sam's well-being."

This made Rodger laugh bitterly. "So, then, Michael, what do *you* think?"

Michael knew this question was coming. Closing the notebook and looking squarely at his partner, Michael said, "Rodger, I currently don't think Sam is our killer. It's true there is something going on, where somehow the details of Rebecca Clemens's murder are identical in fact and fiction, but I am far more likely to believe that someone is getting Sam's information and using it to replicate the crime than that Sam is murdering people and then incriminating herself, Sam of Spades or not. I would need solid evidence that Sam is suffering from true dissociative identity disorder before I could even entertain the thought of her being guilty."

Finishing, Michael looked forward. "Having said that, I do believe Sam Castille is a very deeply troubled woman. I do believe she is somehow involved in everything, twenty years ago and today. But I do not believe she is the copycat killer."

That seemed to satisfy Rodger, who gave his partner the first real smile he'd had all day as he pulled the squad car into Sam's driveway. Unlatching his seat belt, he said, "Good, then. Ready to go talk to her?"

"Yes," said Michael, finding himself relieved that he and his partner were both on the same page again. "Let's go see what Sam has to say for herself."

Chapter 18
Meeting of the Minds

Date: **Friday, August 7, 1992**
Time: **11:30 a.m.**
Location: **Sam Castille's Townhome**
             Uptown New Orleans

Michael looked at his watch as Rodger rang the doorbell to Sam's townhome. It was already eleven thirty. As much as he couldn't stand coffee, he was looking forward to a cup of it. Looking over at his partner's face, and seeing the bags underneath his eyes, Michael concluded that Rodger was probably looking forward to the same.

We're both exhausted. I've had four hours of sleep, maybe five. I can't imagine Rodger's had much more. We're going to need to rest soon, or our investigative abilities, among other things, will start to suffer.

It wasn't the longest stretch, Michael thought, that he and his partner had gone without any rest, which was somewhere at forty-two hours, but it was close. Michael's thoughts were interrupted by the door opening, and a man answering it instead of Sam. Rodger seemed completely surprised, and Michael, who could have sworn he had seen this man's face before, was just as taken aback.

"Um, is Samantha Castille there?" Rodger finally said. "I'm Detective Bergeron and this is Detective LeBlanc. We, um . . . "

"Sam, you were right," called the man to the interior of the house. "It's the detectives."

The man muttered, "One second," before closing the door. A moment later, Sam, who looked like someone had just told her she was scheduled to be executed, opened the door.

"It's about my story in the newspaper, isn't it?" asked Sam. When Rodger nodded, almost whispering a "yes," Sam let the two detectives into her foyer. As they entered, she said, "I've spoken to Kent already. You two don't have permission to look around my house. But we can talk, for now."

That only brings you up higher on the suspect list, Sam, Michael thought. *An innocent person has nothing to hide. However, given everything, I really can't fault your lawyer for advising that, or you for listening to him.*

Entering Sam's study, Michael looked Sam over. She was paler than usual, her face tighter, and her expression less open. The man helped her sit behind her desk in a surprisingly familiar way, as if they were close friends. Michael wondered if perhaps this was that Jacob fellow Dr. Klein had mentioned, even though he couldn't get the nagging feeling out of his head that he had seen this man before.

"Have a seat," said Sam as she motioned for the two detectives to sit. Rodger immediately took a seat, but Michael did not. Although he could not search the house, the law stated that anything "in plain sight" was fair game.

"I think I'll stand for a bit, Sam," said Michael. "I've been sitting a lot today."

Sam nodded and then motioned toward the strange man. "This is Richie. Richie Fastellos. The author. He's"—Sam looked up at Richie and gave what Michael considered a needful smile— "a friend."

Michael and Rodger shook Richie's hand. Michael noted his hands were a bit clammy. Michael figured that he must be as nerve-racked as Sam.

So that's Richard Fastellos. I thought I recognized him from the back of The Pale Lantern *and* Darkness Rising. *Wasn't he supposed to be doing a book signing? I wonder how he's involved in all this.*

Michael's questions were answered as Richie said, "I was here on business for a book signing. Sam and I, well, we're working on a joint project. We were just having some breakfast and brainstorming when we found out about this mess."

As Richie continued to talk about how he and Sam knew each other, giving out information such as his publicist being stranded in Pittsburgh and such—things that Michael deemed irrelevant—he looked around the study.

Michael's gaze happened upon the mantle of the study's fireplace, regarding several pictures of Sam as a child. One particular picture caught Michael's attention. It was of Sam, around seven or eight years old, sitting in Audubon Park, New Orleans's largest city park, in one of those children's railway trains that would circle the perimeter of the park.

Seated behind her was a middle-aged, dark-haired man, wearing a suit without a tie, his hands on the girl's small shoulders, steadying her as she raised her arms in the air, holding on to a balloon that was dangerously close to flying away. The girl was laughing mirthfully.

Must be her father, Vincent Castille's son, Michael remarked to himself, focusing between the man's kind expression and Sam's jubilant one. Michael then furrowed his brow as he felt he should recognize the man.

Odd, where I have I seen this man before? Perhaps a newspaper clipping? Or maybe a painting somewhere? Or a photograph at Rodger's apartment? Was this guy connected to someone else other than Vincent Castille?

Michael's thoughts were jarred as Rodger called out to him. Turning to see all three people looking at him, Michael cleared his throat. "Sorry, I was washed up in my own thoughts. What were you asking me, Rodger?"

"Sam was asking if you wanted any coffee," said Rodger.

"Yes, please," replied Michael. "Light and sweet, if you would."

"I can handle this," Richie said and quickly walked past Michael, leaving the room.

Once Richie was gone, Sam quietly asked, "So Rodger, Michael, tell me the truth." She exhaled softly. "Am I a suspect?"

Michael let Rodger reply, "I'm sorry, Sam. Yes, you are a suspect."

"My story is rather condemning, isn't it?" asked Sam, looking down, her expression devoid of emotion.

"Yes," replied Rodger solemnly. "But neither I nor Michael believe it. Right, Michael?"

Michael nodded his head, saying, "Correct, Sam, I don't believe you're the murderer. I do believe, however, that you are being framed. It would help if you would let us search your house."

"I don't know," said Sam, shaking her head. "I need to protect myself right now. And Kent has always guided me properly. I don't think it's a good idea."

"We understand," replied Rodger. "But Michael just wants to help. We might find something here that could help find out who is framing you."

Sam shook her head and said, "Sorry, let me get my legal ducks in a row, so to speak, and then I'll talk to Kent about it."

Michael looked at Sam and said, "That delay could give the real killer time to make any evidence disappear. It would be best if—"

"We won't pressure you any more, Sam," Rodger suddenly interrupted.

Michael furrowed his brow and sighed. *There Rodger goes again, undermining my techniques. He needs to stop letting his feelings for Sam get in the way of the investigation.*

As Michael stood there, Richie returned with a tray of hot coffee. Michael thanked Richie for his coffee and tasted it, and was surprised that he actually liked it.

Rodger seemed to like the taste, too, as he said, "Well, Richie, this is the best coffee and chicory I've had in a while."

"Agreed," replied Sam with an appreciative smile, sipping from the cup and nodding. "You make it as well as a native."

This caused Richie to chortle softly, and as Michael sipped his cup, he saw the novelist reach over and touch Sam's hand, saying, "Thanks, but I just followed the instructions on the canister. Honestly, I'm not trying to impress anyone."

Michael looked at Richie and shook his head. He knew a guy making a play for someone's attention when he saw it.

Bullshit, Richie. You are trying to impress Sam and you know it. Put the brakes on, cowboy. This is a murder investigation, not a dating service.

Finishing his coffee, Michael set down the cup and turned to Sam, saying, "Sam, I have to ask you a few questions. What were you doing last night between the hours of one and three?"

Sam leaned back in her chair and sucked on her bottom lip for a moment before saying, "I was here, in bed, probably snoring very loudly."

When Michael stared at Sam with an unimpressed look, she added, "I had dinner with Richie at the Ritz-Carlton. Check with the host and my credit card company if you don't believe me. I had a lot to drink. We both did. After dinner, I caught a cab home and pretty much passed right out."

Michael nodded and turned to Richie. "And you, Mr. Fastellos, what were you doing last night between the hours of one and three?"

Richie, who had been sipping his coffee, asked, "Wait, am I a suspect, too?"

Michael said, "No. But you're a mystery writer, correct? Then you should know that we have to ask this. It's police procedure to ask everyone connected to a crime or a suspect what they were doing during the time of the crime."

"Oh right," said Richie, giving a bit of a nod. "Well, I was in my hotel room writing. Um, I was pretty tanked as well. I think I ordered a cheeseburger at two? Or was it a pizza? Or maybe—"

"Thank you, Mr. Fastellos," answered Michael, feeling it was his civic duty to make this man stop talking. "That's all I needed to know."

Looking at Rodger, Michael said, "I don't have any more questions at this time."

"So that's it?" asked Sam. "I mean, how we can prove my innocence?"

Michael answered Sam before Rodger could. "You'll be proven innocent when we catch the real killer, Sam. For now, I advise you to stay in your townhome in case we need you."

"The hell with that," said Sam, slapping her hand on her desk and standing. Michael blinked at Sam's outburst as she continued, "I've been sitting here for the past several days, suffering and feeling like my life is falling apart, because some asshole wants to emulate Grandfather from twenty years ago. I finally get the nerve to write about it, to try to put this behind me, and suddenly I'm a suspect."

As Michael relaxed from Sam's eruption, she leaned toward him and said, "Junior Detective Michael LeBlanc, if you think for a moment that I am going to sit here and wait for you all to catch this guy, you're sorely mistaken."

Well, she won't be the first suspect who forced herself into an investigation. But for her sake, I hope she doesn't think she can physically help out. She's a suspect. If she gets involved in any way, it could—

"You *should* help us find the real killer, Sam," said Rodger. "You could hold information that could prove to be invaluable to solving this case."

Michael felt his carefully built argument crumble.

The idea, however, seemed to bring a smile to Sam's face, who hastily agreed. Richie also chimed in, stating that he could offer his support as an outsider, giving a point of view that would help the others put things into perspective.

Rodger, much to Michael's dismay, thought this was a viable and intelligent idea, and that the four of them, together, stood a fantastic chance of catching the real murderer and clearing Sam's name.

Michael felt that if he didn't speak up before things completely spiraled out of control, the three of them would end up joining hands together in the center, letting out a college-like *"whoop"* and running off to derail the entire investigation in a fashion reminiscent of any badly made seventies cartoon containing a group of amateur detectives and a meddling dog. Whether there would be a freeze-frame and a catchy sound bite was debatable.

"Hold it," Michael finally said, drawing the attention of all three people in the room. "This is not a crime drama on television, and this is not a mystery by Richard Fastellos or Sam of Spades. This is a real-life serial murder investigation."

Drawing in his breath, Michael continued, "First off, Sam, you are a suspect. I hate to say it as much as Rodger does, but it's the way things are, and until you are cleared, anything you do, and I mean anything, will be viewed under a magnifying glass."

Turning to Richie, Michael continued, "And you, Mr. Fastellos, are an outsider. You have almost no idea what the three of us, especially my partner and I, have been through recently. You may be a fantastic writer, but if you get involved in this investigation, and our commander finds out, you'll be arrested so fast it will make you wish you were back in Pittsburgh. And if you are lucky, all he'll do is ship you back home."

Finally, Michael turned to Rodger.

"And Rodger, man, you have got to get your head on straight. I know this is a personal thing for you, but if you hadn't noticed, we've made little to no progress these past three days. Ouellette may like you, but if he knew that you brought civilians into this, especially a suspect, you'd be suspended, if not fired, before you could blink."

Ending his diatribe, Michael surveyed the room, and saw three people both hating him and silently agreeing with him.

Finally, Rodger spoke up. "Michael, you bring up a lot of good points. However, while you yourself have said you believe Sam is innocent, we both know there is no way Ouellette's going to let us strike her from the suspect list based on personal feelings. And you also know that with Aucoin and Dixie on the case, we have to tread carefully.

"But two civilians can find out things we police can't. People open up more to civilians. You know that. If Sam and Richie want to stick their necks out to prove Sam's innocence, they're going to do it regardless of our personal wishes. We might as well direct them toward information we need, instead of letting them wander aimlessly."

Rodger shifted a bit and added, "What I'm saying, partner, is that if these two kids are going to put themselves into this investigation, we can either arrest them now or see what they can find out. I'd prefer the latter. Anything to get this killer off the streets."

Michael bit his upper lip and scowled at his partner.

That was a very sound, logical argument. As annoyed as it makes me, I have to say I'm impressed. Good play, Rodger. Maybe you're not as incompetent as I was starting to think.

Even though he barely knew them, Michael had to agree that Sam and Richie had as good a chance of uncovering something important as anyone else. Sighing softly, Michael decided to take a chance. It was better than following a procedure that obviously wasn't working.

"All right," said Michael, sitting down. "But if we're going to do this, we're going to do this by the book. And you three let me coach you on what that means before you agree. Any divergence and you two are done. It'll just be Rodger and me. That's my condition to help out."

Sam immediately nodded, saying, "I will do anything to clear my name and to catch the person responsible for this, Michael. Name your parameters and I'll follow them."

Richie nodded, saying, "I just want to help Sam prove her innocence. So I agree as well."

Rodger smiled and nodded. "I also agree. Thanks for your help, partner." He patted Michael on the back.

Ignoring the friendly gesture, already being in "work mode," Michael began. "First off, you three do whatever I say. I'm dispassionate enough to keep us from making mistakes that will get us caught. So if I say to do something, you three will do it."

Michael closed his eyes and pointed up, visualizing his mental task list. "Second, we have two new detectives on the case: Kyle Aucoin and Dixie Olivier. They can't know anything about this agreement. Sam. Richie. If you run into them, give them short, honest answers and then disengage. Don't give them reason to suspect anything."

Michael continued, turning to face the two writers. "Third, we have a short period of time for everyone to get on the same page. Sam and Richie, Rodger and I have a lot to catch you up on. Some of it, particularly what happened yesterday, is really horrific stuff. What we need from you two is for you both to just listen. Let us get out this glut of information. Then, in kind, we'll let you all tell us anything we may need to know. Finally, after that, we can plan our next move."

Michael's proposition seemed agreeable to everyone present. So for the next hour, Michael and Rodger, taking turns, recounted their investigation over the past three days. Although Sam and Richie kept to their word and didn't interrupt, both looked positively horrified at what had transpired so far, especially the events at Mad Monty's warehouse.

When they were finished, Sam, who had been sitting on the edge of her seat, leaned back and fanned herself. "Honestly, what's happened to you two is as crazy as what's happened to me."

Looking over at Richie, Sam gently slapped his forearm and said, "You sure we're all not in one of your stories?"

Richie, who had started sweating profusely during the telling of the events with Mad Monty, fanned himself as well. To Sam's query, Richie shook his head.

"I don't think I'd write something about a person getting pulverized by a machine. That's"—he paused for a moment—"a little too dark for me."

Rodger shook his head and said, "You should try living it, Richie. It's a whole different kind of nightmare."

As Richie, who had since gotten the coffeepot from the kitchen, poured another cup for everyone, Sam said, "What gets me is what that Fontenot guy said to you all as you left."

Michael blinked, having forgotten what Sam was talking about. "What do you mean, Sam?" asked Michael. "What about what Fontenot said?"

Sam said, "He said that the snake is the most dangerous creature because the snake knows. That's a warning from the Haitian voodoo religion. It means that your enemy already knows what you are doing, and will likely turn your actions against you."

Sam got a thoughtful look. "Something like that. It's a warning to be careful where you tread."

Michael sighed and shook his head. "Well, folklore and superstition don't really fall into the logical boundaries of a murder investigation. So how is this relevant, Sam?"

"First off," said Sam, standing up and leaning on her desk, "Robert Fontenot knows something he wasn't telling you, but he tried to warn you all, Rodger especially, that the enemy, the killer perhaps, knows you both are investigating.

"Second, it made me think of a possible angle to all this," Sam continued, moving out from behind her desk and walking along the wall of her study toward her sizable bookcase. "It's just that my grandfather had an interest in the occult. He always claimed people were limited by how much of their brains they used. With time, he thought, we could live forever, and that pain and suffering brought out the full potential in people."

Michael nodded at Sam. "Yes, and during his trial, your grandfather was shown to have occult magazines, dealing in voodoo and witchcraft and other nonsense. Again, what does that have to do with the investigation now?"

Sam reached her bookcase and started looking for a book. "While that stuff is superstition, like you say, there is always a kernel of truth. Usually, it's people making things happen to manipulate others, other times it's science that appears to be like magic. I'll show you what I mean."

Richie and Rodger seemed engaged with whatever it was Sam was talking about, as they were watching her intently. Michael, on the other hand, felt that the conversation was going off topic. However, trying to be patient, he asked, "Sam, please explain what you mean."

Sam nodded, pulling out a large black book titled *Modern Vodoun*. Opening it, Sam turned the book around to show a picture of a dark-skinned man directly in front of what looked like half a dozen shambling people with dead looks in their eyes. The caption read "Zombi."

Sam began to explain. "See, we fictionalize zombies as reanimated corpses, while in voodoo, they are people who have been heavily drugged for forced menial labor. The reality is that there are no zombies, but the fictional idea we have of them is based on this fact."

Michael spoke again, "That's nice, Sam, but please explain to me how this pertains to the investigation."

Sam shuffled through the book. "What Robert Fontenot was talking about, with the comments about snakes, are called loa, powerful spirits that serve the voodoo version of God. They can be animal spirits similar to Native American totems. Or spirits of the dead that have ascended to minor deities. Or even gods from the old world. Loa, according to voodoo, not only guard us, but can influence us, harm us, empower us, and even possess us."

Michael shook his head in disbelief that this conversation was even taking place. He also wondered why someone like Sam would give it any credence.

Sam, seeing Michael shake his head, said, "Now wait a minute, Michael, I'm not saying this is real, but stuff like voodoo is powered by belief. A lot of people allow the occult or superstition to influence their everyday decisions. Many world leaders, good and bad, have placed faith in the supernatural. Abraham Lincoln had dream interpreters, for example, and Adolf Hitler routinely used astrologers."

Michael, who was feeling increasingly less tolerant, said, "I don't allow ridiculous beliefs to influence my decisions. And I think it's preposterous that a grown woman like you would place any stock in ghost stories."

Sam looked hurt for a moment, then furrowed her brow and said, "Michael, it's not about whether what you believe is real or not, it's about what others, like the killer, believe. I mean, there are too many occult references in my grandfather's past, as well as what is happening now, to be a coincidence. Someone in the past, like my grandfather, and someone presently, is using the concept of voodoo and loas as either a motivation or an excuse to commit murder."

Sam turned the page in the voodoo book. "Take this passage, for instance: 'Loa can physically influence the world around them by piggybacking on, and in extreme cases, possessing a host after a ritual is performed to call down, or summon, the loa. The direct influence of a loa is always preceded by—'"

"Stop right there, Sam," interrupted Michael, who felt his patience finally wearing thin. "So you think someone is using, or did use, these serial murders in a more sacrificial or religious way?"

Sam sighed, a look of pity crossing her face. Michael arched an indignant eyebrow at her.

Placing the book back where she got it, Sam nodded to Michael. "Why not? There has to be a reason for these murders, right? Why not have them be connected to voodoo or something similar? This is New Orleans. Haitian voodoo is practiced here. Why can't the murders be connected to a voodoo cult?"

"Because of one reason," said Michael, trying to get the conversation back on track. "Unless Rodger and Edward, along with everyone else in the New Orleans Police Force, missed something, there was never a single shred of evidence pointing to any voodoo cult. Even less so in the current investigation."

Richie suddenly spoke up. "What about that person or group you mentioned who contacted Topper Jack and Mad Monty? You know, the Nite Priory."

Everyone turned to Richie, who continued, "Sounds religious to me. Maybe Sam is right, Michael? Think about it for a minute. Vincent Castille had an interest in the occult, all that loa and zombie stuff Sam just mentioned. So what if this Nite Priory is a cult, or something similar, that is romanticizing what Vincent Castille did, and is using his interest in the occult to act like some kind of directive or something for murder."

"I hate to say this," Rodger said to his partner, "but Richie and Sam both have points. We've been looking at these murders as being the work of some sort of lone psychopath. But what if it is a cult? What if it's more organized than we thought?"

Before Michael could answer, Rodger continued, "And as for twenty years ago, Michael, you can't be sure there wasn't something that might have been religious. When the doc was arrested, there was a glut of occult magazines and clippings with him. He never spoke of it in trial, even though the defense tried to use it for an insanity defense, but there *was* evidence that he might have been involved a cult of some sort. Who's to say that this Nite Priory, as Richie was getting at, isn't a remnant of that now?"

Sam nodded and said, "Right. I don't know why my grandfather committed those murders. No one does. And you, Michael, even mentioned that no one looked into 'why' twenty years ago."

Michael nodded, feeling his incredulousness dropping as the other three started to make more sense to him. "Agreed. I've always felt that the 'why' is vital to this investigation and that it being overlooked was a big mistake."

Michael looked over at Rodger.

Rodger frowned, saying, "We were all in such a hurry to stop the murders that we did drop the ball on why he did it. And no one wanted to follow up on the voodoo thing once the trial had started. What did Ouellette say back then? Ah yes, that it was better to focus on putting Vincent on death row and being done with it."

Nodding at his partner, Michael wasn't too surprised to hear that his commander didn't put much stock in the occult back then. Ouellette had always struck him as being an extremely logical person, not one to buy in to nonsense.

Michael looked back at Sam and said, "All right, I'm willing to entertain this cult angle in things, especially since there is a 'Nite Priory' that keeps popping up."

Michael shifted in his seat. "But now, Sam, I have a question for you."

As Sam returned to her seat, Michael asked, "In your story, who is the murderer?"

Sam looked about as surprised as could be at that question. "Wait, what? Why do you want to know?"

"Because I believe someone is setting you up," replied Michael. "We need to show that this is the result of someone getting ahold of your notes or your manuscripts. The sooner we do that, the sooner you won't be a suspect. If you tell me now who your murderer is, we can use that to start setting a trap."

Michael chuckled and added, "Besides, you may give us a lead."

Sam lowered her head in thought. After a long moment, she looked up and said, "My murderer is Dallas Christofer."

Michael, Richie, and even Rodger sat there in total silence. Michael had no idea who this person was, and from the look of confusion on Rodger and Richie's faces, neither did they.

Finally, Michael shook his head, shrugged, and said, "I'll bite. Who is that?"

Sam looked a bit annoyed as she began to explain herself. "Dallas Christofer was the only survivor of a Bourbon Street Ripper murder. He was buried alive with his mother, Maple Christofer—Grandfather's last victim."

"Holy crap," said Rodger suddenly. "I remember that! Wait, it was Kyle Aucoin who found Maple and her son. He was alive? Holy shit, I thought he had died. Wait, no, he was committed to an institution, right?"

Sam nodded. "Yeah, committed to the Acadia Vermillion Hospital in Lafeyette. As far as I know, that is where he is to this day."

Michael was silent, but his eyes were widening. In his head, a lightbulb went off.

Acadia Vermillion Hospital. Wait, wasn't that where Sam *was committed?*

Michael got excited. This couldn't be a coincidence. "Sam, that is sheer brilliance. You may have solved this case."

Again, the room got silent.

Sam asked, "Are you serious, Michael?"

Michael cleared his throat. "I mean, has anyone else in this room thought to check up on Dallas Christofer?"

The obvious "no" came quickly, and Michael continued, "Okay, it's a long shot, I agree, but it can't hurt, Rodger, for us to follow up with the Acadia Hospital and see if Dallas is still there, or if he was discharged, or even escaped."

"Brilliant idea," said Richie, giving Michael an approving nod. "We should get going right away, yes?"

"Not so fast," said Michael, asserting his control over the scenario again. "Remember, we do this my way, and while this Dallas thing is a great lead, it could just as well be a red herring."

Michael's statement got agreeing nods from the room, and so he continued, "Rodger, we still have two accomplices left. I believe that Fat Willie is next. One of us should head to Angola

State Prison to talk with him. The other should head to Lafayette and check up on Dallas. We can deal with Blind Moses in Jackson Square tomorrow."

After a few moments' thought, Rodger said, "Let me handle Fat Willie. I have contacts—old friends—in Angola and should be able to get myself in easily."

Michael nodded approvingly. "Good. I'll handle going to Lafayette and the Acadia Hospital. Sam, you—"

"I'm going with Rodger to Angola," replied Sam.

"Um, no," replied Michael. "First off, we're doing things my way, and I want you to search old articles for references to that voodoo stuff. Second, I can't imagine them letting a civilian into the state penitentiary. Third, why would you want to go?"

Sam inhaled, then sighed, saying, "Because Rodger is going."

Michael looked at Sam, who had the most adamant and un-yielding look on her face, and then at Rodger, who looked simply terrified. Michael blinked and starting rubbing the area between his eyes.

This is a mess, but maybe these two need to talk their problems out. Maybe, just maybe, for once I should follow my gut and let these two go together.

Michael looked to his partner, and asked, "Is there was a way to get Sam into the state prison?"

Rodger, who still looked horrified, managed to mutter, "I can swing it if I pull in some favors."

Sam nodded and smiled at Michael. "Good. We'll take my car. Michael, that should give you use of the squad car, yes?"

Michael, still rubbing between his eyes, nodded.

"So?" asked Richie, who at this point was looking around the room. "Um, what do I do? Go with Sam and Rodger? Go with you, Michael?"

Jump off a cliff, Michael thought to himself.

After a moment, Michael said, "You can check up on the old Bourbon Street Ripper murders and see if there is any voodoo cult connection. Also, see if there is anything about this 'Nite Priory' that you can find."

Richie nodded, then patted Sam on the back, saying, "So we'll meet back here tonight?"

"Probably a good idea," said Sam, getting up to start tidying up the room. "We can meet back here, compare notes, have dinner. That sort of thing."

Rodger said, "Dinner would be nice." He looked like he was starting to recover from his shock at the idea of being alone with Sam. He got up, patted Michael on the back, and went to help Sam with the dishes.

Michael went back to rubbing between his eyes. This was going to be a long day.

Richie, left alone with Michael, asked, "Hey, you okay? Can I get you anything?"

Feeling an overwhelming surge of sarcasm, one that supplanted the desire to simply cry and give up, Michael answered, "Cyanide, please."

Chapter 19
Richie's Routine Day

Date: **Friday, August 7, 1992**
Time: **1:00 p.m.**
Location: **New Orleans Public Library**
               Downtown

After leaving Sam's townhome, Richie headed straight back to the Ritz-Carlton, got changed, ordered a quick lunch of fried oysters, and did an Internet search on where the public library was located. Wading through web directories, Richie eventually found what he was looking for—the library was located on Loyola Avenue. Jotting down the address and grabbing a briefcase filled with pens and notebooks, Richie wasted no time in leaving his hotel room and catching a cab to the library.

On the way to the library, Richie organized his thoughts on what he needed to accomplish. Part of him had become extra-anxious over the sudden pressure of being involved with two members of the New Orleans Police Department in a real-life investigation, while another part saw this as the perfect chance to help Sam.

Richie hadn't been particularly fond of the idea of Sam gallivanting off with Rodger to Angola, even though it seemed they had something that they needed to talk about. What he had wanted was to be the one to pair off with Sam.

As Richie exited the cab and paid the driver, he suddenly realized he was jealous of Rodger. As the taxi pulled off, the novelist stood there and stared into space for a long moment, then became half-cognizant of his legs carrying him to a nearby bench, a sudden dizziness having overcome him. His head was spinning, and suddenly he felt like he was going to be sick. The sudden onset of the nausea was unsettling, and he bowed his head and thought for a moment on why this might be happening.

Richie was not the kind to fall just for any woman, but as he looked back at his behavior since he had met Sam, he began to wonder. Every time he thought about her, Richie felt his heart start beating harder, his hands start shaking, and his throat start to get dry. It was the most unsettling feeling he had ever had. As he sat there on the bench, vision and sense coming back into focus, the sudden dizziness fading away, Richie said, "Holy shit . . . I think I'm falling in love with her."

Turning his attention back to the task at hand, Richie headed inside the library. He wasn't sure what he was expecting, but it wasn't what he ended up seeing. Perhaps it was due to him spending most of his youth in the Carnegie Library of Pittsburgh, with marble floors, flying buttresses, and sweeping, elegant staircases, but upon seeing the interior of the main building of New Orleans Public Library, he couldn't help but feel disappointed.

It was just a typical library, with rows of bookshelves, a reading area full of tables and chairs, and an area with a dozen or so computers. Directly in front of Richie was the large semicircular desk of the librarians, with the card catalog wrapped all the way around it.

Taking a breath in, Richie gathered himself and stepped forward, up to the librarian desk. Most of the librarians were busy checking out books, checking in books, or updating the card catalog. Overseeing the entire operation was a woman who looked to be at least two hundred years old, her skin more wrinkled than a sun-dried prune, her nose pointier than the tip of a knife, and her lips puckered so tightly that just being alive must taste exceedingly sour to her.

Avoiding Madame Skellington, Richie headed over to another librarian, a young woman with shoulder-length brunette hair and hazel eyes, who looked to be college age, just as she finished updating a card. Clearing his throat, Richie got the young woman's attention. He was completely shocked when she took one look at him and gave a loud gasp.

"It's you," said the young woman so loudly that several dozen heads turned toward the commotion. Richie felt his ears burn and instinctively shrank back.

"Yvonne Baudelaire," snapped the living mummy of a librarian, "that is not a proper way to act. Keep your voice down."

"Sorry, Miss Dubois," said Yvonne, blushing hard. Turning back to Richie, she asked, "How can I help you today, sir?"

Despite being caught off guard by Yvonne's outburst, Richie quickly recovered. Figuring this woman to be a fan of his, he turned on the charm and asked, "If you don't mind, maybe you can you show me where the microfiche readers are located?"

As quick as a roadrunner, Yvonne was out from behind the desk and, motioning for Richie to follow, headed between the rows of books.

"This is so cool," Yvonne said in a low voice as she led Richie through the stacks of books toward the back. "I had heard that you were in town, but I could never have dreamed that I'd ever meet you in person."

Feeling the rush of being in control, Richie said, "And I never dreamt such a pretty young lady would be helping me."

Yvonne's ears turned bright red.

Once in the back, the young woman showed Richie a door marked "microfiche" and unlocked it for him. Still flushing, Yvonne said, "Sir, you'll have to sign in to use the room, but I'll make sure you aren't bothered about it until you're done."

"That's very sweet of you, Yvonne," replied Richie. Looking into her eyes, he touched her hand gently. "Please make sure that I'm not disturbed for the next couple of hours, okay?"

If Yvonne had nodded and run off any faster, she would have gotten whiplash. Watching her leave, Richie chuckled to himself and shook his head. "So easy it should be a crime."

Letting himself inside the microfiche room, Richie turned on the lights. The room was quite cool and had a scent of acetate.

There was a single long table on the back wall to lay out microfiches ready to be scanned, and through another door was the reader and film catalogs.

Richie put his briefcase down on the table and moved to the catalog room, where the acetate scent was positively pungent. He started thumbing through the archives, looking for slides related to the investigation, trial, and execution of the Bourbon Street Ripper. After a few minutes, Richie had pulled several slides and decided to take a break. Leaning against the catalog, his mind started to wander, and thoughts of Sam began to emerge.

Despite his charm, Richie rarely gave any woman a thought once she was out of his presence. The fairer sex, although enjoyable, never had a lasting reaction in him. And yet, for the second time in less than hour, Richie started thinking about Sam. And for the second time in less than an hour, Riche began to wonder if he was falling for this woman.

His thoughts started with her smile and blue-gray eyes, then that sandy blond hair that she usually wrapped back. Then his thoughts went, literally, southward, Richie visualizing the curve of her chest in the blouse she had worn that morning, the way her jeans hugged her womanly hips, and the way they swayed as she walked. As Richie caught himself fantasizing about Sam, he felt a sudden surge of anxiety wash over him. It didn't make any sense to him, but it felt like something inside was clawing away at his gut. Taking out his bottle of pills, Richie popped one into his mouth and swallowed.

"What the hell is wrong with me?" Richie said to himself, taking out another pill. He was about to swallow it when he felt the anxiety within him start to subside, the placebo effect he had come to rely upon lately kicking in once again.

"When I get back to Pittsburgh, I'm going to make an appointment with my therapist," said Richie as he put the extra pill in his shirt pocket.

Placing the pill bottle on top of the cabinet, Richie returned to the task of fishing through the microfiche for articles pertaining to the Bourbon Street Ripper.

It was a quarter past five and Richie was still scanning articles when something caught his eye.

It was a photograph taken several months before the murders started. Vincent Castille was posing with a gaunt-faced woman, a heavier-set man, and a younger gentleman outside of some kind of mansion. The caption read, "Modern Priory donates millions to Southern Baptist Hospital. Social elite give sizable donation for restoration and upgrade of medical facilities. Shown here: Vincent Castille, Gladys Castille, Gerald Robichaux, and Jonathon Russell."

"Priory? Could this be the same as the Nite Priory?" Richie asked out loud, starting to feel a rush of excitement. He read through the article.

While it didn't use the term "Nite Priory," the article did detail the group as being a society related to the carnival krewe Comus. Checking back through his notes, Richie remembered that Comus was the most exclusive of the carnival krewes, with membership often restricted to the wealthiest families with the highest status. Highly exclusive and highly ritualized, the members were known for secretive initiations, midnight gatherings, and a rigid hierarchal structure. They even wore black, hooded robes for their meetings.

"Creepy stuff," Richie said to himself as he copied all the information down.

A sudden knock on the door to the microfiche room jarred Richie out of his research. From the other side of the door, he heard the harrowing voice of Miss Dubois.

"Sir, the library will be closing soon, and you are required to sign in and out of the microfiche room. If you do not come out this instant and do so, I will be forced to call the police."

Richie felt his heart increase at that threat. This was exactly what Michael had told him to avoid, getting on the police's radar. As quickly as he could, Richie turned off the reader, grabbed his notes, and headed out the door. Standing there, looking like one of those loa from Sam's voodoo book, was Miss Dubois, holding out the microfiche room form.

Richie smiled nervously as he signed in and out, nearly dropping the pad as he handed it back to the old woman. After she looked it over and snorted dismissively, she said, in a tone that could skin a cat, "Have a nice day."

Wanting nothing more to do with the mummy's wife, Richie hastily headed toward the exit.

He was halfway out the door when Yvonne, like a true groupie, was right beside him, holding the door open for him.

"Sorry about Miss Dubois," said Yvonne as the two stepped outside. "She can be a real bitch sometimes."

"Ah, it's fine, really," Richie replied with a smirk, forcing down his anxiety. "I'm used to working with difficult people. You should meet my publicist, Gordon. He can be a real ass sometimes."

As Yvonne giggled at that comment, Richie hailed a cab. Smiling at Yvonne and turning back on the charm, he said, "Thanks again for your help. Because of you, my next book will be even better."

This really seemed to make Yvonne's day, and as Richie got into the taxi, two girls about Yvonne's age came up to her. They squealed just as girlishly as she pointed Richie out.

Keeping up the suave smile, Richie gave them a polite wave and told the taxi to pull out. Just as he closed the door, he heard one of Yvonne's friends say, "I can't believe you actually met Dean Koontz!"

Richie's face fell, and his expression didn't change until he arrived at the hotel.

By the time he was back in his hotel room, Richie had recovered from his experiences at the library. Instead, he was focused on ordering dinner—a steak with potatoes and steamed vegetables—and then he sat down to call Sam.

Instead of Sam, however, Richie got the answering machine, and Sam's message was as subdued and sedate as one would expect. Leaving a message for her to call him, and that he had some important news, he then booted up his laptop computer and started to check his e-mail.

Amongst the usual junk, Richie saw an e-mail from Gordon, asking Richie to call him. The tone of the e-mail was curt and formal, and it made Richie's hair stand on edge. Quickly picking up the hotel phone, Richie called his publicist.

"Hello," answered Gordon, in what Richie could only call a monotone voice.

"Hey, Gordon," started Richie, trying to sound as jovial as possible. "How are things in Pitts—"

"Richie, where the hell are you?" interrupted Gordon. "I thought you'd be back here by now!"

Richie gritted his teeth, not liking the sharp tone of his publicist at all. Gathering himself, he replied with, "And I thought you'd be in New Orleans by now. What gives?"

"Check your e-mail, Richie," replied an unimpressed-sounding Gordon. "I was delayed so badly that I just canceled my flight. I caught your interview, by the way. Good job there. But that's not the point. I've been e-mailing you for two straight days. When are you coming back? We have only ten days to prepare for your trip to Seattle and Los Angeles. And Letterman wants you back after you return from California. And—"

"Jesus, slow down," retorted Richie. "You're giving me a headache." He took a deep breath. "So I am pretty much booked solid after ten days. I get it. But Gordon, you have to hear this. I am on the verge of something huge."

"What?" exclaimed Gordon. "What's going on over there? What are you doing?"

"Look, you remember the Bourbon Street Ripper story I was going to write after we were done with *The Pale Lantern*?" Richie began, hurriedly trying to come up with the words.

"Yes," replied Gordon. "What of it?"

"Well, check the news tonight, Gordon," Richie excitedly continued. "There is a copycat killer right now who is doing the same thing. And the granddaughter of the original Ripper, Samantha Castille, is a friend of mine."

There was a pause before Gordon said, "I'm listening. Go on."

Hurriedly, Richie laid out his plan to Gordon, emphasizing that he and Sam were working very closely. He left out the part about assisting in the actual police investigation.

"Hmmm," Gordon said as Richie finished. "Imagine that. Well, when do you think you'll be done with this little side trip?"

"I think that in three to four days, the investigation will wrap up," replied Richie. "From what I've seen, the police are really serious about catching this killer."

"Well, all right," answered Gordon, his voice not nearly as excited as Richie's, but still sounding quite interested. "You just keep me up-to-date on things, okay? I don't want to be left in the dark anymore."

Richie scribbled down a note to e-mail Gordon every morning. "Right. Will do."

"Okay, then," replied Gordon, sounding a bit tired from the conversation. "I trust you, Richie. And I guess it was a good thing that my ticket got lost. Otherwise, I don't think you'd be doing this right now, because I would have dragged your ass back to Pittsburgh."

Richie gave a sharp, forced laugh and said, "Probably. Anyway, I'm starving and my dinner should be here any moment. I'll e-mail you tomorrow morning."

"Good," said Gordon. "Take care, Richie."

Richie hung up the phone and walked over to his luggage.

"Good luck, my ass," he said as he reached into the recesses of his bags. Pulling out a plane ticket with the name "Gordon Rockway" on it, Richie slowly ripped it up. At first, he wasn't sure why he had stolen Gordon's ticket. It was something he had done almost on a whim, and guilt had been nagging at him. But now, with everything that had transpired so far, he was glad he did it. Gordon would have made meeting and working with Sam very difficult.

"Sorry I had to trick you, Gordon, but something inside tells me this is for the best."

Richie was just finishing up dinner when there was a knock on the door. For a moment, he sat there, holding a glass of wine, and wondered who it could be. A sudden rush of excitement overcame him as he thought, for a moment, that it might be Sam. Quickly, he got up and opened the door.

What he was expecting to see was Sam, and possibly Rodger. What he saw was a woman a few years older than Sam, perhaps in her midthirties, with auburn-red hair that fell to either side and partially over her face. The woman had auburn eyes and was attractive in that "I can kick your ass" sort of way. She wore a long black coat over a dark blue shirt and a pair of black pants.

Even before Richie could ask who this tough chick at his door was, the woman whipped out a police badge and said, "Mr. Richard Fastellos? I'm Detective Dixie Olivier. My partner and I would like to have a word with you." Richie closed the door to his room.

Why are the police here? Are they already on to me? Did they follow me from Sam's house? Wait, why would they even be at Sam's house? Holy shit, did they arrest Sam already?

Richie reached into his pocket to fish out his pill bottle. Instead of feeling the comforting plastic tube, he felt only emptiness and lint. Richie's heart started pounding. Where was his anxiety medicine?

"Mr. Fastellos, please open up the door," said Dixie, knocking on the door.

Richie's mind raced as he tried to remember where he had left his pill bottle. Sweat began to bead up on his brow as he remembered taking the bottle out and popping a pill in the microfiche room at the library. The library!

"Oh God. I can't believe it," moaned Richie to himself.

There was another knock on the door, followed by Detective Olivier saying, "Mr. Fastellos. It's very important that we talk to you immediately. If necessary, we will come back with a warrant."

Richie's hands were trembling as the anxiety attack continued to come on. Sliding down to his butt, he buried his face in his hands.

"Mr. Fastellos," Dixie said, now clearly agitated, "I'm giving you one last chance to open up, then I'm going to get a warrant."

One last! The detective's words triggered something in Richie's mind. He had one last pill in his shirt pocket! His fingers trembled as he reached into his pocket, searched around, and pulled out the pill. He could take this pill now, deal with the police, and then go get his prescription refilled in the morning.

Richie took three deep breaths, fighting back the nausea from the anxiety attack. Forcing the pill down, he got up and began composing himself. Just taking the pill was enough to start settling his nerves. *It's okay. Tell them they scared you. Play it off. It'll be okay.*

Continuing to breathe in and out, Richie formulated an explanation for his behavior. Finally calm enough, he opened the door and smiled pleasantly at Dixie, who was noticeably scowling at him.

"Sorry," Richie said. "I was just writing something very hardcore for my next book, and you scared the crap out of me."

"Scared you?" replied Dixie. "Do you have reason to be scared of the police?"

Richie chuckled, shook his head, and winked at Dixie. "No, of course not. You know who I am, correct?"

"You're Richard Fastellos," replied Dixie flatly, "the author of *The Pale Lantern.*"

"Right, right," replied Richie. "Well, I was writing something for my next book from the killer's point of view and I'm afraid you got me while thinking like a murderer."

Dixie smiled pleasantly enough at him and nodded her head toward the interior of the hotel room. "May I come in?"

Richie smiled back, the situation with Sam giving him a clear course of action. "I think I'd rather talk out in the hall. Unless you have that warrant you talked about?"

Dixie's pleasant turned into a smirk. She shook her head as she stepped back and said, "Well, why don't we go downtown, then? We can give you some coffee and have a nice long chat."

Richie's lips ached as he kept his smile up, the pill fighting back any more anxiety. He exhaled, chuckled, and then asked, "Well, am I a suspect? Do I need to call my lawyer?"

"If you were a suspect, Mr. Fastellos, I'd be treating you completely differently," said Dixie.

Richie felt her eyes searching him, as if sizing him up.

"Right now, you're a potential witness. However"—Dixie's voice suddenly got stern, her eyes piercing—"if you keep acting like this, like a suspect, then I'm going to start treating you like one."

Richie felt he had more to lose than to gain by continuing to be evasive. He said, "Let me get my wallet. I'll be with you in a moment."

In the hotel lobby, Richie and Dixie were joined by another detective, a man about Rodger's age, but with considerably less hair.

"This is my partner, Detective Kyle Aucoin," said Dixie.

"A pleasure to meet you, Mr. Fastellos," said Aucoin as he shook Richie's hand. "Thank you for speaking with us this evening."

The two detectives escorted Richie through the lobby toward the outside.

As Richie walked along, he glanced toward the bar and restaurant. A flash of red caught his eye, and life slowed down for Richie as he caught the gaze of the Lady in Red. Seated at the bar, between two heavy-set and dangerous-looking men, the lady gave Richie a serious look, and then shook her head.

In a moment, the novelist was past the entrance of the bar, life having sped back up to normal, and the Lady in Red was out of eyesight.

What's going on? Why would the Lady in Red do that? Am I now in some sort of danger?

The two detectives escorted Richie to their squad car and drove him downtown to the 8th District police precinct. The building was abuzz with activity, and as Aucoin and Dixie led Richie to one of the interview rooms, the novelist saw that there was a large board with the pictures of both serial murderers' victims on it, and a handful of uniformed officers being given orders by a bald man who looked to be in charge.

Richie looked at everything thoughtfully. *The copycat killer thing must really have everyone riled up.*

Richie was shown into a room with a table and a set of chairs. It was like any police interview room he had ever imagined, complete with barred windows, a one-way mirror, and a thermostat, for literally "sweating out" a potential perpetrator.

"Really?" asked Richie, looking over at Aucoin and Dixie as they led him inside, motioning toward the table. "I'm a witness, and you're interviewing me in an interrogation room? Are you serious?"

"Sorry about that, but we don't actually have comfortable lounges for witnesses," Aucoin said as he slid back a chair for Richie to sit in. "Can we get you anything? Water? Coffee, perhaps?" Aucoin turned toward his partner. "Dix, can we get some coffees in here?"

"Whatever, Kyle, sure," Dixie snapped at her partner and then left the interview room. Richie rolled his eyes and shook his head.

As Aucoin turned back to him, Richie, who had folded his arms and was feeling rather indignant, said, "Look, Detective Aucoin, I write mysteries for a living. I know the good cop, bad cop routine. I also know that the way detectives try to get confessions is by buddying up to their suspects. You're going to be the good cop, Dixie's going to be the bad cop. It's really boring.

"And lastly," Richie said, cocking his head to the side and staring right at Aucoin, "I know that, unlike in every crime drama ever written, I can end this interview whenever I want."

Aucoin just smiled at Richie. "Well, you have all the answers, don't you?"

Standing up and loosening his tie, the detective walked over behind Richie, and patted his shoulders. "And I assume you know that me touching you is police brutality, and me calling you a fucking smartass"—Aucoin leaned down and whispered in Richie's ear—"and saying I'm going to rip your nuts off if you talk down to me again, is abuse."

Standing up, Aucoin patted Richie gently on the back, walked over to the other side of the tables, and took a seat, still smiling. "I can assure you that for now, Mr. Fastellos, you are a witness. But if you keep copping an attitude with me, considering the immense strain I'm under right now, I'll find a reason to lock your smart ass up until this investigation is over."

Richie's face had grown stony, and his eyes had gotten very focused on the detective in front of him. His jaw clenched and he felt a rush of rage. He imagined what it would be like to punch Aucoin in the face repeatedly for giving him such a hard time. It would be satisfying to see Aucoin's teeth punched out, his nose broken.

Closing his eyes, Richie inhaled slowly, then exhaled just as slowly. When he opened his eyes, the dark feelings had passed, the pill still doing its job. Richie said in a steady voice, "My apologies. I was out of line."

Holding out his hands in a friendly gesture, smile broadening, Aucoin said, "See? Now we can be friends.

"And speaking of friends," Aucoin continued as Dixie returned with a tray of coffees, "what we want to talk about is your new friend, Samantha Castille."

Richie wasn't the least bit surprised. "Sam Castille," he said. "Well, we've only just met. What about her?"

Handing Richie a coffee in a disposable cup, Dixie said, "You call her Sam instead of Samantha? You sure you two have just met?"

Richie frowned for a moment, thinking to himself that Dixie was way more perceptive than he was comfortable with. Looking her in the eyes and seeing a calculating look, Richie realized that he was about to enter a battle of wits over information that could be used to incriminate Sam.

He was just glad that, by now, the anxiety medicine was flowing through his system. He could think clearly. He could psyche them out like he had psyched Kent out yesterday. *I just need to make sure they don't get anything that can be used against Sam.*

Taking the coffee cup, Richie sipped at it thoughtfully before saying, "Well, she asks everyone to call her Sam. It's like saying Chris for Christina, or Alex for Alexandra, ya know?"

"Ah, so that explains the familiarity," said Aucoin, taking the coffee handed to him by his partner. Aucoin took a sip. "And yet, you were seen at Miss Castille's house this morning."

With that, Richie realized that his initial fear was true. They were staking out Sam's house. Biting on his bottom lip, he wondered just how much the two detectives knew.

Do they know about Rodger and Michael?

Deciding that it was entirely possible, Richie chose his next words very carefully. "We're both writers, Detective. It's a bond that's as strong as, well, the bond between fellow policemen. For someone like myself, that's one of the things I live for—visiting with a fellow author."

"I find it hard to believe that there isn't something else there," replied Dixie, having taken her seat. "Fellowship is one thing, but who goes over to a single woman's house early in the morning just to talk about writing?"`

"She's not bad-looking," added Aucoin, winking at Richie. "Are you two, ya know, closer than just professional?"

Richie sipped his coffee and stared at Aucoin. He was really starting to dislike this guy. Having Dixie hit him with the hard questions was one thing, but Aucoin's attitude had a cockiness about it that made Richie want to throw boiling oil on his face.

Richie decided to take an over-the-top approach. He chuckled and shook his head, saying, "Between you and me, Detective Aucoin, I wish. I think Sam is pretty hot, but that's not how she sees me. Nope, our relationship is purely professional."

Richie leaned back and swished his coffee around in his cup.

That seemed to derail the routine Aucoin and Dixie were working on, and from what Richie could see, they were immediately changing tactics. Dixie sat back, tapped her index finger on the table three times, and turned to Aucoin. "Ya know, this is all fun and everything, the testosterone trip, but we should start asking him the questions we're supposed to ask him."

Richie caught on to the three taps and felt a sense of satisfaction. He easily recognized it as some sort of code between partners.

"Right, right," replied Aucoin as he leaned forward, looking more intently at Richie from across the table. "We have some questions about this morning. First off, Mr. Fastellos, what did you and Miss Castille talk about this morning?"

Richie considered his answer. The two detectives seemed pretty good at what they did. Aucoin seemed to have the "act" down, and Dixie was uncomfortably perceptive. Richie reasoned that bullshitting them probably wouldn't work and figured that being transparent would best give him a chance to push Sam's alibi forward.

"We're working on a joint project concerning these serial murders," Richie said, swishing his coffee around some more. "I'm going to be writing a True Crime novelization of the investigation while Sam is writing a fictionalized version of the murders."

"Yes, we saw her first chapter," Dixie said, looking steadily into Richie's eyes. "Hardly a 'fictional' account of the murders."

Before Richie could reply, Aucoin spoke up. "Yeah, that was pretty disturbing, Richie, to have her chapter be identical to the murder scene."

Aucoin shrugged at Richie, asking, "Any idea how that happened?"

Again, Richie felt that honesty was the best course of action.

"Believe you me," he said with a shrug of his own, "if I knew the answer to that, Detective, I wouldn't have spent the entire morning comforting a grown woman who was having a nervous breakdown."

"Pretty convenient, Mr. Fastellos, that you are the only one to be at that grown woman's house to say how she was reacting," replied Dixie, smirking at him as if she didn't believe a word he was saying.

Before Richie could respond, Aucoin asked, "Were you with Miss Castille last night?"

Richie nodded and said, "Yes. We were having dinner at the Ritz-Carlton."

"Can you show us a receipt to prove that?" asked Dixie.

"No. Sam paid for the meal."

"What time did you two part ways for the evening?" asked Aucoin.

"I don't remember. We were pretty drunk."

"Again, this is all very convenient," replied Dixie, steadily gazing at Richie. "You and Sam have dinner last night, she pays for the meal, then she invites you over to her house the next morning." She shook her head. "Sounds like someone was creating an alibi last night, Mr. Fastellos. And you get to be that alibi."

Richie stared back into Dixie's eyes, feeling that she was gaining the upper hand in this interview. His mind raced, trying to sort through a way to take back the lead from her. He got a gut feeling that Dixie would momentarily abandon logic if she got angry. Thinking back on her questioning, Richie realized she was fixated on him being alone with Sam.

A moment later, Richie knew what he had to say.

Leaning back in his chair and adopting a playboy's sneer, Richie said, "Okay, Detectives, you got me. I wined and dined Sam last night in hopes of tapping that sweet ass of hers. Even though I got her shit-faced drunk, she wouldn't put out, so I sent her home to sleep it off. This morning, I went over to her house in hopes of getting some morning nookie. No dice, but I'll try again tomorrow."

The sound of a chair sliding against the floor resounded throughout the room as Dixie stood up with an angry look about her, her voice raised as she said, "You son of a bitch. I'll kick your teeth—"

"Whoa, whoa," said Aucoin, suddenly standing as well, gesturing for his partner to relax. "Calm down, Dix. Take five, okay? Take five."

Richie kept up the smirk. Again, the detectives were derailed. *Gotcha, bitch.*

Dixie walked to the back end of the interview room, running her fingers through her hair and huffing softly.

Aucoin sat back down and said, "Hey, sorry about my partner. She's on edge. We all are on edge. And she really hates chauvinistic comments like that."

Richie smirked, his guess about Dixie being a feminist right on target. "That's okay," he said, "because I'm bullshitting you both."

That seemed to catch both detectives off guard.

Richie felt a sense of accomplishment. With Dixie angry and both detectives derailed, all he had to do was give them the information he wanted them to walk away with, and end the interview.

Before either detective could respond, Richie said, "This interview has been a lot of fun, but it's starting to drag. So here's what you need to know from me, even if you don't want to hear it."

Clearing his throat, Richie began, "Last night, while Rebecca Clemens was being murdered, Sam was sleeping off being drunk. Like I told you, we had dinner at the Ritz-Carlton. She had an entire bottle of Lucien Le Moine 1983. I was just as sloshed. I put her in a cab. She went home. She passed out. I can promise you, Detectives, that Sam was in no condition to stalk, capture, and kill anyone last night."

The expressions on the two detectives' faces showed that they weren't expecting this turn in conversation. Slowly, Dixie's hands dropped and Aucoin's smile faded.

Richie continued, "When she saw that her story had the exact same timeline as the murder, she was genuinely terrified. You can't fake that kind of reaction. So I don't know who did it, or how, but it's not Samantha Castille."

"And why should we believe a goddamn word you're saying," asked Aucoin, his eyes narrowing, "when you just admitted you lied to us?"

Richie put his hands behind his head. "I don't care if you do or don't believe me. You two are treating Sam as a suspect. You're trying to get me to slip up and give information away that could incriminate her. I'm telling you that I don't have anything to give other than Sam was drunk last night and a nervous wreck this morning. So continuing this interview is a waste of time."

And just like that, Richie had taken control of the interview.

The two detectives straightened up, looked at each other, and nodded.

Dixie offered to take Richie's coffee, and he said, "I'm not quite finished, but thanks." She took hers and Aucoin's coffees and left. Aucoin stood up and straightened his tie.

"I guess we're wasting our time, then," he said. "Sorry for having taken up your evening."

Richie waved off Aucoin's comment and winked. "This was fun. And for the record, I am a smartass."

Shaking his head, Aucoin said, "Well, I'm glad you can laugh at this shit, Mr. Fastellos. People are dying out there and my partner and I are wasting time with your sorry ass."

Richie shrugged at Aucoin and said, "I don't solve mysteries, Detective. I just write them."

It was probably the biggest lie Richie had told all day.

Richie finished his coffee and put the cup down as Aucoin went over to the intercom and pressed the button, saying, "Interview's done. I'm getting Mr. Fastellos out of here."

While Aucoin had his back to him, Richie took a handkerchief out of his pocket and wiped down the coffee cup. He didn't know how desperate or crooked the New Orleans police department was, but he wasn't about to leave fingerprints that someone could use to frame him later on.

Richie had hidden the handkerchief before Aucoin returned to the table.

"One last thing," the detective said. "What did you do after leaving Sam's house?"

Richie nodded and said, "I went to the library to do research for my book—on something that came up in conversation."

"Oh?" Aucoin asked curiously, leaning in a bit. "Care to tell me what it is?"

Richie thought to himself that it couldn't hurt to be truthful about this one detail. "I was checking up on information pertaining to the 'Nite Priory.'"

That seem to satisfy Aucoin, who got a thoughtful look, nodded, and motioned for Richie to stand. "Thank you very much, Mr. Fastellos. You've been a great help."

"My pleasure," said Richie as he rose, wiping his sleeve over the area that he just touched. "I hope you all catch the sick bastard who's doing this."

"We will," replied Aucoin solemnly, looking at Richie with a piercing gaze and a slow nod of the head. "So help me God, we will."

With a return nod, Richie followed Aucoin out of the interview room. As he did, he reflected back on what should have been a fairly routine day of brainstorming a writing project. So far, he had gone on two dates with a murder suspect, found potentially important clues to the biggest mystery in New Orleans, and been interrogated by the police.

Richie chuckled inwardly.

Can't say today has been boring at all!

Chapter 20
Introducing Dr. Lazarus

Date: **Friday, August 7, 1992**
Time: **2:00 p.m.**
Location: **Acadia Vermillion Hospital**
               Lafayette, Louisiana

As he drove along the interstate heading toward the Acadia Vermillion Hospital in Lafayette, Junior Detective Michael LeBlanc mulled over recent events involving the investigation.

To say that he felt derailed was an understatement, and to say that he was more than annoyed by it was an even bigger one. Despite his disagreement with Rodger and him separating for the day, Michael had come to the realization that he needed time to himself. It was the perfect chance for him to think over this case.

First, there was the problem with letting civilians be a part of the investigation. Having Sam and Rodger go off together was bad enough, but Michael knew the two had to reconcile whatever was between them.

What really annoyed Michael was that they allowed someone not even related to the investigation get personally involved. To Michael, Richie was nothing more than a useless liability.

Another problem Michael had was that not enough effort was being put into discovering how the real killer was able to learn of Sam's manuscript before it was published.

While having lunch, Michael was able to come up with two plausible explanations: One, the killer worked at, or had connections with, the *Times-Picayune*, and therefore could intercept Sam's work before it went to publication. Two, the killer had somehow gotten a copy of Sam's work right after she wrote it.

Sam had stated that she had dropped off her manuscript at four o'clock the day of the murder. Michael had verified that drop-off time by calling the *Times-Picayune* and speaking with Jacob Hueber, Sam's liaison to the newspaper.

Therefore, of his two theories, the first was more possible, allowing for a warm body to easily take Sam's writings and tailor the murder to it; however, it gave very little wiggle room for time: the murderer would have had only five hours to get the manuscript, memorize the information, and commit the crime in a similar fashion.

But what disturbed Michael about this timeline was that Sam had several hours unaccounted for, having no solid alibi after dropping her manuscript off. If Sam was the killer, her time unaccounted for could be enough to prepare the location. And if Sam had already chosen the victim, all she would have had to do was leave the Ritz-Carlton after dinner, reroute her taxi to a location near where the victim was located, and commit the crime.

It's unlikely that Sam could pull this off if she was as drunk as she claimed to be, but if she was acting drunk—if she was deceiving Richie—then it's not impossible that she could have done it.

Putting that aside, Michael's mind turned to the third problem he was having in the investigation: people were withholding information from him. To Michael, it seemed that every time either Sam's father, Rodger's former partner, Edward, or details concerning the original Bourbon Street Ripper murders started to come up, something derailed the conversation.

There is something about the relationship between Rodger, Edward, Sam, Sam's father, and Vincent. It's almost like Sam's father stumbled upon something that got him killed. What was it? Did he solve the murder and die because of it?

Despite trying as hard as he could, Michael could not figure it out. Resigning himself to there still being something missing— some key piece of evidence—he instead focused on getting safely to his destination.

Soon, he was within the city limits of Lafayette, developed on the interstate cutting through Southern Louisiana and built primary on wetlands. Following his handwritten instructions, Michael turned north off the interstate, traveling just a few minutes before reaching the hospital.

Michael had expected the hospital to look more run-down, more ominous, considering that the hospital had been around for several decades. So he was pretty surprised when he drove past a motorized metal gate, up a paved driveway, past groves of freshly pruned cypress trees, and saw white-stucco, sparking clean buildings that looked fairly modern.

Parking in a space marked "visitor," Michael looked again at his notes on the hospital. Sure enough, this was the correct place, and looking out of the car window, he saw a covered walkway leading up to a building marked "Administration."

It was a short, brisk walk. Out and about on the lawn, patients dressed in white robes were walking, sitting, or being pushed along in wheelchairs by orderlies and nurses. The atmosphere was serene, and Michael found himself genuinely at peace.

Inside the hospital lobby, a comfortable room with gentle music, soothing aesthetics of cool colors, and large windows letting in healthy amounts of sunlight, Michael approached the front receptionist, a nurse who looked to be in her early twenties.

The nurse smiled at Michael and said, "Hey there, handsome, welcome to Acadia Vermillion Hospital. How may I help you today?"

Michael smiled and replied by showing his badge and saying, "Detective Michael LeBlanc, New Orleans Police, Homicide. I have an appointment to speak to Dr. Lazarus."

The nurse looked at Michael's badge, keeping up that pleasant smile and saying, "Director Lazarus is expecting you. Come this way, Detective."

With thanks, Michael followed the woman, who hugged a clipboard to her chest as she walked along the halls. Soon, Michael found himself being ushered through a door that had a plaque with "Director Lazarus, Ph.D." written on it.

The interior of the office was similar to Dr. Klein's, only far less neurotic and much more tasteful. The office had large windows along the exterior walls, with comforting artwork covering the interior walls. Soft flute music, melancholic and beautiful, played in the background. At the far end of the room was a single oak desk.

Dr. Lazarus sat behind his desk, looking outside the window, his back to Michael and his hands resting behind his back. The man had gray hair and wore a white doctor's coat.

"Director Lazarus," said the nurse, who had come in with Michael, "this is Detective Michael LeBlanc, from New Orleans."

"Thank you, Miss Cormier," replied Dr. Lazarus, with the kind of calm voice you'd expect from an older doctor who had seen it all. "You may go now. The detective and I have a lot to talk about."

"Yes, sir," replied Miss Cormier, who winked at Michael and then left.

Michael ignored the wink. Approaching the desk, he started to say something, but the doctor spoke instead. "Have a seat, Detective. So, you're here to talk about Dallas Christofer, correct?"

Dr. Lazarus turned to Michael. It was then that Michael realized that the doctor's chair was actually an electric wheelchair, controlled by a small stick on one of the rests. His face was old and had a burn scar on the right side, but otherwise he seemed very congenial. Smiling pleasantly, the doctor said, "I had a feeling, after hearing about the new serial murders, that someone would come."

He's lame. And a burn victim.

As Dr. Lazarus motioned for Michael to sit down, he noticed a strange tattoo on the doctor's wrist—a circle with an eye in the middle. Filing that away for later, Michael asked, "Before we get started with him, I have to ask you a strange question, Doctor. What do you know about Blind Moses?"

The doctor's gentle smile never faded as he shook his head. "Not as much as I'm sure you'd hoped. I am not surprised to hear her name come up, however." Now Michael realized why Douglas had chuckled at Rodger calling Blind Moses a man.

I get it now. Blind Moses is a woman. Ha! Old Rodger got the same stunt pulled on him that he pulled on me about Sam!

Michael's momentary amusement was pushed aside as the doctor invited him again to take a seat, this time with a more visible motion. As Michael did so, taking out his notebook and pen, he asked, "Well, if you don't mind indulging me a bit further, what do you know about Blind Moses?"

Dr. Lazarus replied, "Only that she worked closely with the original Bourbon Street Ripper, Dr. Vincent Castille. When I visited him in prison, Vincent mentioned her several times. I never actually met her."

Michael nodded, theorizing that Blind Moses must have had something to do with the voodoo stuff Sam was talking about. Even though he still found it ridiculous that a grown woman would believe in something like that, he was beginning to wonder if the theory of the present-day killings being carried out by a cult had some credence to it.

Filing that information away in his memory, and coming back from his thoughts, Michael followed up. "One more question unrelated to my visit, if I may. What was your relationship to Dr. Vincent Castille?"

Keeping up his soft smile, Dr. Lazarus said, "He was a colleague of mine in the field of neuroscience. We studied together at Tulane's School of Medicine. He was also a dear friend."

"Neuroscience?" asked Michael, his voice obviously perplexed. "I thought Vincent Castille was a surgeon."

"He was a surgeon, and a brilliant one at that," replied Dr. Lazarus, a reminiscent quality to his voice. "Never before and never since have I known a man with hands so skilled on the operating table. However, his true passion was the study of the mind. Like many in his field, Vincent believed that man could overcome any limitations by unlocking this." The doctor reached up and tapped the side of his head.

Michael sat there, thinking. This was the first time something like this had come up in the investigation. Wondering if Dr. Lazarus had even more pertinent information on Vincent Castille than he did on Dallas Christofer, Michael asked, "So, given our conversation, Doctor, do you have any idea why Vincent Castille became the Bourbon Street Ripper? Why he committed those horrific murders?"

To Michael's disappointment, Dr. Lazarus shook his head. "I am afraid not, Detective. I really wish I knew. Vincent was a good friend of mine, and we often traded research information. I was horrified to find out that he was the Ripper. I, and many other colleagues, all felt like he had betrayed everything we held dear as doctors."

Michael frowned. Another brick wall.

"But Vincent did become reclusive several months preceding the murders," the doctor said so suddenly that Michael was jarred out of his disappointment. "He wouldn't return my phone calls. He missed lunch dates. He missed guest lectures. He just shut himself off in that mansion of his at the lake."

As Michael took notes of that information, adding the Castille Mansion at Lake Pontchartrain to his list of places to investigate, Dr. Lazarus added, "Perhaps that will help your investigation."

"Perhaps," replied Michael, finishing his notes on the conversation so far.

A moment or so later, Michael said, "So, on the matter of Dallas Christofer. I'm here because one of the leads in the case points in Dallas's direction. I'm here to see if he's here, talk to him if possible, and find out what I can about him."

"Ah yes, indeed," replied Dr. Lazarus, shifting to sit up more in his seat. "The subject of Dallas Christofer is a delicate one at best. You see . . . well, perhaps it's best that I start by explaining what Acadia Vermillion Hospital is, as opposed to what it used to be."

"All right," replied Michael as he started taking notes again.

"This hospital is an addiction and behavioral modification facility," began Dr. Lazarus. "Over ninety percent of our patients are dealing with some kind of addiction, be it a substance addiction, gambling addiction, or even sexual addiction. The rest are patients who suffer from serious behavioral problems, such as uncontrolled anger, impulse control, or severe discipline issues."

Michael nodded, taking notes as Dr. Lazarus continued speaking.

"This facility is the best in the state at treating addiction and behavioral problems because of the research done during the seventies. During that time, and before then, this hospital housed people with severe emotional and traumatic disorders, often leading to violence and psychotic behavior."

Michael thought Dr. Lazarus's statement certainly made Dallas a favorable suspect. Michael wondered if Sam really was on to something with naming Dallas as her murderer.

Dr. Lazarus concluded, "So Dallas Christofer, and several others, are leftover patients reminiscent from those days. They are housed in the old building at the heart of the facility, and kept separate from the general populace."

"I see," said Michael as he finished his notes. "In your opinion, then, is Dallas Christofer dangerous? Would he be capable of murdering someone?"

At that, Dr. Lazarus chuckled. It wasn't a particularly unpleasant chuckle, but it had a sinister air to it. Finally, the doctor shook his head and said, "No, but I can see why you'd ask that."

Michael cocked an eyebrow. "Is that so? Why would you say that?"

Instead of answering, Dr. Lazarus turned on his wheelchair and moved to the front of the desk, saying, "Come with me, and I'll show you and explain everything."

Michael looked down and realized that Dr. Lazarus wasn't lame. He just didn't have any legs below the knees. *My God! What happened to this guy?*

Michael quickly got up, moving alongside the doctor. Surprisingly to Michael, Dr. Lazarus seemed adept at moving around his office. Michael, although impressed with the doctor's ability to maneuver an electric wheelchair, wondered how he lost his legs. However, he was unable to bring himself to ask.

As he headed out of his office and toward the elevator, electric wheelchair zooming along with a *whirring* sound, Dr. Lazarus said, "If you are investigating the old Bourbon Street Ripper murders as well as these new ones, Detective, then you undoubtedly know who Samantha Castille is, correct?"

"Yes, Dr. Lazarus," replied Michael, walking alongside the doctor. "I am well acquainted with Miss Castille. And I do recall that she was housed here for a short while after her father's death. What does that have to do with anything?"

Taking the elevator down, Dr. Lazarus continued, "I was the attending physician for both Dallas and Samantha. I'm guessing you know these details because of a certain so-called Dr. Klein, yes?"

The distaste he revealed as he said Klein's name was enough for Michael to ascertain that Dr. Lazarus had no use for Sam's psychiatrist either.

"Correct again, Doctor," replied Michael. He was impressed with the doctor's deductive abilities.

As the pair exited the building, Doctor Lazarus said to Miss Cormier, "The detective and I are heading toward the old building, Hold my calls, please."

Once he and Michael were outside, Dr. Lazarus continued, "That man has no business caring for someone like Samantha Castille. That girl's mind is so badly fractured that she, like Dallas, will likely never live a normal life. As it is, I'd wager that her ability to form emotional bonds is virtually nonexistent."

"I don't know about that," replied Michael, noticing that the foliage of the cypress trees was starting to thicken. "Sam seems very emotive and very friendly. I really don't think there is much wrong with her, outside of the obvious anxiety issues."

"And you're a doctor now, Detective," quipped Dr. Lazarus so quickly that Michael blushed.

Dr. Lazarus took in a breath and said, "When I first started treating Dallas and Samantha, I could see it. Inside them both was a ticking bomb of unfathomable rage and violence, just waiting for the right trigger to set them off. Remember, Detective, both children, at the age of ten, watched their parents tortured to death by that murderer. And in the case of Dallas, he was buried alive with his mother's remains."

"Yes. I remember the story of Dallas and Maple Christofer," replied Michael, who watched absently as Dr. Lazarus wheeled effortlessly along the now darkened path toward an old brick building, which indeed looked ominous, and in some places darkened, as if the mortar had been charred. "They were the last known victims, not counting Sam's father, of the Bourbon Street Ripper."

"Correct," answered Dr. Lazarus. As the two approached the door to the old building, two security guards, armed with side arms, opened the doors for them both.

Michael looked the two over and realized that the side arms were tranquilizer guns. He mulled over the presence of those weapons, thinking that this Dallas must pose a threat to people's safety after all.

Sam, if you end up being right about Dallas, I will buy you a steak dinner at Commander's Palace.

Once inside, Michael and Dr. Lazarus were joined by a pair of burly orderlies, who led the two downstairs and along a long corridor. Dr. Lazarus was silent during the walk, which gave Michael a chance to look around. Despite the exterior of the building looking dilapidated, the interior of this building was even more modern. The walls were made of polished metal, the ceilings had recessed fluorescent lighting, and the floors were made of tiled ceramic.

Michael did not know what to make of this facility. It was like he had just stepped into a science fiction television show. He was both amazed and incredulous. All he needed now to have his suspension of disbelief utterly destroyed was to pass by an open doorway where a group of surgeons were performing an alien autopsy.

But nothing of the sort happened. At the end of the corridor, right after a sign marked "Block A," they emerged in a larger circular room with many metal doors all around. The room itself had a raised ceiling with a balcony all around the outer rim, a second floor of sorts. Standing along this balcony at regular intervals were guards with what Michael recognized as tranquilizer rifles.

From inside those doors, Michael heard all sorts of sounds. From some rooms, he heard the sounds of laughing. From other rooms, he heard the sounds of conversation. And from other rooms, he heard the sounds of wailing, crying, and even screaming. It was extremely unpleasant, and despite his own emotional detachment, Michael found himself wanting to leave. *What is this place? How does such a facility exist?*

"This is Block A," explained Dr. Lazarus as the group moved past metal doors, screams of torment from within. "This block was one of four in this old building, and used to house children and adolescents suffering from psychotic conditions. Now it holds patients who are too unsafe to be part of the general population."

Eying the room where the horrendous screams were coming from, and wondering what demons could make a human make those noises, Michael found himself asking, "What happened to the other blocks?"

"Destroyed," said Dr. Lazarus. "Ah, here we are." He stopped in front of a metal door with the number six on it. One of the orderlies unlocked the door with what looked like a touch telephone's keypad.

Michael asked, "Wait, is it safe to go in like this? Shouldn't we have a guard with us?"

But Dr. Lazarus didn't answer, and instead just wheeled into room six. Clenching his jaw in a manner that felt uncharacteristically anxious, Michael followed him inside.

Inside the room, which was small and plain but comfortable-looking, and had a single bed, a sink, and a toilet, Michael came face-to-face with whom he could only assume was Dallas Christofer.

He was the complete opposite of what Michael had expected.

Crouched in the corner of the room was a man in his midthirties, short hair bald in several places, with a skinny frame. His entire body was badly scarred, as if he had been burned long ago. Every piece of his body was covered in scar tissue, his lips and most of his nose and ears were gone, and he wore a simple white patient gown. In his scarred hand was a piece of white chalk, and the man was busy rubbing the chalk along the wall and floor of his cell.

"This is Dallas Christofer," said Dr. Lazarus, "son of Maple Christofer, and the only survivor of the Bourbon Street Ripper."

Michael just stared at Dallas in disbelief. The burnt man didn't seem to notice that there were two people in his room, and instead just went on scribbling. Michael didn't know what to think, so he just turned to Dr. Lazarus. "So, what happened? Was he burned by Vincent?"

Dr. Lazarus shook his head and said, "No. When Dallas came to me, he was physically whole." He gave a heavy sigh.

"Let me start from the beginning. When Dallas and Samantha were brought to me, both children were suffering from severe psychotic fits. Both arrived here on the same day. If I remember the timeline, Dallas was found buried with his mother's remains underneath a cypress tree in a field owned by Vincent Castille, the police led there by an anonymous tip. He was very weakened from repeated blows to the chest and back with whatever was used to bury them. It took a short time for a judge to issue a search warrant for Vincent's properties, which is how the police discovered the evidence needed to get an arrest. It was right afterward that Vincent was arrested, minutes after murdering his son in front of his granddaughter."

That all seemed to add up to the old case as Michael knew it, so he nodded and said, "Yes, Doctor, that's the events as they were told to me. So it was just a matter of hours between the Christofers being found and Vincent being arrested. So subsequently, both children were sent here on the same day?"

"Correct," replied Dr. Lazarus, giving a curt nod. "As I said, both were suffering from severe psychotic fits when they arrived. Dallas was housed here in room six, while Samantha was housed in room five."

Dr. Lazarus motioned to the room on one side of Dallas's.

Michael nodded, figuring that Samantha and Dallas being housed right next to each other had to mean something. He just couldn't figure out what.

"Both children arrived switching between psychotic fits and a catatonic state," said Dr. Lazarus. "At first, we simply observed. Dallas's fits continued much as you'd expect of a child who was suffering from such severe trauma. Very soon, he had to be medicated to keep from hurting himself."

Dr. Lazarus's tone started darkening as he said, "But Samantha quickly lessened with the fits and withdrew instead. Not catatonic, but calm, deliberate, quiet. She talked to Dallas through their wall and talked to herself while cuddled in the corner of her bed."

"Sounds more than a little creepy, Doctor," said Michael, who was beginning to wonder if maybe he was underestimating Sam.

Nodding, Dr. Lazarus said, "'Creepy' is a good word to use here. And her condition continued to improve at a remarkable pace. Three days after Samantha arrived, she was completely normal."

Michael picked up the tale, saying, "Which is when the Castille attorney had Samantha released, correct?"

The doctor nodded and said, "Correct. Samantha's fits had completely stopped. Dallas's had not. Dallas had to be heavily medicated. Samantha had a full recovery and walked out."

Dr. Lazarus's voice lowered. "Do you see the problem here, Detective?"

It only took a moment before Michael answered. "Dallas did what one would expect someone in his situation to do—suffer a complete breakdown. Samantha, in the meantime, reacted in an unbelievable way."

Dr. Lazarus nodded and said, "Correct again. Samantha's reaction was one of psychotic repression. I am convinced that she took all of that shock, all of that rage, all of that hatred, and locked it away deep inside the darkest recesses of her mind."

Nodding, Michael found himself frowning, his mental scale of Sam's innocence starting to tip in the other direction. "When a person represses that much hatred and anger, it's bound to come back, correct?"

"Yes," replied Dr. Lazarus, folding his arms and tilting his head back, as if recalling the memories for the first time in years. "If there was ever a person with a demon inside them, waiting to come out, it was that little girl."

Michael continued to stay silent. He understood that Lazarus wasn't being literal with the term *demon*, but even he could think of no words other than *demon* or *monster* to explain the darkness he was being told existed within Sam Castille.

"Every test I gave Samantha before her release led me to believe that she would, sooner or later, snap and become a monster. I tried to warn Mr. Bourgeois, but that Dr. Klein had a proverbial bug in that man's ear. I believe he wanted her committed at his own facility in New Orleans, perhaps to experiment on her himself. Dr. Klein used his influence to shoot down every emergency hearing to commit Samantha. I could not hold her here. I'm just glad that Mr. Bourgeois betrayed Dr. Klein and kept Samantha out of his care as well. However, after the night of the fire, I had no legal recourse to try to get her back, so Samantha has since then been without the proper, in-patient care that she needs."

Michael heard skid marks in his head. "Fire? What fire?"

"Ah. I thought you knew," replied Dr. Lazarus, unfolding his arms and cocking an eyebrow curiously. "The night Samantha left here, there was a terrible fire that broke out in this building. You were never told this?"

Feeling like a deer in headlights, Michael said, "Actually, this is all news to me, Doctor. What are you talking about?"

"That is most unusual," replied Dr. Lazarus yet again, tapping his fingers together in a thoughtful manner. "It was a deciding factor in the court's decision to put Samantha into Dr. Klein's care. Let me tell you the details on what happened.

"You see, for one hour a day, we let the patients of each block out to walk around the central rotunda. Samantha was collected by Mr. Bourgeois during that hour. I remember Samantha said good-bye to Dallas, then left. Less than ten minutes later, the power box in a nearby utility closet shorted and exploded, starting a fire that quickly spread and consumed the entire building."

Michael shook his head in disbelief. "This is pretty unbeliev-able. And the patients were inside or outside of their rooms when the fire started?"

"Outside in the rotunda," replied Dr. Lazarus. "And they were just about to go inside for lockdown. That is why everyone in this block, Block A, was not killed."

Dr. Lazarus's voice was thick with distaste as he said, "The other three blocks were not so lucky. We lost every other patient and all of my staff that night, Detective."

Dr. Lazarus motioned toward where his calves should be. "I was trapped underneath some burning debris. The damage to my lower legs was so bad that they had to be amputated."

"I'm sorry," replied Michael, giving a canned response.

Dr. Lazarus, saying nothing at first, rolled over to Dallas, and laid his hand very gently on the burnt man's shoulder. The patient stopped scribbling and looked up at Dr. Lazarus. That was when Michael saw that Dallas's eyes looked dull and lifeless.

As he rested his hand on Dallas's shoulder, Dr. Lazarus said. "It was like in a fairy tale. As soon as the fire started, while I was trapped underneath that debris, flames all around me, this young boy, Dallas, came up to me and pulled me to safety. I remember Dallas saying, 'Don't you dare die on me, Doctor. No one who is kind to me deserves to die.'"

Looking between the doctor and patient, Michael asked, "So, how did Dallas get like this?"

Dr. Lazarus gently rubbed Dallas's shoulder while saying, "After rescuing me, he went back to help the rest of the children. However, Dallas's heroics proved to nearly kill him. He was ter-ribly burned that night. And the smoke inhalation was so bad that it caused permanent brain damage."

As Dr. Lazarus patted Dallas's shoulder and turned away from him, heading back toward Michael, he said, "Even with all my knowledge about neuroscience, I am unable to help reverse the damage done to this boy. So, I take care of him, locked away from the world that could hurt him, the hero who saved my life."

Michael found himself looking away as if he was intruding on the tender moment between doctor and patient.

Finally, he asked. "So you believe Samantha Castille started this fire?"

"I do indeed," replied Dr. Lazarus as he wheeled out of the cell. "I remember seeing her near the utility closet several times in the previous days, as if she was examining it. So look at the facts, Detective: Samantha Castille seemingly recovered from the trauma of seeing her father murdered in three days, and then the only living person linked to those murders is nearly killed, the night she leaves. Dallas is a shell of what he once was. In many ways, Samantha nearly finished what her grandfather started."

Waiting for Michael outside of the room, Dr. Lazarus turned to him and said, "You cannot tell me that this is all coincidence, Detective. My belief is that Samantha Castille started that fire to kill Dallas Christofer. I also believe that she is like her grandfather, and only needs the proper push to become a psychotic murderer."

Michael frowned again. *I hate to think this about Sam, but Dr. Lazarus does have a point. She's looking more like a suspect every minute.*

Just as Michael was preparing to leave, he turned to give Dallas Christofer one last good look. Dallas looked back at him, his blank, mindless eyes staring dully. However, from this angle, Michael could see what Dallas was scribbling.

What the hell!

Michael quickly moved over to where Dallas was, which made the young man slip back anxiously, as if expecting an attack. Michael paid Dallas no mind, crouching down and looking over what Dallas was scribbling. The words were unmistakable.

Michael called out to Dr. Lazarus, "Doctor, Dallas is scribbling some words down here. Has he been doing this much lately? Or is this a new behavior?"

"If it's the same two words over and over again, then he's been doing that off and on for the past twenty years. What is he writing down?"

Michael looked back over the shell of the man who used to be Dallas Christofer, then looked back at the writing on the wall. Taking in a deep breath, he read the words off the words to the doctor.

"Nite Priory."

Chapter 21
Michael's Busy Day

Date:　　　**Friday, August 7, 1992**
Time:　　　**4:00 p.m.**
Location:　**Lafayette Police Department,**
　　　　　　　Lafayette, Louisiana

It was well past lunchtime and much closer to dinner, by the time Michael left the hospital, having been given a couple of boxes from Dr. Lazarus containing dossiers on every employee and patient of the facility from twenty years ago. Michael was surprised that Dr. Lazarus would break doctor-patient privilege in this way, but the doctor had just smiled and shaken Michael's hand. Michael had again noted the strange tattoo on the doctor's wrist.

"I'll be keeping an eye on you, Detective LeBlanc. Do your very best," Dr. Lazarus had said.

Michael didn't know what to make of that statement.

Stopping at a café for a very late lunch, Michael took time to compare and organize his notes. After an hour, he realized that he was running out of both leads and daylight. He was just about to pay his bill and head out when he saw a note from his and Rodger's trip down to the bayou to talk to Robert Fontenot. Curious, Michael read over the note:

Fontonet's mistress
Jean-Laffite Theater
Lives in Lafayette now

"Looks like I've found a missing lead," Michael said to himself, paying his bill and heading out of the café.

It didn't take Michael long to find what he was looking for—the Lafayette Police Department. Pulling up in a visitor parking space, Michael entered the precinct and headed over to the front desk, where a uniformed officer sat looking very bored.

Michael showed his badge and identified himself, saying, "I'm working the New Orleans serial murders. I need to call in to the New Orleans Eighth Precinct and check up on something. Mind if I use the phone?"

"Not at all," replied the officer, who let Michael in behind the desk. "I needed a chance to make some fresh coffee anyway."

Scratching himself, the officer headed off to the back, leaving Michael to wonder two things: first, if there was anyone in southern Louisiana who did not drink coffee, and second, who would be manning the front desk.

Picking up the phone, Michael dialed his precinct and asked to be connected to Homicide. A few moments later, a familiar female voice answered, "Homicide Department, this is Detective Dixie Olivier."

"Dixie, they have you answering the phones, eh?" asked Michael, glad to hear his friend's voice.

"Hey, Michael," replied a tired-sounding Dixie. "Wait, the caller ID says . . . Hey, are you calling from Lafayette?"

"Yeah, the case is leading me here," Michael said. "Long story, I'll be sure to include it all in my report. You sound exhausted. Still jet-lagged?"

"Yeah, and Gino is still asleep, poor dear. Kyle is distracted with Cathy and Cheryl. It's a real mess, Michael," Dixie replied.

Michael leaned against the desk, looking down and focusing on his call with Dixie. He was still not pleased that his closest friend had to come back from vacation so early, but he knew why Commander Ouellette had put the four of them together.

Fortunately, Dixie soon changed the conversation. "So, Michael, what did you need?"

That snapped Michael back into the present. He quickly straightened up and said, "Right. So I need some information dug up from the archives. From the Bourbon Street Ripper case. Robert Fontenot, the suspect who Rodger and Edward arrested, had a mistress. She worked at the Jean-Lafitte Theater. She lives in Lafayette now. Can I get a name and address?"

"Sure thing," replied Dixie. "I just got finished sorting all the information from the original case. Man, Rodger takes terrible notes. I think the information on Fontenot is over on Kyle's desk. Mind holding for a few minutes?"

"Not at all, Dixie, thanks," replied Michael, who then leaned back as an officer entered the precinct. He was a clean-cut guy about Michael's age with a handsome face, soft blue eyes, and crew-cut hair.

Seeing Michael behind the desk, the officer came over and asked, "What's going on? May I help you?"

Michael showed his badge and said, "New Orleans Homicide. I needed to stop by to check back in with my precinct."

The officer nodded, smiled pleasantly, and headed toward the back.

Michael took a moment to let his gaze linger on the departing officer and how he walked with an admirable posture. Michael had a pleased smile on his lips as he heard Dixie get back on the phone. "Here we go, Michael. You ready?"

Michael slipped out his notebook and said, "Go for it, Dixie."

Dixie sounded like she was reading off a list. "Okay, her name is Rosemary Boucher. Her stage name was Rose and she lives in West Lafayette. Ready for the address?"

Stating that he was, Michael proceeded to write it down. Once he had the entire address in his notebook, he asked, "Dixie, is there any other information about Miss Boucher?"

"Nothing, really," replied Dixie, yawning.

Michael was about to thank Dixie and hang up when she added, "Oh wait, she was dismissed from the club about a month prior to the beginning of the Ripper murders. Edward took a note here. It says 'M and M.' Does that mean anything to you, Michael?"

A light went off in Michael's head as he recalled their visit to the ruins of the nightclub. He remembered a poster of two women in red—twins. *The M&M Sisters. I remember Rodger mentioning that they were a staple of the club. What was Edward's interest in them? Would Rosemary know about them?*

Michael said, "Yeah, might be a lead. I'll follow up on it. What about you, any leads yet?"

"Just one for now," replied Dixie. "Kyle and I have a potential witness we need to interview later this evening. Gotta go pick him up at the Ritz."

Wondering if that was Richie, and hoping it was not, Michael said, "Thanks for the help here, Dixie. I really appreciate it."

"Don't mention it, Michael," replied Dixie. "I hope you have more success than Rodger and Sam do. Talk to you later."

And just like that, Michael's brain went on a coffee break.

For a long time after Dixie had hung up, Michael just stood there, stunned. Then, slowly, very slowly, he hung up the phone. *She knew that Rodger and Sam went off together. But how?*

Michael forced his mind back to analyzing the facts. Once he had refocused, it took a short amount of time to determine that Aucoin and Dixie must have staked out Sam's townhome.

So they saw Rodger leave with Sam. Which means either we're in deep shit, or they think we're playing a card with a potential suspect. Either way, we can't bullshit our way out of this, and I'm not about to let my partner take the fall for this alone. I'm just as guilty of not following the rules. I'll just have to accept whatever happens.

Once he had come to that conclusion, quelling any panic and mentally returning to the investigation was easy. Michael gathered up his belongings and left the precinct, thanking the front desk officer again for use of the phone.

Driving along a heavily wooded back road, comprised more of dirt and gravel than concrete, Michael looked out for the address of Miss Boucher. Finally, a weather vane–topped mailbox with her number came into view from amongst the foliage, and a small metal gate provided an entryway to the well-secluded property.

Michael carefully pulled up behind an old Oldsmobile Cutlass that had seen better days. Getting out of his car, Michael heard loud barking coming from inside the house, some of it very high-pitched and some low and deep.

Great. She's a dog person. I'll bet there are a dozen mutts in there.

Michael looked over the house and figured he was right. The smell of dog shit and doggie chew toys were everywhere. Overall, the yard looked and smelled like it had seen better days.

Going to the front porch, Michael rang the doorbell. When he didn't hear anything, he knocked.

The riotous sound of dogs got closer, right against the door, as a woman's voice called out, "Get back! Back, you mutts! Get back!"

Michael expected the door to swing upon, and was a little surprised when he heard, "Who the fuck is there? Tell me now, or I'll sic my mutts on your sad ass."

With a bit of a start, Michael replied, "New Orleans Police Department."

The blinds on the side window parted and a woman's finger tapped the glass. "Show me your shield then. Show it here. Where I can read it."

Sighing inwardly, Michael slowly took out his badge and held it up over the glass. "Junior Detective Michael LeBlanc, ma'am. How's this, Miss Boucher?"

"It's fine," came the reply, and then silence. Looking toward the glass, Michael saw a rather bright blue eye looking at the badge from behind the blinds. In the dark interior of the house, it looked almost disembodied. The eye suddenly looked up and locked eyes with him, and then the blinds snapped shut. A few moments later, there was the sound of three locks unlocking, and the door opened.

On the other side was a woman in her forties who looked like she, at one point, had been quite attractive. However, the lines on her face, the faded look in her eyes, and the wrinkles over her brow showed a woman who had had the fire in her extinguished a long time ago.

She was wearing a bathrobe, and had her hair up in rollers. A lit cigarette hung from her lips.

Rosemary looked Michael over and smirked, shaking her head and saying, "Christ, are they letting babies on the police force now? How old are you, kid?"

Not giving an answer to that question, Michael nodded his head toward the interior of Rosemary's home and said, "I'd like to speak with you about Robert Fontenot and the Jean-Lafitte Theater. May I come in?"

Rosemary stood there for a few seconds and looked into Michael's eyes. Michael could see the hardness there, the edge that he was used to seeing in the eyes of vagabonds and prostitutes. It was not what he expected to see in the eyes of a woman who had once been someone's mistress.

Rosemary stepped back and turned around, leaving the door open for him to come inside. Michael considered her for a few moments, thinking, *This woman has been through a lot of crap. But she doesn't see the police as the enemy. And she doesn't come across as hiding from anyone. She's like a person who just doesn't give a shit anymore.*

Stepping into the house, Michael saw the dogs. Not just three or four dogs, but at least a dozen, were all lounging about the front room as if they were the house's rightful owners. There were dogs of several breeds and all sizes, from Pekingese and toy poodles to rottweilers and a pit bull.

Almost all were facing a large, bulky television that was showing an afternoon soap opera. A few feet away was a sofa, a small wingback chair, and a coffee table with an ashtray and a slew of magazines on it.

Michael couldn't help but wonder how this woman cared for them all, much less was able to function with this many animals. Several of the larger dogs, such as the rottweilers, came up to Michael, sniffing him curiously before heading back to wherever they felt like sitting.

"When I saw on the news that someone was copying the Bourbon Street Ripper, I knew it was only a matter of time before the police came by asking questions," said Rosemary as she sauntered to the sofa, picked up a lazy-looking Scottish terrier, and sat down, placing the dog back in her lap. She motioned for Michael to sit on the wingback chair, which currently had a sedentary and quite comfortable-looking bulldog on it.

"Is that so, Miss Boucher?" Michael moved to remove the bulldog from the chair, only to have the dog look up at him and give him the most condescending snort he had ever heard.

"Butch, go on and let the nice man sit down," called out Rosemary, petting the dog in her lap.

The bulldog, moving only its eyes, looked over at Rosemary, then looked back up at Michael. After a second of what must have been deep contemplation, the bulldog let out a tremendously loud fart and jumped off the chair, trotting off to lie down on a patch of carpet.

It took Michael a second to come to terms with being both snorted at and farted at by a dog. He finally fanned the area around the chair a bit and took a seat. Then he picked up where he had left off in the conversation. "Well, why would you say that you expected the police? What did you know about the original case?"

"Not much, hon," said Rosemary, taking a few drags of her cigarette, "but I was acquainted with one of the suspects. But you already knew that, didn't you?"

Chuckling softly, Michael leaned back and said, "So then, what was your relation to Mr. Robert Fontenot?"

"I fucked him," said Rosemary, her lips curling around the cigarette almost lewdly. "Every night if he wanted. Bobby was what you would call my sugar daddy."

"Right," replied Michael, who tried to rest his hands in his lap, only to find a toy poodle there instead, looking up at him and panting merrily. Remembering Boudreaux, Michael figured that being good to the dogs would build a rapport with Miss Boucher. And so, petting the small dog, Michael continued the interview. "What doesn't make sense is this: how can a man like Robert Fontenot, an offshore worker, afford to, well, keep a woman like you?"

Much to Michael's surprise, Rosemary started laughing, smoke blowing out her nose. After a few moments, she said, "Is that what you think? That he was an offshore worker? Kid, where do you get your information? I already told that detective twenty years ago that the offshore bullshit was a front!"

Michael felt himself again in the maddening position of being a deer caught in the headlights. His hand stopped caressing the toy poodle, which did its best to restart the petting with a few choice licks. Holding his frustration inward, he asked, "Which detective was that? Rodger Bergeron?"

"Oh hell, no, not that dolt," replied Rosemary in a shocked tone. "Rodger's partner. What was his name? I should know, because I saw him every—Edward! It was Edward. I told him."

Michael was relieved this wasn't another secret of Rodger's; however, he was just as annoyed that this was another case of Edward having a sizable role that had been hidden from him. *Again.*

Rosemary, who had since taken another long drag off her cigarette, said, "I'll tell you what I told Edward, hon. Robert Fontenot, my Bobby, only worked offshore to keep his cover up. In reality, he was the Black Bayou Boatman."

It took a few seconds for Michael to register what Rosemary was talking about, for the Black Bayou Boatman was well before his time. As it dawned on him what Rosemary was saying, Michael shook his head in disbelief.

"The Black Bayou Boatman, so named in honor of Charon, the boatman to the Underworld, was one of the most prolific hit men to ever work for the Marcello family. In both the sixties and the seventies, he was implicated in over two hundred contract murders, although no one was ever able to identify him. Witnesses would vanish without a trace, and there were even whispers that the CIA had him on retainer."

Michael recalled that some of his more conspiracy-minded friends from college believed that the Black Bayou Boatman was involved in, among other things, the John F. Kennedy assassination.

"He also etched his initials into his victim's bodies," finished Michael, making a cutting motion with his free had. "Three interlocking *B*s."

"That's right, hon," replied Rosemary, taking a final drag and putting out her cigarette.

Leaning back, Rosemary said, "Bobby was a cold-blooded killer nearly sent to death row by an even more cold-blooded killer. He worked directly under Carlos Marcello, the head of the Marcello family back then. If someone crossed Carlos, they'd get a midnight visit from the Boatman."

Michael's mind was a whirl of activity, trying to make a connection between Robert Fontenot, alias the Black Bayou Boatman, and Vincent Castille, alias the Bourbon Street Ripper.

"You're trying to figure out why the Ripper framed him, aren't you, hon?" asked Rosemary, reaching into her robe and pulling out a cigarette case and lighter. She took a few seconds to light the fresh cigarette. "So was Edward. Drove the poor dear nuts, but he finally figured it out."

"He did? What did he figure out?" asked Michael, a bit shocked that what seemed to be such an important lost connection was just within reach.

Rosemary sat back and took a long drag of her cigarette before leaning back and crossing her legs. Every movement of hers seemed to Michael like she was putting on a show.

"Well, hon, it's a long and sordid story. You ever heard of the M and M Sisters?"

Again, a light went off in Michael's head. He had been waiting for the conversation about Robert to lull before bringing up Edward's note about them, and here was Rosemary bringing them up herself. What luck!

Michael sat up straight, full attention on the reclined woman before him, and said, "Yes. I have heard of them. They were a staple at the Jean-Lafitte Theater, correct?"

"Correct, hon," replied Rosemary, who took a few moments to get comfortable. "Magnolia and Marigold were their stage names. Now, see, they weren't the best act. They could sing well enough, and they had a look that belonged in the fifties, but that isn't what made them so popular."

"Oh? So what made them so popular then?" asked Michael, as the toy poodle in his lap fell asleep, snoring softly. Looking down at the sleeping animal, Michael rested his hand on it and looked back at his hostess, waiting for her answer.

"They were the hottest damn pair of blondes you'd ever seen, hon," said Rosemary, smirking. "Two women in red who just slipped out of your most sensual fantasies. Ruby red lips, blue eyes, and bodies that were too fucking perfect—they made me sick."

"Is that all?" replied Michael, cocking an eyebrow at the "big surprise." "They were really attractive?"

"You were expecting something more?" asked Rosemary, who leaned forward to flick some ashes off her cigarette, the embers fluttering down into the ashtray. Looking back at Michael, Rosemary shook her head. "You don't know much about women, do you?"

Michael's brow furrowed, his countenance growing indignant as he said, "That's not relevant to this conversation, Miss Bou—"

"Oh hon, but it is relevant," interrupted Rosemary, leaning back and looking at Michael for a long time.

Just when Michael started to feel his patience wearing thin, Rosemary said, "Well, maybe you don't think with your dick, hon, but most men do. And back then, Carlos's grandson, Giorgio, decided that Magnolia was going to be his woman. But what Giorgio didn't know was that Magnolia already had a sugar daddy, someone who she was in real tight with."

Michael thought for a moment, considered the logical direction the story could go in, and then said, "Let me guess, Vincent Castille, right?"

"Close, hon, real close. It was Dr. Castille's son," Rosemary said, taking a drag on her cigarette.

In the depths of Michael's mind, a bell went off. Suddenly, Michael sat up so fast that the toy poodle nearly fell out of his lap. "Wait, if Vincent's son was with Magnolia, then does that make her Sam's mother?"

Rosemary gave a wicked little smile to Michael. "That's what Bobby and I thought. Of course, we never saw the two together, but it made sense. Edward was always protective of the sisters, even though he had no investment in them. And why not keep it a secret? After all, it wouldn't be proper for the mother of someone as well-bred as a Castille to be a lounge singer, so I'm sure that family did their bit to keep her their dirty little secret. Besides, if that bitch Magnolia had a child, how she was able to perform afterward is beyond me."

"Why do you say that?" asked Michael, who was thirsting for any information Rosemary could offer.

"Hon, she had a weak heart," replied Rosemary, pausing to take another drag. "Was born with it, poor girl. That's what killed her. One night, the two of them were performing and Magnolia just fell over."

Rosemary looked up at the ceiling for a moment, her brow furrowing as if parting the haze of twenty years spent trying to forget. After a few moments of what must have been furious thinking, she looked back at Michael and nodded. "Dr. Castille was there. He was the one who ran to her side and had someone call for an ambulance. He tried to resuscitate her, but she never regained consciousness."

Rosemary took a lingering drag of her cigarette and said, "She died that night in the hospital. That was back in May of 1972."

Michael added Magnolia's death to the timeline he had been constructing, saying, "So about a month before the Bourbon Street Ripper murders began, correct?"

"Correct," Rosemary replied, leaning forward and putting her cigarette out. "After Dr. Castille's arrest, I started thinking that Magnolia's death was what set him off."

The toy poodle in Michael's lap apparently decided it was time to part ways with him, and wiggled to get free. Michael helped the small dog get back on the floor. "Well, that's just as a good a theory as anything else I've heard, but do you have any hard evidence?"

"None, hon," said Rosemary, shaking her head. "Just a woman's hunch and thirty years of knowing men."

That was enough for Michael. Mentally noting Rosemary's theory, he then asked. "So, why did you get fired from the nightclub about the same time as Magnolia's death?"

Rosemary's expression grew serious. For a moment, she looked around as if expecting someone to be eavesdropping on their conversation. When she finally did speak, her voice was low. "Because I know who murdered Magnolia."

Michael's brow furrowed in confusion. He was getting tired of being caught unaware with surprises pertaining to the investigation.

"Excuse me? Magnolia was murdered?"

At that moment, the door opened and a voice so thick with a Cajun accent that it was nearly foreign called out, "Mama, I'm home! Whew, it's so hot out there, the sweat's going down my ass and makin' my spine tingle like it's December, ya!"

Looking up, Michael saw a massively muscular Cajun man, with a ruddy face and a big nose. In one hand, he held a large hatchet, in the other hand what looked like a dead oppossum.

Immediately, the big man stormed over to Michael, his brow furrowing, his manner quite threatening. The dogs went wild, barking like mad, as he stood right before Michael.

The big man boomed, "Hey you, what you doing with my mama? You fucking with her? You got a problem, boy?"

Michael kept his wits about him, in case the man got violent. He was physically repulsed by the heavy scent of dirt and sweat about him.

Immediately, Rosemary called out, "Eustace! You be nice! This is the police, and he's here to talk to Mama, not bother her."

That made Eustace back off immediately, even though he stared down at Michael.

"Now apologize to the nice police detective, Eustace," Rosemary said to the big man.

"Sorry, sir," replied Eustace, his voice suddenly quite contrite. "Don't like no men messing with Mama. You understand, right, sir?"

Amazed at how quickly this burly truck of a man went from nearly attacking him to being as polite as possible, Michael said, "It's all right, Eustace. Good for standing up for your mama."

Michael looked up at Eustace and watched as he just stood there and nodded his head, mumbling apologies underneath his breath. Michael wondered if Eustace was simple. "Yours and Robert's son?"

Rosemary stood up and walked behind Eustace, rubbing his back gently.

"Eustace, honey, go put that oppossum outside to drain for skinning. Mama will make a mess of jambalaya tonight."

Eustace hugged his mother and walked off at a plodding pace. Rosemary watched him leave with the fond look one gives a puppy. When he was gone, she turned to Michael and said, "No. Bobby and I had a beautiful baby, but I wasn't able to keep him. Eustace, on the other hand, is what you'd call an unexpected gift from God after one too many beers."

Michael nodded his head, mentally filed away that Robert and Rosemary did have a son, and said, "Seems like a nice enough fellow."

Rosemary shrugged, gave what Michael could only call an uninterested smile, then said, "Well, I think I'm all talked out today, Detective LeBlanc. And I need to make dinner for my boy. Mind if we chat some other time?"

Michael said nothing, but inwardly he found himself annoyed that, once again, he was interrupted by something before a piece of information could be handed out. However, Michael just smiled and nodded, standing and saying, "I should be getting back to New Orleans anyway. It'll be dinner for me, too, by the time I'm back in town."

Rosemary nodded and showed Michael to the door, saying, "All right. You come visit me again in a few days. I'll tell you the rest of what I know. Until then, you stay safe, Detective. There are bad things out there. Snakes waiting to strike. The snake always knows what you're going to do, hon, always."

As he headed outside, Michael said, "Yeah, I've been told. Thanks for that."

As soon as Michael was out on the front porch, the door closed and locked behind him.

Michael went to the squad car and got inside. *Superstitious idiots. The only snakes I have to worry about are the people who are lying and withholding information from me.*

Michael stewed over the information all the way back to New Orleans and the 9th Precinct. By the time he was walking to his desk, carrying a bag filled with comfort food—fried chicken and mashed potatoes—it was ten o'clock and Michael was in a thoroughly bad mood.

"Hey, Michael," called out the familiar voice of Dixie. Looking over at his friend, he saw that she was looking worse for wear, too. He didn't see anyone else.

"Hey, how did your investigation go today?" asked Michael, opening his bag and pulling out his unhealthy but hopefully worry-numbing dinner. He tried offering his friend at least a tired smile, but found he just couldn't muster up the energy to care.

Dixie leaned over Michael and gently rubbed his shoulder. It felt good, and Michael was grateful for it. Despite being only friends, Dixie had a way of making Michael just feel better. And Dixie was known for being one of those rare types of people whose smile and laugh could turn your day around.

"It was shitty. We questioned that prick of a writer, Richard. We might as well have asked a Ouija board to divine answers from Vincent's ghost. Richard, or Dick as Aucoin now calls him, was completely unhelpful."

Michael wasn't surprised to hear that. He was glad that Richie, despite not belonging in this investigation, had managed to follow the instructions given earlier that day. However, this train of thought made him think about her parting comment on the phone, and the advance knowledge that others knew Rodger had taken Sam with him. "So, be honest. Am I in hot water, Dix?"

Dixie got up, slid a chair over and turned it around backward, and sat next to Michael.

Once she was leaning forward on the chair, Dixie said. "You? No. But Rodger's going to have a lot of explaining to do. We all know he's protective of Samantha Castille, but Ouellette's pretty pissed at him for this crap he's pulled."

"This entire investigation is crap," replied Michael, trying to eat his dinner and finding he wasn't hungry. "I just had a long conversation with Dr. Lazarus, and an equally long one with Miss Boucher, and while I've got some great information, I still feel like I'm being left in the dark."

Michael's diatribe earned him a sympathetic look from Dixie. He was glad there was someone he could talk to, especially when he had never felt more estranged from his partner. "You're angry, Michael," Dixie finally said. "I wish you'd just go ahead and admit it."

Michael shook his head. Admitting that he was angry with Rodger was something he was hesitant to do. The flood of emotion would be too strong.

Instead, Michael said, "I just want to know why he's so invested in Sam Castille that he's risking both the investigation and his career. I really want to know that, Dix."

Dixie started to open her mouth when a strong but gentle voice called out, "Dixie. Honey."

Both detectives looked up. Standing at the doorway was a handsome man in his midthirties, with long black hair, dark eyes, and olive skin. Michael recognized him as Gino, Dixie's longterm boyfriend.

"Hey, honey," Dixie replied, getting up and going over to Gino. Michael looked away as the two embraced, focusing on his fried chicken.

"Evening, Michael," said Gino at last, prompting Michael that it was polite to look back at the two.

"Evening, Gino. How goes work?" Michael asked.

"Slow. Thank you for asking," Gino replied.

He nodded toward Dixie. "I was just here to take Dixie home. Will that be okay?"

Michael nodded to Gino, whom he had a lot of respect for. He considered Gino to be one of the more courteous people he knew. "That's fine with me. Dix, I'll see you tomorrow. Gino, take good care of her."

"Of course," replied Gino, putting an arm around Dixie.

"You make sure you get some rest, okay, Michael?" said Dixie. She paused for a long moment, looking down at Rodger's desk. Finally, she spoke up.

"And Michael . . . "

He looked up and saw his friend tapping a photo on Rodger's desk.

"Sometimes, the truth is right under your nose. Take care of yourself, and even more so, take care of your partner."

As the pair walked off, Michael noticed what Dixie was tapping. A framed photograph. Looking at it, he realized it was a picture of Rodger and Edward posing with Ouellette for the press. It was signed: "We did it, buddy. Edward."

Looking at the picture, Michael smiled to himself, remarking how similarly Edward and he dressed, only Edward wore a suit without a tie.

Suddenly, Michael's pulse quickened, and something in his memory clicked. He studied the photograph of Edward closely. Something seemed familiar about the clothing Edward was wearing.

Suit without a tie. Suit without a tie. Suit without—

Suddenly, it hit Michael where he had seen a picture of Edward before. The same man in the same suit, only this time with hair a little grayer and face a little older, riding a children's train ride in City Park.

"Son of a bitch," Michael said, a sudden feeling of anger, rage, and betrayal welling up inside of him. "How could you not tell me this, Rodger! How is this 'minor shit' that's 'not relevant'? How can you expect me to trust you now?"

With a sudden and uncharacteristic spark of fury, Michael slammed the photograph facedown onto his partner's desk, glass shattering. Particles of glass sparkled in the homicide department's dimmed light like angry tears.

"Edward was Sam's father!"

Chapter 22
Fat Willie

Date: **Friday, August 7, 1992**
Time: **5:00 p.m.**
Location: **Louisiana State Penitentiary**
             Angola, Louisiana

The cold clanking of metal bars sliding resonated in the background, and together with the stark and unforgiving glare of the fluorescent lighting, created an atmosphere devoid of warmth. From the courtyard, where inmates were engaging in outdoor activities, to the dormitories, where the sound and smells of human defecation oozed from the walls, to the silent and isolated death row, every part of the prison complex felt like it had been abandoned by hope.

Every time he came to the Louisiana State Penitentiary, Rodger felt that lack of warmth and hope, and it chilled him to the bone.

As he sat in an interview cell at a table, across from Sam Castille, both wearing "Visitor" name tags, Rodger reflected back on the long drive to Angola, where the state prison was located.

He had expected Sam to waste no time in having the talk he dreaded, but Sam had remained silent, concentrating on driving. By the time they had gotten halfway to Baton Rouge, Rodger had fallen asleep. Sam had woken him up as they arrived at the penitentiary's entrance.

Rodger had had a quick smoke. He'd been craving one since morning. The check-in procedure had gone quickly. Rodger's main contact within the prison, Assistant Warden Charles Daigle, had been understandably perturbed when Rodger showed up with a civilian. It wasn't until Rodger made certain to assure Daigle that Sam was there solely to act in an observational capacity that tensions lessened.

Coming back from his thoughts, Rodger became aware that Sam was now looking over at him. He wished he hadn't lied to Daigle. He knew Sam would be asking questions. He also knew he would be allowing it.

"Everything okay? You've been tense since we got here," Sam asked, her arms folded and her shoulders hunched. She had a tired look on her face and dark circles under her eyes. Despite that, she looked genuinely concerned for him.

Rodger shrugged and said, "I've just got a lot on my mind right now, Sam. I'm trying to figure out how to catch this killer before anyone else dies, how to keep my ass out of hot water, how to keep your ass out of jail, and how to keep Michael from hating my guts."

Looking at him, Sam smiled a little and relaxed her shoulders. Rodger couldn't help but notice how much like her father she looked like at times, despite inheriting both her hair and eyes from her mother.

Finally, Sam said, "You're too harsh on yourself, Rodger. You're trying to do too much. That's why Michael and Richie and I are here—to lessen your burden, and to take some of the pressure off your shoulders."

Rodger shook his head. "A nice sentiment, Sam. But let's be realistic. It was your father who figured out the case last time, and he was a genius. Michael isn't that good yet, although he will be one day, when he gains the intuition that Edward had back then. And you are a brilliant woman, much like your father, but you're too deeply involved in this, on account of you being both a Castille and a suspect, to provide the objectivity I need. And, Richie, well, he seems like a nice guy, but . . . "

" . . . he's a bit of a goof, I know," replied Sam, almost giggling for what seemed like the first time in two decades. "But he's a lovable goof and a real sweet guy. Despite his lack of *grace and poise*, he has been essential in helping me come out of my shell for the first time in many years." She accented that last statement with a faux French accent, arching her blond eyebrows at the old detective.

Rodger chuckled at Sam's girlish ways, having not seen this much life in her since before her father's murder.

Rodger's thoughts were interrupted by the metal bars sliding aside, a sound soon eclipsed by the sounds of feet shuffling and chains sliding. Daigle's voice could also be heard, saying, "Come on, Willie, the sooner you talk to the detective, the sooner you can get back to your books."

"That's a good thing," replied a Southern gentleman in what sounded to Rodger like a thick voice, the kind of voice that sounds like someone with a throat too big to open properly. Pulling his emotions inward and seeing Sam do the same, Rodger mentally prepared himself for the interview.

Then Fat Willie rounded the corner, and Rodger instantly felt disgust. Calling him fat was like calling a volcano hot—it was a gross understatement. Fat Willie was obese, at least four hundred pounds, and could pass for a Caucasian Sumo wrestler.

He wore the same bright orange prison uniform one would expect of an inmate, but it was obviously tailored to his size. His face sported unsightly reddish stubble, and his hair, a mixture of red and spots of gray, was short and messy. His hands and feet were handcuffed and chained, loose enough so that he could walk, but not so that he could run.

And he smelled of hamburger grease.

Fat Willie, being escorted by Charles Daigle and a prison guard, entered the cell. Daigle sat Fat Willie down at the head of the table, patting him on the shoulder and saying, "Now, Willie, this is Detective Rodger Bergeron, and the charming lady with him is—"

"Samantha Castille," interrupted Fat Willie. He nodded cordially to her. "William K. Benedict, otherwise known amongst members of the esteemed Louisiana Penal System as Fat Willie. It's a pleasure to meet such a celebrated young lady, Miss Castille."

When Sam just nodded, her lips tight and her face emotionless, Rodger could tell he needed to take control of the interview right then, or Fat Willie's putrescence would make Sam lose her cool.

"Sam won't be talking to you, Willie," said Rodger. "She's just here to watch. You will be talking with me."

Fat Willie turned to look Rodger up and down, saying, "Weren't you Edward Castille's boyfriend?"

The jibe did nothing to Rodger's mood, but he held his tongue and said, "Partner, Willie. He was my partner."

Fat Willie nodded and scratched under his nose, saying, "My mistake. No offense intended."

Not buying that for a second, Rodger turned to Daigle. "Give us about thirty minutes alone to interview him, okay, Charles?"

Daigle snorted and shook his head, saying, "You have fifteen. Any more and Whitley will have my ass."

As Daigle and the guard started to leave, Fat Willie looked back and over his shoulder, saying to the assistant warden, "Hey, Daigle, give Warden Whitley my love."

Fat Willie then puckered his lips and blew a kiss in a manner that was both obscene and unsettling. Turning back to Rodger and Sam, Fat Willie said, "See, Whitley is such a decent fellow, he wants to fix all of Angola's violence problems. But what our venerable and honorable warden forgets is that man's own nature is to fuck each other up, figuratively and literally."

Leaning toward Sam, Fat Willie said, "Isn't that right, Samantha Castille . . . sweetie pie?"

Rodger slapped the tabletop. When Fat Willie looked over, Rodger made a motion and pointed toward his eyes. "Talk to me. Not her. Me."

"Fine," replied Fat Willie, shifting his weight to look over at Rodger. "So, what can an exclusive lifetime member of the Louisiana State Penitentiary do for you?"

Rodger leaned forward to lock eyes with the repulsive convict. "You can start by telling me what manner of accomplice you were to Dr. Vincent Castille—the Bourbon Street Ripper."

"Oh, come now, *accomplice* is such an ugly word," replied Fat Willie with a sort of indignation about him. "And it's so inappropriate for what I was assured would be a gentleman's conversation."

Rodger couldn't believe what he just heard. "Excuse me, what?"

Leaning forward, Fat Willie started to rub a pudgy finger over the surface of the interview table as if he were caressing the skin of a lover. The motion was crude and left a trail of oil on the faux wood.

"You see, *accomplice* denotes assistance with the execution of the crime, or otherwise points to personal participation. Dr. Castille always kept to himself during those most intimate and, might I add, satisfying moments. No, I was more of an independent contractor facilitating the events leading up to the crime, instead of actually participating in a *ménage* à *trois* of suffering with the Bourbon Street Ripper."

Fat Willie's eyes trailed over to Sam, who visibly stiffened. Then the man leered back over at Rodger. Keeping that look, he said, "Besides, my weapon of choice is not a scalpel, but a seven-inch-long piece of spicy Cajun Boudin that makes the girlies cry."

"You're a serial rapist," Sam said, her voice and gaze as cold as ice.

Fat Willie returned her gaze. "Guilty as charged, sweetie pie. And lucky for you, ladies with small tits and wide hips are my favorite. You see, I can easily pretend a woman like you is any age I want."

Leaning forward, his mouth slightly open, the obese convict ran the tip of his tongue over his teeth.

Disgusted, Rodger said, "I think, Fat Willie, that you are full of shit, and that you never worked with Dr. Castille on anything. You're just a two-bit rapist who could never keep up with someone like, oh, Giorgio Marcello."

Slowly pulling his tongue back in and shutting his mouth, Fat Willie, who suddenly sounded less playful, said, "Well, now, Detective, you certainly hit below the belt. And here I was going to make our short visitation into something entertaining."

Straightening up, he said, "As far as Marcello goes, he is how Dr. Castille found me. You see, when Blue-Eyed Marcello would get bored picking women up the old-fashioned way, he'd hire me to add a bit of spice."

Returning to rubbing his pudgy, oily finger over the table's surface, Fat Willie continued, "So I would make certain that Marcello's nightly companion was grabbed, sacked, and delivered unharmed and . . . unspoiled."

There was a loud sliding sound as Sam pushed back her chair, got up, and started to pace, eventually standing on the far side of the room, a look of repulsion and rage on her face. Rodger could empathize—Fat Willie was not only a serial rapist, but he had helped another serial rapist commit his crimes by kidnapping the victims.

Rodger was now easily able to figure out how Willie had helped Vincent. "So, you're the one who kidnapped the Bourbon Street Ripper's victims. Am I right, Willie?"

"Bingo," replied Fat Willie, sitting back and shrugging. "In my defense, I had no idea what Dr. Castille was doing with the women. I thought he was trying to create another granddaughter."

"That's a load of bullshit," said Rodger. "There's no way you could not have known the women you kidnapped were being murdered. That shit was all over the news."

At that, Fat Willie smirked. "I tend to keep to myself, Detective, and if I'm not playing directly with the goods, I don't really think twice of them. Truth is, I didn't know until his last victim, that Maple woman, had been kidnapped that Dr. Castille was the Ripper."

Rodger, who was following along in disbelief, suddenly stopped and considered what Willie had just said. His brow furrowed for a moment as he said, "Wait a minute. You aren't the one who kidnapped Maple and Dallas?"

Shaking his head, Fat Willie said, "Nope. Not at all. I do believe, if I may be allowed to theorize, that the doctor took them himself."

Trying to figure out how a man in his seventies could accomplish such a feat alone, Rodger asked, "So, then, other than the Christofers, you kidnapped every other one of Vincent Castille's victims?"

"I did," replied Fat Willie. Then he scratched his head thoughtfully. "Are we counting Sam's father as a victim? Because, if I remember from the newspapers, he kidnapped himself."

Sam, who had been standing there and staring narrow-eyed at Fat Willie, sucked in a breath and gave him a look that spoke of premeditated murder. Her fists were clenched and she had almost-inhuman rage boiling in her eyes.

Rodger watched as Sam closed her eyes and turned away from Fat Willie. Looking back at the convict, Rodger asked, "So then, Fat Willie, have you been contacted by someone or something called the Nite Priory?"

This question seemed to take Fat Willie by surprise, and rearing back, he looked Rodger up and down as if he were a long-lost relative. "Well, I'll be damned."

Suddenly, Fat Willie laughed out loud, a great booming laugh, and clapped his hands. "You have got to be shitting me. I honestly thought I was the only one to get a letter from this Nite Priory thing. But with you asking me about it, that can only mean one thing. This copycat is going around and contacting all of the Ripper's old contractors, ain't he? Sweet Josephine, that is too much!"

Taken aback by Fat Willie's reaction, Rodger found himself growing more and more intrigued. From his point of view, both Topper Jack and Mad Monty seemed to be on the outer edge of the Castille murder ring, while it currently looked like Fat Willie was further inside.

The only loose end was how Blind Moses fit into the equation. Rodger shelved that thought for the time being.

"Do you have it with you? The note from the Nite Priory, I mean," Rodger asked in a voice low enough to force Fat Willie to come closer.

Fat Willie grinned and said, "It's in my cell. I will have my esteemed assistant warden, Mr. Daigle, get it for you after this interview."

Rodger was glad there was no dirty joke or disgusting quip for once.

Sam spoke up. "I have a question for you." She had returned to her seat and had her left fist clenched over what looked like a key chain.

Fat Willie rolled his head over to look at her, leaned forward, letting out a small fart toward Rodger, and said, "You can ask me anything, sugar-cooch."

Sam's fist squeezed the key chain several times in a pumping motion, her face getting less tense with every pump. "I'd like to know how Grandfather contacted you with instructions, Fat Willie. Did he leave notes, like the Nite Priory is doing?"

With a *smack* of his lips, Fat Willie leaned back, shook his head, and said, "He had his own personal courier who did all the messaging and shit for him. That bitch would show up in the middle of the night while I was sitting on my couch watching porn, or soaking my fat ass in the tub, or taking a goddamn shit. She'd stare at me all creepy like for a few moments and then start giving instructions. When she'd leave, there would be money stuffed in an envelope waiting for me."

Rodger was keenly interested in this piece of information. He got Fat Willie's attention and asked, "Who was this courier, Willie? We need a name."

Fat Willie shrugged and said, "Why, Blind Moses, of course."

The room went silent. Sam's eyes grew, and Rodger, who was hit with two realizations—Blind Moses' role in the original murders and her gender—just shook his head. He had never seen it coming.

Finally, Rodger said, "So, then, Blind Moses is a woman and was Vincent's courier, correct?"

"Yes, indeed. And damn, that bitch was freaky," replied Fat Willie, lifting up his belly and dropping it as if he was trying to make it bounce. "You ever had a blind woman stare at you? It was like the bitch could see. She had this misty look in those blind eyes, like there was something else inside there. Something inhuman."

"What did she look like?" Sam quickly asked.

"How the hell should I know?" replied Fat Willie in a tone of increased annoyance. "You seen one nigger bitch, you seen 'em all. She worked for your granddaddy. You should know who it was. Really, it's like you inherited your brains from your mother's side of the family."

Sam's chair slid back, and she stood up and leaned forward, her eyes narrowing and her face full of rage. "What did you say?"

In a flash, Rodger was also standing, putting his hand out to get Sam's attention. "Whoa! Whoa! Sam, calm down! This slime ball isn't worth it." He shook Sam's shoulder, trying to get her to relax a bit.

Sam quickly turned to glare at Rodger, and for a moment, her countenance was that of a predator, a killer's look, that same inhuman look as before. Rodger was taken aback by the sudden glare and stepped back. *What the hell? That ain't the Sam I know.*

Lowering her head, Sam took a deep breath, then looked back up. All was suddenly normal with her expression. Turning to Fat Willie, she asked, "How can you know anything about my mother? She died soon after I was born. Childbirth complications. You never knew her. She wouldn't associate with swine like you."

Fat Willie gave a short laugh and said, "Is that what they told you, sweetie pie, that your mother died of complications from childbirth? That's funny. Real funny."

As Sam stared again at Fat Willie, Rodger spoke up, wanting to preserve the peace, as well as Sam's dignity. "Mary Castille has nothing to do with the questions we're asking you, Willie."

Even though Sam again stared at him, Rodger ignored her and continued, saying, "We'll get your letter from the Nite Priory. Now answer this, if you were the copycat killer, how would you get your victims to their point of execution?"

Fat Willie crossed his hands over his chest, his fat face crinkling up in what looked like deep thought. "Honestly, Detective, I'd lure them there. People are a lot more street-savvy nowadays, so unless you have a series of vacant alleyways to drag your victims along, you need them to come to you. You'd have to convince them to meet you, alone, at a certain time of night."

For the first time since the interview, Fat Willie seemed serious. He continued, "Once she arrived, I'd drug her, probably with chloroform, but maybe with something more potent. Then I could get her and my equipment set up for the party. When she woke up, she'd wish she hadn't."

Nodding, Rodger thought about the two victims, Virginia and Rebecca, as well as how Mad Monty mentioned that at least one of them had been contacted on a pay phone.

"Has your question been answered satisfactorily?" Sam asked Rodger.

Rodger came out of his thoughts and nodded his head.

Sam turned back to Willie and said, "Good. Now you will tell me what you know about my mother."

The clanking of iron from the hallway signaled the return of Daigle and the prison guards. Fat Willie gave a nasty grin and shrugged, saying, "Them's the breaks, sweetie pie. Maybe you need to look further into how your daddy met your mommy, and how your grandpappy was involved in all that."

Sam glared at Fat Willie. Rodger starting getting nervous.

"You know what the worst part about all this is, sweetie pie?" said Fat Willie. "Ain't no one been honest to you your whole life, girl. You need to question why the Ripper killed your daddy. You really need to question that."

Just then, Rodger heard the sound of a door opening and closing loudly. Daigle and the guards came up from the hallway, unlocked the cell, and entered it.

"All right, Willie," said Daigle as the guards helped Fat Willie to his feet. "That's enough being a dick for one day. Back to your cell."

As Fat Willie was ushered out of the cell, he turned his head back to the duo and said, "And sweetie pie, if you ever want some real lovin', come see me. I bet my Boudin link could split you down the middle and soak up your sweet Burgundy. You'll scream for me, won't you, baby?" He accented the question by blowing a final lewd kiss.

Rodger felt a strong desire to punch Fat Willie square in the face. Fortunately, the convict was soon gone, and Rodger was left standing there with Sam, who looked both fatigued and disgusted.

As if handling a stick of dynamite, Rodger placed his hands on Sam's shoulders and said, "Let's get that note and then get back to your car. You want me to drive?"

"Yes, please," Sam said from in between her teeth.

It took them only a few minutes to tell Daigle about the note. Rodger was exhausting the last of his favors with his friend, but soon had the note in his hands. Fat Willie had sealed it in a plastic bag. Rodger decided to wait until he got back to the precinct to open it.

Once on the road out of Angola, Sam reached into her glove compartment, took out a notebook and her silver pen, and started scribbling furiously. Rodger, who had one eye on the highway and one eye on Sam, watched her with increasing caution.

Soon Sam had scribbled so hard in her notebook that the pages started to tear. Her jaw was clenched and tears were forming in the corners of her eyes. She was whispering to herself in what Rodger recognized as Haitian Creole, and her eyes once again had that murderous, inhuman look.

"Whoa, whoa, calm down," Rodger said, reaching over to touch Sam, only to have his hand slapped away. Hearing a truck's horn, he looked forward again.

What Rodger saw scared the shit out of him.

While dealing with Sam, he had pulled into incoming traffic. An eighteen-wheeler was barreling down on them, the grill mere yards away from smashing them both to pieces. Rodger's spine tingled as he felt his body unlock from the shock, a burst of adrenaline rushing through his system. His body snapped into action of its own accord, and with a sudden quick turn, Rodger pulled off the road onto the grass, narrowly missing a head-on collision.

It took Rodger a few moments to collect himself, and when he turned to say something to Sam, he saw that she was still scribbling hard, tears in her eyes caused by what he could only gather was anger.

"Sam," Rodger called out. When he got no answer, he called out again. Then, reaching over, he grabbed her hands and made her stop writing. She looked up at him, her blond hair falling to either side of her face, her eyes filled with tears. Her jaw was tightly clenched and her ears were red.

"Dammit, Sam, we very nearly just died!" Rodger said as he looked down at the page she was writing on, half-torn with the strokes of her pen. He looked back at Sam. "Look, I know you're upset and everything, but you have got to get it together. If you don't get your shit together, people will think you're a nutcase. And if they think that, then they'll think you're guilty. And once they think you're guilty, that's it—it doesn't matter if you're innocent or not. To them, you will always be guilty."

As Rodger slowly took the pen out of Sam's hands and the notebook from her lap, Sam looked down. To his surprise, Sam's tears began to flow freely, and she sniffled several times. To Rodger, Sam looked like that ten-year-old girl who used to look up to him as an uncle—a girl who desperately needed someone to listen to her, to be there for her.

"Do you think I'm guilty?" Sam asked, her voice thick with tears.

Rodger shook his head and said, "No. No, not at all."

"Do you think I'm a nutcase?" Sam asked, her voice quieter.

Again, Rodger shook his head. "No, I don't think you're crazy. I do, however, think you are suffering a lot right now. And that Fat Willie guy got to you."

Leaning back, Rodger looked at the page Sam was furiously writing on. It was detailed notes of a scene where a character, Big Charlie, was killed in a horrible accident while in prison. All sorts of brainstormed ideas were there—falling and getting impaled on a metal pole, getting burned alive from an explosive furnace, even falling into a laundry press—and those were the less gruesome ones. Turning back to the previous page, Rodger saw a note saying:

"Fat Willie = Big Charlie"

"Okay . . . " Rodger said, a touch of concern readily apparent in his voice, "Fat Willie really got to you."

And then the notebook was gone from Rodger's hands, Sam having snatched it back. Her expression was stern and hurt, and she held the notebook protectively to her chest. "I can't kill him in real life, but I can kill him again and again in my stories."

Rodger cracked a small smile and handed Sam her pen back. "It's a good outlet, Sam. Therapeutic, right?"

With a sardonic chuckle, Sam put both back into her glove compartment. "Sorry about that outburst. It was that stuff about my mother. You have no idea how hard it was to get any information about her from Father. It was like he was hiding something. Grandfather, too. Grandfather would always say that I was the only important one."

Sam turned to Rodger and, wiping her eyes, asked, "Did you know my mother?"

Rodger shook his head and said, "I wish I had known Mary Castille. She and Edward were married in a private ceremony at the Castille Estate. And just the Krewe of Comus was invited. Strange, I know. He never talked about her, and by the time you came along, I was told she had died in childbirth.

"I always wondered why Edward kept Mary a secret. Wouldn't even tell me where he met her, only that she was a singer. I used to joke with him that she was a celebrity, just like I used to joke with him that you got all the traits from her side of the family, since he had dark hair and brown eyes. He never liked that joke. He always told me not to talk about shit I didn't understand."

Sam looked down at her lap and nodded, saying, "Thanks for telling me what you know."

Soon, the two were on their way again, Rodger driving back toward the city of New Orleans. Looking at the clock in the dash, he noted to himself that they still had time before they reached the city. He had gotten so comfortable with this pseudo-closeness with Sam today that he had all but pushed the idea of the "important conversation" out of his mind. He knew, however, that until they actually talked about it, they couldn't move past it.

"Hey, Sam, it's going to be a few hours before we get back," Rodger said, focusing on the road before him. "Anything else you want to talk about?"

"Let's talk about my father and his death," came Sam's curt reply.

Rodger's expression grew very serious. "All right, the hell with it," was his decisive reply. He looked over at Sam. "But you go first, Sam. I don't have the nerve."

"Very well," Sam quietly responded, then straightened up and began. "It's really obvious that you have been avoiding talking to me for, well, close to twenty years. At first, I thought it was like Kent said, that you wanted to put the murders behind you." Sam wasn't looking at Rodger. Instead, she was looking outside as the scenery passed by.

"However, as time went on, and you still didn't contact me, didn't even drop me a line, it became obvious—painfully obvious—that you didn't want to talk to me. Hell, you wanted nothing to do with me."

The bitterness in Sam's voice had finally started to come out, a strain in the back of her throat.

"You were there throughout all my childhood, Rodger. You'd come over to my father's townhome for dinner almost every night. You'd sit for me when Father was busy with that Comus stuff. You'd take me to City Park and Pontchartrain Beach. Hell, until I was seven years old and Dad explained it to me, I thought you were my honest-to-goodness uncle. And then, my life falls to shit, everything I ever cared about is torn from me, and you . . . you . . . " Sam quickly turned her head to look directly at Rodger. "You fucking abandoned me!"

Rodger, who had been choking up more and more as Sam talked, and using all of his concentration to avoid swerving off the road, found himself flinching at the end of Sam's speech. His grizzled jaw was clenched, his old, tired eyes were tearing up, and it was all he could do to avoid letting them spill.

Rodger's voice cracked, in spite of himself. "I'm sorry. I'm sorry, Sam. It was just, I . . . your father . . . I couldn't face you."

Sam's voice had an incredulous tone. "You couldn't face me? Rodger, no one blames you for my father's death! Dad went to confront Grandfather alone. He made his choice, and—"

Rodger couldn't take it anymore. The gnawing pain that had been eating away at his guts for twenty years became unbearable. A secret pain, one he had hidden from everyone, burst forth. "You don't get it, Samantha! I'm the one who sent Edward to his death!"

Sam just stared at Rodger. The older man, unable to keep the tears from pouring down the side of his face, had enough mental acumen to pull off to the side of the road before getting into an accident. Once the car was stopped, Rodger rested his head on the steering wheel—partially because his head had never felt so heavy, and partially to hide the tears streaming down his cheeks.

For the first time in years, Rodger's voice was shaking as he spoke. "The investigation really wore on us, Sam. It was like it consumed our lives. Your father and I. We couldn't eat. We couldn't sleep. All we could concentrate on was the evidence, those photos of the crime scenes. After a while, it started to get into our heads. Every time we closed our eyes, we'd see the victims, their faces, the agony, and what was left of their bodies. We became so engrossed in this nightmare that we started to lose track of everything around us."

Shaking his head, rubbing his brow on the steering wheel, Rodger continued.

"When Aucoin found Maple and Dallas, though, Edward lost it. It was like someone set off the crazy bomb in his head. I had never seen him so angry. He came to me, babbling, saying he had figured it out. He knew who the Bourbon Street Ripper was—your grandfather. His father."

Lifting up his head, Rodger stared straight ahead, seeing nothing before him but his own obscured vision. Like Sam, the floodgates of emotion, held back twenty years, had opened, and nothing would close those gates.

"No one wanted to believe that Dr. Castille was the Ripper. But your father was convinced. He begged me to go with him, to arrest Vincent. To kill him if necessary. He begged me, Sam! He goddamn begged me!"

Finally Rodger looked over at Sam, his face drenched in tears. Although he could barely focus, he saw that Sam's face was covered in tears as well.

"I didn't believe him, Sam! I was so exhausted, so wrapped up in my own bullshit that I told him I wouldn't go in without proof. He went off by himself. Sam, your father never went to arrest a suspect without backup. But he went to the mansion that one time, alone, and . . . and . . . "

"My grandfather murdered him," Sam replied, her voice still choked with emotion.

Rodger said nothing at first. He wanted to tell Sam what Dr. Klein had revealed, but decided that this could only hurt the situation more than help it. To Rodger, letting Sam know she had witnessed that murder wasn't just unnecessary, it was cruel.

Instead, Rodger nodded and said, "If I had only believed him, Sam. He'd still be alive. And maybe, just maybe, that sweet little girl I used to take to Pontchartrain Beach would still be around."

As Rodger wiped his tears away, he heard Sam's voice. It sounded softer, gentler than usual. "She's still around, Rodger."

Rodger was suddenly aware that a handkerchief was dabbing the tears off his unshaven face. Turning, he saw Sam giving him a soft, sad smile, and using what looked like a pocket kerchief to dry off his face.

"She's not gone. She's just very frightened of getting hurt again. She never knew her mother. Her father was murdered by her grandfather. And her "uncle Rodger" never talked to her, never visited, didn't even send so much as a birthday card."

His face dry, Rodger sniffled hard and gave Sam a weak smile. "I guess I've been pretty foolish, haven't I? Thinking you'd hate me if you knew the full story."

At this confession, Sam chuckled, putting away her kerchief. "And it looks like I was too proud to seek you out. I guess we've both been pretty stupid."

Rodger felt the weight lift off his shoulders. "Yeah, we've been pretty stupid."

Then Sam did something that Rodger was not the least bit expecting. Leaning forward, she wrapped her arms around Rodger and held him, her head against his shoulders. Rodger rested his head on hers. For a moment, it felt like he was being hugged by little Samantha again.

When Sam broke the hug, she wiped away the remnants of her tears and said, "Sorry. I've been having a lot of, well, emotional catharses lately, and I feel like I'm, well, feeling again for the first time in years."

Rodger noted that Sam was again squeezing that key chain of hers, the one with the red plastic shoe. He figured it must be an emotional safety net, much like him and his cigarettes. He gave Sam a small smile and nodded, then, taking the car out of Park, casually mentioned, "Besides, I sent you cards, remember? Every year. Christmas, birthdays . . . ?"

As he pulled out onto the road, Rodger saw Sam shaking her head.

"No, you never sent me a card, Rodger. I've never gotten anything from you," she said.

Rodger said nothing. He knew he had sent Sam cards many times. But he didn't want to argue. Not after everything they had talked about.

For many long minutes, only the loud *hum* of the road underneath Sam's car and the sight of the passing mile markers kept Rodger's attention.

Finally, Sam spoke up. "Rodger?"

"Yes, Sam?"

"Are we . . . are we on good terms now?"

Rodger smiled, saying, "Yeah. We're good, Sam. I'm glad we got this settled."

Sam closed her eyes and seemingly went to sleep.

Rodger focused on the road, but his mind was elsewhere.

I sent her two cards a year. Two cards a year, one on Christmas and one on her birthday. I also sent a card for her confirmation and one for her graduation.

Rodger didn't like how this made him feel at all.

Why didn't she get them?

He gritted his teeth in rising frustration.

Who's been cutting off communication between Sam and me?

Chapter 23
The Nite Priory

Date: **Friday, August 7, 1992**
Time: **7:00 p.m.**
Location: **New Orleans Police Precinct, 8th District**
              French Quarter

Upon following Detective Aucoin to the police precinct floor, Richie saw a middle-aged woman with gray hair, dressed in drab clothing and carrying a box, approaching the detective. The woman had a teenage girl with her who was dressed in clothing that made her look more like a streetwalker and less like a high school student.

The girl had Walkman buds in her ears and was apparently listening to something dripping with angst, her expression one of a jaded soul who had seen and suffered it all, and could be impressed by nothing. The woman, who looked rather plain in comparison to the daughter, had a world-weary look about her.

"Cathy. Cheryl," Aucoin said with a surprised start, for the moment completely ignoring Richie, instead approaching both ladies. "What are you—"

"Your box of college yearbooks," interrupted Cathy, a twinge of what Richie detected as sadness in her voice. "I found it while cleaning out our rental storage. I had left you a message, but"—the woman offered the box to her husband—"you didn't return any of my calls."

Taking the box, Aucoin said, "I've been busy with this case, Cathy, you know that." His voice was, in Richie's mind, a bit harsh, because Cathy's face seemed to age almost a year from the comment. Apparently Aucoin caught on to that, because immediately, he rubbed the woman's shoulder.

"Thank you, Cathy," said Aucoin before turning to the girl.

"How's school, Cheryl?" Aucoin asked the girl, who was busy cracking her gum at the world. "Still acing your trig classes?"

Cathy made a motion of putting something into and plucking something out of her ears. "She can't hear you, Kyle. She's listening to that Manson guy again. Remember, her world is one big dark room right now."

"Right, that Manson guy," Aucoin replied as he put the box down on a desk. "I'll never understand the music kids listen to these days." His voice lowered as he leaned in toward the woman. "How's everything at your mom's?"

"Fine," replied Cathy. "We're gonna stay there until, you know, we've had a chance to start going to—"

Aucoin's voice dropped, as if he were embarrassed to be having this conversation. "Cathy, honey, I said that wasn't necessary. We just need a chance to talk this out, you and me. There's no reason—"

It was at this point that both Aucoin and Cathy, whom Richie could only assume was the detective's estranged wife, realized that Richie was standing a few feet away, watching. Cathy's face started to flush while Aucoin, who looked to be holding in his temper, nodded at Richie and said, "You mind, Dick?"

Dixie, who was walking up to the group, said, "I've got him, Kyle. This way, Mr. Fastellos."

Richie walked alongside Dixie, who neither looked at or spoke to him. Soon they were in the precinct lobby. Dixie was showing Richie to the door when the officer at the front desk said, "Hey, Dixie! Gino's on the phone. Want me to tell him that you'll call him back?"

Dixie shook her head and said, "No. Tell him to hold. I'll take it over in the squad room." She then escorted Richie outside.

As the warm night air washed over Richie, he felt Dixie pull on his arm until she was eye-to-eye with him. Her voice was low as she said, "I've got my eye on you, Mr. Fastellos. Don't screw up."

As she went back inside, Richie rubbed his arm, wondering what the hell was wrong with the police in this city. As he started walking through the French Quarter, heading back toward the hotel, Richie began to wonder if the stress of the investigation was already causing these seasoned cops to crack.

It was almost like something was making a bad situation worse.

Richie's thoughts were interrupted by someone stepping in front of him, having come out of an alleyway. Richie froze in his tracks as the large person with a thick square jaw, dressed in a pinstriped suit, looked down at him. Just as quickly, he realized that an equally large man was right behind him. Then it clicked in Richie's head—these were the two men who had been with the Lady in Red at the Ritz-Carlton bar!

Again, Richie's muscles started to coil, and his fists started to tighten, when a voice nearby spoke.

"Good evening, Mr. Fastellos," said a weasel-like voice. From behind the big man in front of him came a smaller man, about a foot shorter than Richie, his hair slicked back, his nose pointy, and his shoulders obviously artificially enlarged by his jacket. The short man grinned up at Richie.

"Lovely evening for a drive, don't you think? Why not come for one? I have someone who wants to talk to you." Just as the short man said that, a black Cadillac pulled up beside the four of them, and a burly black man with dreadlocks and sunglasses got out of the driver's seat. Richie suddenly realized he was getting "taken for a ride" by mobsters.

"Nice night for a ride?" asked Richie, looking for a quick exit. "Who are you guys? What did I do?" The fear he had about the Lady in Red suddenly bubbled to the service. "I swear, I've never touched her!" Richie immediately regretted the outburst.

The short man just laughed and held out his hands in the least genuine gesture of goodwill Richie had ever seen. "Just a conversation, Mr. Fastellos. Nothing more."

"Well, can't we have a nice chat back in the hotel bar?" Richie asked, feeling more out of control by the second. His last panic pill was no longer at its full strength.

"You're a funny man, Mr. Fastellos," replied the short man, eying Richie as a predator would his prey. "Please try not to piss your pants. We just got the car cleaned."

The short man addressed the chauffeur. "Damarco, is Mr. Marcello ready?"

The black man nodded, speaking in a decisive Jamaican accent. "Of course, Mr. Ernesto. He's just having himself some dinner right now."

Ernesto smiled toothily at Richie as he motioned toward the car. "See, Mr. Fastellos? You get to have dinner with Mr. Marcello. How lucky of you! Now, come this way, and please"—the short man's teeth glittered like fangs—"don't make a scene."

Richie felt that he was trapped, a feeling he did not like at all. Looking around again, he quickly realized that he had nowhere he could run. He was too far from the police station to call for help, and there weren't enough pedestrians to see that he was in trouble.

He must have hesitated a bit too long, because Ernesto made a motion toward Richie, and the two men on either side of him grabbed him, one hand under each arm, and pulled him into the car.

Richie's heart pounded in his chest, his head beginning to hurt, as he felt the situation spiraling totally out of control. He was sure that the Lady in Red was indeed some mob boss's woman, and that he was being taken to get fitted for a pair of cement boots. *I've got to explain to this Marcello guy that it's all a misunderstanding!*

Mr. Ernesto got into the front passenger seat, while Richie, who was seated in the middle of the backseat, had the two large goons on either side of him. This situation did not help set him at ease.

Neither did Mr. Ernesto's chatter during the ride, which was about how easy it was to hide dead bodies.

The car took them to the Riverwalk, an elevated shopping mall located right on the Mississippi River. The white polished exterior rose up from the end of Canal Street, near the ferry, and extended along the river all the way toward Poydras.Right next to the entrance to the Riverwalk was a building Richie recognized as the Rivergate, which currently sported a large sign titled "Future Site of Harrah's Casino and Resort."

This time of the evening, the entrance to the Riverwalk was mostly deserted, and the Rivergate, which had people walking in and out of it, was too far away to shout at. Richie focused on keeping himself from panicking, knowing that if he gave in to fear, he'd be good as dead. Doing all he could to keep his anxiety down, Richie tried to focus on how he would talk his way out of this situation.

As the car stopped, Ernesto finished his useless babble with, "But the best part is that the mudbugs and fish in the river will eat any kind of carrion, Mr. Fastellos. It's really an amazing way to get rid of something you never want to be found."

It took all of Richie's willpower to keep from freaking out. He really wished he had just one more pill, something to help him get through this. Shutting out Ernesto's comments, Richie put all of his focus into appearing completely normal as he was walked up the ramp and into the Riverwalk.

The mall was closed, and except for a few janitors, who paid the five people no mind, no one else was there. The interior of the mall was very attractive, with stores lined up around a center atrium that traveled alongside the bank of the river. Ceiling fans were rotating nice and slow, keeping the muggy August air from getting too stagnant. The shops all had metal mesh doors over their entrances, and in the air hung notes of Brahms's Fourth Symphony. The entire place smelled of pine.

As the group headed upstairs, Richie spotted a lone security guard at a station, and he was about to call out to him when he saw that the guard was both listening to headphones and reading the newspaper. Richie felt his stomach sink. It was obvious to him that this guy was on the payroll of this Marcello person.

The second floor, which overlooked the atrium, sported an area near a long outside balcony, café-style seating everywhere. The seats and tables were moved to the side, and sitting at a large round table was an older gentleman with a brunette women sitting opposite him. The older gentleman, Richie noted, was quite handsome, with that charming, lady-killer look about him. His hair was obviously dyed black, slicked back in the traditional "wise-guy" manner, and his suit, clearly tailored, sported a red rose on the lapel.

The woman was wearing a red and black dress that was both revealing and uncomfortable-looking, and apart from having an obviously inflated chest size, she seemed positively bored to tears with her dinner.

All around were big, strong-looking goons, all wearing pinstriped suits. As Richie approached, escorted by Ernesto, he wondered if he really had left reality and entered into a film noir.

"Mr. Marcello," Ernesto said as he and the others stopped with Richie a few feet from the table. "This is Mr. Fastellos, as you requested."

Marcello, who was trying to enjoy a particularly juicy cut of steak, turned to look at the short man, with some of the most blue eyes Richie had ever seen staring at Ernesto. Looking back at his dinner, Marcello motioned toward his glass. Out of seemingly nowhere, a butler appeared with a bottle of wine and refilled Marcello's glass.

Maybe it was the almost casual dining atmosphere, or the soft classical music, or even the nonthreatening way in which Marcello nodded, but Richie felt any fleeting remnants of his anxiety, like what he felt when he saw that the security guard was ignoring him, melt away. It seemed like maybe he was anxious over nothing, and that this Marcello person just wanted to talk to him. Instead, Richie focused on getting his charm up, so that he could smooth-talk his way out of this situation and back to his nice, safe hotel room. *Keep it simple. Sit down. Find out what he wants. Give it to him. Leave.*

Ernesto's introduction finally got the attention of Marcello, who in turn waved the short man off, then turned to his dinner companion and said, "Doll, why don't you wait in the car for me? I'll be about thirty minutes."

"But, Giorgio, I haven't finished my dinner!" whimpered the woman in a particularly spoiled-sounding voice.

"She hasn't finished her dinner," replied Marcello with a chuckle, turning to some of his associates. "You guys hear this? She hasn't finished her dinner!"

The associates started chuckling as the woman folded her arms and huffed.

Marcello, cutting another piece of steak, said, "Then take your damn dinner back to the limo, doll. Take the whole fucking bottle of wine, too, for all I care. Just get the fuck out of here."

Scowling at Marcello, the woman got up, looked over at the butler, and said, "Bring my plate, my glass, and the bottle, Robaire."

The butler nodded and replied, "Yes, madam." He then placed all three articles onto a silver tray and followed the woman.

"And take the elevator," called out Marcello over his shoulder. "I don't want you to break those five-hundred-dollar heels!"

"Fuck you, Giorgio," called back the woman as she left with the butler.

With a shrug, Marcello looked over at Richie and said, "Seriously, I don't know sometimes who runs this outfit—me, her, or my cock." The man motioned toward the empty seat and said, "Take a seat, Mr. Fastellos. Let's talk."

As Richie took a seat, Marcello asked, "Do you want something to eat?" He looked around and said, "Can someone get Mr. Fastellos something to eat? Maybe another steak, or some fried catfish?"

As Richie was about to reply that he wasn't hungry, Marcello looked at him and asked, "What do you all eat up in Pittsburgh, anyway? Cheesesteak?"

Richie couldn't help but chuckle, saying. "That's Philadelphia, Mr. Marcello."

"Right," Marcello replied with a chuckle of his own, and cut at his dinner, popping a juicy morsel into his mouth. As he chewed on it, one of the goons placed a plate in front of Richie with blackened catfish. A glass nearby was filled with white wine.

Marcello motioned to the food and said, "Eat up. Drink up, too. Don't worry, it's not poisoned or anything."

Richie, who hadn't even suspected poison, found himself not very hungry. Suddenly, he was very aware that he was sitting there with a New Orleans crime boss, from a bona-fide crime family, surrounded by cronies, in an isolated place where he couldn't be heard.

The situation reeked of murder.

"If it's all the same, Mr. Marcello," replied Richie, looking at his host, "I'd really like to know why I'm here."

Giving a nod, Marcello said, "Just get to the point, eh? I can respect that kind of attitude, Mr. Fastellos."

Taking a long drink of his wine, Marcello sat back and began, "The truth, Mr. Fastellos, is that we've been watching you for a couple of days now, and we know what you've been up to in this fair city."

Richie found his lips tighten and his gaze narrow as it suddenly became apparent that Marcello wasn't talking about the Lady in Red.

Deliberately, he said, "What do you mean, Mr. Marcello?"

Marcello waved his fork and knife around, saying, "I mean, that you've been cavorting with Miss Castille. You know, the Ripper's granddaughter."

Richie's gaze remained focused. "She has a name," he replied dryly. "Samantha Castille. Or Sam, to her friends."

"She ain't got no friends, Mr. Fastellos," replied Marcello in conversational way. "And that's how we like it. No friends. No outside influences. Nothing to bring out the evil that family committed."

Richie felt emotions bubble up inside of him. Strong emotions. Like with Aucoin, he imagined punching Marcello in the face until he had no more teeth.

Gritting his own teeth, Richie hit the table and growled out, "What is wrong with everyone in this city? Why are people persecuting Sam over something her grandfather did twenty years ago? Why can't you people just let it go?"

Immediately, Richie regretted his actions. Anxiety started to bubble up inside him. Remembering that he was out of pills,

Richie concentrated on pushing those feelings down. All he had to do was get through this meeting and get back to the hotel room.

This outburst seemed to make everyone present grow more alert, with some of the goons who had been slouching straightening up. Even Ernesto, who moved forward with an outstretched finger, started to say something when Marcello waved him back. Placing both hands together, fingertips tapping against each other, Marcello looked right into Richie.

"Let's get one thing straight," Marcello began. "I don't have to explain shit to you, Mr. Fastellos. New Orleans is my fucking city, just like it was my grandfather's. Now we do some shady shit, Mr. Fastellos, but that's just business. But the Bourbon Street Ripper, well, that was just plain sick shit. If my grandfather, God rest his soul, had known what Vincent Castille was all about, there would have been no business partnership, no nothing. Money from the Castille fortune wasn't that important to Grandfather."

"Business partnership?" asked Richie, the revelation of that catching him off guard. "Wait, your grandfather and Sam's were business partners?"

Marcello smirked, looking both smug and uncaring as he said, "Shit like that stupid nightclub. Grandfather and Vincent were, what do you call it, anachronistic and stuck in the fifties. I guess the club was just a way for them to hold on to the old times."

Richie blinked in confusion.

Club? What club?

"But that's not why you're here," continued Marcello, swishing around his wine and sipping at it. "I just want to know how Miss Castille is pulling this off. That's all."

"Pulling what off?" asked Richie, cocking his head to the side and peering at Marcello.

Marcello again looked into Richie. "The murders, Mr. Fastellos. The murders."

Feeling himself bristle like a male protecting his female, Richie replied, "Sam is not the murderer, Mr. Marcello."

Sniffing at his wine, Mr. Marcello asked, "How can you be so sure?"

Richie was getting tired of explaining things over and over again. "She was drunk the night of the last murder, and there's no reason for her to incriminate herself by writing about the very thing she did. God, why is everyone so convinced that Sam is behind the murders?"

Marcello started laughing, and some of his men soon joined in. The long laugh made Richie bristle up even more, and only when the mob boss seemed to calm down, did he say, "Oh, she's behind the murders, Mr. Fastellos. I can promise you that. You see, the Castille bloodline is filled with evil. It started with Vincent, and it's continued to Miss Castille. Only her father, who was a regular pain in the ass anyway, was innocent."

Richie wasn't sure how Sam's father fit in to this, but he was sure it was important.

Richie's ponderings were interrupted by Marcello saying, "Again, Mr. Fastellos, any idea how Miss Castille is doing it? Any information would be richly rewarded."

Richie frowned at that statement. If he could guess at how ruthless these kinds of people were, he was sure that they'd never leave Sam alone.

I have to get out of here and warn her.

Richie finally said, "Sorry, I honestly don't know anything. I wish I could help out, but my dealings with Sam have been purely professional."

Eying him, Marcello asked, "Are you sure? Is that your final answer?"

Folding his arms, Richie nodded. "Yes. I don't know anything."

The look on Marcello's face was one of pure disappointment. "That's really a shame, Mr. Fastellos, because I was hoping to find a use for you."

Snapping his head toward Richie, Marcello went back to eating.

Suddenly, Ernesto and the goons from the car were upon Richie, grabbing his arms and legs and carrying him toward the balcony.

"What the hell?" screamed Richie, his body suddenly going hot as his heart rate exploded. "What the hell are you doing, you lunatic?"

"I can't have you warning Sam that we're on to her," replied Marcello, casually cutting his steak into small chunks. "And as soon as we figure out how she does it, we're gonna do her the way Vincent did that poor bitch Maple. So I'm afraid you're gonna have to wait for her in hell, Mr. Fastellos."

"Are you out of your damn mind?" cried out Richie, flailing his arms and legs in an effort to get free. The goons held tightly on to him, and Ernesto, who was grinning sadistically, drew a switchblade out from underneath his coat.

Richie, sweating bullets, anxiously called out, "You seriously are going to kill me because I couldn't help you? Christ, you could just send me back to Pittsburgh! You could lock me in a room for a week! You could do anything to stop me from talking to her!"

"Please don't insult me," replied Marcello as he sipped his wine, smacking his lips. "If I let you live, you'll find a way to warn her. That's how you guys think. With your dicks. Just die with some fucking dignity."

The goons carried Richie dangerously close to the edge of the balcony railing. One toss, and he'd end up swimming for his life in the mighty Mississippi. Trying to kick free, Richie called out, "You know the police are gonna come looking for me, Marcello! Don't think they'll notice a famous author missing?"

"You aren't all that," replied Marcello. "You're just a flash in the pan. In a few weeks, someone else will be a best seller, and you'll be a memory in the newspapers. I was just gonna have you shot, but your whining's pissed me off. Ernesto, carve this guy up and toss him over."

Marcello emptied his wineglass. "Good-bye, Mr. Fastellos."

Ernesto, flipping open the blade, called out to the goons. "Open his shirt."

Suddenly, Richie felt the rough hands of the goons rip open his shirt, and he cried out again as he struggled to get free. His heart and head pounded. His eyes were glazed, and every breath seemed to grow heavier and heavier. He thought that if he hadn't left his pills at the library, he could have taken one and he'd be able to think clearly now. If only he could get to his medication.

As he felt his shirt rip open, Richie could only think of how he'd never see Sam again. Deep inside of him, the thought of being kept away from her made every synapse in his brain start to fire off wildly. He became aware of every breath he was taking, every sensation around him.

"Hold him steady," called out Ernesto, as Richie felt the hot night air on his chest and stomach. "I don't want to cut my fucking fingers. I said—"

Richie never heard Ernesto finish his statement. The next time Richie looked up, he saw the short man flying over him and over the balcony, hurtling toward the river. Richie felt the goon holding his feet let go, and as his feet landed on the ground, he looked up and saw the same goon falling to the ground in a heap, his neck bent so hard that his spine protruded from the base.

Richie then felt himself being pushed down, and was vaguely aware of someone in black ramming together the heads of the two goons holding his arms. Suddenly his arms were free, and Richie felt himself fall to the floor.

Everything was happening so fast, yet all Richie could feel and hear was the pounding of his heart. The world seemed to be moving in slow motion.

Looking up, he saw one of the goons falling back, his throat cut and crimson blood squirting out like in a movie, his jugular torn open. The sight of blood started Richie's motor skills again, and he quickly scooted back. As he looked at the last goon remaining, the Jamaican named Damarco, he finally saw it—a person in a black hooded robe landing from a jump.

Damarco reached into his coat, presumably for a gun, and the figure in black stabbed into the Jamaican's abdomen with Ernesto's switchblade and ripped upward. Damarco's intestines almost immediately spilled out onto the balcony.

Richie scooted back in terror, and then started to hear gunfire and screams from inside the Riverwalk. Looking inside, he saw more people in black hooded robes landing near him from the roof above and rushing in toward the goons inside, who were drawing their guns and firing. Instinctively, Richie rolled out of harm's way as stray bullets sprayed past him.

As he rolled onto his stomach, he suddenly felt warmth in his left hand. Looking down, he saw that the person in black who had saved him was pressing Ernesto's switchblade into his hand.

From underneath the hood, Richie only saw a dark mouth, which said, in a thick Creole voice, "Protect yourself."

Wide-eyed, Richie pushed himself up, his hands slipping on a puddle of Damarco's blood. Falling down, the red junk splashing all over him, he could only watch as the people in black tore through Marcello's goons with blades and bare hands.

Some had their necks broken, some were used to absorb other goons' bullets, and some were eviscerated. All around Richie, the screams of the dying mixed with the music of Johannes Brahms in a symphony of death.

It was beautiful, in a horrific and blood-chilling way.

Richie was aware that he had finally gotten up, the shock of what he was seeing still registering in his brain. Wading through the carnage, still holding the switchblade, Richie noticed how everything seemed so distant, so unreal.

By the time he finally approached Marcello, the only one left alive, who had fallen back and was scooting away from everything, time had sped up back to normal, and Richie was aware that the people in black were behind him, moving in on the mob boss.

"What the fuck?" screamed Marcello in a bloodcurdling panic, his blue eyes boggling. "This is fucking not happening! This is fucking not happening!"

"Giorgio Marcello," said a sultry voice from beside Richie. "You picked the wrong person to mess with."

Richie looked at the hooded figures, remembering the article he had read in the library. He turned, his eyes widening as he saw the Lady in Red beside him. Suddenly, everything made sense—

her sudden interest in him, her warning, and most importantly, her being here right now.

"Nite Priory," Richie said, looking at the Lady in Red.

The Lady in Red smiled with those pouty red lips and replied, "We can talk later, Richie. For now, what do we do with Blue-Eyed Marcello?"

Richie looked back over at Marcello, his eyes narrowing murderously. He vaguely remembered the name from his research, but who Giorgio was didn't matter to him. Here was a man who had threatened to kill Sam, and tried to kill him. Rationality and humanity were thrown out the window—Richie wanted revenge.

"Fucking stop this shit," cried out Marcello. "You fucking psychopath! You are . . . oh my fucking God, everyone is dead! What the fuck just happened?!?"

Richie reared back and kicked Marcello right in the stomach, shouting down at him, "You could have just let me go, you stupid fuck! You brought this on yourself! Fuck you and your family!"

Looking back at the Lady in Red, who was watching Richie dispassionately, Richie said, "Do whatever you want with him. Just make sure he can't hurt Sam."

The Lady in Red nodded at Richie and then motioned toward Marcello. "Carve him."

"You're fucking insane," cried out Marcello, as three of the hooded figures moved in. "Fucking insane!"

Richie turned away. As angry as he was at Marcello for trying to kill him and Sam, he didn't want to watch a human being murdered that way.

An hour later, Richie sat at the stairs leading down to the bottom floor of the Riverwalk. His blood-covered clothes were, for the most part, gone, taken by one of the people in black, and he was wearing a spare janitorial uniform given to him—most likely from the employee locker room. The blood and bodies had been cleaned up, every corpse tossed into the river. Richie's heart rate had returned to normal, but his head still pounded. Everything seemed completely unreal, like he was walking in a dream.

Richie was sure he was suffering from shock.

"Coffee?" asked a sultry voice above him. Richie turned up to see the Lady in Red holding a cup of coffee out to him.

"Thanks," replied Richie, taking the cup and sipping it. It was warm. It was real. In the muddy waters of this insane dream he had been dumped into, along with this mysterious Lady in Red, that coffee was real.

"Giorgio deserved the death he finally got," said the Lady in Red, looking away from Richie. "The slime has been a serial rapist since the seventies. We just needed a reason to go after him and his people."

Richie nodded in understanding. He was beginning to realize what he had gotten himself into, and he wanted answers. Standing up, he turned to the Lady in Red and asked, "Who are you? Who are you all?"

The Lady just smiled, tapping Richie's lips. "You already know the answer to that, Richie. You just need to find out why we're here."

Again, Richie said, "Nite Priory."

The Lady in Red just smiled and walked down the stairs.

Quickly, Richie followed her. "But why? Why are you all committing these murders? Why are you framing Sam?"

"Is that what you think, that we're a group of serial killers?" asked the Lady in Red, stopping to motion to a person in a black robe, who had just finished mopping up the blood from the bottom floor, to go upstairs. She then turned to another two people in black, who were disposing of the bodies of the janitors and security guard, and nodded in approval. "Because if it is, that's a hell of a way to thank me for saving your life."

Richie suddenly felt embarrassed, and his headache didn't make him feel any better. Hurrying after her, he said, "Wait!"

When the Lady in Red stopped, Richie quickly cleared his throat. "I'm sorry. It's just that . . . those notes. I mean, the police think—"

"The police think what the real killer wants them to think," said the Lady in Red. "Nothing more and nothing less."

The Lady in Red folded her arms and stared straight into Richie. "You know, you're lucky as hell that Marcello owns this place, that he has the security cameras turned off when he's here, and that he pays off the police to stay away from it. Otherwise, Richie, you'd be in serious trouble."

Biting his bottom lip, Richie nodded, then asked, "So, if you all aren't behind the murders, but someone is using your name, then . . ."

Richie's voice trailed off, and then hurriedly he said, "That is why you asked me to try to solve this murder! Someone is framing you all!"

The Lady in Red gave a sexy smile, leaned in, and pressed her lips over Richie's. The taste was like strawberries, the scent like exotic fruits, the feeling like silk. There was no emotion to the kiss, just the physical act. When she parted from it, she said in a low, sexy voice, "I knew you were the right pick, Richie."

Stepping away, the Lady in Red was approached by the big Cajun-sounding man who had initially saved Richie from his attackers. "Madam, we're done here. We're clearing out."

"Good," replied the Lady in Red, who then looked back to Richie. "We'll be watching you, Richie. I'll be watching you, like I have for a long time. Solve this case, Richie. And be careful." The Lady in Red's pouty lips frowned. "It's imperative that Sam stays alive until this is over. So watch out for yourself, and keep Sam safe."

"I will keep her safe," Richie replied, looking down at the ground. "I care for her. We'll solve this together. Thank you."

Richie looked up, and the Lady in Red and her companions were gone. He muttered, "I hate it when she does that."

A few minutes later, Richie was standing outside, looking at the nearly vacant parking lot of the Riverwalk. Only the car that had brought him, along with the Marcellos' limo, were still there. No one else was around.

Sitting down on the stairs leading up to the Riverwalk, Richie started to feel his emotions surge forth and his psyche start to melt. Despite having kept himself together during a meeting with a cutthroat lawyer, an interview with two detectives, and an interrogation with a mob boss, this was too much.

For a long time, Richie sobbed into his hands, rocking back and forth and feeling wave after wave of anxiety run through him. Over and over again, he thought the same thing: *What the hell am I supposed to do now?*

Chapter 24
Mending of the Ways

Date: **Friday, August 7, 1992**
Time: **10:00 p.m.**
Location: **Sam Castille's Townhome**
                Uptown New Orleans

By the time Rodger drove up to Sam's house, it was pretty late. Sam, who had fallen asleep, was easily roused, and Rodger helped her inside. As she turned on the lights in the hallway, then onward leading to the kitchen, Rodger looked in the front hall's grandfather clock and took out Edward's gun.

When Sam came back, Rodger was looking over the gun, a wistful smile on his face. He looked up and saw Sam looking at him, a mixture of amusement and annoyance on her face.

"Your father's service revolver," Rodger said, looking at the gun with a fondness that only a memory could bring. "He always kept it in this clock, right here in the hallway, when he wasn't at work."

He opened the barrel of the gun and, seeing six bullets, said, "You keep it loaded. Are those the same bullets he had in his gun twenty years ago?" Recalling the report of Edward Castille's murder, Rodger knew that Edward's gun was found without a single shot fired.

Sam took the gun, politely but firmly, from his hands. She closed up the barrel and put the revolver back in place. "Yes. And now I keep it here for protective purposes. I'd like to think that my father's spirit is watching out for me in that gun."

Rodger put his hands in his coat pockets and nodded. "Maybe it is, Sam. Your father thought the world of you. You should know it. You should remember it."

"Yeah, I know," was Sam's reply as she latched the grandfather clock's door closed. "It just seems so distant to me, my memories of Dad. I know it sounds awful, Rodger, but I have much better memories, especially lately, of Grandfather."

Sam leaned against the wooden and glass frame of the grandfather clock. "It's like, I don't know, it's like he's the one watching over me and not my father. Isn't that creepy? That a monster like Vincent Castille would be my guardian angel, keeping watch over me from beyond the grave?"

Rodger rested his hand on Sam's shoulder, saying, "Sam, your grandfather is nowhere near you. You and I both know that if there is an afterlife, he's burning in the lowest levels of it—pardon me for saying that."

"No, it's okay," Sam said, shaking her head, a hint of bitterness in her voice. "Grandfather was a monster. I hope that he is burning in hell."

For a few moments, neither said anything. Then Sam, with a chuckle, detached herself from the grandfather clock and said, "Well, this is a morbid conversation." She pointed back at the kitchen with her thumb. "I was just making some coffee. Richie should hopefully call and check in soon. Did you want some coffee while we wait for Michael?"

Rubbing his chin, Rodger replied that coffee would be wonderful.

An hour and some Chinese takeout later, Rodger was sitting in Sam's study, enjoying his second cup of coffee, and feeling very relaxed. Sam, who had gone upstairs to take a shower, still hadn't come back down. There was no sign of Michael or Richie, and Rodger was beginning to wonder if he'd need to give the precinct a call and inquire as to where his partner had gone.

Rodger's thoughts were interrupted by a knock on the front door. Looking around and realizing that he was the only person on the first floor, Rodger got up and went to the front door.

"Just a minute," he said gruffly before unlatching the front door and opening it up.

Michael was standing there. For only a moment, Rodger could see the most pissed-off look on his partner's face. Then Rodger's vision was obscured by Michael punching him directly in the nose.

Stars and fireworks went off in Rodger's head as he stumbled back, landing on his ass, his vision momentarily blurred from the pain of the blow to his nose. Above him, he could hear Michael, his voice low but trembling. "You son of a bitch. Why didn't you tell me?"

As Rodger's senses came back, so did a rush of anger. Who the hell did Michael think he was to hit him like that? Getting back on his feet, Rodger shook off the pain and looked at his younger partner.

Seeing Michael moving to grab him, Rodger, more out of instinct than anything else, dropped his shoulders and punched Michael twice in the gut. His own voice was much angrier, much louder, as he said, "What the fuck is your problem, Michael?! Tell you what?"

Rodger couldn't figure out what had his partner so angry, but that thought was quickly spinning into oblivion as the white-hot anger of being coldcocked in the face was taking over. Moving to put his partner in an elbow lock, Rodger was a moment too late in seeing Michael's head rise up. The top of Michael's head struck the underside of Rodger's chin.

Rodger saw red stars.

Stumbling again, Rodger fell flat on his back. Michael, who was panting and grabbing his gut, limped to stand over the fallen older man. His voice was still angry as he said, "Sam's father. Your partner. Edward Castille. Same damn guy. Why didn't you tell me?"

Lying there on the ground, Rodger felt fear at Michael having figured out that he had still been keeping a major secret from him, even though he had sworn not to tell. However, as he felt Michael grab his collar to lift him up, that fear was replaced by anger at being assaulted. Rearing his head back for the second time in two days, Rodger head-butted Michael in the face.

Michael stumbled back against one of the walls of the front hall, while Rodger, who got to his feet with considerable trouble, fell back against the other wall. For a long moment, Rodger, who was both exhausted and had a bloody nose, just tried to catch his breath.

Finally, when he could speak, he said, "I guess it's too late to apologize, eh?"

Michael glared back at him, blood coming from his mouth, and said, "Yeah, a bit late."

Nodding, Rodger asked, "Will an explanation do?"

"Maybe," was Michael's response.

Blood was trickling down the back of Rodger's throat from his busted nose, but he ignored it. Instead, he began to explain. "It's really simple, Michael. I've felt ashamed for letting Edward go off alone to confront Vincent, which, of course, led to him getting killed. I've been beating myself up over it for twenty years. That's why."

To Rodger's surprise, Michael laughed some, shaking his head. "You really are a stupid ass, Rodger. Don't you realize that this one piece of information could destroy the entire investigation?"

Rodger shook his head. "How the hell could that possibly derail everything?"

Michael's tone was bitter. "Because you're making it damn near impossible for me to trust you or your motivations. You've withheld so much information from me, it's like you've been purposefully impeding the investigation. And now this? You know that Sam is a suspect, but you withhold who her father was. It makes it look like you're protecting her. And since I can't see Ouellette not knowing, it looks like you and he are in this together. How can we work together if I can't trust you?"

Rodger continued to glare at Michael. Shaking his head, he said, "It's not what you think it is, Michael. We all kept that quiet because of Edward's dealings with the Marcello family. We—"

Rodger stopped midsentence when he heard some footsteps coming downstairs.

"What the hell is going on?" Sam said, stepping down to the bottom of the stairs and looking around. She was freshly showered, her still-wet hair pulled back in a ponytail.

Standing there, still bleeding from his nose, Rodger decided it was better not to try to make up a lie just for appearances' sake. "Michael and I had, well, a disagreement," he said, nodding his head at his partner. "We were just working our differences out."

"Sounded like the two of you were beating the hell out of each other," said Sam as she reached the bottom step, shaking her head at both men. "What the heck is happening? Is the stress of this investigation getting so bad that you are all starting to fight like you and Father did, Rodger?"

Rodger didn't say anything at first, aware that Michael was, once again, glaring at him. Looking at Sam, who was standing at the base of the stairs, arms folded, staring back at him with a look of concern and exasperation, Rodger suddenly felt very old, like he had lived past his usefulness long ago. Michael didn't seem to be saying anything, and Rodger wondered if his partner would say anything to Sam about what the fight was really about. However, as the seconds passed, and no such comment came, Rodger realized that Michael wanted him to respond to Sam.

"It's that and some other problems," Rodger said, giving a small nod to Sam. "Michael and I have some talking to do, and I have a lot of explaining to do." He looked over at his partner.

Michael didn't give much of a nod, but it was enough to show Rodger that, indeed, there would be an uncomfortable conversation forthcoming.

"I see," replied Sam as she moved forward to look at Rodger's nose, going so far as to tilt his head up to look at the injury. As much as he wanted to stop her from fussing over him, the pain in his nose was pretty intense, having turned into that kind of throbbing pain that lingers.

"Let me clean the two of you up," said Sam, who started heading toward the kitchen, motioning for both men to follow her.

Rodger followed Michael and Sam into the kitchen, thinking, *We've fought before. But not like this. He must be seriously pissed off.*

Rodger didn't say anything as Sam fixed him up, stopping the bleeding in his nose and making sure it wasn't actually broken. Once Sam determined everything was okay, she tended to Michael, who was equally banged up. As she finished up, the phone rang.

"Crap, I bet that's Richie," said Sam.

She hurried up front. Rodger could barely hear Sam say "hello" before her voice dropped too low for him to hear. Not wanting to eavesdrop, he soon refocused his attention on his partner.

Michael was standing and looking at a piece of artwork on the wall. Rodger had a good view of his partner's back, and Michael seemed to be keen on making sure that was all of him that Rodger saw.

Rodger spoke in a low voice. "Okay, I don't know about you, but I don't want to keep this kind of tension up. I've had too much happen lately, and my old ticker can't handle it. So, what do I need to do to make this right?"

Michael's reply was hushed and sharp. "Tell me every goddamn thing you've been hiding about this case, about Edward, and about you."

Rodger inhaled slowly through his mouth, the throbbing pain in his nose still prevalent. "Right, so after we leave here, we'll go somewhere and I'll tell you everything. That's fair?"

"Yeah, that's fine," replied Michael. As Michael didn't say anything else, Rodger figured that the matter, for the moment, was done. He knew he still had a lot to get through, though. This was turning out to be a very uncomfortable day. *I'm not used to being this emotionally worn out.*

Sam returned. "Richie's not coming over tonight," she said, a tone of regret to her voice. "He has apparently had a rough day, too. He said he'd catch us up on it tomorrow, and that he's got some major news."

Rodger shook his head, just as Michael did, not sure that Richie was someone to take seriously. One look at Michael, and he was sure his partner felt the same way. *Richie is completely out of his element.*

Michael said, "That's just as well, Sam. Rodger and I need to get going. We have to compare notes and get ready to meet with Commander Ouellette tomorrow morning."

Immediately, Rodger felt his blood pressure rise at the mention of meeting with Ouellette, especially since there was no advance notice. Rodger started to wonder if that meant he and Michael just got put on the hot seat.

One look at Michael, who seemed completely composed, and Rodger suspected that it was just a story by Michael to give them an excuse to go have their "talk."

"It's okay, really," Sam said. "I need to get some more coffee and then start on the second chapter in my story. Lord knows, with the details of the last murders identical to my story, I'm half-way considering not writing anything at all."

Before Rodger could say anything, Michael spoke up. "Actually, Sam, don't do that. Write the story just as you intended, especially if there is another murder in chapter two."

Sam nodded, saying, "There is. Do you want me to tell you who gets killed?"

"No," was Michael's reply. "Telling us about your next victim will only make me want to search a city filled with hundreds of thousands of people for a single person based on nothing more than a description."

"Michael's got a good point," Rodger, who had been feeling left out of the conversation, said. "Your last character victim didn't have the same name as the actual victim. So it wouldn't help."

Michael went on, "So what I need you to do, Sam, is create a list of everything you do, from the moment you finish typing the manuscript, to the moment you drop it off at the *Times-Picayune.* Every little thing you do, no matter how insignificant, you need to list. Then, when you have that list, give it to me."

That made Rodger experience two different feelings. First, it made him grumpy that Michael was blatantly cutting him out.

Second, it made him feel hopeful that Michael had an actual plan to crack this case. The look in Michael's eyes, for that moment, eerily reminded Rodger of Edward.

Sam nodded and said, "All right. I can do this. I'll give you a detailed list of what I do tomorrow. Also, I won't allow myself to be sidetracked."

"Thank you," Michael said in reply, then turned to Rodger. "Are you ready to leave, Rodger?"

"I am," replied Rodger, who was starting to feel tired. The day had been long, and this was after the hell that had been Mad Monty. While he knew the value of getting everything with Michael out in the open, Rodger really just wanted to go back to his apartment, have a whiskey, and go to sleep.

Rodger followed Sam to the foyer while Michael got his jacket. Out of earshot of his partner, he gave Sam a brief hug and said, "You be careful, Sam. Remember, you are still a suspect."

Sam, who seemed all too pleased to hug Rodger back, replied that she would be very careful. By the time Michael came out of the kitchen, Sam was unlatching the door to let both men out.

"Good night, you two," Sam said, closing the door behind them.

As Rodger heard the latches slide back in place, he felt that she would indeed be safe.

"You want to drive, Rodger?" Michael asked as they walked to the squad car.

"Honestly, I really don't," Rodger said, taking a moment to enjoy the warm night air. "Do you mind?"

"I don't care," was Michael's reply, the cold way he said it giving Rodger a shiver.

As Rodger got into the passenger seat, his partner was struggling to get the latch on the driver's side safety belt to catch.

"This stupid belt hardly works," Michael briskly commented, finally getting the seat belt to stick.

"It is a piece of shit, partner," Rodger said, the passenger seat belt easily catching. "I've told Ouellette about it several times.

I'm sure when the next quarter budget gets approved, we'll get it fixed."

"Probably not," Michael said as he started up the car. "But we'll see, I suppose." He put the car in Reverse and pulled out of the driveway of Sam's townhome. "So, where to for conversation?"

"The usual place," suggested Rodger, who wasn't feeling too adventurous after such a long day.

"It's probably packed this time of night," replied Michael, as he headed out toward the French Quarter. "Besides, Danny O'Flaherty is singing tonight, isn't he? We won't be able to hear ourselves think, much less talk. How about Jean Lafitte's Blacksmith Bar?"

Rodger chuckled, then nodded, saying, "Somehow, that is terribly appropriate."

Michael's expression didn't seem to soften, so Rodger tried again to lighten the conversation. "That was a good excuse you gave Sam to getting us out of staying late, that Ouellette wanted to see us tomorrow morning. Pretty ingenious."

"It wasn't an excuse," Michael said curtly. "Ouellette wants to see us both at nine in the morning, sharp."

Suddenly, Rodger felt that the mood of the conversation didn't need to be messed with anymore.

Thirty minutes later, both detectives were sitting at a table in a dark, private corner of the Jean Lafitte Bar, far on the Dauphine side of the French Quarter on Bourbon Street. While it was not their usual spot, Jean Lafitte was typically more quiet on any given night. People could actually hear each other.

Rodger liked Jean Lafitte's, although the irony of this bar and the nightclub that had become an important part of the case was not lost on him. The bar, which had once been a blacksmith shop, had a cozy quality to it.

The atmosphere was kept comfortable and dark, due to the illumination of palely lit lanterns, the tables and chairs had an Old World feel to them, the walls were still made of cobbled stone, and the centerpiece of the bar was the old forge and anvil.

Both detectives had gotten a pint of their favorite beers. While Rodger was looking around at the customers, most of them natives who were enjoying Bourbon Street, he noted that Michael was getting out his notebook and pen. Rodger's expression soured. As he sipped on his beer, he thought to himself that Michael wasn't capable of relaxing.

"All right," Michael finally said, taking a sip of his beer and getting ready to take notes. "Start talking, Rodger. No more bullshit. Tell me everything."

Rodger decided the best place to start was with Edward.

"You want to know about Edward Castille," Rodger said, the pale light of the bar's lanterns cascading off his tired face, "I'll tell you about Edward Castille. But a word of this isn't to get to Sam. Ever." He made sure there was a serious quality to his voice—one that conveyed to his often socially obtuse partner the severity of his "request."

Rodger went on, "Edward was what one would have called a model cop. The guy fought for the good guys simply because he wanted the world to be a better place. Or so that is what people like Ouellette and I would have you believe. The truth is that, at the time of his death, Edward was under investigation by Internal Affairs."

Michael, who had been scribbling notes, looked up and blinked. From where Rodger was sitting, the lantern light shone completely on his partner's face, and every etched line of confused suspicion shone through.

Michael looked Rodger in the eyes and asked, "So, then, Edward was a dirty cop?"

Rodger shifted so that the light of the lantern fell off his face. He didn't like talking about this ugly part of his former partner's life, but as Michael had asked for the truth, and a lot more was at stake than Rodger's comfort, he pushed himself to continue.

"If it were only that easy," said Rodger, "because the investigation was never concluded. You see, Vincent Castille was business partners with the head of the Marcello crime family, Carlos Marcello."

"I know that," Michael replied, looking back down at his notes. "I found that out today. They were, what did she say, 'real tight,' right?"

Instantly, Rodger knew who Michael was talking about. Leaning forward and narrowing his eyes some, Rodger said, "You spoke with Rosemary today, didn't you?"

Michael looked up at him, his surprise evident.

With a smirk, Rodger continued. "Yes, Dr. Castille and Mr. Marcello grew up near each other along Pontchartrain Lake—you know, the area in Mandeville where all big mansions are."

Rodger didn't need to elaborate. Unless his partner knew nothing of New Orleans, he'd know the part of Lake Pontchartrain—Northshore—where the obscenely rich lived.

When Michael nodded in understanding, Rodger continued. "One went on to become the head of the biggest crime family in New Orleans, and the other became a respected and beloved doctor. But they remained in contact. So in 1960, the childhood friends funded, built, and managed Jean Lafitte Theater. Why? To live out the glory days of the forties and fifties, I suppose. It's not really important, because the real meat doesn't come with those old geezers, but with their sons."

"Edward and Giorgio," replied Michael.

With a nod, Rodger leaned back into the darkness, taking his beer with him. For a few choice moments, he sipped on it. It had a bitter taste, but it was cool and felt good going down.

"Fathers knew each other, sons knew each other. You could call the two pals, even though they ran in obviously opposing circles. Fast-forward to the seventies. As Blue-Eyed Giorgio came under suspicion of being a serial rapist, the police put him under more and more surveillance. And Giorgio got better and better at dodging the heat."

"And let me guess," Michael said, scribbling like mad. "Edward was under suspicion of protecting his friend, right?"

"Yeah. At first, it seemed ridiculous. Edward was an upstanding cop. He had a young daughter, Samantha, to care for. And together, he and I had closed hundreds of tough murder cases. It was inconceivable that Edward would be dirty."

Michael looked up for a moment, obviously trying to see Rodger in the shadows. "But I don't get it, Rodger. Internal Affairs back then wasn't what it is now. What made them focus so heavily on Edward?"

"The Jean Lafitte Club," Rodger said. "That damn club. I hated going there, but Edward went there all the time. And guess who else was there?"

"Giorgio," was Michael's reply.

"You got it, partner," Rodger said, taking another long swig of his beer. "When I stopped going, and Edward continued to go, and Giorgio started dodging the cops, suspicious eyes fell on Detective Castille."

Rodger paused for a long time and then said, "And me. Giorgio and Edward would often be heard arguing behind closed doors, and the next day the trail of Blue-Eyed Giorgio's activities would go cold."

Michael looked up, and Rodger could see that his partner finally got it. "So you had to distance yourself from Edward, while maintaining the illusion of being close to him, in order to keep yourself from being investigated."

Rodger leaned forward, his face fully in the lantern light. He knew the tired lines on his old face showed. Nodding, he said, "It was the hardest balancing act I have ever had to play. I cared for Edward. He was a friend. And I honestly believed I was better friends with him and Blue-Eyed Giorgio. Not to mention that I loved Samantha like my own daughter. But this . . . this sucked. And it happened during the worst possible time."

Michael's face again registered comprehension. "During the Bourbon Street Ripper murders."

"Correct," Rodger said. He took a sip of his beer, and then sighed. "So, when you think about it, Edward should not have been buried with full honors. But considering that he gave his life to bring down the most infamous serial killer this city had ever seen, it was no surprise when Internal Affairs sealed the case and swept the matter under the rug."

Michael asked, "So, how many of you covered it up? How many are left who still know?"

Rodger thought about it long enough to get an accurate count. "Myself; old Dugas, who headed up the investigation against Giorgio; Ouellette, who, believe it not, was already bald back then; and Kyle Aucoin. We're the only ones left who remember."

Michael nodded his head and, after a few seconds, finished writing. Looking at Rodger, he said, "So that is why Sam is being observed and treated so carefully as a suspect. Her grandfather was the Ripper and her father may have been on the take."

Rodger nodded, figuring that the matter of Edward was closed. He started to drink his beer, but nearly choked when Michael said, "Rodger, I think Edward was innocent. Rosemary said something that resonated with me. I don't think that the arguments had to do with Blue-Eyed Giorgio being under suspicion of rape."

"Whoa, slow down, Michael. Old Rosemary hasn't opened up to anyone before. And believe me, the pressure was put on her. So what's the story there?"

Michael said, "It's simple. I know that Blue-Eyed Giorgio wanted to have a relationship with Magnolia of the M and M Sisters, while she already had a relationship with Edward."

Rodger thought for a moment, sure that the situation didn't add up, swirling the ideas around in his head. After a moment, Rodger shook his head and said, "No, you got that backward. It was the other one, Marigold—Magnolia's twin sister—who was Edward's lover."

The look on Michael's face showed that he wanted to argue, but was fighting it.

Sucking in his breath, Rodger said, "I could have it wrong, partner. It's been twenty years. Magnolia died shortly before the Ripper murders began, and Marigold ran away soon before Dr. Castille was arrested."

Michael didn't say anything for a long moment. When he finally spoke, his voice was very firm. "We need to get that straight, Rodger. I'm sure it's important. Rosemary stated, before I left, that Magnolia was murdered."

This revelation made Rodger blink, and again he was sure the confusion shone on his face.

"Magnolia was murdered? Hmmm. I thought she had a heart attack. Man, this shit from twenty years ago, it just won't go away."

While it was obvious that Michael was tensing up again, Rodger could tell his partner was still managing to keep his cool.

"It is relevant, Rodger," said Michael. "Even if it's not linked to the current case, figuring it out should give us an idea of the big picture. Besides, wouldn't you like to be able to go to the office of the police chief with evidence that Edward Castille was an honest cop caught in a dirty game?"

That thought made a part of Rodger that had been tense for years start to relax. With a tired nod, he said, "I would love that. For his sake. For Sam's."

Michael turned the pages in his notebook and said, "Now, that brings me to the current investigation. Rodger, I am sorry, but the circumstantial evidence points to Sam as the killer. She has a history of mental illness, she was as messed up as Dallas, who I met, by the way, and who is completely off the list of suspects—the guy couldn't hurt a fly—and she has the access to everything her grandfather had, including his property on Lake Pontchartrain, where the torture chamber is located and where the last murder was committed. I don't want to believe it, and I'd want hard evidence before I'd consider arresting her, but it doesn't look good."

Rodger felt his stress level return. Shaking his head, he said, "No freaking way. Sam didn't do it. My gut tells me—"

"Your gut, I am sorry to say," Michael replied, his voice elevated, "hasn't been worth shit lately. In fact, Rodger, who really solved the Ripper murders? You and Edward? Or just Edward?"

Rodger's brow furrowed. As he pulled himself back in the shadows, obscuring his face, he said, "Fuck you, Michael."

From the darkness, Rodger could see his partner's expression soften, Michael getting a look that showed he realized that he had gone too far.

"I'm sorry."

Rodger didn't feel like accepting that apology. He had been wrestling with this for a long time, and Michael's lack of social graces were bringing him to the very edge. He knew the answer, but admitting it out loud would take a surplus of courage that he no longer had—not after today.

After a few moments, Rodger said, "Let's just say that I have as much to prove this time around as you do, and leave it at that."

That seemed to be good enough for Michael. He nodded and sipped his beer. "Well, Sam could be cleared if we could just search her apartment. But that damn Kent keeps stonewalling us from doing so."

"Kent is just looking out for Sam," Rodger replied coolly. "The real thing that concerns me is that someone has deliberately sabotaged my relationship with Sam. Can you believe this shit, Michael? Today, I discovered that someone had stopped her from getting every card I'd ever sent her. All those years of trying to foster goodwill, while nurturing my own injured ego, fucked over because someone decided to block my efforts to be Good Uncle Rodger."

Michael looked up for a second and then nodded. Rodger wondered, through the haze of his mind, muddled now with exhaustion and alcohol, what his partner had figured out. Rodger was sure he'd figure it out later and slid it into the messy stockpile of information that was his memory to sort through later.

Michael turned the page of his notebook and read a note. "By the way, Rodger, Blind Moses is a woman."

"I know," was Rodger's relaxed reply. "Fat Willie told me. And that reminds me. I've got some shit to tell you on him, but let's save it for after I've sobered up."

Michael nodded and said, "That's fine. Anyway, assuming Sam and Richie can keep themselves out of trouble, I have our next two locations figured out. We need to go back to Robert Fontenot and drill him on some particulars that Rosemary said. Then, we need to go to the Castille Mansion on Lake Pontchartrain. I've already got a search warrant in the works, in case the proprietor there tries to stop us."

"That's a good idea," Rodger said, the feeling of booze and sleep deprivation mixing like a Zen cocktail. "If this Magnolia,

Marigold, and Mary thing is going to get sorted out, the Castille Mansion could very well be the place to do it."

Michael looked at Rodger with a confused expression, and asked, "Who the hell is Mary, Rodger?"

Rodger started to answer when someone out the corner of his eye caught his attention. Rodger got up, ignoring his partner calling after him, and headed over to the person in question.

"Kyle," Rodger said, approaching Aucoin, who was still in his suit, standing in the middle of the bar as if he were lost, and looking around. "Here for a drink?"

Aucoin turned toward Rodger, a surprised look on his face. "Rodger, what the heck are you doing here?"

"Having a drink with his partner," replied Michael, who was by now at Rodger's side. Rodger felt a bit of his tension release and some of his pride return at Michael calling him his partner again. "If you're here about Ouellette, we already know. I found out from the commander himself."

"Ah, right, the meeting tomorrow," Aucoin said, looking around the bar again and then back at the detective duo. Patting Rodger on the shoulder, Aucoin managed a small wry smile and said, "Just so you know, you better not plan on having any balls tomorrow after the commander gets done with you."

Apart from helping to sober Rodger up, Aucoin's comment grounded Rodger back into reality. Looking over at Michael, Rodger realized that he had brushed him off again, and said, "I'll tell you about Mary later. Sorry, I got distracted."

"It's okay, thanks," Michael replied. "Detective Aucoin, if I may ask, what are you doing here? You're looking like you're waiting for someone. Is it Detective Olivier?"

Aucoin chuckled and shook his head. "Dixie? No. No. She's probably having a Greek gyro right now. No, I'm looking for someone. Although I guess this is not the place. Man, I am really out of touch with the hot spots in the Quarter."

"Well, there's any place on Bourbon Street," Rodger said. "And there is O'Flaherty's on Toulouse, and House of Blues on Decatur. Why, who are you looking for?"

"My daughter, Cheryl," Aucoin replied. "We got into a fight earlier this evening and she ran off with her friends. With that copycat killer on the loose, Cathy is sick with worry and wants me to find her and bring her home."

Rodger looked over at Michael. As his partner nodded, Rodger realized that the Ripper copycat investigation was going to get put on pause for the night, and all three of them would be getting to bed late after trying to find Cheryl.

"We'll help you," Rodger said to Aucoin. "Let's split up and search for her until we find her."

Michael said, "Right. And if Rodger or I find her, we'll detain her and call Cathy to come pick her up."

Aucoin, who had been looking around again, looked back at the two detectives and gave the kind of tired smile that only a grateful father could give.

"Thanks. I'll remember this, guys. So let's get started. She didn't disappear by magic."

Chapter 25
One Last Chance

Date: **Saturday, August 8, 1992**
Time: **9:00 a.m.**
Location: **New Orleans Police Precinct, 8th District**
           French Quarter

"Rodger, Michael, I am trying so hard not to have a reason to suspend you," Ouellette said to the two detectives, his palms resting flat on the surface of his desk. The tension in the office was palpable, hanging in the air like thick smoke. The door was closed and the shutters were drawn over the windows. Outside the office, the conversations were hushed at best.

Michael was standing to the side of his partner, who, like him, had his hands at his sides and was in an attentive, almost military stance. Sitting to the other side, looking less tense but equally troubled, were Aucoin and Dixie, the former of whom kept looking at his watch. Michael noted that, with the exception of Dixie, everyone in the room looked haggard, tired, and on edge. Even Ouellette, who held himself together with admirable military discipline, seemed like he had not slept in days.

"I am trying so very hard not to have a reason to suspend you," Ouellette repeated, his hands lifting from the surface of his desk and leaving sweat marks, "but your behavior yesterday broke so many rules that I have basically two choices."

Lifting a finger, Ouellette said, "One, I suspend you both right now without pay, and hand the investigation to Aucoin and Dixie. After this case is closed, we can review why Rodger saw fit to take a suspect to Angola, and why Michael saw fit to allow a known witness, who, might I add, gave my other two detectives a real piss-poor attitude, to perform a private investigation."

Michael stood there, unflinching, allowing the accusation to be laid upon him. He had already decided to take the sole blame for suggesting Richie go investigate at the library, since Rodger faced the far more serious charge of carting Sam around.

"Two," said Ouellette, producing a second finger, "I can sweep this shit under the rug with the boys in City Hall, and you two can walk with a very short leash for the rest of this investigation."

Lowering his hand to point at Rodger and Michael, Ouellette said, "I just need from you both a good reason to do the second option instead of the first."

As Michael stood there, formulating what to say, Rodger spoke up. "Michael and I are making some strong headway with the case now. If you'd give us just a few more days, I'm sure we can catch this guy before he kills again."

As soon as Rodger was finished, Michael spoke up. "Commander, we're on the verge of connecting the old Ripper case to this copycat one. We just need a few more key pieces of evidence, and we'll be ready to make an arrest."

Lowering his hand, Ouellette glared at both men, then turned to Aucoin and Dixie. "What do you two think?"

Dixie said, "I think Michael and Rodger have a good point. We should hear the evidence that they've found so far. I'm sure it's more than enough to make up for what they did yesterday."

There was a long pause as everyone, including Ouellette, looked at what was obviously a very distracted Aucoin. They hadn't found Cheryl the night before.

"Aucoin, you wanna come back to work now and offer your opinion on this problem?" Ouellette said.

Aucoin seemed to snap back into place, shaking his head and sitting up straight.

"Right, sorry," he said, clearing his throat. "We've got a solid idea of who it could be with Sam Castille, but as Michael pointed out, we lack hard evidence. Maybe she's guilty, maybe she's not.

But our best bet is to hear what they have to say and then make a decision."

Ouellette stared at Aucoin for a long time, then nodded and turned back to Michael and Rodger. "All right, tell me everything you have learned so far. I'll make my decision then. Michael, you go first."

Michael began to recount everything he had experienced the day before, starting with the trip to Lafayette to meet Dallas Christofer. He then recounted his surprisingly successful visit with Rosemary Boucher, and wrapped it up with the conversation he and Rodger had at Jean Lafitte's—leaving out the fistfight in Sam's townhome.

When Michael was done, Ouellette turned to Rodger. Michael didn't feel snubbed by Ouellette's brisk response. This was serious business.

Rodger gave his report, and while Michael had heard most of it, the retelling of the meeting with Fat Willie just confirmed what Michael had suspected—that this investigation and the one twenty years ago were interconnected. Michael wasn't surprised to hear about the letter Fat Willie received, but he was surprised to hear "Mary" being mentioned. Michael recalled that Rodger had been about to talk about this Mary when Aucoin's appearance had derailed them, and Michael filed away a mental memo to ask his partner about it again later.

Ouellette nodded as Rodger finished up, saying, "I see. So the bloated bastard got a letter as well, giving us three letters total. What do they say?"

"Topper Jack's and Mad Monty's are almost identical," answered Michael. "They both point out knowledge of what the men had previously done and asked them to do it again. Payment was offered in advance. For Topper Jack, it was morphine. For Mad Monty, it was cash."

Rodger picked up for Michael at this point. "Fat Willie's letter was different. In it, this Nite Priory claims to know about all of Fat Willie's crimes, both the rapes and helping the Bourbon Street Ripper by kidnapping the victims. But then the letter asks

Fat Willie for a list of his rape victims from twenty to fifteen years ago."

This was news to Michael, and apparently to everyone else, including Ouellette, who asked, "Well, did the bastard send such a list?"

With a sigh, Rodger said, "I wish I knew. I didn't read the letter until after the interview. I'll have to call and find out again, pull another favor."

Ouellette nodded sternly and said, "Be sure you do. So, have either of you had any luck in tracking down Blind Moses?"

Michael said, "No, we haven't had any luck with her."

"All right," Ouellette said and turned around, looking over his military photographs. He seemed to take only a few seconds to reach a decision. "I run a tight ship, and you two nearly brought the weight of Internal Affairs down on me yesterday. Luckily for you both, Aucoin is great at talking bullshit to those ballbusters, and Dixie knows when to shut her mouth."

Michael looked over at the other two detectives, his eyes widening just a hair for a moment as he realized they had covered for him and Rodger. Trading understanding glances with Dixie for a moment, he knew that the two other detectives understood what was at stake. *They know that we have to solve this case before a third or, God help us, a fourth victim turns up. It will be a serious mess. Who else is putting their careers on the line?*

Michael looked back at Ouellette, and suddenly understood the real reason his commander was so angry—the risk and consequences eventually came to rest on his shoulders.

Ouellette was saying, "But you are going to tell me where you are going, and when you get back, until I say otherwise. Also, I'm not inclined to give you all another chance if you fuck up again."

Ouellette then pointed at each detective in turn.

"So, Michael, no more independent investigations by Mr. Fastellos. You see him snooping around the case again, you arrest him, or your ass is desked for a month. And Rodger, you get over your fixation with Samantha Castille. She isn't your little niece, or whatever she was twenty years ago, anymore. She's a grown woman and a suspect. I catch you near her again, your ass is suspended for a month."

"Understood, sir," replied Michael.

"Understood, Commander," said Rodger.

Ouellette sat at his desk. "Now, what are you two going to do today? And will it include nearly getting yourselves killed?"

Before Rodger could speak up, Michael said, "We're heading back to Bayou Lafitte to speak with Mr. Robert Fontenot again. Rosemary Boucher mentioned Magnolia was murdered. We feel it would beneficial to find out what was meant by that. As we have no jurisdiction in Lafayette, this is the only course of action we can take to get reliable information about that."

Ouellette nodded. "I see. Unfortunately, I don't remember the M and M Sisters very well, but I seem to recall Magnolia had some kind of health problem. Very well, go talk to Fontenot. I'll give Jefferson Parish a call again. Head directly over to the police station near the Bayou. But, make sure you get your ass right back here afterward."

"Right," said Michael, who started to leave.

"Wait a second," replied Ouellette, making Michael stop and turn around. "Call me when you arrive at the police station and before you leave. You all can check in with your buddy J. L."

As Michael rolled his eyes at the thought of seeing "good ol' J. L." again, Rodger responded with, "Checking in and out is a bit excessive, Ouellette. This isn't Houma all over again. You don't need to track our every movement."

The temperature dropped several degrees. Michael and Dixie traded nervous, unsure glances. Rodger, who looked like he realized he had screwed up, shrank like a turtle into its shell.

"Get out of my office," Ouellette exploded, pointing at the door on the way out. The room outside suddenly got very quiet.

Rodger quickly left the room, Michael right behind him, the two detectives emerging right into the open floor, where almost every single person in the homicide department stared at them. From inside his office, Ouellette could be heard yelling, "So, Aucoin, what the hell has you so distracted today, huh?!"

The two detectives got to their desks, sat down, and started getting ready to depart. Michael gathered up his notebook, the three letters from the three accomplices, and his jacket.

Rodger was almost finished getting ready when Aucoin stormed up behind him and shoved him into his desk. "You wanna piss the boss off, asshole, so he can take it out on me?"

Rodger turned around, looking ready to belt Aucoin in the face, and said, "Back off, shithead. Don't blame me for you being distracted with your kid."

"I should bust your teeth out," Aucoin said, raising a fist.

Michael started to move to intercept the blow when Dixie grabbed her partner from behind and pulled him back, saying, "Kyle, it's not worth it! Just let it go!"

As Dixie pulled Aucoin back, Michael moved to stand beside Rodger.

Aucoin finally calmed down enough to get Dixie off of him, then, dusting off his jacket, he pointed at the two detectives. "Next time you two screw up, you're on your own." He stormed off.

Dixie stayed behind a moment to say, "Sorry, it's just that—"

"Cheryl is still missing," Rodger interrupted, pulling his trench coat on. "I know. Michael and I stayed up all night helping Mr. Grateful look for her. I still say she got drunk with some friends and is over at one of their houses."

Michael found himself hoping that was the case, as he was telling himself the same thing, hoping that nothing terrible had happened to Aucoin's daughter.

Dixie gave them a worried smile and said, "We all hope that. Unfortunately, this case takes priority, and Ouellette just turned down Kyle's request for some time off."

Michael wasn't surprised to hear that. "This case is rapidly becoming a high-profile case, Dix. One more victim, and Ouellette will probably have to form a task force."

Dixie, shaking her head, said, "I know. Let's just focus on getting the job done. We can quibble about this some other time."

"Agreed," said Rodger, who was ready to leave.

Michael watched as Rodger walked over to where Aucoin was sitting. Dixie started to move forward to say something, but Michael put his arm out to slow her down.

"Trust me," Michael said to his friend, certain he knew what his partner's action would be. "Rodger needs to do this."

Michael and Dixie watched as Rodger stood next to Aucoin until the latter noticed and looked up at him. Then Rodger put his hand out and said, "I'm sorry for what I said, Kyle. I promise that as soon as we get back, I'll help you find Cheryl."

Aucoin stared at Rodger for a long time before shaking the other man's hand, saying. "It's cool, man. Just . . . just stay out of trouble. We don't need to lose any more veterans to stupid shit."

Dixie turned to Michael and gave him a small grin. "How'd you know that?"

Giving her an equally small wry grin, Michael replied, "I figured at this point, those two could only make up or kill each other."

Dixie chuckled, shook her head at Michael, and reached over to rub his shoulder fondly. "You never cease to amaze me, Michael. But I swear, Rodger is starting to rub off on you."

"Ouch," Michael said in mock hurt, "no need to insult me."

Dixie headed off as Rodger returned. Fluffing up his trench coat, Rodger said, "Ready, partner?"

"Yeah, let's go," Michael replied, and headed out alongside Rodger toward the garage.

The two were almost to the car when a uniformed officer came running up to them, a bit out of breath and holding a folded piece of paper.

"Detective Bergeron?"

Rodger said, "Yeah, I'm Detective Bergeron. What's going on?"

The uniformed officer held out the folded paper, saying, "A faxed report just came for you from a Charles Daigle up at Angola." The officer finished catching his breath and handed the paper to Rodger before heading back toward the building.

Michael leaned against the car, watching as his partner unfolded the report and started reading it. After a few moments, Rodger leaned heavily on the side of the squad car, his face showing incredulity.

"I can't fucking believe this," Rodger said out loud.

Michael was at a loss. He didn't know who Charles Daigle was, or why he'd be writing from Angola. After waiting several long seconds for his partner to recover and answer, but with no answer forthcoming, Michael asked, "So, Rodger, what's going on in Angola?"

Rodger slowly folded up the paper and handed it over to Michael, who read it as his partner explained.

"Last night, there was a riot at the prison. A couple of dozen inmates were injured. However, Fat Willie, well, he tripped on the stairs while he and some others were being ushered by the guards to a secure area."

Michael looked up from the fax and asked, "Is Mr. Benedict badly hurt?"

Rodger shook his head, saying, "He broke his neck, Michael. He's dead."

Michael wondered just how much bad luck he and Rodger were capable of having with this investigation.

The first thirty minutes of the ride were filled with complete silence, and while Michael wasn't fond of driving the squad car, he had volunteered due to Rodger's physical condition continuing to deteriorate. *He's going to need to get some sleep soon. He's not functioning as well as he could be. Hell, I'm younger, and I know I'm not at a hundred percent.*

As they pulled onto the highway that would lead them south into Bayou Lafitte, Michael's thoughts focused on the recent death of Fat Willie. To Michael, foul play was definitely a possibility. After all, of all the accomplices so far, Fat Willie would have been the best possible material witness, someone to testify as to the way the copycat killer was operating.

And with him dead, another lead, that list of rape victims, is done. Unless . . .

Michael suddenly snapped out of his thoughts and turned to his partner. Rodger was snoring softly, and as much as Michael didn't want to wake him up, he needed him to do something.

"Rodger," Michael said, softly at first, and then again more loudly when his partner didn't wake up. After the second attempt, Michael abandoned all subtlety and shook Rodger awake. "Rodger, wake up!"

"Uhh!" was Rodger's jarred reaction, the older man shaking himself as he awakened and sat up. "Are we already there?"

"No, sorry," was Michael's response, sounding unusually apologetic. "I need you to do something for me. When we're done, you can go back to sleep."

"All right, all right," said Rodger gruffly, sitting up straight. "What do you need?"

"Get my notebook and pen out of the glove compartment," Michael began, concentrating on driving. "Go to a fresh page of paper, and write down, in a box, four words per row, 'Call Angola and see if they have a copy of Fat Willie's letter to Nite Priory.' Then circle it."

Rodger, who had the notebook opened to a fresh page, and the pen in his hand, said, "Do what now?"

Michael sighed. This was why he hated to get others involved in his processes. They always managed to mess it up. Only Dixie seemed to take to it well, and only after many nights of working late with her did Michael trust her enough to be a part of his logical methods. Their last all-nighter, about a month ago, ended with both of them going out for drinks after closing the reporting on close to fifty cases.

Taking a breath, Michael explained, "Whenever I write a note that is arranged in a box shape and circled, it means I need to do it as soon as possible. It's a physical symbol for me to see that registers a necessary action in my mind."

It took a few tries for Michael to convey the concept to Rodger, especially the fact that the box was the arrangement of the words and not a drawn box, as well as that he chose four words per row because he knew the entire note was sixteen words, but Rodger finally got it.

Once Rodger had the note down correctly, he commented, "That's an, um, interesting way of doing things there, Michael."

"It's what works for me," Michael replied, trying not to get irritated. "What's your method of organizing your notes, scribbling them down catawampus and hoping to find them later?"

Rodger chuckled and snorted. "I write them on napkins and Post-it Notes. Back off. We each have different ways of being detectives."

Michael apologized, noticing that he was becoming more emotionally sensitive as this case wore on. "Sorry. I think trying to crack this case is making us crack. Is this how you and Edward were near the end of the first case?"

"We were like this near the middle. It got a lot worse near the end," Rodger said, having settled down to go back to sleep.

Michael looked over at his partner, and remembered something he wanted to ask. "Hey, before you go to sleep, partner, what is Ouellette's deal with Houma?"

Rodger stirred a bit and sat back up. "Well, about five years ago, Ouellette, his wife, and their only son were visiting family in Houma. Ouellette's son, Jason, was in his early twenties and had enlisted with the army. He had just completed basic training and was going to be shipped off to Panama—ya know, to help take that bastard Noriega down—and Ouellette thought that it would be a good idea to have a boat party with the entire clan."

Michael nodded, taking it all in. "So what happened?"

"Well," Rodger said, rubbing his brow as if warding off a headache, "Jason and some of his cousins and their friends want to take a midnight alligator cruise of the bayou down in Houma. Ouellette usually kept a pretty close watch on his son, but this being his last weekend in the States for a while, figured the boy could handle himself."

"So, what," Michael asked, a bit leery, "he was eaten by an alligator?"

Rodger seemed jarred by Michael's question, the senior detective suddenly looking over. "What? No! Nothing like that. Jason had too much to drink, slipped and fell off the boat, and drowned."

"Oh," Michael replied, feeling a bit silly for suspecting an alligator-related death. But at least that helped him to understand the reason for Ouellette getting so upset with Rodger over the Houma comment. "So his son dies in an accident, and suddenly he becomes the most overprotective commander in the world? That doesn't make any sense."

Rodger shifted a bit in his seat and frowned. "There's a bit more to it than that. You see, Ouellette was convinced that it wasn't an accident. Autopsy showed a trace amounts of Amobartbital, a barbiturate."

Michael wasn't familiar with the barbiturate Rodger had named, but he knew that those kind of drugs didn't mix well with alcohol. "Sounds like Jason mixed pills and booze, then took a spill off the side of the boat. How is that not an accident?"

"Because," said Rodger. "when the boat came back right after the drowning, Ouellette had it scoured and all of Jason's boat mates searched. No traces of anything like that were found."

"Ah," replied Michael, "so Ouellette thinks that one of the people on the boat dosed his son up and caused the accident."

"Correct," Rodger said, shaking his head. "It was a mess. Ouellette was mad with grief and was certain his son had been murdered. His wife, who was beside herself, just kept begging him to stop acting that way. For a year, until the chief shut him down, Ouellette spent all his free time trying to find a killer that possibly didn't even exist. It ruined his marriage and pretty much killed his chance of getting promoted beyond commander. Since then, he's sort of like me, stuck in the same job, the same situation, until he retires."

Michael wanted to ask a question, but his partner must have sensed it, because before the junior detective could ask anything, his partner said, "But don't worry about me, I'd rather do this more than anything else. Desks bore the shit out of me."

Chuckling in spite of himself, Michael agreed with his partner. Rodger was just settling down again when Michael asked, "So, Rodger, who is Mary?"

"Huh? Oh right, Mary. I did promise to explain that," Rodger replied, looking like he was very comfortable and had no plans on changing that position. "Mary was Sam's mother. Mary Castille. Edward married her in a private ceremony. I never met her. A shame, too—Edward used to tell me that she was a beautiful woman."

Michael's brow wrinkled in confusion. He was certain that Rosemary had heavily hinted that Magnolia of the M&M Sisters was Sam's mother. After all, wasn't that the one whom Blue-Eyed Giorgio wanted, but who had Edward as a sugar daddy? According to Rosemary, Edward was protective of the M&M sisters. Why else would he show them that much attention, unless one was the mother of his child?

But Rodger seems to believe it's the other sister, Marigold, who was Edward's lover. And "Marigold" does shorten to "Mary" better than "Magnolia" does, if that even means anything. Damn, this is going to get confusing. We need to figure out which sister was with Edward, and soon.

Michael looked over at his partner, who was falling asleep inch by inch, and asked, "Rodger, do you remember what Mary Castille supposedly did for a living?"

Rodger gave a sleepy yawn before saying, "Oh, she worked at St. Jude's Hospital. Her and a sister, I think. Both were nurses in the recovery ward."

As Rodger's breaths turned to snores, Michael focused more on his thoughts than the road.

That clinches it. Mary must have been Magnolia or Marigold's real name. And she and her sister worked at the same hospital as Vincent Castille. Yes, that makes sense. Edward would know her from a venue other than the Jean Lafitte Theater. So when the two nurses became lounge singers at the Jean-Lafitte Theater, and one of them got the attention of a known serial rapist, Edward . . . um . . . married one and had a kid with her?

This doesn't add up. What am I missing? What's going on here? What the hell happened twenty years ago with these two sisters?

It was a little over an hour later when the detectives arrived at the Jefferson Parish Police Department near Bayou Lafitte. The building was a dirty white-brick single-floor building complete with a weather-worn American flag fluttering on a flagpole out front. The parking lot was filled with several older-style Crown

Victoria police cars that looked more like old, rusty white bricks than serviceable vehicles. Leaning against the outer wall near the glass front door, the window tinting half stripped off, were three police motorcycles. The rest of the parking lot was littered with at least two dozen pickup trucks, some with flat boats attached to the backs, others filled with various assortments of furniture, lawn equipment, and fishing gear. Pulling up in a free parking space, Michael gently shook Rodger until his partner woke up.

"Huh? What?" Rodger snorted himself awake, and then looked around. "Where the heck are we?"

Michael looked outside in time to see a stout African-American woman waddling toward the building with four children, all joined hands with the oldest and tallest in front. The woman was mumbling to herself. Michael could only make out the words "that good for nothing" and "son of a bitch."

The heat was coming off the pavement in waves of steam, and the car's air-conditioning started sucking up the smell of trash baking on asphalt.

Turning to his partner, Michael smirked and said, "We're in hell."

Chapter 26
Lonesome Hearts

Date: **Saturday, August 8, 1992**
Time: **12:00 p.m.**
Location: **Sam Castille's Townhome**
             Uptown New Orleans

When Richie arrived at the front door of Sam's townhome, he had already memorized what he wanted to say to apologize to her for being so late. He had already apologized on the phone the previous night, and she had accepted his apology with what sounded like a genuine sigh of relief. However, he felt like he needed to apologize again. Part of that feeling came from his guilt at standing her up after she made sure he was included in the plan, while the other part was that he didn't want to ruin his chances with her.

On the subject of Sam, Richie wasn't completely sure that he even had a chance. While it was obvious to him that there was a chemistry between them, he wasn't sure if it could or would go anywhere. He just knew that when he focused his thoughts on Sam Castille, every part of him reacted.

After waking up and getting the morning newspaper, Richie had gone back to the library to get his pills. But the bottle had long since been thrown away. What was remarkable to Richie was that he felt he didn't need them. He hadn't had a panic attack all day, and for once he felt in control—a feeling he had never known without medication. It was eerie, yet refreshing.

So by the time Richie was knocking on the door to Sam's townhome, he had again come to terms with being "in love" with Sam, and hoped that she would return those feelings. He had spent the entire morning mentally rehearsing the apology, as well as certain key and particularly suave comments to make to Sam. He had also made sure he looked and smelled like a gentleman—an effort that was hilariously ruined by the humidity of New Orleans in August.

So when Sam answered the door to her townhome, wearing a pair of black jeans and a white loose blouse, Richie was, by contrast, sweaty and far from perfect.

Sam had an anxious look about her. Fearing that she was upset with him, Richie managed a small wave and started to say, "Hey, Sam. Look, I just wanted to apologi—"

And then Sam yanked Richie inside by his shirt.

"Richie, thank God you're here." Sam hugged him for a lingering moment, then pulled back. Her voice was thick with relief. "You have no idea how good it is to see you."

Bewildered, Richie gave a nervous chuckle, the solidly cool exterior that he used to obliterate Dixie and Aucoin's interview techniques cracked like an eggshell. Before he could reach up and hug Sam back, Sam had pulled away. Still, he grinned and replied, "Well, I know we have some catching up to do and everything, but—"

"No, that's not it," Sam interrupted. Her voice grew hushed and cautious as she said, "I think someone has been in my house."

Immediately, Richie grew serious, the cheesy grin on his face vanishing behind a mask of seriousness. Suspicions, ranging from a burglar to the copycat killer to the Nite Priory, assailed his thoughts, and without thinking, he moved protectively in front of Sam. "Where do you think he is?"

Sam sighed and shook her head. "Richie, I can defend myself, but I was hoping you could—"

"Where do you think he is?" Richie repeated, this time his voice even less emotive and more focused. Something within him felt an instinctual desire to protect Sam.

Behind him, Sam sighed and said, "Well, Tony Testosterony, I don't think they're here now. But if you're that determined to go forging ahead, I'll show you what I found. Just don't get in front of me if there is an intruder here. I might kill you by mistake."

Coming out of his moment of bravado, Richie saw that Sam was carrying her father's service revolver, her thumb on the hammer, her forefinger on the trigger. From what he could see, Sam knew how to use that weapon proficiently.

Giving Sam a nod, Richie said, "All right, lead the way." He motioned for Sam to pass him. As Sam walked by, and then up the stairs, Richie followed. From his vantage point, Richie had a fantastic view. He did his best to not stare, but found it harder with every passing moment. Finally, he gave in to his desire and indulged himself in a long look, only tearing his eyes away just as Sam reached the top of the stairs.

Fortunately, Sam didn't notice Richie staring, and she just marched up to the third floor. Turning right, she entered a bedroom.

Once they were inside, Richie stopped and looked around. His eyes widened with surprise as he looked into what must be Sam's bedroom.

If it was, it was not what Richie expected. The entire room was furnished with hand-carved furniture—everything from an armoire to a vanity to a Queen Anne chair. The walls were lined with hand-painted art of the bayous and French Quarter. A four-poster king-sized bed made of mahogany wood, with an ivory canopy, was the centerpiece of the room. There were candles burning everywhere in brass votive arrangements, and the entire room smelled of coconut and lime.

Holy shit, Sam is loaded.

Suddenly, the small fortune Richie had amassed from the sale of *The Pale Lantern* seemed like peanuts. This was the kind of furniture that people with real money bought.

Sam moved directly to the vanity, up to the terra-cotta vanity mirror. "It was about an hour ago. I was just coming out of the bathroom." She pointed at a small unassuming door leading into what was presumably an equally expensive bathroom. "I came out here, and saw this in the vanity mirror."

From his original angle, Richie couldn't see what Sam was talking about, but as he stepped just to the side, he saw it.

Someone had used beige lipstick to smudge the otherwise pristine vanity mirror with the word *Murderer.* A spent tube of the stuff lay on the surface of the vanity.

Immediately, Richie found himself looking around, an unsettling sense of not being so secure momentarily overtaking him. Pushing hard at his emotions, he forced the fear reaction out, breathing in a deep breath, then exhaling.

"I see," Richie finally said, leaning back and shaking his head. He was just about to ask Sam if she had called the police yet when she briskly walked past him to a small mahogany bedside table.

"I found this in my office, in my typewriter," said Sam as she shoved a piece of paper in Richie's face. He took a step back, but he took the paper and looked at it. In type, most likely from Sam's own typewriter, the word *Torturer* rested in the center of the page.

"Jesus, Sam, what the hell is going on?" Richie asked rhetorically, real fear for Sam's safety welling up within him.

But Sam didn't respond to Richie's comment. Instead, she opened the drawer to the bedside table and took out a large kitchen knife and a piece of paper with a knife-shaped stab wound in it.

"And when I went to my kitchen," Sam said, waving the knife and paper carelessly in front of Richie's face, an act that made him flinch, "this shit was stabbed onto my back door—from the inside!"

The paper had a threat handwritten on it—"You will die like your victims did, bitch!"

Quickly Richie grabbed the knife and paper from Sam, figuring she was too upset, or pissed, to realize how dangerous her waving the weapon around was.

"Here, I'll take those," was the only thing Richie had to say about that.

Setting them to the side, along with the typed paper, Richie exhaled again and looked up at Sam. Her face had two distinct emotions on it, fear and anger, mixed with what almost looked like incredulousness. As Richie leaned in and put a hand on Sam's shoulder, he struggled with what to say to her.

How does one deal with what Sam is going through?

Sam's reaction to Richie's touch was for her shoulder to relax some.

Smiling softly at her, he said, "Sam, we should call the police."

And just like that, Sam swiped Richie's hand from her shoulder and stormed away from him, her arms folded, her right hand still clutching her father's gun.

"No, no police," she said, an adamant stubbornness in her voice. "You and I both know they'll use this as a chance to search my house."

Richie followed Sam, trying to reason with her. "Maybe that's not a bad idea, Sam. I mean, if they search the house and find nothing, that can only prove your innocence, right?"

"Yeah right, Richie," Sam retorted, "unless that bastard Ouellette tries to plant something and frame me, like he tried to frame my father!"

Richie's mind halted for a second as he processed what Sam had just said. "Wait, whoa, hold on, what? Ouellette? Your father? Okay, outsider here who knows nothing, remember? Wanna fill me in on this, Sam?"

With a sigh, Sam walked over to her bed and leaned against it. The way she did only accented the slenderness of her womanly form to Richie, who had to look around the room to avoid staring at her.

"You're a smart guy, Richie," Sam said, "so you know my father was a cop, right?"

Richie nodded, looking into her cool blue eyes. "I figured it out from the service revolver there." He pointed to the weapon in Sam's hand as he leaned against the wall opposite Sam. "So, who is Ouellette? Another cop? What happened to your father?"

Drawing in a breath, Sam said, "Ouellette is the commander for the Eighth Precinct, where my father worked. Let me explain."

Richie listened.

"More than twenty years ago, my father, Edward, was Rodger's partner. Unless Dad was busy with a big case, I'd stay with him in this townhome."

"This one?" asked Richie, motioning around the room.

Sam nodded and replied, "Yep. I'm not sure if you know this, but the Castille family is very old and very wealthy."

Richie chuckled. "Yeah, I pretty much worked that part out."

Sam nodded and continued, "Good. So, anyway, my father and grandfather shared custodial duties. Whenever Dad was busy with a big case, my grandfather would take care of me. I'd spend those days at the Castille mansion on Lake Pontchartrain." Sam stopped, then asked, "Richie, are you familiar with the Marcello crime family?"

His brow furrowing, Richie thought for a long moment. He didn't want to jump into recounting his tale from last night—not yet—but he knew who the Marcello family was, especially now. Nodding his head, he said, "Yeah, I've heard of them."

"Good, that'll save me some time explaining things," replied Sam. "So, my father was friendly with Giorgio Marcello, the son of Carlos Marcello, the famous crime boss."

Richie showed no emotion, clenching his jaw tight. He knew exactly who Giorgio *was*—the past tense being the operative one.

Sam continued, "They used to go to this club, the Jean-Lafitte Theater. I remember Dad used to go there a lot. He said it was for business. He used to meet Giorgio there a lot."

"Did you know Giorgio?" Richie asked suddenly.

"Oh, did I know Giorgio? Um, yeah," replied Sam, a look of remembrance on her face. "I didn't see him as much as Rodger, who I honestly thought was my uncle for years, but every now and then Giorgio would come by. He'd always bring a present for me, like a dress or a doll. He told me I was as beautiful as my mother."

Richie suddenly felt guilt travel down to his gut. The Nite Priory had killed this man in his defense just last night, and Sam was talking about him as if he were a member of her family.

"So, what happened?" Richie asked, pushing back the feelings of guilt and focusing on Sam's story.

"Well, again, you may not know this, but it turned out that Blue-Eyed Giorgio used to, well . . . " Sam's voice lowered as she appeared to struggle for what to say.

Richie knew where that look was coming from. Gently, he offered, "I know, Sam. I read up on Blue-Eyed Giorgio while studying the history of crime in the Big Easy—er, New Orleans—sometime back." He bit his bottom lip. It was a small lie, but a lie nonetheless.

Nodding, Sam continued, "When Dad found out that Giorgio was, well, a rapist, he hit the roof. Of course, at the time, I was ten years old and had no idea what a rapist was. He sent me to stay with Grandfather for weeks while he tried to stop Giorgio. I had no idea what was going on, and Grandpa refused to tell me anything. Then that damn Ouellette got involved.

"He was convinced my father was helping Giorgio cover up his crimes. The one night I stayed over at my father's townhome, he and Rodger were downstairs talking when Ouellette came over. They thought I was asleep, but I had crept down the stairs and sat, listening."

The look on Sam's face darkened as she said, "I heard what Ouellette said to Dad. He said he knew Dad's dirty little secret, and unless he served Giorgio up to the police, he was going to make sure the police chief and mayor found out about it."

Richie had been listening intently to Sam the entire time, following along with what she was saying. However, as Sam revealed what she had overheard, Richie felt stalled. There was nothing for him to grab on to and work with. Everything Sam reported Ouellette as saying was outside of any context he understood.

"Wait, wait, Sam," Richie said, "maybe he wasn't talking about your father being a collaborator with a serial rapist. Maybe he was—"

"Of course that's what it was," screamed Sam, her countenance suddenly becoming violent. She waved the gun in Richie's direction, making him jump back, hands out to defend himself.

"Whoa, Sam, chill the hell out," Richie exclaimed, caution and shock in his voice.

Sam, who apparently didn't notice Richie's outburst, or even that she had a gun pointed at him, continued to rant. "Because right after that, Internal Affairs started to investigate my dad! I heard him talking to Grandpa about it. Grandpa told him to leave town for a few months, to get the heat off, but Dad wouldn't. He said he had his job! He said he had his honor! He said he had me to look out for! His little magnolia!"

Sam was near tears, and as Richie inched toward her, she started to shake.

Richie realized he had never seen someone in this much emotional pain before in his entire life. He wondered just how much anguish Sam's heart held, and how deep that pain went. Richie saw that inside her tear-filled blue eyes lay more emotion than he ever thought possible within another human being.

Then Richie moved. With a quick motion, he slid the gun out of Sam's hand—she wasn't resisting—and pulled her into his arms. Her arms wrapped around him, and she started sobbing into his chest, dampening his shirt with her tears.

"Sorry," Sam sobbed. "Sorry. Sorry. Sorry. Sorry."

"It's okay," Richie said, pressing his face against the top of her head. "Really, it's okay. I'm here, Sam."

As Sam sobbed on, Richie realized his intuition was right on the money with Samantha Castille. This woman really needed someone to help her. For the moment, thoughts of lust were nowhere in Richie's mind. Likewise, there were no thoughts of being a macho man and protecting "the female." It was just him, Richard Fastellos, comforting and caring for her, Samantha Castille.

That settles it. I'm in love with her. God help me.

An hour later, Sam and Richie were back downstairs, having some tea and conversation. Edward's service revolver was back in its usual place, and the two had searched every inch of the townhome without finding any intruders. They had decided to wait until they heard from Rodger and Michael before doing anything else with the case.

"So, Sam, have you seen or spoken to anyone else today about this incident?" Richie asked, sipping his tea, a refreshing change from all the coffee he'd been drinking lately.

"You're the first one I spoke with since it happened," Sam said, sipping her tea with small, less-than-confident sips. "My best friend, Jacob, came by this morning. He told me he wasn't certain if the *Picayune* could continue to run my story, and that Caroline, the editor, would call me later today about it."

Richie nodded, having heard Sam mention Jacob Hueber in passing. "But Jacob believes you are innocent, yes?"

"Oh yes," Sam said, smiling softly into her cup. "Jacob has had a rough past, too. I'm not sure I can tell you anything. Suffice it to say, however, Jacob knows what it means to be alone. To not let others inside your heart."

Richie nodded in understanding. He had become increasingly aware that the people involved in this sordid copycat tale were all misfits who had a hard time letting others into their lives. To him, it seemed appropriate that the people to hunt down a true psychotic killer were those who were, in fact, messed up themselves. *It's almost like, in order to find a monster, you have to be a monster yourself.*

Richie was drawn out of his thoughts by Sam saying, "So he made some copies of something for work while he was here, said he'd be back tomorrow to check up on me, and left. He's one of the editors at the newspaper, so he has to go in to work today. Ya know, with tomorrow being Sunday and all."

"Right," replied Richie, sipping his tea. "The big print day for a newspaper. So, Sam, um . . . you are one hundred percent certain that I cannot convince you to call the police and let them know you have a potentially dangerous stalker after you?"

"I'm certain," Sam replied in a very matter-of-fact tone. She had already told Richie, under no uncertain terms, that she would let Rodger and Michael know the situation when they showed up, and that all four of them would figure out a plan. Richie decided he did not want to push it.

"All right," Richie said, finally giving up the fight. "But I'm staying here until they show up. No compromise there."

To his surprise, Sam smiled into her teacup, batted her eyelashes, and said, "That's a bonus."

Richie blinked. *Did she just . . . flirt with me?*

Suddenly, thoughts of getting cozy with Sam didn't seem so far out of the ballpark.

Coming back to reality, and clearing his throat, Richie said, "So, Sam, I need to tell you about what happened last night."

"Probably not a good idea to talk about it before Rodger and Michael arrive," Sam replied.

Richie frowned and sucked in his breath. "I'm not talking about the investigation, Sam. Something . . . happened last night. Something that is, well, bad and yet holds a lot of answers."

Noting that Sam was staring at him, Richie added, "And I could get arrested if the cops find out about it."

After gently setting her teacup on her saucer, Sam rested her hands on her knees. Her expression was neither disapproving or judgmental, just coolly observant. "Go on."

Drawing his breath in, Richie focused his thoughts on getting the story out as concisely as possible. The novelist in him came out as he sipped his tea, wet his lips, and began his tale.

Richie recounted how he was picked up and interviewed by Aucoin and Dixie, how he had been kidnapped by Giorgio Marcello, and how the Nite Priory had saved him by killing Marcello and all of his thugs.

Sam blinked, then registered surprise. "Wait, everyone is dead? Blue-Eyed Giorgio is dead? His men are dead?"

"Yes, yes," replied Richie, knowing he was sweating. "I've never seen anything like it, Sam. They moved so fast that the thugs didn't have a chance. And I was rushing so hard from adrenaline that the whole thing seemed to go in slow motion. But it was a massacre—a total massacre, Sam. No one survived."

"Jesus, are you sure this happened?" asked Sam. "This wasn't some crazy drug trip or something?"

Richie's voice snapped some as he exclaimed, "Sam! I may be a writer, but even I can't make that shit up! The entire time it was happening, I thought I was crazy! It was . . . surreal. Even now, my rational mind tells me that I was dreaming, but it can't be a dream, because of this!"

Reaching into his pants pocket, Richie took out a folded piece of paper. It was an article taken from that morning's edition of the *Times-Picayune*. He had originally assumed all this time that Sam had already read the headlines, but given how her morning had gone, Richie now assumed she hadn't.

Richie unfolded the paper and showed it to Sam. There an image of human bodies being fished out of the Mississippi River took up a large portion of the page.

The text was as bold as the image: "BODIES OF BLUE-EYED GIORGIO AND ASSOCIATES FOUND."

As Sam looked over the newspaper clipping, shaking her head in disbelief, Richie continued, "If I hadn't seen that, I would have thought the events of last night were some kind of psychotic dream. But seeing this headline proves it was no dream. Last night, I witnessed a mass murder the likes of which I have never seen before."

Sam skimmed over the article. "So, you said the Nite Priory saved you? I thought the Nite Priory were the bad guys, the ones committing the murders."

Chuckling, Richie waved for Sam to wait, saying, "It may seem like that, but that's not what's going on. Let me explain."

Then, just as Richie was about to talk, Sam's phone rang.

Sam lurched, a bit startled, and got up, going over to her desk. Picking up the phone, she said, "Hello?"

A few moments later, Sam's face tensed with rage and she screamed, "Fuck you, asshole!" Slamming the receiver into the cradle, she paced a bit, seething.

Finally, she said, "I need a drink." With an angry scowl, Sam headed over to a small cabinet in one of her bookshelves. Opening it revealed rows of liquor. She stood there, considering for a few moments, before taking out a bottle of black label Jack Daniels and pouring herself a drink.

Richie was standing by the time Sam slam-dunked the drink, and he watched her with silent concern. He could see she was mixing her emotional problems with alcohol, a combination that meant she was spiraling out of control. *I need to do something, and quick!*

Going over to Sam, Richie took the bottle and began to screw the top back on and put it away. When Sam glared at him, he said, "One drink is enough on a stomach with nothing but tea in it. You may need a drink, but your body is going to need some food with that, or you're going to get sick."

Sam's reply sounded like horse snorts. She downed more of the whiskey, only to wince from the alcohol seconds later.

Man, that woman can drink.

"Telling me they know where I live and that they are coming for me. The hell with them," Sam said into her drink.

Hearing what the threat had been only made Richie tense up more.

The silence of the afternoon was again pierced by the sound of the phone on Sam's desk ringing. Sam froze in place, her face starting to turn red.

Wanting to nip this in the bud, Richie held out his hand and said, "Let me. They may piss off if they hear that someone else is here."

Before Sam had a chance to reply, Richie was at the desk, picking up the phone. Putting the receiver to his ear and speaking in his manliest-sounding voice, he said, "Hello? What do you want?"

A woman's voice was on the other line. She sounded like someone who could only be described as a class-A bitch. "Hello, is Sam there?"

Richie wasn't convinced this wasn't a threatening call. "Who wants to know, eh?"

The woman replied in a very cold-sounding voice. "Caroline Saucier. Editor-in-chief of the *Times-Picayune*. Who the hell are you?"

Richie was caught off guard. Again that suave smooth-talker who made two seasoned detectives throw in the towel had been beaten by a single, calculating female.

By the time Richie mentally recovered, the woman on the other line had apparently grown impatient, as she was saying, "Look, whoever you are, just tell Sam to get her ass down here by four o'clock with her submission for tomorrow's paper, or she's fired. Got it, stud muffin?"

Caroline hung up.

Slowly, Richie hung up the receiver and gave a sardonic chortle, shaking his head before looking over at Sam and saying, "Well, that was decisively rude and unfriendly."

"Let me guess," replied Sam, leaning back against the liquor cabinet. "Caroline wants me to turn in my submission."

Richie was both surprised and impressed, although more the latter than the former. "How did you know?"

Finishing off her whiskey, Sam chuckled and winked at Richie. "The look on your face was enough. Also, I remembered that I never turned in my submission. You know, intruder-slash-stalker crap. I should probably get it to Caroline before I get canned."

Sam then tilted her head at Richie, her voice dropping a little in volume and rising a little in pitch as she said, "Wanna come with?"

Richie felt his heart race. On the outside, though, he played it cool and said, "Sure thing. I'd love to see what the inside of the *Times-Picayune* looks like. Been dreaming about it every day for a year."

Sam smirked and said, "Smartass." She put her hair back in a ponytail, gathered her boots, watch, and wallet out of the foyer, and sat down to lace up her boots. Richie watched her move and felt a small smile come to his lips. Just watching her put him in a good mood.

Soon, Sam was picking up her manuscript and heading into her home office, where she started up the copier and started making a copy of her manuscript.

Richie watched with interest. "So you make copies of your writing, eh?"

"Yeah," Sam said matter-of-factly as the two watched the copier spit out page after page. "Originally, I was going to go to Kinko's, but then I found out that using those places isn't very secure. Nothing would stop an employee or someone from stealing your work and publishing it themselves. So I asked Kent what I could do, and he said it would be easiest to have a copier at home."

"So Kent really looks out for you, doesn't he?"

"Oh yes, absolutely," replied Sam, as she gathered the first copy of her manuscript and put it in a manila envelope. "Kent is one of the few people I trust. He's always looked out for me.

"In fact, before I met you"—Sam paused as she wrote *The Bourbon Street Ripper—Chapter 2* on the envelope—"Kent and Jacob were my only friends after my father died."

Richie nodded. He understood that all too well. He was barely acquaintances with Gordon, rarely spoke to his mother about anything substantial, and hadn't spoken to his father since he was a child. For a moment, Richie felt very lonely.

"So, Richie . . ." Sam said, leaning forward on the copier, her hips jutted back as she swayed absently.

Richie was entranced for a long moment, before asking, "Yeah, what's up?"

"Tell me about the Nite Priory." Sam turned around and looked seriously at him.

Richie's expression returned to being serious, matching Sam's pace stride-for-stride. Slipping his thumbs into his pockets, he recounted everything that had happened the previous night pertaining to the Nite Priory, and how the Lady in Red, their apparent leader, needed their help to find out who was framing them.

"What do you think?" Richie asked.

"I think you're nuts," Sam replied.

Richie felt his ego deflate like a balloon.

Before Richie could think of how to respond, however, Sam smiled and said, "But I must also be nuts, because I believe what you're saying."

Breathing a sigh of relief, Richie wiped his brow. "I'm so glad. You have no idea how worried I was that you'd just call me crazy and kick me out."

Sam smirked and turned around to gather up the second copy of her manuscript, which had been sitting there finished for a while, and placed it in another manila envelope. Making the same scrawl on it as the first one, Sam said, "Nah. Lately, I've been thinking Grandfather was up to something."

Richie cocked an eyebrow and asked, "Oh?"

Sam nodded. "There was something my grandfather was up to before the murders, or maybe during the murders, that seems off. Something I can't quite put my finger on. But it reminds me of that voodoo cult stuff we talked about. And Vincent Castille was a member of New Orleans's elite. We're talking families that have been in the city for over ten generations.

"That makes him nobility as far as this city is concerned. They even had a Mardi Gras krewe exclusive to them—the Krewe of Comus. If there is a secret organization like the Nite Priory that has some kind of weird voodoo thing going along with it, and there is a frame job, maybe from a traitor or something, and it's all cultish . . . "

Sam turned and shrugged at Richie, saying, "I don't know. It's all speculation right now, but I'm finding out stuff about my family every day that I never knew. A secret society is not too far off from the crazy shit I've seen lately."

Richie, who had been silent the entire time, nodded in agreement. Everything Sam had just said made perfect sense. "I think we're on the same page then. Shall we get going? And get you some lunch before you get sick from drinking whiskey like that?"

Gathering her manila envelopes, Sam again smirked, saying, "Yeah, I'm a tough Nawlins girl, Richie. I grew up on red wine, White Russians, and a street named Bourbon. I'll be fine."

Richie couldn't help but laugh out loud at that one. As he held the door open for Sam, he asked, "So, give me a sneak preview. Who gets axed in this chapter?"

Sam chuckled nervously. "Oh yeah, that. I was thinking of changing it, after what happened yesterday morning. But Michael told me not to change anything." Any trace of amusement vanished from her countenance, her look suddenly gravely serious. "I hope what happened Thursday night doesn't happen this time. This time, my victim is a teenage girl."

Chapter 27
The Scent of Fruit

Date: **Saturday, August 8, 1992**
Time: **2:00 p.m.**
Location: **Bayou Lafitte Police Department**
             Jefferson Parish, Louisiana

The two detectives entered the Jefferson Parish Police Department. It was a mostly open room, with doors on all three sides leading off to various other rooms and hallways. The air inside was hot and thick with the smell of human odor.

Ceiling fans slowly turned above, doing little to alleviate the heat. All around, people of all ages and colors sat around, waiting to see the police, or stood around talking with the police. The large African-American woman muscled her way past a small line of people, and immediately laid in on some poor clerk who looked like he desperately needed a day off.

"Can I help you, gentlemen?" came a deep voice to the side of the detectives. Turning, Michael saw a large man in a Jefferson Parish uniform. His skin was as dark as pitch, and he looked like he could be Mad Monty's long-lost cousin. The badge on his uniform bore the title "Sergeant."

Rodger moved in first, taking out his badge. "Detective Rodger Bergeron of the New Orleans Eighth Precinct. This is my partner, Michael LeBlanc."

Michael nodded and showed his badge as well. Once the officer seemed satisfied, he introduced himself as Sergeant Calvin Carter, and asked what had brought the two detectives all the way to Bayou Lafitte.

"Why, they're here to see me, C. C.," called out a rip-roaringly thick-accented voice, from the doorway to another room. Michael felt his heart sink and his blood pressure rise as he saw Deputy Sheriff Jean-Luc Thibodaux.

"Hey there again, Shreveport," cawed out J. L. as he sauntered over to the two detectives. "Couldn't get enough of me, ya?"

"My day is not complete without hearing your voice, J. L.," came Michael's dry reply. This was not the person he wanted to see, not ever again, but he knew it couldn't be helped. These small towns didn't have too many deputies, so it wasn't like he could pick and choose.

J. L. shook Michael's hand, much to his chagrin, and then shook Rodger's. "Man, Rodger, you look like the shit that came out of my dog last night. What happened to you, bud?"

Rodger shrugged. "I've had a rough couple of days, J. L. This investigation has been pretty rough."

Michael could tell his partner wasn't in the mood for J. L. any more than he was.

"No shit?" said J. L. in the most insincere display of sympathy Michael had ever seen. "Well, you big-city detectives'll figure it out. Especially since you're back to speak to Old Man Fontenot."

"Right, have you checked up on him?" asked Michael. "Also, where is your phone? We have to call in and let our commander know what's going on."

J. L. moved to the side, showing the way to a back room with a sweeping motion. "Phone's in the break room, Shreveport. Help yourself to some good old-fashioned bayou coffee while you're at it."

Michael couldn't help but feel that coffee, in his state, would just make him feel ten times worse.

Fortunately for Michael, Rodger spoke up, saying, "I'll go make the call, Michael. I need some coffee."

As Rodger was shown to the back by J. L., and as Michael couldn't help but feel snubbed yet again, he turned to Carter, who had been standing there watching the whole thing, and asked, "So, is J. L. always this much of—"

"Yes, although he's going easy on you," interrupted Carter, as if the question had been asked a million times before. Michael found the thought disconcerting.

Half an hour later, the detectives were on their way, following J. L. and Carter, who were in a squad car ahead of them. Michael had wanted to leave early, but J. L. had been called in to help calm down Mrs. Williams, the large African-American woman who had bullied her way to the front of the line, when she got irate at the police for "not arresting that son-a-bitch to-*day*."

Michael had asked if this sort of thing happened all the time, to which Carter replied that it did.

Earlier, on the ride out to the bayou, Michael had told Rodger about Robert Fontenot being the Black Bayou Boatman. Both agreed that, at this time, it was not a good idea to openly accuse Robert of that. They'd go back with Ouellette and have him and the district attorney make that decision.

"For all we know, Robert's got an arrangement with the district attorney that we don't know about," Rodger had said. "Plus, even at his age, I doubt a hit man like him has lost all of his skills."

Michael, who had not relished the idea of going toe-to-toe with a professional assassin, agreed.

Soon, the dirty roads were replaced by just plain old dirt roads, and the pair of cars pulled up to the entrance to the boathouse owned by Robert Fontenot. The Jefferson Parish car's door opened, and J. L. came out, aviator glasses and all, and told Carter to wait. When Carter nodded in agreement, Michael, who had just stepped out of the car, got confused.

"Wait, Calvin's a sergeant, J. L., how is that you're telling him what to do?"

J. L. turned and pulled back his sunglasses, looking right at Michael. "Shreveport, I know Old Man Fontenot better than anyone else, and that old fucker hates men of color. I gotta look out for my superior here, so it's best that C. C. just stay out by the car."

"It's cool," Carter replied to Michael, his relaxed demeanor indicating that he actually didn't care one way or another. "They have a lot of bigots back here, and they don't care that I'm second in command at the police station. Fuck 'em, Detective LeBlanc. But I still ain't getting shot at."

Michael just shook his head slowly. Racism, in any form, was as alien to Michael as putting emotion before logic. But Michael knew it existed everywhere in this city, and on all sides. It wasn't a problem that was going to go away. So Michael had to admit that Carter's decision to not talk to a bigoted man with a gun was a good philosophy. Giving the sergeant a nod, Michael followed his partner and JL to the boathouse.

As they approached the house, Rodger put his arm out to stop Michael. Michael stopped, unsure what was wrong at first. Then he saw the door was open, and Robert Fontenot was nowhere to be seen.

"This could be a trap if he knew we were coming," Michael whispered. "Maybe Rosemary tipped him off?"

A nod from Rodger told Michael that his partner suspected something similar. As he and his partner drew their weapons, Michael said quietly, "J. L.!"

J. L. turned around and, seeing the detectives with their weapons drawn, furrowed his brow. Coming over toward them, the deputy asked, "What's going on here, Shreveport?"

"Precaution," Rodger said. "Remember, this is a murder investigation. This area could no longer be secure."

It took J. L. a few moments to comprehend what he was being told. "Wait, you think Old Man Fontenot is . . . ? Oh hell, no, not him. Really?"

"I'm being serious, J. L.," replied Rodger. "Just have your weapon ready, just in case."

"All right, all right," J. L. replied, unholstering his sidearm. "But just . . . Don't shoot at the guy unless you have to, all right? He's jumpy, but he's not a bad guy."

Michael couldn't think of anything more ridiculous that J. L. could have said, but he dropped the subject, as the deputy was at least going along with the idea of not entering the darkened boathouse without protection.

The three detectives crept onto the front porch of the boat-house, the area eerily quiet. There was no nutria to be found, and the shotgun rested next to the rocking chair as if it hadn't been touched all day. The entire boathouse stank, and it looked messy as hell—dirty dishes and filthy towels everywhere.

J. L. spoke in a hushed tone. "Hell, I ain't never seen it like this before. Think we should go inside?"

Rodger nodded to J. L., then to Michael.

Michael said in a hushed voice, "Rodger, I'll go in with J. L. while you stake the perimeter outside."

"All right, partner. But be careful. No unnecessary chances."

With a nod, Michael entered the boathouse with J. L.

The boathouse seemed only a few yards across. The screen door opened into the messiest and smelliest kitchen Michael had ever had the displeasure of stepping foot into.

A door on the opposite side of the kitchen opened to the other porch on the boat, a small doorway led to a bathroom, and a third doorway led to the bedroom. The bedroom door was slight-ly ajar.

"Think he's sleeping, Shreveport?" asked J. L., voice still hushed, with a notable tension to it.

Michael shook his head and motioned for J. L. to wait while he went first. The deputy nodded and waited while Michael crept toward the doorway leading to Robert's bedroom.

His heart was pounding as he reached the door. He breathed slowly to calm his nerves. It felt like a pressure was on him, a cold and unyielding pushing on his back, his shoulders, and his spine.

Why am I so on edge? I feel like something really bad is on the other side of this door. I feel like I'm being stalked by a predator I can't see or hear. What's going on? This isn't rational!

Michael slapped himself with his free hand, blinking away the sweat that was trying to run into his eyes. His heart was pounding in his chest. It was like pure coldness was pushing on him from behind to enter the room, yet every survival instinct inside of him told him not to do it.

Get ahold of yourself, Michael! You're exhausted, you're extremely stressed out. Just get through this! Finish up here, go to the Castille mansion like you and Rodger decided, and then you can take the rest of the day off.

Straightening up, gun at the ready, Michael opened the door to Robert's room and stepped inside.

What Michael saw immediately burned itself into his memory.

Robert was lying in his bed, arms and legs tied to the four corners by thick wire. His head was strapped down with wire, and a gag was inserted in his mouth. Completely naked, Robert's chest cavity had been opened up forcibly, and most of his internal organs had been scattered about across the walls of the room. Only his heart was recognizable, sitting on a nearby nightstand, secured to it by way of a kitchen knife. The macabre still life was surrounded by a circle of strange symbols.

Robert's nutria hung above him, bled out over his former master's body, the animal's blood filling Robert's empty chest cavity. The room smelled as bad as the two serial murder scenes had so far.

Michael's body was momentarily paralyzed with fear.

My God. My God. My God. Richie and Sam were right. This isn't just a murder—this is a ritual killing.

Regaining his motor functions, Michael crept to the table with Robert's heart attached to it. Michael looked over the designs around the heart. He swore he had seen those symbols before.

Wait, are those the same symbols from Sam's book on voodoo?

Michael detected an odd smell coming from the heart. It was a distinctive fruity odor. Looking closer, Michael saw a small brass bowl beside the heart with a pinkish substance burning inside. Small pink fumes were wafting up, and when Michael sniffed them, the scent of fruit was almost overpowering.

What is that stuff?

For a moment, Michael felt odd, like he had imbibed too much caffeine. His heart continued to race, and he started to feel cold, like the air around him had suddenly chilled.

What the . . . what's happening to me?

"Oh my God! What the bloody fuck happened here?!?"

Turning around, his own body's strange changes momentarily forgotten, Michael saw J. L. coming in the room, a pale look of horror stark on the deputy's face. With a lurch, J. L. turned his head outside the bedroom and vomited, then stumbled out toward the kitchen.

Michael sighed and followed, the chilling sensation still rippling through him. He stepped out after J. L., who went to the back porch to finish vomiting. Michael called out, holding out his hand, "Hey, J. L., when you've emptied your guts, come back in and help—"

Michael cut his sentence short as a small *cracking* sound resonated in his ears, and with a *whoosh*, something moved right past his face, like a mosquito or a fly. A few strands of Michael's bangs flitted down, falling to his hand.

For a long moment, Michael looked down at the strands of hair in his hand, his eyes widening as the *cracking* sound, the *whooshing* sound, and the cutting of his hair added up.

That was a bullet.

Turning to the side, Michael saw J. L., a hole in his head the size of a baseball, falling into the bayou.

In an instant, Michael's weapon was ready, and he pointed it at the doorway. All he saw was Rodger rolling into the kitchen, screaming, "Get down!" Looking back up, Michael stared into the foliage ahead and saw the assassin.

A person dressed in dark indigo robes with a face mask painted to look like a skull held some kind of rifle, which looked military grade. Michael's eyes widened as he saw the indigo-clad figure pull the trigger. The chill around him increased as his heart rate shot up even higher.

Feeling a tingle of sensation ripping down his spine, Michael threw himself to the side as three bullets ripped past him. His adrenaline was pumping like never before.

Neither the chase on the rooftop nor the run-in with Mad Monty's friends had gotten his blood moving and his senses as on fire as this moment did.

As Michael landed, Rodger called out, "That's the person who killed Mad Monty. Shit, he's getting away!" Rodger's voice seemed to come from a distance.

Looking out of the boat, following his partner's gaze, Michael saw the assassin running up the path toward the cars.

Shit! Carter is out there!

The world seemed to be moving in slow motion for Michael as he got up and started running. He felt invincible, like he could do anything, like he could catch this assassin. He ignored the sounds of his partner calling out to him and rushed forward with everything he had.

When he reached the road, he saw Carter, weapon drawn, leveling it at the assassin. However, the assassin jumped and, sliding over the hood of the old Crown Victoria, kicked the large African-American cop in the face even as he cocked the gun.

Carter might as well have been a puppy. He flew back more than three feet from the impact, landing with a heavy thud.

Michael heard himself scream out, "No!" before leveling his gun at the assassin and pulling the trigger.

The assassin's head cocked at the sound, and with a leap, the figure landed on the other side of Sergeant Carter, the bullet whizzing past. Securing the rifle on what looked like a harness on his back, the assassin took off down the road, moving at an uncanny speed.

Michael rushed forward, jumping onto the hood of the squad car and then leaping off, launching himself over Carter. As he landed, Michael tore off running again. His heart was pounding harder than it ever had, so loudly he could only hear the rushing of his own blood. He felt he could all but fly.

What's happening to me?

The assassin tore into another driveway, leading toward another boathouse. Michael followed, coming across a boathouse about the size of Robert's. A couple was out front, grilling something.

As the assassin ran past them, he stopped and kicked the grill, launching it into the air. As the grill came down, the assassin spun around and kicked it, sending sizzling hot steaks and flaming coals right at Michael.

Seeing the burning coals and meat come at him, Michael quickly ducked and performed a baseball slide. The fiery debris flew over him as if tumbling silently through space. Michael noted that the meat still looked a bit undercooked. Looking forward, he saw the assassin heading toward the railing of the boathouse. A much larger tour boat was passing by at the same time.

He's going to jump for it!

Pushing with his free hand, Michael launched himself out of his baseball slide and back into a running position. Leveling his gun at the assassin, and barely hearing the screams of the couples on the tour boat as they dove to the ground, Michael fired off three shots. The sound of the bullets leaving his chamber sounded distant.

The assassin jumped on the railing and, head cocking toward the bullets, did a leap in the air, flipping heels overhead. The bullets whizzed underneath the figure, who had turned to face Michael, albeit upside down. From a leg holster, the figure withdrew a pistol and, pointing it at Michael, fired off three shots. Then the assassin landed on the tour boat, about a dozen tourists scattering.

Quickly, Michael threw himself into the air and twisted his body, slamming himself against one of the exterior walls of the boathouse and sliding along it toward the waterside of the boat. The bullets whizzed past, although one grazed his cheek. Michael couldn't feel the pain.

Landing on the water side of the houseboat, Michael looked up and saw that the tour boat had nearly passed where he was standing. Gripping his gun hard and taking a few steps back, Michael rushed along the length of the houseboat until he was nearly at the opposite end.

At the last moment, he jumped up and, swinging his legs to the side, ran along the wall for a few steps before vaulting off the side of the houseboat and over the water, his body spinning as he rolled onto the deck of the tour boat.

Once he was on his feet, Michael looked around and saw the assassin racing toward the back of the ship. The tourists were running toward Michael, effectively blocking his path to the killer.

Move!

Rushing toward the panicked crowd of tourists, Michael jumped up and, landing on the railing of the tour boat, slid past the dozen or so now completely shocked tourists before landing on the stern area of the boat. The assassin had reached the railing and was looking to jump into the water.

Michael was aware of himself screaming out, "Stop!" and leveling his gun at the assassin. The assassin turned, pistol focused on Michael, and the two pulled the trigger at the same time.

Michael rolled to the side, avoiding the bullet as it whizzed past him, and the assassin did the same. The two leapt to their feet and the assassin spun around, aiming at Michael's gut with a kick. Michael barely brought his hand up in time to deflect the blow. Holding the assassin's foot, Michael smashed his elbow against the assassin's knee.

As the assassin fell back, his weapon spinning to the edge of the tour boat and going over the side, Michael saw the shape of hips and the outline of a bust.

A woman? The killer is . . . a woman?!

Michael didn't have time to ponder that fact, as the assassin sprang to her feet and leapt at him with a flying kick. Michael barely had a chance to bring up his hands, his right hand—the one holding the gun—taking most of the blow. His own gun went spinning off across the deck as he flew back against an exterior wall of the tour boat.

Damn! She hits hard!

Michael only had a second to re-collect himself before the assassin rushed at him, going for a series of punches. Michael deflected them. He was far more comfortable with close combat. Counting over a dozen strikes at him, and certain they came in a matter of seconds, Michael finally caught what must have been the fifteenth one. Grinning at the assassin, Michael jumped and flipped back, kicking her square in the chest.

The assassin flew back, landing on the deck and skidding back. Michael's victory was short-lived, as he saw that the assassin had landed near his gun. Landing from his attack, Michael cursed himself for being so showy in his attacks and, with everything he had, he rushed at the assassin.

The assassin lay still as Michael neared her position. Michael rushed toward his gun, reaching where the assassin's feet were splayed out.

Suddenly, the assassin moved, one of her legs flying up. The foot connected with Michael's groin. The junior detective saw only bright lights and felt only pain, the world still moving slowly as he stumbled back.

Then he was suddenly aware of a new pain, a stabbing sensation in his gut. Looking down, Michael saw a throwing knife sticking out of the right side of his stomach. Looking back at the assassin, he saw her throwing another knife, this one at his neck.

Michael's right hand was down at his side, and his left hand flew to close around the flat of the blade, the sharp point less than an inch from his throat. Just as he prepared to throw the knife back at the assassin, he saw that she now had his gun in her hand.

There was a *crack*, and Michael stumbled and crumpled back, pain exploding in his left shoulder. He slid back along the deck. He felt his strength and the rush that had made him feel invincible start to falter.

The assassin advanced over him, pointing his gun at his head. Her eyes shone like lifeless steel.

Michael could only think, *I'm dead.*

Then the sound of thunder erupted.

Michael felt the world return to normal as the assassin leapt back, dropping his gun in the process. Turning to the side, Michael saw Rodger on the deck of Robert's ship, firing his revolver at the assassin. Landing on the railing, the assassin took a look at Rodger, and then a look back at Michael. Leaning back, the assassin dove into the waters of Bayou Lafitte.

What the hell just happened?

Michael's thoughts were suddenly interrupted by an incredible pain in his groin, his gut, and his shoulder. Looking at his left shoulder, he saw fresh blood welling up, turning his white shirt red.

I've been shot, Michael thought, the coldness of shock starting to overcome him. *I've been stabbed and shot.*

Crawling to the edge of the tour boat, even as the pain became overwhelming, Michael saw the assassin emerging on the shore of the other side of the bayou. The rifle was still harnessed to her back, and her mask was still on. Without so much as a backward glance, the assassin ran off into the foliage.

"Damn it," Michael muttered to himself. "I almost had her."

Michael then passed out, the pain too great for him.

When Michael awoke, he was aware he was on a stretcher, and that about half a dozen people were around him. He was also aware it was late in the afternoon, and that he must have been out for at least several minutes, if not longer. The paramedics who were around him were loading him up into an ambulance.

Looking around a bit, Michael saw Rodger and Carter nearby. Rodger was smoking a cigarette like his life depended on it. Behind them, Michael could make out that he was back outside Robert's driveway and that at least a dozen police cars were there. Tourists from the tour boat were being interviewed, and a news reporter was giving a broadcast.

Michael didn't care about that. All he wanted was to make sure that everything was okay with his partner.

"Rodger," Michael called out weakly.

"He's awake," one of the paramedics said. Michael saw Rodger and Carter immediately come over to him, Rodger putting out the cigarette.

"Michael," Rodger said, by his partner's side. "Man, are you okay?"

"I've been better," Michael said with a wry smile, the pain only lessened in the sense that he was sure the knife wasn't stuck in his stomach anymore.

"Damn, Michael," Carter said, shaking his head in what looked like disbelief. "Those were some superman stunts if I ever saw it."

"What do you mean?" Michael asked.

Shaking his head with a look of pure disbelief, Rodger said, "You, partner, started pulling some seriously crazy stunts. People were talking about you leaping from boat to boat. It was like the stuff you see in the movies. Where did you learn that?"

Did I do all that? Michael wondered, trying to think through everything that had happened. It was all a haze, and his head was aching like someone had been banging on an anvil inside of it.

"Fruit," Michael said to himself.

Rodger looked down at Michael, his confusion obvious. "Fruit? What do you mean?"

"In Robert's bedroom, from a metal thing next to his heart. Something fruity. I remember feeling . . . " Michael struggled with the words, saying, " . . . like I could do anything. I felt invincible."

"Sounds like PCP," said Carter, shaking his head. "Never heard of it being that strong or fast-acting."

"Maybe," Michael said weakly. "I really don't know."

"I'll make sure the CSU boys check it out. They've already identified the bullet from the rifle the assassin was firing. It was a 7.62 millimeter. Military issue." Carter shook his head. "Poor J. L. never had a chance." That said, Carter patted Michael on the calf, as if to say "Atta boy," and then headed back to the crime scene.

Rodger watched Carter leave, then turned back to Michael. Michael gave him a weak smile and felt, for the first time in a while, grateful to see his partner. "You saved my life, buddy," he said. "I guess you're not so incompetent after all, are you?"

Rodger chuckled, shaking his head and saying, "Man, you are a pain in the ass, Michael, you know that?"

In spite of the pain, Michael laughed. After he stopped, he asked, "So what happens now?"

Rodger thought about it for a moment. "I'm heading back into the city to talk with Ouellette. It seems this Nite Priory thing is a real threat. Then I'm going to go check on Sam and see if she got in touch with Richie."

"How can I help?" Michael asked.

With a chuckle, Rodger said, "You get better. The EMTs say it's not likely life-threatening, but you'll be out for at least a few days. Meanwhile, I'll follow up on those clues you gave me. Of course, I'll visit you at the hospital."

Michael groaned. Being in the hospital could have him out for the rest of the investigation. Conjuring up a small smile, he said, "You'd better not solve this case without me, partner. I'll be pissed."

To Michael's surprise, Rodger laughed and said, "Partner, I don't think I can solve this case on my own, so don't you go dying on me, okay?"

Michael felt a real smile pass his lips. "Okay, bud. You got it."

As Michael was loaded up into the ambulance, the paramedics again swarming over him, the haze in his mind slowly parted, and the pain slowly became unbearable again. Struggling to focus, he wondered how everything was connected. The Bourbon Street Ripper. The copycat. The Nite Priory. The odd smell from Robert's heart. The sensation of incredible power. The indigo-clad assassin. Everything.

Mercifully, Michael soon passed out again.

When Michael next awoke, he was in a recovery room, his body in a hospital gown, and his wounds obviously in postoperative dressings. Michael wasn't sure how long he'd been out. Looking around, he saw that he was in a private room. Flowers and cards littered a table nearby, gifts from his coworkers. A huge bouquet of carnations, his favorite flower, bore a large card saying, "From Dixie and Gino."

But what caught Michael's eye was his notebook on his bedside table, with a card labeled, "To the World's Best Partner. Let's get him together."

Michael had never been so happy to have Rodger as his partner.

Chapter 28
Meeting at The Times

Date: **Saturday, August 8, 1992**
Time: **3:30 p.m.**
Location: *Times-Picayune*
            Central Business District

It was three thirty in the afternoon, and Richie was sitting with Sam in the waiting room of the *Times-Picayune*. They had just arrived and were waiting for Caroline Saucier to see them.

The complex of buildings itself was rather modern for such an old paper, and while Richie wasn't sure what he had expected, he was certain it wasn't what he saw. Several buildings, dedicated to news offices, printing, and distribution, made up the working gears of New Orleans's largest print newspaper.

By comparison, he hadn't expected such a clean, modern waiting room for the editor-in-chief, with comfortable lounge-style seating, a television showing the local news, and a cappuccino machine—which seemed so out of place to Richie it somehow managed to work.

He and Sam had enjoyed a quick yet filling meal at Café Beignet, one of the more famous New Orleans cafés, located on Bourbon Street. Richie had eaten jambalaya, one of his favorite Cajun dishes, while Sam had put away half a muffuletta. The two finished off their lunch with a cup of coffee and chicory and were on their way in about an hour.

While they had been sitting there, however, Richie had noticed a difference in the atmosphere of the French Quarter's busiest street. There wasn't any less traffic, but it seemed less casual and relaxed. Richie hardly saw anyone traveling alone, and there were almost no solitary women about. Even the men seemed to be grouped together, and everyone almost appeared to looking over their shoulder as they went along with what otherwise was a normal day.

While watching the French Quarter traffic, Richie thought to himself how the city's change in attitude had to be due to the recent string of serial murders. He had been thinking about the overall situation, finding it odd that an entire city would react this way to only two deaths. But after carefully contemplating everything, he determined it was almost like the city, for whatever reason, had never completely healed from the original Bourbon Street Ripper murders.

By the time they had gotten on the bus to head toward the *Times-Picayune*, Richie had pushed those thoughts away, deciding that for the most part, he was relieved that the public didn't know who Sam was yet. He had figured it was because she was still relatively anonymous, and the media wasn't publishing information about her. But he knew that the moment her face and name were made public, Sam Castille could end up in considerable danger.

And that will make things really difficult for her, Rodger, Michael, and me. So long as Sam stays out of the public eye, we'll all be okay.

Richie was jarred out of his memory of lunchtime, and his subsequent ponderings, by the sound of the secretary's voice saying, "Sam, Miss Saucier will see you and your friend now."

The office of Caroline Saucier was, much like the waiting room, not what Richie had expected. A black metallic desk was the central piece of the room, with a comfortable-looking leather chair resting behind it. The wall behind the desk was lined with a large bookcase, sparsely covered with books and binders of various shapes and sizes.

The outer wall was comprised almost completely of large glass-paned windows, the tinted kind that almost made the world look a grayish-blue, and the interior wall was lined with plaques, pictures of famous moments in New Orleans history, and some of the most famous headlines of the *Times-Picayune*.

Without a thought, Richie went over to the wall and examined a few of the headlines.

"Shuttle *Challenger* Lost"

"Governor Long Assassinated"

"In Memory of Pearl Harbor"

Richie, who had never before had an interest in journalism, was surprised that the wall of headlines emotionally impacted him. Perhaps, he felt, it was because he was looking at history, frozen in time, behind those panes of glass. Or perhaps it was something else, a sort of macabre interest in the fact that every headline he saw was about a negative event. Thinking to himself that the media was following a disturbing trend of sensationalizing bad news over good news, Richie shook his head.

That's a sad statement on humanity.

Richie's musings were interrupted by the sound of a stern feminine voice making a throat-clearing sound. Turning, he realized he had walked into this person's office and taken a left turn to check out the wall of headlines. Sam, who was already seated at one of two chairs before the editor's desk, was staring at him, and the other person, whom Richie could only assume was "Miss Saucier," looked several shades of irritated.

Ms. Saucier was a woman most likely in her early forties with a stern and businesslike demeanor about her. As thin as Sam, there was something about her that screamed "bitch" to Richie. Perhaps it was the age lines already showing, perhaps it was the dark auburn-red hair that was styled into a bob cut, perhaps it was the charcoal-gray suit she wore, or perhaps it was the cold stare from her dark blue eyes. Whatever it was, Richie felt an instant, almost hostile dislike toward this woman.

"Caroline," Sam finally said, motioning toward Richie, "this is my friend, Richard Fastellos, author of *The Pale Lantern*. Richie, this is—"

"Caroline Saucier," said the stern woman, holding out her hand, not to shake it with Richie but to show him where he could sit, "and while it's an honor, and all that, to meet an up-and-coming author, I have a very tight schedule today. So if you would please have a seat, Mr. Fastellos, Sam and I can conclude business, you two can get back to doing whatever it is you writers do when you're not writing, and I can go back to running my newspaper."

Richie scowled inwardly as he took the offered—more like appointed—seat.

What a bitch! What the hell is her problem?

As Richie sat down, pushing back down his surprising anger, he noticed a single picture that stood out on Caroline's desk. It was a double frame. One frame displayed a younger Caroline, dressed in a relaxed pair of jeans and a T-shirt, looking uncharacteristically happy with a very pretty brunette woman, posing in front of Cinderella's Castle at Disney World. The other frame had that same woman, with a close-up of her face, smiling lovingly at the camera while in a park. The two photographs looked old and dated, Richie noticed, and both the pretty girl and Caroline looked to be in their early twenties.

As soon as Caroline saw Richie looking at the pictures, she briskly turned it away from him and gave him a nasty stare. Richie stared back, curled his upper lip, and rocked his head from side to side a bit. He did not like this woman.

"So, Sam," Caroline said, sitting back down and holding out her hand, "what do you have for me?"

"Here, everything you want," was Sam's reply, giving Caroline the manila envelope with her story's second chapter. "Five thousand words, an engaging story, and lots of tension for the readers to sink their teeth into."

Caroline opened the envelope, took out the manuscript, and started to scan it. After a few minutes, she said. "A teenage victim, eh? Good stuff. Now, one won't show up dead tomorrow morning, will it?"

Richie watched as Sam's cheeks grew red. She shook her head vigorously, her ponytail bobbing from side to side. "I swear, Caroline, I have no idea how that happened. It's a terrible coincidence. The police"—Sam paused, and Richie could tell that she was struggling with what to say—"think I'm being set up somehow."

"I bet," replied Caroline, putting the manuscript down. "In fact, I was thinking we should probably not publish this for a few days. After all, this little 'coincidence,' as you call it, has created a major shit storm. If you knew how many phone calls we've gotten about this, how many other newspapers want to write a story about my paper, you'd be pissing in your pants right now."

Richie felt like an outside observer watching a boxing match, with Caroline in one corner and Sam's ego in another. Sam just winced at Caroline's harsh words, her face and jaw tightening as stress started to build up again. Richie's own blood pressure rose as he felt the protective desire toward Sam welling up in him again.

"Caroline, that's not really fair," Sam finally said. "I mean, I'm a victim here, too. After all, my family is—"

"Your family," Caroline interrupted, "that is, the entire Castille family, is comprised of some of the richest people in this city. You and I both know that your aunts, uncles, and cousins don't give a crap about you. This is not about the Castille family, Sam, this is about you."

Surprised at this sudden turn in conversation, Richie arched an eyebrow at Caroline.

Sam, sighing heavily, nodded her head. "Yeah, you're right, this is about me. But, Caroline, you have to believe me, I have no idea how this happened."

For a long moment, Caroline stared at Sam, her cold eyes holding a calculated look. Finally sighing, the stern woman leaned back and shook her head, saying, "Sam, I'll be honest, this has really hurt my business. I have people from all over, rich and powerful to poor and hungry, trying to get from me as to who Sam of Spades is. In the public's eye, Sam of Spades is the copycat killer."

Richie watched as Sam's face went a few shades paler. It was then that he spoke up. "Miss Saucier, I think I get what you're saying. Do you think Sam is guilty?"

Caroline looked over at Richie, her brow furrowing. "Honestly, Mr. Fastellos, I haven't a clue. I don't know Sam as well as Jacob does, but I've known Jacob for years and trust him. He's torn up over this, so much so that tomorrow he is going on vacation to try to find a way to help her. However, that doesn't change the facts. Sam's story and Miss Clemens's murder were frighteningly similar."

"I know," Sam said, chuckling morbidly. "Believe me, I know."

Richie looked over at Sam and gave her a weak smile. He honestly didn't know what to say. Unlike with Kent and the detectives, this wasn't something Richie felt he could talk his way through. Feeling uncomfortably powerless, Richie consigned himself to just being there for Sam.

"If you need to pull my story, I'll understand," Sam said, avoiding eye contact, a thickness to her voice. "If you need to fire me, I'll understand that, too."

There was a long pause as Caroline sat there, leaned back and stared intently at Sam. Richie noted that Sam eventually was unable to avoid the stern woman's gaze any longer, and for a long time, the two locked eyes in what Richie could only assume was a battle of wills.

Apparently Sam measured up, because finally Caroline said, "No. I don't think I'll be firing you today, Sam."

Richie, more so than even Sam, breathed a sigh of relief.

Sitting up, Caroline said, "Besides, I want to see what happens next." She pointed at Sam, saying, "But if another 'coincidence' happens, Sam, I don't think anyone can protect you. Not your family's social standing, not Mr. Bourgeois, and even not Mr. Fastellos here."

Richie wondered why Caroline felt compelled to bring him into it. His temperature started to rise again as he envisioned getting up and slapping the taste right out of her mouth.

"Thanks, Caroline," Sam replied, getting up to shake the older woman's hand, "you won't regret this."

"I hope not, Oh-Entitled-One," said Caroline as she shook Sam's hand, then Richie's, who also stood up. "I sincerely hope not."

On the way out the office, Richie turned one last time to look at the editor-in-chief. To his surprise, Caroline was staring straight at him, her eyes narrowed and her jaw tight. Richie, narrowing his eyes back, smirked and shook his head before walking out.

He had never met anyone who had pissed him off that quickly, and already his darker nature was in the admittedly childish act of fantasizing about harming her. In the back of his mind, Richie decided that if he were the serial killer, Caroline Saucier would be the next victim.

I hope you die in a fire, bitch.

The two had taken the bus when heading out to the *Times-Picayune*, and now they took the bus back to Sam's home. On the ride back to Sam's house, Richie finally asked, "Okay, Sam, so, I give up, what's Caroline's problem?"

Sam, who had become quiet after leaving Caroline's office, her face very tired, looked over at Richie and gave him a half smile. "What, you can't tell that she's one of those angry, male-hating stereotypes?"

Richie gave a short laugh as he shook his head. "No, I worked that part out myself. I mean, why is she such a hostile bitch toward you personally?"

"Ah ha, I see," replied Sam, nodding and looking forward. "Did you see that pretty girl in the picture with her?"

Nodding, Richie said, "I saw that, yes. It was an old picture. Looked to be about ten, maybe twenty years old. Who is she?"

"You mean who *was* she. She was her lover, Richie. Her deceased lover, Allison Surette." Sam glanced over at Richie. "Grandfather killed her. I believe she was victim number four."

"No wonder she's so . . . hostile . . . toward you," Richie said, the scenario with the stern woman making more sense.

"No kidding, right?" Sam said, her voice sounding more tired and strained. "To be honest, I don't think I'd have that job if Jacob hadn't pushed me so hard. I don't think Caroline hates me, but I do think she is so broken over what happened to Allison that just looking at me reminds her of that awful event."

As Sam closed her eyes, seemingly resting, Richie stared at her. The more time he spent with her, the more he felt that he understood the Lady in Red's edict to "keep Sam safe." Closing his eyes, he rested as well as the bus drove them back to Uptown.

When Richie opened his eyes, he noticed two things. First, he noticed that Sam's hand was resting on his arm. Second, he noticed that they were approaching the stop where they needed to get off. Half-tempted to miss the stop, just to feel Sam's touch on his arm a bit longer, Richie finally decided to be prudent and, reaching up and over, gave a tug on the "stop wire."

His movement caused Sam to rouse from what must have been a peaceful nap. Her hand was off his arm before she noticed she had it there. Smiling softly at Richie, Sam let him help her get off the bus. Richie felt at peace as he walked alongside Sam down the block to her townhome.

As the two approached the townhome, Richie saw a police squad car waiting outside. Putting his hand on Sam's shoulder, he pointed it out.

After looking at it for a few moments, Sam said, "I think that's Rodger's."

Sure enough, waiting outside of the car, sitting on the front steps to Sam's home, and finishing a cigarette, was Rodger Bergeron. Richie immediately noticed two things about the senior detective. Rodger looked awful—worse than before—and his face showed a level of exhaustion that Richie didn't think was possible on someone Rodger's age. Also, Richie noticed that Michael was nowhere to be seen.

"Hey, Rodger," Sam said as she and Richie approached the townhome.

Rodger stood up and gave them a tired smile, nodding his head at Richie. "Hey Sam. You doing okay?"

Sam shrugged her shoulders. "I've been better. But how are you?"

"I've been better, too. Very sore right now."

"You look awful, guy," said Richie as he nodded and looked around for Rodger's partner. "Where's Michael?"

"Eh, long story," was Rodger's reply.

Sam had moved past both men and was unlocking the door to her townhome. "Well, you can tell us all about it over tea. Want to come inside?"

To Richie's surprise, and presumably Sam's, Rodger shook his head. "I can't come in, Sam. Oullette's on my ass about going to Angola with you. Michael was right, this nearly cost us both. If I don't watch myself, I'll lose my job and my pension."

"Oh," was Sam's reply. Richie could hear the disappointment thick in Sam's voice. Instantly, he felt bad for her. He knew she cared for Rodger like an uncle. Again, Richie felt uncomfortably powerless.

"So," Sam finally said, "was there a reason you came here then?"

"Yeah, there's a reason," Rodger said, lighting up another cigarette. "Mainly to tell you that it's best if you lie low for a while. Don't do anything more with the investigation. Let me handle it."

"You mean you and Michael," Sam said.

As Rodger shook his head, Richie, for a moment, thought that maybe tragedy had befallen Michael. His eyes shifted between Sam, whose worried look told him that she feared same thing, back to Rodger, whose haggard look did nothing to dissuade the worry that Michael LeBlanc was dead.

So when Rodger said that Michael had been injured in the line of duty and was in the hospital, but would recover, Richie felt a surge of relief rush through him. One look at Sam, who had her hand to her chest and was exhaling softly, and he knew Sam felt the same way.

Still, Richie noticed something about the way Rodger looked that told him Rodger wasn't being forthcoming with all the information. Holding that to himself for the moment, Richie decided to let the conversation between Rodger and Sam play out.

"So what happens now?" asked Sam.

Rodger shifted a bit, looking tiredly at the ground, then back up at Sam. "For now, you stay home, work on your writing with Richie here, and do anything other than continuing to investigate things. I mean it, Sam. You stick your nose out again, and Ouellette won't hesitate to have you arrested."

Sam frowned. Richie could tell she was not pleased.

"If you won't do this for me, Sam," came Rodger's more assertive reply, "then do it for Edward. Don't make your father watch his daughter screw her life up."

Richie looked intently at Rodger. It was obvious to him that the senior detective meant "from heaven." Richie recalled from his research into New Orleans that it had a heavy Catholic influence. So, it wasn't completely out of place for Rodger to make such a comment, even if he didn't seem to be the religious type.

With just that one statement from Rodger, Richie felt like he saw through Rodger's gruff, hardened exterior to the deeply spiritual person inside. It was a surreal moment of cognizance, and with it, Richie realized that most of the people in New Orleans, to some degree, wore masks that disguised and guarded the real person. *It's like the people of New Orleans live within their own perpetual Mardi Gras masquerade, never showing their real selves. I wonder why.*

That revelation in his mind, Richie glanced over at Sam. Her face was steely and determined as always. Richie wondered what was underneath the mask Sam wore. *To live your life wearing a mask. How awful. Sam, I have to set you free.*

The expression on Sam's face was unreadable at first, but the more Richie looked at her, the more he could tell she was wrestling with her emotions. Finally, giving Rodger a nod, Sam said, "All right. I'll stay here. Good luck, Rodger. Please be careful."

Leaning in, Sam moved to embrace the detective. Rodger pulled back and shook his head. "If someone is watching us, that'll get me in trouble."

Richie detected the regret in Rodger's voice.

"Take care, Sam," Rodger said.

As Rodger headed back to his car, Sam went inside. Watching the two depart, Richie realized that he had, at this moment, the ability to make things right. He realized that now was the right time to tell Rodger about his encounter with the Nite Priory.

Quickly, Richie followed Rodger, who was opening the door to his squad car.

"Hey, Detective Bergeron," Richie said, catching Rodger's attention and keeping him from entering the vehicle.

"Yes, Mr. Fastellos," replied Rodger. "What is it?"

"Look, I wanted to give you the information I found. About the cult. About the Nite Priory."

Rodger leaned forward against the door to the squad car and just looked at Richie.

Richie sweated. He didn't want to get arrested over this, but at the same time, he couldn't help but feel he held a key piece of evidence.

Richie must have taken too long to say something, because Rodger said, "If you have something to say, Mr. Fastellos, go ahead and tell me now."

"Okay," Richie said, sucking in his breath. "Vincent Castille and the social elite of New Orleans could be the Nite Priory's ancestors. I found an old microfiche article with him, someone named Gladys Castille, Gerald Robichaux, and Jonathon Russell. The article referred to them as a Priory. I know it's a long shot, but it's all I could find."

Rodger nodded and wrote that information down in a small pocket notebook, saying, "I know who Gladys is. That was Vincent's sister. I'll check up on Gerald and Jonathon. They could shed some light on things."

"It very well could," Richie said.

"Anything else about the Nite Priory?" asked Rodger tiredly.

Richie nodded and said, "They seem to be some kind of secret organization. I don't know much about them, but their members wear, or wore, black hooded robes. They seem to be assassins or something, but I'm not sure. Their trademarks are the use of cutting weapons and their bare hands. They appear to go after high-profile targets, like high-ranking members of crime families or public officials."

As Rodger's eyebrows rose some, Richie smiled nervously. He had just lied to Rodger by altering his story to make it sound like he had researched the Nite Priory instead of meeting them.

"Interesting," came Rodger's reply as he looked Richie in the eyes. "And where did you get this information?"

Richie didn't show his reaction, keeping that cool exterior he'd used to shut down Aucoin's and Dixie's interview of him. Internally, however, he grew concerned. He was certain that if he told Rodger about being at the Riverwalk, even if he didn't get arrested, he'd be hauled in for questioning.

They'd never believe me about the Nite Priory. I'd be arrested for sure.

Giving Rodger a placid smile, Richie came up with what he believed was a good lie that would have immediate credibility with Rodger. "I came across that information while going through Sam's library of voodoo stuff. Pretty crazy, don't you agree? The answer was right there in front of us the whole time."

As Rodger looked at Richie intently, the novelist kept up his smile.

What is with this guy?

"All right, I'll be sure to pass that along. Thanks," Rodger finally replied, leaning in and keeping his voice low.

Richie kept up his smile and inwardly felt much better about the whole thing.

"However, you need to watch your ass," Rodger said, his voice remaining low so that, Richie suspected, Sam couldn't overhear them. "Ouellette, my commander, also has his eye on you. If you're caught doing any more independent investigating of your own, you'll be back in jail or on the first plane to Pittsburgh."

Richie gritted his teeth and nodded. "This is not good. So there is nothing I can do anymore to help out?"

Rodger leaned against the door of his car and nodded. "You can stay with Sam." Rodger's voice, still low, had taken on a deadly serious tone. "Ouellette has me on a short leash, so I can't look out for her. Stay with her and make sure nothing happens to her."

Richie looked back at Rodger, the two men locking eyes in what Richie felt was an unspoken understanding. To Richie, Rodger looked wild, as if he hadn't slept or eaten all day, like he was running on sheer willpower. There was an almost twitchy quality about him. Richie thought to himself that there was something seriously wrong with the senior detective, like he was giving off the kind of vibes of a man who was dangerously close to the edge.

Realizing that he was staring too long, Richie broke his gaze in a manner that would look like defeat and nodded, saying, "I understand, Detective Bergeron. I'll keep an eye on Sam. I'll keep her safe. I'll stay with her."

"Good," Rodger replied, starting to get into the squad car. He stopped at the last moment, pointing at the sky and shaking his finger as if to say that he had forgotten to mention something.

"Although, Mr. Fastellos," Rodger said, his voice remaining hushed and taking on a sudden primal gruffness, "I know you have a thing for Sam."

Richie felt himself beginning to sweat.

"And that's okay," Rodger continued. "She needs that kind of normalcy in her life." Again, Rodger stared into Richie, and there was something dangerous to his gruff voice. "If you use her, or hurt her, or fuck her and leave her, what will be left of you won't fit into a small box."

With that said, Rodger gave a frighteningly pleasant smile and said, "Have a great day, Mr. Fastellos."

Richie stared as Rodger took a moment to struggle with the front seat belt, started the car, and drove off. For the second time today, he felt the sudden urge to punch someone right in the face. Instead of anxiety or panic, he felt the intense urge to hurt someone really badly. The mental image of punching Rodger's teeth right out was unsettlingly satisfying.

You fucking dick! Don't you dare threaten me!

Richie took a few minutes to shake it off and rationalize why Rodger Bergeron, a normally very nice old guy, would suddenly become so defensive and vicious. Richie finally determined that it had to be due to this "uncle" status he had with Sam. After all, if he was Sam's father's partner, and was like an uncle to Sam, being so protective of her, especially with what had been happening lately, made sense. His sudden anger finally abated when he decided that Rodger's threat was more obligatory than anything else.

"Still, there was no reason to threaten me like that," Richie said to himself as he headed up the front porch steps back to Sam's townhome. "I'd never hurt Sam. And I'd sure as heck never, what did he say? 'Fuck her and leave her.' Sheesh. Give me more credit."

But I love her. She will be mine, old man, and hell on you if you think you can get between us.

With his manhood mentally restored, Richie headed back inside Sam's townhome, remembering to close and lock the door from the inside.

Chapter 29
Dessert at Muriel's

Date: **Saturday, August 8, 1992**
Time: **7:00 p.m.**
Location: **Sam Castille's Townhome**
                     Uptown New Orleans

After saying good-bye to Rodger, Sam had headed back into her townhome's kitchen to make tea for herself and Richie. However, before she could even put the kettle on the stove, she had begun to feel faint and was forced to sit down at the small breakfast table. She was still sitting there, pressing her hands to her face, her consciousness fluctuating, when Richie came back inside. While she had been sure it was exhaustion, Sam had no idea why her fainting spell came on so quickly.

Richie had been understandably concerned, and after a brief discussion had persuaded Sam to go lie down for a while. So Sam, despite wanting to continue with the investigation, allowed Richie to help her upstairs to her bedroom, where she lay down.

Once in bed, Sam closed her eyes, her consciousness sinking into the mattress like a body sinking deep into water. Her thoughts were a mire of anxiety over her current predicament and the drowning nostalgia that had been circulating in her heart recently. Her mind finally drifting far away from the pain, Sam began to dream.

It was a hot afternoon in the summer of 1972, and ten-year-old Samantha Castille was lying in bed with a slight fever. In her arms, she clutched a small porcelain doll wearing a Southern lady's dress. Next to her sat one of the Patterson sisters, Tania. The young black girl was taking the cool rag, soaking it in a basin of fresh water, wringing it out, and then dabbing it over young Samantha's face and forehead.

"You certainly did a number on yo'self, Miss Samantha," said Tania, rinsing out the cloth and folding it up to place on Samantha's head. "You need to be more careful, else your grand-daddy gonna think we don't take care of you."

Samantha didn't say anything, simply staring upward and letting the cool rag on her head lull her into the place between consciousness and unconsciousness. It had been an abnormally hot day, and Samantha, as ten-year-olds are apt to do, had played outside too long with no sunscreen.

So besides having a painfully pink sunburn on her cheeks, ears, and the front of her neck, she was overheated. Grandfather, who had been taking his tea out at the gazebo in the backyard, had instructed Miss Patterson to take Samantha to her room and for Tania to tend to her.

"Is Grandpa coming?" Samantha finally asked Tania.

"Oh, I'm sho' he will come in time, Miss Samantha," Tania responded, resoaking the cloth to dab it to the girl's face again before resting it on her head. "He said he had some important business he had to tend to first."

"Important business," Samantha repeated. It was a term she'd been hearing her grandfather use a lot more lately. The girl was only vaguely aware that something bad was going on in the French Quarter, something that kept her father and Uncle Rodger busy all the time, so to have her grandfather get busy as well left her with very few people to play with.

And she could only interfere with Miss Patterson, Miss Cooper, Mr. Reginald, or Mr. Mason so many times before she found herself in trouble.

"It's because of that horrible stuff happening in New Orleans, Miss Samantha," blabbed on Tania, increasing the pace of her cloth rinsing and the dabbing of Samantha's face. "Mommy don't want Violet and me talking about it, but how can you not talk about it? Not wit' those ladies missing!"

"Ladies missing?" Samantha again repeated and then looked over at Tania. "What is happening in New Orleans, Tania?"

The Patterson twin looked like someone had slapped her in the face. Flustered, she shook her head and waved her hands, saying, "Lord me, I have said too much. Don't you mind me, Miss Samantha, I'm just talking out the side of my mouth!"

Samantha didn't reply. She genuinely liked Tania Patterson. She was the more simple of the two Patterson twins, but she was nice and had a good heart—unlike her sister, Violet, whom Samantha regarded as mean and moody.

"Anyway, Miss Samantha," Tania droned on, "I don't know what your grandfather is up to, but I seen him talking to Mama late last night about something. All I heard was them talking in old Creole. Mama said she won't teach me Creole."

Samantha looked over at Tania and blinked, the cool rag on her head making it very difficult for her to keep her eyes open. "Why not?"

"Because she's too stupid to learn Creole," said a much slower-paced and sterner voice from the entrance of Samantha's bedroom. Both Samantha and Tania turned to see Violet standing there, hands on the door frame and looking in their direction, her gray eyes staring blankly and showing the usual lack of emotion.

"Oh Violet, why you gotta be so mean to me?" cried out Tania, her face showing genuine upset.

"Because you are an idiot," was Violet's reply as she leaned against the frame of the doorway. "You shouldn't go talking to your betters like you're equal to them. Also, you need to watch what you say, or Mama will skin your ass."

Tania's lip wobbled from Violet's chiding. Samantha's brow furrowed, even though that pinched her sunburned skin together. She really didn't like Violet Patterson. Everything about her screamed "mean" and "bully."

"Tania can talk to me all she wants," Samantha said, reaching out to pat the visibly upset Patterson sister on the knee. "She's my friend, and I like her. You should apologize to your sister right now, Violet!"

Tania looked from Samantha to Violet and back again, tears on the rims of her eyes.

After a few seconds of silence, Violet stoically said, "I apologize, sister."

Tania got up and rushed over to her twin sister, hugging her tightly. "Oh sister, I knew you was just being tough," she said. "I always knows you love me."

Samantha watched as Violet slowly placed a hand on her sister's back, the insincerity of the hug more than apparent from Samantha's angle. Violet looked over Tania's shoulder, focusing on nothing at all. "Idiot. You make a big deal out of everything."

Samantha thought to herself how horrible Violet was, watching the exchange with growing contempt for her. The little girl wondered how someone could be so mean to her own twin sister. *If I had a sister, she'd be my best friend.*

"Tania," Violet finally said, still in the embrace, "Miss Cooper wants you to go and peel onions for tonight's dinner."

Tania stepped back and said, "Oh, but what about Miss Samantha here? Can you tend to her?"

Violet immediately said, "Mother has me on a task from the master. I cannot."

"It's okay," Samantha said to Tania. "I'll be fine. I'm already feeling much better." It was a small fib, but Samantha knew better than to distract Tania from her duties, lest the girl get her ears boxed by the cook.

"All right then, Miss Samantha," Tania said, giving Samantha a thumbs-up. "I will sees you at dinner!"

With that said, Tania scampered off toward the kitchen.

Samantha closed her eyes and relaxed her breathing. She felt the motion of the air in the room, and felt the coolness of the rag on her head. These sweet and comforting sensations were soon overshadowed by a cold feeling of unease. Her brow furrowing, Samantha opened her eyes.

Standing directly over her was Violet Patterson. She had moved to Samantha's side without making so much as a sound, and seemed to be staring blankly at her. Up close, Violet's grayish eyes were like polished steel, showing no emotion.

Samantha gasped, her little heart racing. She clutched her doll tightly, as if it were a protective blanket that would keep her safe.

Without a word, Violet took the rag off Samantha's head. Never shifting her blank gaze, Violet wet the rag in the basin, rinsed it out, wrung it out, folded it, and placed it back on the girl's head. Then, taking the basin, Violet backed up and left the room, never looking away from Samantha until she was gone.

Despite the deadness of her eyes, the look on Violet's face was unmistakable—a cold, remorseless hatred.

As soon as she was gone, Samantha breathed again, her little heart pounding in her chest. Tears formed in her eyes. She hadn't been frightened like that in quite some time.

For a long time, Samantha lay in her bed, looking up at the ceiling and trying to shake the fear. She found that she couldn't. Violet's odd behavior had terribly frightened her, and resting was now impossible. Samantha knew what she wanted. She wanted her grandfather. She wanted Grandpa Vincent.

Getting up, still clutching her doll, she slowly crept through the hallways of the Castille mansion to her grandfather's study. Soon the large oaks doors loomed before her, and Samantha knocked gingerly on them.

No response.

After waiting a few seconds, Samantha knocked again, this time more assertively.

Still no response.

The girl fretted as the memory of Violet's creepy behavior assailed her, and finally, just wanting to be near her grandfather's things, Sam pushed open the door and entered the study.

All the lights were off, casting the room into eerie shadows, save for one light on her grandfather's desk. Holding her doll to her chest, Samantha crept toward the desk and, scooting up on her toes, looked up on it.

Nothing really caught her eye, just some boring letters written in calligraphy and a ledger of household expenses. Her grandfather, caught in what Father often referred to as the "time of antiquity," still wrote with a quill, and Samantha had learned at an early age not to mess with the inkwell. So when Samantha saw that the inkwell's cap was still off, lying on a nearby book, the girl slipped up onto her grandfather's writing chair, swiped the cap, and placed it back on the inkwell.

As she leaned back, she noticed that the book the inkwell cap was on had a funny design, something that looked like a triangle, but with flourishes coming out of the sides and the points. Above the design, written in gold leaf, was the word *Vodoun*.

"Vodoun," Samantha said out loud, pronouncing the word as *voh-dune*.

It was a curiously thick book, with a bookmark jutting out in one place. Samantha, in spite of herself, found opening the book to be irresistible. The girl excitedly thought to herself that "voh-dune" was something new and different. She figured it would be best for her to learn about it, and then maybe she'd have something new to talk to her grandfather about.

Because she was a small child, she had some difficulty opening the book. Once it was open, however, Samantha looked at the pages and immediately wished she had left well enough alone.

On one page of the book was a whole bunch of writing in a language that reminded Samantha of French, but clearly was not. She had heard Miss Patterson and Violet speaking in a French-like language before, and knew what it was called, but had never seen the language written down. However, this is what this had to be—Creole.

On the other page, however, was a detailed drawing of a skeletal figure, dressed elegantly in a black tuxedo, with a black top hat and dark glasses. A cigar stuck out of his skull-faced mouth and a bottle of rum was in his bony hand.

The caption underneath said, "Baron Samedi."

"Baron Samedi," Samantha said to herself. As she started to turn the page to see if there were any more drawings, the girl heard the sounds of footsteps and voices approaching the doorway to the study.

Quickly, Samantha closed the large book—quite a feat while kneeling on her grandfather's chair—arranged it as best she could, and hid herself underneath the desk. She had never snuck into her grandfather's study before, but she knew it made him very angry when someone did that. So, clinging to her doll, she held her breath and waited.

The first voice she recognized as Miss Patterson, the housekeeper, who said, "Are you sure you want to go through with this, Master Castille? It's still not too late to turn back, Madonna help us all."

"I am certain, Miss Patterson," said Vincent's voice as he stopped at the door. "Besides, at this point, I'm rather besieged into this arrangement. Our interested party isn't known for patience. And while there may be some stupid enough to cross him, I am not one of those people."

The door to the study opened, and Vincent, dressed in his doctor's attire, entered the study. Miss Patterson walked in behind him. From her vantage point, Samantha could only see their feet, but her grandfather's highly polished shoes, and Miss Patterson's thick shoes and thicker ankles, were unmistakable.

"I do understand that, Master Castille, but what about them murders going on in Nawlins right now? You know, the Ripper murders?" There was a real caution to the housekeeper's voice. "If you were to do anything with all that happening, wouldn't it send the poh-lice your way?"

Vincent, who was standing at the desk, seemed to stall out while rifling through objects on his desk. Samantha continued to hold her breath, breathing shallowly and only when she dared. She remembered that her grandfather had a keen eye for detail, and wondered if he would notice something off about his desk.

Oh no! The inkwell cap. He'll notice that the inkwell cap is back on! Oh dear!

Wanting to be an honest girl, Sam thought about getting up and turning herself in now. However, she stopped any movement the moment she heard her grandfather say, "Yes, the Bourbon Street Ripper murders in New Orleans are indeed unfortunate, Miss Patterson. You are being smart and keeping your daughters indoors, yes?"

"Oh yes," replied Miss Patterson. "I keep them inside at night just like you said. No one is gonna butcher my girls!"

"Good," replied Vincent as he walked away from the desk. "Now, Miss Patterson, I believe I will be requiring the services of Blind Moses again. Can you contact her for me?"

Samantha wondered who Blind Moses was.

Miss Patterson's voice grew quiet and subdued as she said, "If that's what you wish, Master Castille. I'll bring her to you."

"I'll meet her out back, Miss Patterson," said Vincent as he headed toward the door, the housekeeper following him. "That way I can finish my tea. When Sam wakes up, I want to go riding with her."

"Of course, Master Castille," Miss Patterson said, following Vincent out of the study.

For a long time after they left, Samantha lay there, her breathing slowly returning to normal. What she had heard didn't mean anything to her, and the girl wondered just what the "Bourbon Street Ripper" was, what "Baron Samedi" was, and who "Blind Moses" was.

"What is Grandfather doing, and who is he working with who's all impatient?" Samantha asked herself out loud.

Heading toward the hallway, Samantha pushed the door open and—

—suddenly Samantha was standing inside the basement of her grandfather's mansion. The room was bathed in a dim and cold blue light. All around were wooden and metal devices of torture: a rack for stretching limbs, a Saint Andrew's cross for flogging, an iron chair for cooking flesh, and an iron maiden for puncturing bodies. But the centerpiece of this chamber was a large metal table, with thick leather straps on all four corners, and a tray covered in all sort of equipment, from scalpels to drills to soldering irons to hooks to circular saws.

Samantha gasped and dropped her doll, which shattered like glass as the room took on a red hue, heat rising everywhere about her. In the center of the room, strapped to that table, was her father, Edward, his chest cavity opened up as if an autopsy were being performed on him. Standing next to her father's corpse was Vincent, dressed in his doctor's scrubs. Her grandfather was removing Edward's heart with the forceps, while pausing to write down notes in a notebook with a bloody, but otherwise shiny, silver pen.

Samantha eyes were wide and her lips were curling in terror. Her small frame was shaking violently, and her head hurt, bells ringing in it. Suddenly, she screamed, "Noooooooo!"

Slowly, Vincent turned and looked over at Samantha, Edward's heart still and unbeating held in those forceps. Putting down the pen, Vincent pulled down his mask. His expression was one of confusion. "No?"

His voice had a tone of stern reprimand as he said, "What do you mean, 'no,' Sam? This is the very thing you asked for, the very thing you wanted. How can you say 'no' to me now, Sam?"

As Samantha backed away, Vincent stalked toward her, holding out her father's heart. "You wanted this, and I gave it to you. I told you, you are the most alive when you are in pain. Edward's suffering, all of my victims' suffering, it made them more alive than they ever were before."

Vincent was upon Samantha, holding her father's dead heart right before her eyes. "Did you see it, Sam? Did you see the life leaving his body? Wasn't it wonderful, Sam? Wasn't it wonderful?"

Samantha felt her tongue loosen, and she screamed, "Why are you doing this to me?"

"Why? You want to know why?" replied Vincent. "Can't you remember why?"

Suddenly, Samantha the child was Sam the adult, standing there in front of the table where her father's dead body lay. In Sam's hands, she held a scalpel and a pair of forceps—in them was her father's lifeless heart. With a gasp, Sam dropped them both, the heart making a *shploop* sound as it hit the ground. Sam backed up, right into Vincent.

Sam froze as her grandfather's hands came to rest on her shoulders. Leaning forward, his lips parted, and Vincent Castille muttered, "It was all for you, Princess. All so that you might live . . ."

Vincent's breath was like ice on her skin.

" . . . a life without fear."

With a start, Sam Castille awoke from her nightmare. The sky was already starting to darken. Looking over at her alarm clock, Sam saw that it was already seven in the evening. Her stomach rumbled and her head, though still feeling full, was no longer in terrible pain.

Getting up, Sam headed downstairs to the kitchen, and was surprised to see that the lights in her study were still lit. Wondering if she had left the downstairs light on, Sam cautiously walked into the study, wary that there might be another intruder.

Sitting in one of her chairs was Richie Fastellos. He had a book—one of Sam's, entitled *Branston's Bungle*—in his lap, and his head was leaned back. His mouth was open and he was snoring slightly.

Sam felt herself smile as she took in the sight, pressing herself against the frame of the doorway. Whether she had wanted to or not, Sam had grown quite fond of him. His awkwardness and cavalier attitude, although unwarranted, was very appealing. Moreover, he was nice to her, going out of his way to help her out in this difficult spot.

Sam, remembering it had been Richie who had helped her to bed earlier, and then left her alone, also realized, when you cut away at the layers of attitude, machismo, and charm, Richie was a real gentleman.

As Sam watched Richie sleep, she took in the shape of his face, the broadness of his shoulders, and the leanness of his form. Feeling her heart flutter a bit and a heat rise to her cheeks, Sam looked away, trying to push those thoughts out of her head. When she looked back, she found her eyes sliding down to Richie's pants. Her body began to ache with a desire she hadn't felt in years, and with an embarrassed gasp, Sam quickly turned away.

I cannot believe I just checked him out! What's wrong with me?

Still, Sam felt her gaze returning to look over Richie as he began to stir, and once again Sam found herself smiling softly.

Well, he is nice to look at, and I've always been attracted to guys with a lot of intensity.

Sam's perusal only lasted a little bit longer before Richie woke and sat up suddenly, the book dangerously close to sliding off his lap. Sam quickly looked away, so as to not be caught staring at her guest. Clearing her throat, she said, "Hey, it's about dinnertime. You hungry?"

Richie, who was still waking up, looked around and presumably saw what time it was, because he muttered, "Crap, I fell asleep. Dinner? Yeah, sounds good."

As Richie got up, Sam's book fell to the floor. Richie made an *"ack"* sound before picking it up and checking the book for damage. Sam watched the incident and chuckled, shaking her head and saying, "Goof."

"Sorry about that," Richie said, dusting off the book and starting to put it away, but not before tapping the book and saying, "Good story, by the way. You're not a bad writer, Sam. You just need to work on your narrative."

As Sam led Richie to the kitchen, she said, "Is that so? Is that some of the professional coaching I get as part of my end of the bargain?"

Entering the kitchen, Sam started to search the cupboards and refrigerators for something to make a meal out of, and found she was sorely lacking in groceries. Frowning, Sam barely heard Richie's response—that he was just giving advice because he liked her writing and wanted to see it improved.

"That's nice, thanks," she said as she scanned the cupboard for food that was not there. She finally shook her head, saying, "You know, I just think we're either doing takeout or eating out tonight, Richie. My cupboard is bare."

Richie, who apparently hadn't noticed Sam's dismissiveness toward the writing conversation, or didn't care, said, "Honestly, Sam, either would be lovely."

"Let's eat out," Sam said after a bit of thought. "I don't want to be stuck here in case some whack job decides to harass me again. Let's pick a place and then go eat. My treat."

Richie, who had been looking around Sam's bare cupboards as well, asked, "That's twice you're paying for dinner. Are you sure?"

"Yeah, it's cool. I've got it covered," Sam replied, looking over at Richie and winking with a grin. She liked how, even with the level of comfort they had gained with each other in just a few days, he was still a little awkward. It was cute.

"Well, all right then, but I'll get it next time," Richie replied. "So, what now?"

Sam looked at the time. "I slept in my clothes and am kind of sticky. So, if you can wait down here for a few minutes, I will go shower and be down in a jiff."

Richie laughed in agreement and nodded. "Sticky, eh? Okay, Sam. You go un-sticky yourself and I'll wait down here. Don't take too long, all right? I'm so hungry I could eat my own toe with a white wine and lobster sauce!"

"Then I'll hurry up, lest you become an entrée at your own fancy dinner party." Sam smirked and headed upstairs.

Fortunately for Sam, the headache she had been fighting off was completely gone; however, the memory of her nightmare was not. Even as she let the hot water run over her body, she couldn't get the images out of her head—her grandfather standing over her father's body, her own hands bloodied by her father's viscera, and her grandfather's taunts that the awful murders were for her— something she had asked for.

A life without fear.

Also, the name in the book kept popping back up in her mind. *Baron Samedi.* Along with that name came the memory of her grandfather mentioning Blind Moses to Miss Patterson.

Sam recalled that one of the detectives had mentioned, during their meeting yesterday, that Blind Moses was in Jackson Square. Closing her eyes and letting the water stream over her body, Sam remembered that someone from her past owned a shop in Jackson Square.

I believe it's the Patterson sisters who own a shop down there. God, I haven't seen Tania Patterson in years. Calling on her would almost be worth running into Violet. I wonder if Tania would have any idea where we could find Blind Moses.

As Sam dried herself, she decided that, since it was a Saturday night, the Patterson shop, if it was still there, should still be open.

When Sam was done with her shower, and was dressed again in similar black jeans and a white poet blouse that opened in the front, her hair loose and drying, she went downstairs. She found Richie in the kitchen with two glasses of freshly made iced tea.

When Richie looked up and saw Sam, he smiled and bowed to her. "Cold tea on a hot summer's night, my lady?"

"Ham bone," came Sam's reply. However, she couldn't help but smile back, feeling herself melt a little on the inside. The gesture was genuinely touching.

As Sam sipped on her iced tea, which had that lemony flavor she so loved, she said, "Hey, Richie, do you want to go to Jackson Square for dinner? The restaurants there are wonderful. And it's a Saturday night, so it should be pretty exciting to explore afterward."

Richie gave her a thoughtful look and nodded, saying, "Sure thing, why not? I still haven't seen Jackson Square, and it's not like I have anything else going on. Let's just make sure that wherever we eat, they serve a good dessert. We've earned it."

"Dessert? Oh, then we have to go to Muriel's! They have the most delicious red velvet cheesecake there," replied Sam, relishing the thought that, amongst other things, she would be able to take in a part of New Orleans she really liked. Sam was thinking of the sights she and Richie could take in, after talking to the Patterson sisters, when he spoke up.

Richie chuckled and said, "Well, I'm a guy, so cheesecake is not going to ring my bell like it will ring yours. But sure, Muriel's it is."

His voice then lowered.

"Hey, Sam, there is something I need to tell you."

Sam looked over, still sipping on her iced tea. She tilted her head to the side curiously and asked, "What is it, Richie?"

"It was, well . . . " Richie seemed, for the first time that afternoon, to really struggle with his words. Finally, he said, "Rodger told me to also stay out of the investigation. So I can't even help out while you're keeping a low profile."

Sam frowned. She has always thought of Rodger as being on her side, but it sounded now like he had to choose being a cop over being her "uncle." She frowned and finished off her tea before exhaling in frustration and staring up at the ceiling. "Well, hell, I guess that sort of shuts us down, doesn't it?"

Richie nodded and said, "I'm really sorry, Sam." He finished his tea.

But Sam was thinking about something else, and didn't pay any attention to her guest for the moment.

If we happen to go to Jackson Square for dinner, happen to pop in on the Patterson sisters, and happen to find out about Blind Moses . . . Well, that's not investigating, now, is it?

Sam looked back at Richie and gave a sly grin as she firmly set her empty glass down on the counter. "Well, then, we're not investigating tonight. We're just going to have dinner and take in the sights."

With that said, Sam and Richie, for better or for worse, left for Jackson Square to go have dinner and dessert at Muriel's.

Chapter 30
Sam's Special Day

Date: **Saturday, August 8, 1992**
Time: **9:00 p.m.**
Location: **Jackson Square**
            Downtown

It was a little past nine o'clock when Sam and Richie left Muriel's, having finished an incredible, albeit expensive dinner, topping it off with a generous slice of red velvet cheesecake. Sam's cheeks were still flushed from the dessert, and she had a spring in her step. Walking side by side, she and Richie entered Jackson Square.

During the daytime, Jackson Square was just another example of New Orleans's unique architecture, but at night it was a wonderland of lights and music. All around the outside were a myriad of shops ranging from quaint and old-fashioned to modern and trendy, several historic landmarks such as the Cabildo and the Presbytere, and the gloriously beautiful St. Louis Cathedral.

Within the center of the square was a small but well-kept park, lined with Old World gaslights and wrought-iron benches. The centerpiece for the park was the statue of General Andrew Jackson.

All around, festive Cajun and Zydeco music played, the most common being any rendition of "When the Saints Go Marching In." The smell of freshly cooked and heavily spiced meats and seafood wafted in the hot summer air. All around, dozens upon dozens of artists, performers, and mystics peddled their services and wares.

Sam loved Jackson Square. It was undoubtedly her favorite part of the French Quarter.

As she and Richie passed the Café du Monde, where she had had lunch with Jacob Hueber just a few days prior, Sam said, "You know the history of Jackson Square, right, Richie? That it used to be the central town square for New Orleans?"

Richie chuckled. "I do now," he said, and reaching over, took her hand in his.

Immediately, Sam's face flushed, her body temperature increased, and her breath sucked in. Looking over at Richie, who was walking along with a small smile, Sam quickly yanked her hand away, softly muttering, "Wha—what'd you do that for?"

Looking over at her, Richie just shrugged, still smiling, and said, "There's a serial killer on the loose. Gotta protect my friend, yes?"

Sam felt her flush die down, but as she looked around, she could see that although natives and tourists alike were enjoying themselves, everyone was sticking to groups, and just about every woman was holding on to someone else's hand. Feeling a bit out of place, Sam agreed to let Richie hold her hand—but only because she'd look suspicious otherwise.

Sam noted that his hand felt strong and warm.

A few minutes later, after wading through the crowds of shoppers, tourists, partygoers, and artists, the pair approached a storefront called La Croix Voodoo Shoppe. The exterior of the shop was black with wrought-iron and lit with gaslights. In the windows were what looked like department store displays, but with skeletal creatures in gentlemen's and ladies' clothing, doing activities such as walking in the park or having a picnic. A few ghostly images faded in and out of the background.

"Really, Sam," said Richie, "a voodoo shop? After what we've been through recently?"

Sam just turned toward Richie and gave him a coy smile, looking up at him from behind her lashes and saying, "But they have such nice incense. Surely you wouldn't begrudge me getting some, would you?"

Richie had the look of a man who knew he was being manipulated, and while he gave a thoughtful look, as if heavily considering the options, he was just a hair too quick to agree to fool anyone.

Sam tapped Richie on the nose and said, "Uh-huh. Come on, stud."

Hand in hand, the two entered the store.

Passing through a black curtain, the pair entered a well-furnished store that looked nothing like its exterior. Instead of skeletons and ghosts, there were rows of books, incense, dried herbs, candles, crucibles, and other ritualistic paraphernalia.

Music that sound like drums, bells, and native chants played over a sound system, and the sweet scent of light frankincense wafted in the air. An electronic cash register was set up on the only counter in the shop. Behind it was a staircase leading up to the next floor. To the side was a beaded doorway.

Two employees, a young woman and young man, both dark-skinned Creoles, were tending the store.

A few patrons, mostly locals, were browsing. Otherwise, the place was empty.

"Okay, different and yet normal," said Richie, sniffing the air. "Not what I expected."

Sam didn't say anything in response, instead just looking around. She had never been in the Pattersons' shop, but this had to be the place. She remembered that after Aunt Marguerite had passed away, Aunt Gladys had taken over as executor of the Castille estate, as well as Sam's guardianship.

One of her first acts had been to fire the entire Patterson family, claiming that their "voodoo pagan religion" brought shame upon the "good Christian" Castille household.

Sam had been sixteen at the time and couldn't do anything about it; however, after passionately explaining the situation to Kent Bourgeois, Sam and Gladys reached an agreement—Gladys could live in the mansion as long as she liked, provided that any of the original servants who were released, including the Pattersons, received a severance of a quarter million dollars.

Considering the size of the Castille fortune, Aunt Gladys agreed. A few days after the Pattersons were paid off, Sam moved out of the mansion and into her father's townhome, then filed for emancipation. From that moment onward, she refused to speak to Aunt Gladys unless it was absolutely necessary.

Sam was tugged out of her memories by Richie tapping her arm and saying, "Hey, Sam, I think that person knows you!"

Sam shook her head and looked up, seeing a African-American woman standing on the stairs. The woman was about Sam's age, with sensual curves and deep chocolate skin. She wore a dark purple bustier with a black rim that settled down to a long dark purple skirt, split on the side. Her long black hair was braided in locks, and held back by a dark purple head rag. Her eyes were sensual and dark, and were staring directly at Sam.

It took a few seconds for Sam's brain to register everything, but she was sure she knew who this was. Sam was amazed that in fourteen years, the girl had grown from a gangly, awkward, string bean of a girl into such an amazingly beautiful woman.

"Tania?" Sam asked, walking toward the chocolate beauty.

The dark woman smiled and, holding out her arms, swept forward and embraced Sam. A heavy scent of herbs and incense was evident on her, but underneath, the smell of that goofy yet kindhearted servant still lingered. Sam had never realized until this moment how "kind" Tania smelled, if such a thing were possible.

"Miss Samantha," Tania said, her voice now as sensual as her look, yet brimming with excitement. "*Ave Maria* be praised, it is wonderful to see you again!"

Sam welcomed the familiarity. For one brief moment, everything was normal—her father was alive, her grandfather was not a murderer, and her life wasn't a nightmare. As she parted from the hug, Sam realized this was the first touch of normalcy she had felt in a long time.

"Please, just call me Sam," Sam finally said, smiling warmly at Tania and standing there clasping her hands to the dark woman's forearms. "It is so good to see you alive, well, and"—she looked Tania over again, failing to find a single flaw with her body—"looking incredible."

To Sam's surprise, Tania gave a soft laugh, detached from her, and walked over to the counter, gesturing toward the store. "As you can see, Sam, we've done well for ourselves with this store, our voodoo tour, and Violet's card readings. Sam, this is the best thing that ever happened to us."

Sam gave Tania a real smile, putting her hands on her hips and nodding her head. She was glad that, despite the suffering of so many people associated with her life, the Patterson sisters had turned out well.

"So Violet is reading cards, is she?" Sam said, having trouble picturing Violet doing anything of the sort.

"Yes, she is," replied Tania with a nod, leaning forward. "And before you ask, she is as much of a grouch now as she was back then."

Sam smirked and tried to imagine Violet being any worse than she used to be, and having a hard time with that.

"And how is Miss Patterson?" asked Sam, looking around for the heavyset large woman who used to be her housekeeper.

Tania's voice grew quieter as she said, not sadly but matter-of-factly, "Mama passed five years ago from diabetes. She went peacefully. It was too soon, but being her size . . . Well, I'm sure you can guess."

Sam felt sad that she never got a chance to say good-bye to the kindly housekeeper. "I'm sorry to hear that, Tania. Your mother was a good woman. She'll be missed."

A clearing of the throat, and Sam realized she had forgotten Richie, who was standing next to her and looking utterly left out of everything.

"Sorry, Richie," Sam said in a low voice. "This is Richie Fastellos, a friend of mine."

"Hey, there," Richie said, reaching forward to shake Tania's hand. "Pleasure to meet someone who is an old friend of Sam."

Turning back to Sam, Tania said, "I have an idea! Why don't you check out our voodoo tour, Sam? You and your friend will enjoy it. Mama used quite a bit of money to put it together, and it really promotes and preserves our religion."

"All right," said Sam, giving that soft smile of hers. "Let's see what this voodoo tour is about. How much is it?"

"Ten dollars a person," replied Tania. "The tour lasts a little over twelve minutes. Violet is waiting at the end if you want a card reading."

"Are you okay with this, Richie?" Sam asked her friend, realizing she didn't know his religion or whether a voodoo tour would offend him.

"Sure! I'm fine with it," replied Richie, giving an amused chuckle.

Sam gave Richie a nod and then reached into her pocket to get her wallet out and pay. She was only halfway through getting out her money when Richie slapped a twenty onto the countertop and slid it over to Tania. As Sam looked up at Richie in surprise, he winked at her and said, "Told you I'd take care of the next thing."

What a sweetheart, Sam thought, her heartbeat increasing a little as she reached out, took his hand, and followed Tania through the beaded doorway.

Stepping through the beaded door, Sam and Richie were led into a room lit by black light and up a ramp to a black cart with the visage of Baron Samedi painted on the back. The baron held a cigar in one hand and a rum bottle in the other. The cart, which had a platform for Tania to stand on and a railing for her to hold on to, was on a track that vanished through a black curtain. A backdrop to the loading area had, painted in fluorescent paint, figures of skeletons, ghosts, and nude men and woman dancing around fires. Atop the wall was a banner saying, "The Mysteries of the Voodoo Religion Tour."

Sam was surprised to see that the voodoo tour was a dark ride. She had always loved those things growing up, and to see there was still one in existence was pretty amazing.

"Step into the baron's embrace, mortals," Tania said in a voice that was both seductive and soothing, the dark woman walking back and motioning for Sam and Richie to follow.

Sam looked at Richie, who shrugged at her, and then she walked forward, getting into the car first, with Richie getting in next to her.

Tania settled on the platform at the front of the cart and, hitting a button, launched the ride into action. The cart lurched and then fed into the blackness beyond the curtain.

Sam watched as the tour took them through a scene of clearly animatronic people, slaves in the South before the Civil War, working the fields, playing outside their shacks, and playing music by moonlight.

Tania began to speak. "When the ancestors of the Creole people were brought over to the New World, they brought with them their religion, a religion that divinized the animals, the spirits of their ancestors, and the gods of the spirit world."

The ride went through another curtain, into a scene of animatronic slaves in rows in an outdoor church, praying at a mass led by a white preacher.

Tania continued, "And those beliefs were combined with the religion of their masters, the religion you know as Christianity."

Sam nodded to herself, remembering that from her books. Passing through another curtain, the scene showed people dancing around a bonfire at night. Sam had to admit that she was impressed, as the animatronics were very well done.

Tania's voice rang out as she put emphasis into her speech for this room. "The resulting religion became what is known as Louisiana voodoo. It combined the prayer and concepts of a supreme deity from Christianity, with the ancestral and spirit worship of both Africa and Haitian voodoo."

Sam was fascinated. She had been studying Haitian voodoo as if it were the authentic thing—never would she have guessed that there were so many versions of the religion. Sam felt completely fixated on the tour.

Passing through another black curtain, the cart entered a dark area, a semicircle.

In the center, amongst a large circle of candles, was a priestess in a bloodred robe, kneeling before a large pool of water, a ceremonial dagger in her hand. Above the priestess, a ghostlike apparition hovered, moving in an up-and-down motion. Around her were people in black hooded robes, holding bowls of water.

Sam felt Richie grab her arm and shake it, pointing at the hooded robes. "The Nite Priory!"

Sam swatted Richie away. She felt drawn to the circle. More than that, she felt an uneasy and sickening feeling of déjà vu.

"All voodoo religions have one thing in common," Tania continued. "The ritual! The priest or priestess, preparing themselves with incense of the guava and mango plants, using the blessing of holy water and blood, direct their willpower through an object, called a *focus*, to call down the voodoo spirit—a loa—to attach to their body and communicate with the living. Once the loa attaches itself to the living host, attaching at the spine and riding on its back, the spirit is capable of wielding its magic in this world."

Tania leaned forward and, in a hushed voice, said, "But a loa can only ride on a host's back for a short amount of time. To stay within the host permanently, a deeper and much more dangerous ritual is needed to force the loa to possess—that is, to take up residence within—the host. This persists until either the loa is cast out, or the host dies."

Sam heard Tania's voice, but it seemed so distant. She started to feel sick to her stomach, and her head was starting to pound. Up until the moment when the cart passed through another curtain, Sam couldn't tear her eyes from the animatronic ritual.

Passing through another curtain, the cart entered another dark room. On one side was a bedroom scene, where a priestess, with a ghostlike creature resting on her back, attached where the spine meets the neck, extended her hand over the body of a very frail-looking little girl. On the other side was a voodoo priestess, again with a spirit-like creature attached to her, blessing a bride and groom.

"All ceremonies beneficial, from healings to weddings to tending to the recently dead," Tania continued, sweeping her arm around the room, "use holy water to call down the loa and use their magic to bless the world around them."

Sam leaned to the side and stared at the animated loa attached to the back of the priestess. Her head was starting to throb, and her vision was getting blurry. It was getting difficult to think clearly.

What's going on?

The cart passed through yet another curtain. This time, the room was pitch-black, save for two unsettling scenes—one of a priestess slicing open the throat of a chicken, with crimson blood pouring into a bowl, and one of a priest covered in runes and casting an accusing finger at a pair of wealthy land owners.

Both of them had spirits upon them as well, but these looked scary, like something out of a horror story. The two spirits tormenting the wealthy land owners looked like twin hags made of nightmares.

Tania's voice lowered as she leaned forward and spoke in a hushed tone. "But for ceremonies malevolent, such as curses and the stealing of life, blood was used instead of water. For blood contains life, and to spill it creates both great power, and a great sin."

Sweeping her arm toward the twin hag-like spirits, Tania's voice rose. "These two loa, Marinette and Bwa-Chech, are particularly called down to ride, or even possess, hosts in order to unleash terrible calamity upon others. The sisters, who are forever destined to be in conflict, have a hatred of life and a desire to cause suffering to all living around them."

Sam stared at the two hags and felt, for a brief moment, a primal fear.

Then the pain really started. Sam's head throbbed terribly, and her nausea started to build. Her dinner was starting to try to come up, and her heart was beating uncontrollably. As Sam struggled to fight back the noxious feelings, she began to wonder if she herself was possessed.

Once again, the cart passed through a curtain, into a pitch-black room where Zydeco music played. All around, in the darkness, were skeletons dressed in the attire of the living. Some were dancing. Some were drinking. Some were fornicating. Above the cart, ghosts flew about in dancing patterns. At the far end, where the cart was headed, were three beings.

One was a short, dark-skinned man with a comically tall top hat on his head, wearing a tuxedo with tails, a cigar in his mouth and an apple in his hand. His expression was one of laughter.

Another was a dark-skinned beauty who wore a purple shoulder wrap that showed most of her bosom, a purple skirt that left little to the imagination, and a sash made of gold. Her hair was jet-black, and her seductive eyes were fiery red.

The third was a skeletal man in a tuxedo, top hat atop his bony head, holding a cigar in one hand and a rum bottle in the other.

Sam, who now felt so woozy she was leaning against Richie, recognized the third as Baron Samedi. Richie put his arm around her. Sam wondered, with annoyance, if Richie thought she was trying to cuddle with him.

"The three chief loa of Louisiana voodoo," said Tania, back again to showing off, swinging her arms to motion toward the three at the end of the track, "are Papa Ghede, protector of children and chief of the loa; Madame Brigitte, defender of graves and cemeteries, and queen of the loa; and Baron Samedi, usherer of spirits into the realm beyond, guardian of the crossroads between life and death, and king of the loa."

Tania leaned forward once more. Sam, feeling like she was on the verge of vomiting, couldn't tell if Tania knew how bad off she felt. Sam could smell the sweat on her friend and former servant as she said, "It's said that until Baron Samedi digs your grave, you cannot die."

Quickly, Tania jumped off the platform, and the area with the three loa flew open, parting like double doors, to reveal a grave. From the way the set was built, however, it looked as if the cart was falling down into the grave. Baron Samedi stood on the side of the grave, holding a shovel and looking "up" at the cart. With an earsplitting laugh, Baron Samedi motioned toward the grave as the cart sped up, giving the riders a real sensation of falling into the ground.

Sam felt Richie tense up and grab her protectively, but it was already too late. Sam felt herself vomiting her dinner as her world went black.

When Sam came to, the ride was stopped, and she was out of the cart, being held in Richie's arms. Tania was kneeling worriedly over her, and the Creole man from the front of the store was cleaning out the cart with a mop and bucket, grumbling the entire time.

"Sam," Richie said as Sam opened her eyes, his voice thick with concern, "can you hear me?"

"Miss Samantha," said Tania, reaching out to give Sam a small shake, "are you all right?"

Sam's eyes finally focused. She blinked a few times and tried to sit up, only to have Richie hold her steady, telling her to go slow. Sam was glad she decided to listen, for the moment she started moving, she felt woozy again. With effort, and with Richie and Tania helping, Sam sat up.

She could see that she was back at the start of the tour, near the loading ramp, and that the black lights were off, replaced by fluorescent lighting.

"Ugh," Sam said. "How long was I out?"

"Just a few minutes," replied Richie, concern still on his face. "You had us worried."

"What happened?" Sam asked, looking around.

"You got bad motion sickness, Miss Samantha," Tania replied, her face showing concern as well as guilt. "I should have said something—given the usual blurb I give at the start of the tour. I am so sorry, Miss Samantha."

"Please, call me Sam," was Sam's reply, a small smile and a touch of her hands to Tania's showing that it was okay.

"I guess we won't be doing that tarot card reading," Richie said with a chuckle, the obvious attempt to lighten the mood not lost on Sam.

"More excuses, Princess?" came a voice from behind the beads leading out to the store.

Through those beads came a dark-skinned woman who, other than being skinnier and with a more gaunt face, and with steel-blue eyes as opposed to dark ones, looked identical to Tania. She was dressed in a black robe that covered her entire body, and a dark purple shawl that draped over her shoulders.

"Hello, Princess," Violet said, looking in Sam's direction. Her grayish eyes were just as they had been years before, distant and gazing. And her gaunt face showed that as kind as the years had been to Tania, they had been just as unkind to Violet.

"Sam," Richie said as he started to help her stand, "did you know that Violet is blind?"

As Sam stood up, with some difficulty, she looked at Violet. Hearing Richie's question, Sam nodded. It wasn't something she had ever paid much attention to before. Violet's being blind was as normal as Violet's being mean-spirited.

"Violet, it's good to see you," Sam said, not sure what else to say to someone who had been antagonistic to her for years.

Violet's response didn't help the situation. "To answer your question, Mr. Fastellos, yes, I am blind. I was born blind. And I doubt Princess paid much attention to it, living in her Shangri-la."

"Violet," Sam said, "that's not true. I—"

"Save it," Violet interrupted, then turned toward the young Creole man. "Are you done, Ollie? We have customers."

"Yes, ma'am," replied Ollie, who took the mop and bucket and stowed it away in a nearby closet before scuttling up front.

Tania, who had been kneeling over, was standing up now and, turning to her thinner sister, said, "Now Violet, you need to stop that! It's been too many years. Miss Samantha is our friend now. Our equal."

"If that is the case," said Violet as she walked past Tania, moving around her sister as if she could see her, looking directly at Sam, "then why do you keep calling her 'Miss Samantha' when she's asked you to call her Sam?"

Sam watched as Tania opened her mouth to say something, her bottom lip starting to quiver as it did when they were younger.

Closing her mouth, then opening it again, Tania said, "I'll be up front. It was good seeing you again, Sam. Take care of yourself."

Tania left, leaving Sam and Richie alone with Violet.

Sam felt extremely uncomfortable. She might have never gotten along with Violet, but there was always a restraint to the hostility in the quieter Patterson sister. Now, though, that restraint was gone, and part of Sam felt as if Violet was sizing up her throat for attack—a feeling that made Sam tense up defensively.

Richie had gotten very quiet. Sam could feel him tensing up, as well, his fists clenched.

Sam decided that she didn't want to be alone with Violet anymore, Richie notwithstanding, so she started to head toward the exit, taking his hand. "Well, nice to see you again, anyway, Violet. Good—"

"Stop," Violet said, her voice authoritative.

Sam's legs seized, as if some invisible force had grabbed them and rooted them to the spot. She felt herself grow angry as she unwillingly obeyed Violet's command. *I can't move!*

Violet walked in front of Sam and stared blindly with those gray eyes, her gaze distant. "You came here to ask me and my sister something. What is it, Princess?"

Don't call me Princess! Sam wanted to scream at Violet but couldn't. As unsettling as her gaze was years ago, now it was ten times worse. Looking away, Sam said, "I want to know about Blind Moses."

To Sam's surprise, Violet chuckled and then asked, "And what would you do with that information?"

"Find her," Richie spoke up, moving just enough to pull Sam back away from Violet, a gesture that Sam felt instantly grateful for, "and ask her about the Bourbon Street Ripper murders. And her role in them."

"She was Grandfather's courier," Sam said, feeling stronger now that she was no longer so close to Violet. "She delivered messages to his accomplices."

"And that's all she was to Master Castille? Is that what you believe? Because I never pegged you as that stupid," Violet said, leaning down and looking up, once again staring blindly ahead. Immediately Sam felt indignation within her, like someone had lit a hot coal within her heart, and suddenly the years of Violet's cruel behavior toward Tania and herself came surging forth. Before Sam realized it, she had pulled her hand back and slapped Violet across the face.

"Sam, what the hell?" Richie shouted, pulling Sam away.

She looked at Violet as she stood there, her head cocked to the side from the slap, a welt forming on her face. Feeling her self-control slipping, her body shaking, her eyes widening, and her jaw clenching, Sam waited for Violet to make her move.

"Princess," Violet said, a little blood trickling down the side of her mouth as she looked in Sam's direction, "you're pathetically weak."

Sam felt her body quivering, every single muscle in her body seizing, as if the next logical action would be to leap on Violet and rip her throat out with her teeth.

"Helplessness is a terrible feeling," Violet said, walking away from the pair, her back to them. "Your grandfather's victims knew that feeling while he was torturing them. The families of those victims knew it when they viewed the bodies. And I knew it, every second of my life from the moment I first opened these useless eyes. Now the Princess, the most blessed among us, knows how that feels. She's helpless against her own inner demons."

"You're insane," Richie said, still holding Sam. "People feeling helpless is a horrible thing. So you were born blind. That's unfortunate. But to torment Sam like this? To make her so upset that she hits you?"

"I didn't make her do anything," replied Violet, her fingers running over the railing of the dark ride. "Like the hag sisters, Marinette and Bwa-Chech, the Princess and I are destined to be in conflict."

"You want to fight with Sam?" exclaimed Richie. "You're out of your mind! Why would you want to be at odds with someone you haven't even been around in over ten years?"

"Because she hates me," Sam said, her voice bitter with anger as she moved from Richie's grasp. "That's it, isn't it, Violet? For whatever reason, you've hated me my entire life. Now, more than ever, you hate my guts."

There was a very long silence before Violet answered. Her voice was low, but the venom dripped from it like fangs from a serpent. "Yes, Samantha. I hate you. You would never understand why. You cannot understand why. One day, maybe you'll see the sheer amount of blood spilled for you. Then, just maybe, you'll grasp the depth of my contempt for you."

Sam didn't know what to say. In her wildest dreams, she had no idea how much Violet Patterson hated her.

After a long, tense silence, Violet said, "If you want to meet Blind Moses, don't worry, she'll seek you out soon enough. Your stars and hers are also destined to clash, Princess. You best be ready."

"And the Nite Priory," Richie asked, for Sam was still feeling bewildered by the hatred she felt from Violet. "What about them? How do they figure into this?"

"Idiot," was Violet's reply, her voice contemptuous. "Irrelevant. Don't waste my time."

Sam watched as Richie moved to say something, then shook his head. "Come on, Sam," he said, taking her hand. "The last thing you need is to listen to this hatred. She's clearly mad from bitterness."

Sam started leaving with Richie. Suddenly Violet's voice called out, "Princess!"

Sam stopped, turning quickly, not sure what to expect. Violet, still with her back turned, was holding up her hand and showing three fingers.

"I read your cards while you were unconscious," Violet said. "Your past is the World Card reversed. Your present is the Moon Card. Your future is the Death Card. Take from that what you will."

Sam didn't know what that meant, having never put a lot of stock in the tarot. She filed away a mental note that she'd have to look up what those cards meant later on. She didn't like the idea of the Death Card being in her future. It sounded ominous.

Sam allowed Richie to tug her out. In the front of the store, Tania was busy helping two customers, a young man and woman, select candles. For a moment, the dark woman turned to look at Sam, a sad look on her face.

She started to move toward Sam, who shook her head, not wanting any more contact with the sisters. Tania stopped, nodded, and went back to helping the couple as Sam and Richie left the store.

On the way back to the car, Sam mulled over everything that had just happened. She felt anxiety at being forced to confront Violet. She felt rage at the way Violet treated her. And she felt fear at how strong the negative emotions inside her were. Sam felt as if she had met her mortal enemy, someone whom she would one day have to kill or risk losing her own life to.

That disturbed Sam terribly. Most importantly, Sam was suddenly very tired. She felt drained, like all her willpower had been siphoned out.

On the ride home, Richie, who was driving, said, "Sam, I think we should stop investigating and leave this to the police."

Sam, who was leaning against the side window, staring ahead blankly, looked over at Richie and said, "Why? Why would you say that?"

Richie gritted his teeth, and Sam could tell that he was struggling with what to say and what not to say.

"Out with it, Richie," Sam said. "We're in too deep to start withholding information from each other."

"This voodoo cult shit," Richie said. "It's a bit too freaky. I mean, I don't believe in loa or ghosts or Baron Samedi, but there are people who really believe this shit. And they're crazy. Like that Violet bitch. She probably *is* Blind Moses herself, you know."

Sam shook her head and looked forward, saying, "Violet was twelve years old during the Bourbon Street Ripper murders, Richie. There is no way a twelve-year-old blind girl could run as a courier."

"Then maybe Blind Moses is a title," Richie said, his voice more aggressive. "Maybe those wacky cult people, with their voodoo and Christianity and whatever, just give the name Blind Moses to one of their most important people."

"Good theory," Sam said stoically, starting to feel worn down. Her head wasn't hurting, but her heart was. She wanted to go to bed and forget about today ever happening. She wasn't even sure what was real anymore—if she was insane or under some kind of control. *Maybe I am possessed by a loa after all.*

Feelings of helplessness assailed Sam, and for a brief moment, Sam had an image in her mind of a stone floor covered in blood, a visage of skull-like faces staring at her from the darkness, and a feeling of overwhelming terror.

As Richie continued to prattle on, Sam felt like she was going to cry.

"I'm not trying to theorize here, Sam," said Richie as he continued his diatribe, his brow furrowing as he harshly turned a few corners. "But this shit is getting way out of control. Serial murders? Secret societies? Voodoo cults? Christ, Sam, this is getting serious!"

Sitting up straight, Sam looked over at Richie, feeling a sudden rush of anxiety. She was sure Richie was getting ready to abandon her like everyone else eventually did. The ache in her heart only increased as she furrowed her brow.

"What the hell is wrong with you, Richie?" Sam said, her bottom lip starting to shake. "Why can't you be supportive of me in this? I need to follow this thing through to the end! I need to know what's happening to me! Why are you being such an asshole?"

His voice raised to almost a scream, Richie cried out, "I don't want you to get hurt! I care too much about you!"

Richie's exclamation took Sam by surprise. She sat back and stared ahead, unsure what to say. Too much was happening at once. She had to pull away, get away from Richie and everyone else. She had to be alone. She was safer alone.

"You're too sweet for someone as messed up as me," Sam finally said.

"Sam," Richie replied, desperation in his voice, "don't say that. I—"

Sam interrupted by placing a hand over one of his. Looking over at him, she said, "Richie, I don't want to hurt you. You've been so sweet to me, from the time we met until now. You didn't need to be, and God knows, I don't deserve it, but you have been. That means the world to me."

Sighing, Sam looked away and watched as Richie pulled into the driveway of her townhome. "You should go back to Pittsburgh. I'm falling into hell. It started with my grandfather, and it's ending with me. This is a Castille problem. Whatever is going on, this is a hell I don't want to drag you into. Go back to Pittsburgh. Write your next book. Forget about me and all this death. Live a good life. Good-bye, Richie. Thank you for showing me a few days of happiness."

Sam unlocked the door and got out of the car. The hot August air felt oppressive, but Sam was used to it. All her life people had hated her, and she had been alone. It wasn't a new sensation to her. It was better she do this alone.

Sam was halfway up the steps to her front porch when she felt someone grab her hand. Spinning around, she saw Richie, a look in his eyes she hadn't seen before. Instead of the suave novelist, or the disarming goof, she saw the eyes of a man—a strong and sincere man, looking at her with what only could be compassion.

"If you're going to hell, Samantha Castille," Richie said, his voice low but firm, "let me be there to pull you out. No matter what happens, I swear you won't go through this alone. And when this is done, let me be the wings that carry you back out of hell. I love you, Sam. I always will."

Sam's throat tightened to the point that she couldn't swallow. Her eyes instantly began to water. Her tough exterior, the one she had carefully built up over the past twenty years, cracked like an eggshell.

"Richie, I . . . " Despite priding herself on always being strong and in control, Sam couldn't think of a single thing to say.

Richie pulled Sam into his arms. For a moment, Sam looked up into those crystal-blue eyes, lost in their depth. Then her eyes closed, and she leaned up, her head tilting to the side, her lips parting. She felt his lips press into hers as they met in the center—each coming to the other.

Her mind slipped into autopilot. The taste of his kiss, the scent of his skin, the feel of his strong arms around her, drew her into a feeling of security she had never experienced before. Sam wasn't sure how long the two of them kissed, or when their hands started to tug at each other's clothes, or when they went into the townhome, or up the stairs, but by the time her mind came back to her, she was in her bed and Richie was on top of her.

Sensations overwhelmed Sam, and with them a feeling of completeness that overtook every one of her senses. She couldn't describe it. It was unlike anything she could ever have dreamt it to be. Sam felt as if they were no longer two people, but one person, joined in a way that was more than beautiful—it was sacred.

Her arms wrapped around Richie's neck, holding on to him as if her were her only lifeline, as if letting go would drop her into the abyss. She kept staring into his deep blue eyes, her body tensing from the overwhelming feelings as their lovemaking continued.

After what seemed like an eternity later, Sam was vaguely aware that Richie had sped up his motions, and that she was arching her back and crying out. The pleasure inside her had grown until it overtook her. Then it hit. A tidal wave of unstoppable force, like nothing ever felt before, crested again and again and carried her to a place of bliss.

Sometime later, Sam's mind came back to her. She was lying next to Richie, resting her head on his chest, her finger delicately touching the muscles on his chest. She gave extra attention to a single scar, shaped like a slight crescent, which reached from the top of his chest down to just above his stomach. Richie held onto her tightly, a silent reminder of his vow.

Sam's finger lightly traced Richie's chest scar as if it were fragile. "Where did you get this scar?"

Richie mumbled something incoherent, half-asleep, and turned to fully embrace Sam. His body against hers made Sam feel, for the first time in her life, utterly secure.

Sam couldn't do anything but smile. Never before had she known such joy.

I can't deny it any longer.

Sam's lips pressed over Richie's chest, kissing it gently before resting her head against it and settling down to sleep.

I'm in love with this man.

Epilogue

Date: **Sunday, August 9, 1992**
Time: **3:00 a.m.**
Location: **Somewhere in the French Quarter**

The sound of a rat scurrying across the ground of an abandoned apartment in the French Quarter caught the attention of one of the room's two inhabitants. Wearing a black hooded robe, the man stood over a sink, washing his hands with thick soap. The sink, like the rest of the apartment, was decrepit and stained with mold and rust.

As he finished washing his hands, the man said, "I'm really disappointed in the police, you know. I thought they would be more on their game. Between those detectives following every red herring, and Commander Ouellette being convinced Samantha Castille is me, I have almost no opposition."

Drying off his hands on a surprisingly fresh-looking white towel, the man walked over to the end of the counter where a tray lay, its contents covered with a duty towel. As he lifted the tray and carried it across the room, the man said, "I am still hoping someone will rise to the occasion and challenge me. Maybe that junior detective, LeBlanc. I have high hopes for him."

Placing the tray down on a stand near a covered table, the man said, "The sad part is that LeBlanc is right. The police should really be focusing on the original crimes to figure out who I am."

Looking at the covered table from beneath his hood, the man's pale mouth parted into a smirk. "You're frightened. Don't worry, everything has purpose, even your death."

The man looked up at the single lightbulb illuminating the otherwise dim room. "I've been waiting for this time, my time, for so long. With tonight, vengeance shall finally be mine."

As he lowered his head, the man removed the duty towel from the tray, revealing the metallic shine of a myriad of surgical items—scalpels, forceps, probes, even bone saws. Touching his fingers tenderly to the steel tools, the man said, "It's been too many years, but with Nick's assistance, everything is coming together perfectly. He even managed to get you to me without any problems. I'm very proud of that boy."

Turning to the side, the man turned on the monitoring equipment, which stood next to the covered table. A heart rate monitor, an intravenous machine, and an artificial respirator were all soon beeping away quietly. The man gave a nod to the equipment and turned back to the table.

With a sound of disgust in his voice, the man said, "You'll have to forgive me for starting so late. My prior engagements kept me away later than I'd have liked. Necessary evils to keep up my facade.

"But you'll forgive me, won't you? Of course you will."

Grabbing the corner of the covering over the table, the man pulled it back, revealing a girl no more than sixteen years old, dressed in a skimpy, skin-revealing outfit. Her entire body was secured with thick leather straps, and her mouth had a ball gag with holes stuffed in it. The girl's eyes looked utterly horrified and her entire body quaked.

"So, shall we begin?"

The girl started to scream into the gag as the man picked up a scalpel.

Underneath the black hood, the man's lips parted into a white smile.

"I won't lie. Tonight is going to be very difficult for you."

As the man lowered the scalpel toward the girl's exposed midsection, her muffled screams became even shriller.

"Very difficult indeed, Cheryl Aucoin."

Afterword

Had fun? I certainly hope so!

If you made it this far, you realize by now that the story is only partially over. The truth is that *Sins of the Father* was originally meant to be one book, but after several conversations with my editor and my publisher, we decided to break it into two. This is a good thing. I believe that as two books, the story can be told more completely.

Because of that, *The Bourbon Street Ripper* needed to end with a bit of a cliffhanger. I do believe, though, that we left it with enough conclusiveness to stand on its own merit. That said, you'll have to wait for Book Two in order to see "whodunit."

In all seriousness, I thank you from the bottom of my heart for reading my first novel ever. The moment I decided to become a writer, I also decided I wanted to start with a mystery. And I also decided I wanted that mystery to be set in my hometown of New Orleans, Louisiana. What I didn't expect was to shelve that idea for many years, or for the idea to grow well beyond a mere mystery during that time. Least of all, I didn't expect *Sins of the Father* to grow into what it has become.

So what has *Sins of the Father* become?

It has become several things. Foremost, it's a thriller, a story meant to keep you on the edge of your seat, to riddle you with suspense and apprehension.

Second, it's a mystery, and while I wouldn't call *Sins of the Father* a classic mystery, the entire story has several mysteries within it. But as you can tell by now, the mysteries are more than just

"who is the killer?" There is also "what happened in the past?";
"who was actually involved in what?"; and "what is really going
on?"

Finally, *Sins of the Father* is a story of how the consequences
of the past shape the situations of the present. As you likely see,
there is a strong element of karma present in the story. One could
say that a major theme is how things left unresolved in the past
have come around full circle to haunt the present and the future.

So as you reflect back upon this book and await the conclusion, remember the following: Be skeptical of what the characters
told you unless you saw it unfold yourself. Let your intuition guide
you and your imagination disturb you. Keep an open mind to
solutions that defy convention, but never let go of cold, hard logic.

You might just figure it out all before you get to the end.
Wouldn't that be something?

There are too many people to thank to fit on one page, or
fit in one afterword. But most of my thanks goes to my wife for
supporting me, my family for believing in me, my critique group
for shaping me, my publisher for publishing me, and my editor
for putting up with me. To anyone whom I may have forgotten—
thank you, as well, for sticking it out with me during this amazing
journey.

See you in Book Two!

—Leo King

About the Author

Born in New Orleans, Louisiana, Leo King has always had a taste for the gothic side of life, from the tragic romances to the cast-iron tracery to horrors lingering in the shadows. Growing up, Leo enjoyed ghost stories, murder mysteries, and black humor.

This first love of 'all things dark' did not abate even as Leo grew a secondary love of science fiction and fantasy. In fact, it colored his views of the other genres, painting his word-laden landscape with shades of gray.

After leaving New Orleans in the wake of Hurricane Katrina, Leo settled in Houston, Texas, where he began to write professionally as an article writer and a Ghost Writer, which was strangely fitting. After moderate success, Leo penned a short story entitled *The Sound of Raindrops*, which he submitted successfully for publication to Bayousphere magazine.

Currently, Leo King is writing a collection of short stories that will include *The Sound of Raindrops* and other tales, as well as additional stories from the world of his first novel, the mystery/thriller *Sins of the Father: The Bourbon Street Ripper*. Writing stories with a dark flavor and a sardonic look at the human condition, Leo always hopes he's just controversial enough to make his readers think.

Connect with Leo

Email

leoking@foreverwhere.com

Twitter

@leokingauthor

Website

www.foreverwhere.com

Facebook

facebook.com/leokingauthor

www.ingramcontent.com/pod-product-compliance
Lightning Source LLC
Chambersburg PA
CBHW061610210726

48287CB00001B/71